THE POLICEMAN'S DAUGHTER

Tony Annereau

ISBN NO

9781693314797

ACKNOWLEDGEMENTS

I would like to pay tribute and thanks to the many people who, knowingly or unknowingly, helped to make this book possible.

My late wife, Janet Maureen, for her encouragement and enthusiasm during the early stages of the story.

Mary Brace for her unstinting work and advice as my editor.

Graham Brace for getting the book published.

Thérèse Wisely in France for her helpful suggestions about language usage and other aspects of French life.

Gill Beckett for the cover design.

The staff in the Mont Mouchet Resistance Museum for their unknowing help.

The countless French men and women whose parents or grandparents were caught up in the fight against the Nazis in the early nineteen-forties.

Tony Annereau 2019

FOREWORD

Despite my French surname, I have to admit that I had never been to France until 1961 when a school friend suggested camping over there for a lark. Our recently acquired wives were surprisingly keen to join us and, no doubt, to chaperone us.

So in a late September evening we arrived in Boulogne and it was foggy. We'd planned to set up camp somewhere but decided against it finally and instead managed to get into a small hotel in St Pol, not far from Boulogne. The next morning started bright enough but as the day wore on it began to rain. It persisted for the best part of the nine or ten days we were over there and it was hardly an auspicious start to what nonetheless was destined to become a lifetime love affair with the country.

I had just seen enough of what the country had to offer through the gloom and rain wetted windscreen to want to see more and the following year I suggested to my wife that we take another look. She went along with the idea so in mid-June Janet and I drove down to the Mediterranean Cote d'Azur in our little Renault Dauphine.

It is a curious fact that the more I saw of France, the hungrier I became for more; the mountains, the rivers, the gorges, the forests and the architecture, to say nothing of the food, were all so different to England. We quickly made friends with total strangers on the coast in a campsite and at the camp's small 'buvette', where the owner politely and patiently put me right on some of my broken French.

My French ancestry derives from my grandfather of some ten or more generations ago, Jean Annereau. He was a Huguenot living in the closing years of the sixteenth century and was a protestant in a largely Roman Catholic country, presided over by Louis XIV with the backing of the Pope. The Huguenots were treated to extreme cruelty but it was returned with interest during a period of intense violence when it became known as 'The Wars of Religion'. My ancestral grandfather sickened of it finally, fled the country, eventually turned up in London's Aldgate area, then little more than a country village. He probably became, or carried on as a silk weaver although that is something I have yet to verify.

I carry a strong sense of belonging when I travel about in France. I feel very at home whenever I am there and entirely relaxed, so much so that I have often wondered if our genetic makeup can be programmed by living in the same place for hundreds or possibly thousands of years and those genes are now emerging in me.

It was against this background that I became more aware of the German takeover of the country in the early nineteen forties. Janet and I were endlessly reminded of some of the iniquitous cruelty meted out to the French populace by the Nazi imposed régime. It resonated in me with its echoes of the Wars of Religion. The more we looked the more evidence we found. It inspired me to write an historical, but totally fictitious tale of how it might have been in the early 1940s, for an imaginary village and its inhabitants in south west France. I have played hard and fast with real history and there are wildly imaginative and inaccurate accounts surrounding gendarmeries and other organisations. I have never had ambitions to become a historian nor have I possessed the necessary background or financial support, to ever become one. There exists an entire galaxy of well-educated historians who in turn have published countless deeply researched books and papers dealing with the era during which my fictional tale takes place.

I hope you will find my fictional version of history entertaining and a good read.

Tony Annereau

In 2004 we were making for our holiday house in South West France and had been on the road for several hours. We were bored, weary and very thirsty and needed to get out of the traffic for a while. On the spur of the moment I left the busy autoroute where signs pointed to vaguely familiar names, but which held no special significance for either of us. The new road was quieter but not completely free of traffic so taking pot luck I turned again onto a very minor and empty road. This time more directional signs pointed to numerous small towns and villages, none of which meant anything to us. We continued for a while through spectacular countryside, past deep river valleys, lakes and distant mountains and eventually ran down a long twisting incline into a village. Ahead was a diminutive square overlooked by a small church. Over my shoulder I had spotted some sort of bar or restaurant, adorned at the front with a faded blue, white and red sun awning.

By now we were more than ready to take a break so I drove up onto the square where an ancient Citroën van and a small Renault were parked. It was fiercely hot and apart from a patch of shadow, provided by a moth-eaten plane tree near the middle, there was no escaping the strong sunshine. We parked beneath it and walked stiffly over to the bar where two locals were discussing football with the owner. Behind the counter, high on a corner shelf, a large television was showing some sort of cycle race. The commentary was barely audible as the sound was turned down, and all that could be heard was an excited murmur. I ordered two beers and we sat outside at a metal table under the awning.

An elderly woman perched on a bicycle appeared from around the corner and passed by, crossing the almost empty square diagonally towards the top edge. We watched as she carefully dismounted, leant the bike against the front wall of a house and disappeared inside. The bar proprietor brought out the beers which were gratefully consumed as we gazed about. The shutters on two small shops and a few houses were closed against the afternoon sun and apart from the two gentlemen and the bar owner there were no further signs of life. My wife commented, 'Well it's all happening here!' and I responded by saying something to the effect that I doubted if anything much had ever happened here for about two hundred years.

I was wrong . . . totally wrong.

<u>One</u>

It promised to be another hot day and the village was just beginning to stir. As usual the baker had been up since before daybreak and was already unloading a second batch of loaves from his ancient oven. On the opposite side of the square Madame Hortense Hubert was performing her ritualistic sweeping of dirt, real or imagined, from her immaculate doorstep. She did this every day, regardless of whether or not it was necessary, since it provided her with a reason to be on the outside of her front door more often than she might otherwise be. It was an important part of her daily routine as she always needed to be the first to know if anything of interest had transpired during the night or early morning. Sadly, her life was now very predictable, not to say boring, and rarely punctuated by anything that could be described as interesting despite her diligent observation of the passing scene. The step sweeping was necessarily performed with great care and precision to ensure that no opportunity was missed for information gathering. As was the case on most mornings, very little seemed to be happening and it was with some reluctance that she withdrew to the dark interior of her little house, and closed the door behind her.

Chalhac-sur-Bache is not untypical of many small rural communities across France. It is not particularly beautiful nor does it possess any special claim to fame and has only survived through sheer necessity and the determination of its inhabitants. There are few alternatives for the villagers and in any case this is what they know and understand. Their forebears lived and worked in virtually the same way in the same place, and they too had managed to survive, so there have been little or no imperative and few opportunities for them to change their way of life. The Great War had exacted its terrible toll when Chalhac had seen its population of young men, and not so young men, decimated by the carnage in the trenches in north eastern France and Belgium. A poignant reminder of this was erected at the edge of the little square, with the names of those lost engraved upon a simple bronze plaque on the base of a stone war memorial. Their loss to the village is still hugely felt where strong young men are an essential resource and who had become suddenly conspicuous by their absence. It had shown its effect by the visible lack of young children after the war and now, in 1940 there is a noticeable shortage of eligible young men and women and a disproportionate number of middle aged ladies, still dressed in black mourning. By 1939 what had remained of the young adult male population had once again mostly disappeared into the army in anticipation of another round of conflict with Germany.

There are few records available about the origins of the village. It had probably begun life as little more than a goatherd's shelter by the side of a small river, now known as 'la Bache.' It is impossible to date this with any real accuracy but it was certainly several centuries ago. Over the succeeding years it became a little more permanent, gathering a few more people. It slowly began to grow into a hamlet and then into something more resembling a village. Much later a small church was built under the auspices of Rome. In the intervening years the church had been fought over by various religious and political opponents and the original had been largely destroyed by Protestant Huguenots during the Wars of Religion.

Even now there is not a lot to the village which lies halfway down a long twisting wooded valley. Behind the village there is a steep rocky hillside, above which is a plateau of scrubby grassland. Beyond that the land rises again, culminating in a wild area of causse with scrub, rock, caves and windblown trees. The opposite side of the valley is rather more amenable to human occupation, although for some unexplained reason the village itself grew up on the other, rockier side of the river. It may have been the chance of flooding that was the deciding factor and was perhaps considered too risky to build upon. Whatever the explanation, the area of grassland's only inhabitants now is a small herd of cows accessed by a small bridge of stone and wood that spans the river, allowing access to the animals. In the heat of summer the grass turns yellow so the cattle have very little to graze on. The village has in its centre an open space imaginatively called La Place, overlooked on one side by the church, a modest structure supporting a simple bell tower with its single bell, rung to remind the local inhabitants of their devotional duties. The road to distant towns runs alongside the square and past the church. Beside the road on the edge of the square is the war memorial which is lovingly tended by the local ladies who place flowers at its base as needed.

* * * * *

Apart from the church, from where on Sundays a trickle of the devout can be seen coming and going, La Place provides the location for the weekly market, held on Wednesdays. It creates a focal point to what is otherwise a mostly formless week. People from the surrounding communities and farms bring in their spare produce to trade or barter, so the market is an essential part of the basic supply of food and raw materials for the village, giving the locals the chance to buy, sell and exchange their own produce. There is nothing spectacular about these gatherings and very often the items for sale add up to little more than a few eggs, a bunch of carrots, some fruit and one or two local cheeses. The Wednesday market's most important function is probably the opportunity it provides for the exchange of news, views and gossip as it filters slowly down the valleys from the world beyond. The area's comprehensively agricultural economy was left in a precarious state for a long time following the Great War and by 1940 the problems imposed by military conscription mean farming is once again barely viable. The women in the community have once again been obliged to become farmhands and to do the hard physical work normally done by the men.

Facing the church on the opposite side of the square is a small bar run by Monsieur and Madame Fournier. Jacques Fournier lost his right leg in 1917 and was unable to continue his chosen trade as a joiner. He lived with his parents in the modest house on the square until their rather premature death from pneumonia in the early thirties. Not long after that he opened his 'bar' in one of the two ground floor rooms and has managed to scratch some sort of a living by dispensing homemade liquor to those who can afford it. He married Maria not long after opening his bar, as he had found it increasingly difficult to look after himself and run his little business at the same time. Maria is the younger of two daughters of the local blacksmith, whose forge lies just behind the square in one corner. A derelict building separates his premises from the ageing Madame

Hubert's house which she shares with her daughter, Henrietta Suau. Monsieur Bonnet's bakery faces up the square towards the Hubert house.

Behind the buildings on Bonnet's side of the square 'la Bache' winds its way slowly towards the old water mill, a crumbling structure a little further down the road leading out of the village. It still functions, although how often it can actually work depends upon the amount of water running. A mill pond was dug many years ago to create a head of water to drive the ancient wheel in times of drought. More often than not the river becomes little more than a stream or dries up completely on occasion, resulting with the pond quickly becoming depleted. The other problem is the availability of grain for milling. The immediate area is not suitable for cereal growing so livestock is the major farming interest, but what little grain is produced is usually brought to the miller, Monsieur Malet. The mill has been in his family for many generations and is now generally regarded as a part of the landscape. Monsieur Malet has two sons Daniel and Claude and a daughter, Monique.

At the other end of the village is a small, rather dilapidated house belonging to a stone mason, Jules Gaillard and his Russian Jewish wife Sarah. Jules' own father had found work in Russia as a stonemason when work was becoming short in France. His young son Jules, had followed in his father's footsteps and eventually became a restorer of parts of Tsarist Russia's palaces. It was by no means an easy life and had become difficult and dangerous during the revolution and the years that followed. Jules had met his Jewish wife Sarah during that time and they had their two sons, Marcel and Guy. Fortuitously, Jules' distant cousin Maurice Chambon had died and left him his house in Chalhac. It was particularly timely, as it had given them the opportunity to leave Russia, where life was becoming more and more precarious in the post-revolutionary period during the early twenties. When they abandoned Russia in 1925 they had been accompanied by their two sons Marcel and Guy then aged only six and four. They had with them very little by way of possessions – an old perambulator and an even older bicycle. The pram contained a few clothes, some bedding and Jules' stone working tools. Their excitement at the prospect of having a house they could call their own was quickly dispelled when they arrived in

Chalhac to be eagerly directed by young Madame Suau to the slightly derelict building just out of the village. They were tired and exhausted from the many weeks they had spent walking from southern Russia, across the Balkans and Italy. Jules had barely known of his late cousin's existence, let alone what sort of property he had inherited. That his cousin Maurice had been aware of Jules' whereabouts at all, had been quite surprising and it was even more remarkable that Jules had been traced to Russia where he had lived for nearly thirty years.

It was obvious that the house had been unoccupied for quite a time whereas Jules had assumed that his cousin had died quite recently. It was only later he discovered that cousin Maurice had succumbed to Spanish 'flu in 1919. The house had fallen into a state of disrepair and it took Jules and Sarah a great deal of time and effort to bring it back to a habitable state. Although the finished product could barely be described as elegant, they were perfectly happy with the results. Compared with what they had left behind in Russia, it was Heaven on earth. Jules managed to get employment at a quarry within cycling range of the village and the family settled down to something like a reasonable existence. Marcel is now nearly twenty, and works with his father in the quarry and Guy is training to become a teacher. He lives away from home with the family of a fellow student in Clermont-Ferrand.

Their arrival in Chalhac-sur-Bache early in 1926 had caused a considerable stir in the village. Henrietta Suau had been sweeping the doorstep of her mother's house early one morning when they arrived in the square. Her immediate impression was that they were Romanies or tinkers, or both. Bedraggled and dirty after weeks of walking, they were an unprepossessing sight and Henrietta was about to close her front door on them when Jules called over to her and asked very politely if she could direct them to the house of the late Maurice Chambon. Henrietta's curiosity was immediately aroused and she replied that they had already passed the house on their way into the village, but she would be glad to walk back with them the way they had come and identify the house for them. Jules was grateful for her apparent concern, so with Henrietta leading the way, they walked the short distance out of the square and up the road to the dilapidated property. Jules and Sarah were to say the least, taken aback when they first caught sight of their inheritance, a four square grey volcanic stone-built structure with a lauze roof that had begun to fall in at one end. The front door was badly split and some of the windows lacked glass or were cracked. They thanked Henrietta again and managed to get into the house without being further accompanied by their new-found friend, who would doubtless have been happy to help with the inspection.

During this first encounter Henrietta Suau quickly realised that although Sarah spoke adequate French, her dialect was heavily tainted with something she was unable to identify with any certainty. Over the next few days she made it her business to pump Jules as hard as she could about Sarah's origins. She discovered that the family had trekked from southern Russia and that Jules' cousin had left him the house, but Henrietta felt sure there was more to Sarah than she had so far been able to uncover. Several days later, and having gone through the usual pleasantries, Henrietta decided upon a more direct approach:

'Do you have any family still living in Russia Madame?' asked Henrietta as casually as she could one afternoon, having stopped outside their house where Sarah was lifting a large piece of timber off the ground. Sarah dropped the wood before replying:

'If I do, I am afraid I don't know where they will be now,' replied Sarah somewhat enigmatically.

'How very sad! You lost contact with them as a result of the Revolution perhaps?'

'Not directly but it is too complicated to explain right now.' Sarah was beginning to feel that Henrietta was becoming just a little too inquisitive for her liking.

'You must forgive me Madame but my husband is waiting for this piece of wood which he needs at the back.'

'Of course, of course!' said Henrietta, who retreated down the road to consider the facts as she saw them.

Two

On the first Monday of June 1940 the news from northern France was grim. Until now the Chalhac populace had been quite optimistic about the possible outcome of events as they unfolded over the previous several weeks. The hugely expensive Maginot line had been promoted and much vaunted as an excellent defence against further German ventures in the French direction. The army was well trained, prepared and sufficiently large to deal with any invasion that the 'Boche' might be considering. Sadly, the planned defensive strategies were thrown into disarray when a large German armoured force made its way into France via the Ardennes Forest. It had virtually ignored the carefully prepared Maginot line defences, leaving thousands of military personnel untouched and effectively stranded in their massively engineered installations, rendering them largely redundant. That the German army would be able to penetrate the Ardennes had been dismissed by the French military as being unlikely. They had unwisely considered that the density of the forest was enough to deter any serious armoured incursion. The British Expeditionary Forces and a substantial part of the French army had been placed in Belgium where it was mistakenly anticipated that they would be confronting the Germans. The resulting entrapment of both the British and French forces and their subsequent humiliating retreat via Dunkirk left the way largely open for the German army to advance upon Paris and elsewhere.

In Chalhac the news that the Luftwaffe had actually dropped bombs on Paris, caused considerable consternation. The mood had abruptly changed from optimism to pessimism. Jacques Fournier's bar was unusually crowded for a Monday and he had his wireless set on the top of the little zinc topped bar and everyone sat or stood as close as they could to hear the latest reports from Paris. The official line was that 'the army had things under control and that people should not worry too much and remain calm.' These words of encouragement were greeted with some scepticism by those assembled in the bar, having earlier been given an imaginatively upbeat and edited version of what had really transpired in Belgium.

The official radio bulletins stating that 'the unanticipated advance by the Germans through the Ardennes was meeting with stiff and heroic resistance' had been met with quiet and barely disguised derision. A general sense of gloom, apprehension and disbelief pervaded Fournier's at that moment. A near silence was broken only by barely audible mutterings. Malet the miller spoke up:

'My God! Is this the best our military can manage?'

'I thought we were going to give the Boche a bloody nose. Now they're bombing Paris!' said someone standing near the doorway.

'What the hell are 'the Anglais' trying to do? I thought they were supposed to be helping us hold back the Boche. As far as I can see all they have done is made a complete mess of it all and ended up running for their lives onto the beach at Dunkerque. So much for alliances!'

'Your boy is up there somewhere isn't he, Malet?' asked someone.

'They both are,' corrected Malet who was exceedingly anxious about his sons as he had heard nothing from them for over three weeks. The last letter from Daniel had said that he and his brother were well enough and were part of a reserve battalion and stationed somewhere near Rouen. That was the last he had heard and with the latest news of the German forces' advances he assumed that prisoners were being taken. He silently prayed that they were safe and had not been captured or worse.

Although the French authorities were doing their best to give the impression that things were under control, it was far from the truth. Much of the population in the North had drawn its own conclusions about the true situation and the first of what was later to become a flood of refugees, was already moving southwards. Shops and businesses had begun to close and others were considering their best course of action. People in the North were panicking and anxious to get as far away as they could. Little of this was being broadcast on the radio for fear of creating an even greater stampede, but it was impossible to disguise the fact that a substantial part of the French populace was on the move.

There were now eight people crammed into Fournier's bar and by any normal standards this would have constituted overcrowding. As the temperature rose outside it was matched by an even greater increase within. Tempers were becoming frayed with the heat and with the alarming news which continued to emanate from Jacques' wireless set. Monsieur Bonnet the baker appeared and elbowed himself into the bar with some effort. He had left his wife in charge of his shop as he had some late news to impart to the assembled crowd in Fournier's premises, which could be clearly seen from behind his own shop counter.

'I have just had a telephone call from my brother-in-law in Orleans,' he announced, 'and he said there are a lot of people streaming into the town, looking for somewhere to stay. It seems they are mostly from Paris or thereabouts. He reckons the hotels are doing very nicely out of it and some of the shops are putting their prices up like mad.'

'It sounds like a few people got the wind up and are getting out while they can,' volunteered a voice near the doorway. 'A few people' barely described the avalanche of humanity leaving Paris and elsewhere. Businesses and individuals were grabbing what they could and heading southwards in the vague hope that the Germans would somehow be halted before they were overtaken. It was only to be expected that there would be some shops and individuals who would see this sudden influx of people heading their way as an unanticipated bonus. Some were prepared to exploit their fellow countrymen quite ruthlessly.'

'How long do they think they can stay in Orleans?' said someone.

'They're not just in Orleans, they are all over the place and the roads are full of them.'

'I can't see the Boche stopping at Paris, even if they do get there. So what are these damned people going to do then? Keep running?'

'Well there are no hotels in Chalhac so they'll be out of luck here,' joked someone.

'It's no laughing matter my friend. If you were being chased out of your town by damned foreigners, you would want to make sure your family was safe.'

'All right, all right. I didn't mean it.'

'Well then, shut up!'

Jacques Fournier decided he'd had enough. 'Let's calm down shall we messieurs! It's bad enough as it is and it will do nobody any good if we argue among ourselves.' Peace within the bar was restored. The next news bulletin was due at midday and the little crowd began to disperse. Fournier poured himself a glass of beer, turned off the radio and sat down outside in the partial shade of the building.

Three

Madame Henrietta Suau lived in the little house on the square with her younger sister, Anne-Marie and their mother, Hortense Hubert. The two men in Henrietta's life had been taken from her in the Great War: her father in 1916 and in the following year, her young husband François. She had married François Suau just before the war began and at the time it had seemed a good idea. Sadly, it had not worked out the way they had planned and there had neither been the time to set up a home and begin a family, nor to achieve any of the normal things that life might have been expected to deliver. Instead, when the war finished in 1918, Henrietta found she was at twenty three, very attractive but widowed and childless, living in her newly widowed mother's house in Chalhac with her younger and pretty sister, Anne-Marie.

Their parents, Albert and Hortense Hubert had produced their two daughters in the closing years of the nineteenth century: Henrietta in 1895 and Anne-Marie two years later. They had been faintly disappointed to have had girls and although they loved and cherished their two daughters intensely, they had still hoped that in time a son or two might be forthcoming. A little over two years elapsed before Hortense became pregnant again and finally went into a long and difficult confinement which culminated in a stillborn son. The birth did irreparable damage to Hortense's insides and doctors were of the opinion that she would be unable to bear any more babies. Sadly the prognosis proved correct and the family was to remain complete as a foursome until Albert was killed in the blistering shelling of Verdun in 1916. Henrietta and Anne-Marie did as much as they could to comfort their mother when the news of their father's loss was made known. All three of them were devastated but the two sisters found enough strength to overcome their own sadness in order to give Hortense some sense of hope for the future. Barely a year passed when Henrietta too, received notification that her own beloved husband, young François, had been mown down by a German machine gunner as he stumbled across a soggy, shell-holed field. Indescribable misery ensued, and had somehow to be dealt with by

Anne-Marie, who was by now barely twenty. There was no work in the village, other than agricultural labouring, and although Anne-Marie was keen to maintain some sort of financial stability within what was left of the family, she was not a strong candidate as a cowherd.

At the age of six years old Anne-Marie had begun what was to become a lifetime friendship with Georgette Vidal, a child she had liked from the start when they found themselves sharing a school desk in the nearby village of la Petite Boude. Georgette was a bright girl and on leaving school in 1911 was obliged to stay at home with her mother, filling her days with needlework, cleaning and learning to cook. Monsieur Vidal was a minor official in the Licensing Office in the town of Domvent d'Olt dealing with agricultural affairs and other matters. Three years later, at the outbreak of the Great War, he had managed to get his daughter a job in the local town hall as a replacement for a young filing clerk, who had been called to arms a few months earlier. When Anne-Marie wrote to Georgette telling her what had befallen the family, and that they were on hard times, she promised she would keep her ears open for any job opportunities which might occur. She had been true to her word and shortly after the conflict with Germany was over, Anne-Marie found herself working face to face with her old school friend in the Domvent town hall, as a self-taught clerk-typist.

It had taken a good deal of imagination on Georgette's part to portray her friend as the ideal employee, for whom the inside workings of the local administrative offices would have probably remained a mystery for evermore, had it not been for her efforts. The fact that a number of junior posts had become vacant as a result of the carnage in north and eastern France, was probably quietly anticipated by the administration at the time and it is very likely that some of the rules had been relaxed, enabling Anne-Marie to land the job she did.

She settled quite quickly into the new régime. It was a busy journey of over half an hour from her home in Chalhac to Domvent d'Olt. The road was twisting and narrow and barely usable in the winter, when the snows made it virtually impassable. When it thawed it flooded and became little more than a muddy lane. The bus service was a fairly rudimentary affair, provided by a 'bus' adapted from an army truck, used previously during the recent war. In the morning it would stop at Chalhac, and reach Domvent at about 7.30, providing the road remained passable. The same bus would stop in Domvent in the late afternoon and deliver Anne-Marie back to Chalhac half an hour later.

Six months passed and one afternoon she arrived home wearing a slightly enigmatic smile. Henrietta, who was highly attuned to her sister's moods, noticed immediately that something had changed in her sister's demeanour.

'So?' It was the briefest of questions.

'So what?' replied Anne-Marie evasively.

'What's happened?'

'Nothing!' She blushed slightly.

'Liar!'

'Promise you won't tell Maman?'

'It depends.'

'Alright, I'll tell you.' She took a deep breath. 'I've met someone.'

'You mean you have met a man?'

'Yes.'

'How? Where? Who?'

'He works at the office. He was at the interview when I went for the job.'

'It's a bit sudden isn't it?'

'Not really – I am sure he liked me from the start and that's why I got the job.'

'What's his name?'

'Eric Farbres.'

That he had a name made Henrietta realise there was actually a real person her sister was talking about. As this was the first and only time this had occurred, she was intrigued to know more.

'What's he like?'

'He is quite tall, slim, short wavy fair hair and a thin moustache.'

'How old is he?'

'I'm not sure, but I would say about twenty-six.'

Henrietta considered this for a moment or two then said, 'so how did he come to be at your job interview when everyone else had been getting killed in the mud in the north? Was he injured?'

'No, he didn't serve.'

'Really?' Henrietta's eyes opened a little wider and her eyebrows rose questioningly.

'His father is something at the Prefecture in Clermont and somehow or other he persuaded the powers that control these matters that his son would be more useful in an administrative post than being an amateur soldier.'

'Lucky Eric,' said Henrietta, less than enthusiastically. It had taken her no time at all to take an instinctive dislike for the man. She was still hurting badly from the loss of her own beloved Francois, little more than a year before. To be told by Anne-Marie that she had fallen for someone, for whom the conscription had been side-stepped, courtesy of his father, did nothing to endear him to her. Moreover, in the very brief time since she had been told of this development, she was already at a loss to understand why her sister could have been so blind to the likely effect this might have upon both her bereaved mother and sister.

'So when are we going to see this wonderful creature?' asked Henrietta, very sarcastically.

'Quite soon I hope.'

'Are you serious about all this Anne-Marie?' Henrietta was beginning to see that her sister was not going to be easily deflected by anything she might say.

'You don't understand, do you? He is a lovely man and he says he loves me and I love him.'

'Oh! I understand that well enough. What I cannot understand is how you can bear to think about him like that, knowing he has been safe and warm, with no risk of being shot at or blown to pieces for the last four years, when his friends, if he still has any friends, family or whoever else he knows did not get that chance.'

'Well, I'm sorry but that's the way I feel.'

'When are you going to tell Maman?'

'The sooner the better I suppose. What do you think she'll say?'

'God only knows.'

* * * * *

Hortense Hubert was surprisingly sanguine when she heard Anne-Marie's news. Henrietta had accompanied her sister to confront their mother, and neither knew what to expect. Hortense was already seriously concerned about her daughters' futures and was well aware that since the last war ended there was now a self-evident shortage of marriageable young men. At first she felt an overwhelming sense of relief when it seemed Anne-Marie was being courted by someone employed in a local administrative office and who was therefore, almost by definition, a respectable person and was holding down a responsible job.

'And what is this young man's name, Dear?' asked Hortense. Anne-Marie had not wanted to promote Eric too early as a possible suitor and was becoming more and more nervous about telling her mother about it even now - or at least not until she felt a little more confident about his intentions.

'Eric Farbres, Maman.'

'An unusual name isn't it. He's not German is he? It sounds almost German. Where do they come from – do you know?'

'I have not asked him very much about his family, although his father has quite an important job in the Prefecture in Clermont.'

'So they are French no doubt. How old is this Eric?' Hortense realised that there were some essential details about this person, which had to be established and this entailed a certain intrusion into her daughter's privacy.

'I believe he is nearly twenty-six.' Anne-Marie anticipated the next question.

'Was he injured during the war?'

'No. He did not have to serve and was in the office at Domvent.'

'Why was that? Is there something the matter with him that he was not called up?'

'No Maman. It was because his father works in the Prefecture, and he knew someone of influence in the defence department. He persuaded his friend to pull a few strings for him, so that Eric could stay where he was in Domvent.'

Anne-Marie realised that she had perhaps been a little too frank with her mother about Eric and his recent history. She was beginning to blush, partly through the excitement of telling her about this new phase in her life and more probably she had begun to understand, somewhat belatedly what effect the bald facts about Eric were going to have on both her mother and her sister. Torn between her basic honesty and trying hard not to disguise the less palatable truth about his avoiding army service was proving to be a delicate path to tread. Hortense sat silently for what seemed to Anne-Marie, to be a lifetime. She was trying to digest this information and to make some sense of it. Finally she spoke:

'What did this young man think about his father's efforts to keep him out of the trenches, I wonder?'

'He pleaded with his father to let him enlist,' she lied. Anne-Marie had very rarely lied to her mother but this required her to quickly extemporise. She immediately had terrible feelings of guilt welling up inside her.

'Well, that's something in his favour isn't it?' Hortense was not altogether convinced by her daughter's response. However, she felt it was necessary to tell her daughter how she felt about it, but conflicting ideas swarmed around inside her head, not the least being her wish to see both her daughters produce some grandchildren for her. Henrietta had been cheated out of this by the loss of her young husband but there could still be someone out there who might wish to pair up with an attractive young widow. Despite the grim statistics recently revealed about the losses of men in the battlefields during the war, Hortense remained ever optimistic. She did not want to be responsible for destroying any opportunity that might arise for her younger daughter to find a likely suitor. She at last made up her mind:

'I am very happy for you Darling. I hope your friendship with this young man will grow into something worthwhile. You are one of the lucky ones!'

'Thank you Maman, you are a dear. Please don't feel badly about Eric and that he didn't serve in the war – it wasn't his fault after all.' She had decided that having told one lie to her mother, compounding it with another would be easier.

Henrietta had sat silently throughout the course of this delicate encounter between her sister and her mother. She always felt she knew her sister rather better than Hortense did and that she was holding back on the truth in some way. It seemed to her as highly unlikely that this paragon of charm and honesty would have found it necessary to plead with his father to allow him to serve in the army. All his friends, assuming he still had some friends, would have enlisted like everybody else. Could he have been so gutless not to have told his father that he was joining his friends and neighbours and gone off to war, regardless of the old man's wishes? Somehow it did not quite add up in Henrietta's view and only increased her dislike of him.

* * * * *

Several weeks passed before Henrietta and Hortense met Eric Farbres but it was finally arranged that he would visit Chalhac to be introduced. He appeared on his motor cycle, the very latest Peugeot, purchased by his father to make it easier for him to get to and from work. At the time, he was living with his parents in their large house, several kilometres from Domvent. There was no usable bus service in that direction and although the railway went through Domvent from Clermont Ferrand, the trains did not stop close enough to their home for it to be any use. So Papa Farbres had once again eased life's problems a little for his son. He arrived in Chalhac on a Saturday afternoon, wearing a sturdy tweed suit and, goggles and gauntlet gloves. Anne-Marie had been waiting anxiously at the window of their house for the appointed hour of his arrival. He was very punctual and before he could remove his goggles and gloves, she was already out of the front door and advancing upon him.

He was a fairly good looking young man: above average height, deep set grey eyes and light brown wavy hair. Henrietta reminded her sister later that she had described his hair as fair. They walked across to the house and the door was opened by Henrietta who greeted him rather coolly:

'Good Afternoon Monsieur.'

'I am delighted to meet you, Madame! I have heard a great deal about you.'

'Have you indeed?'

'I have told Eric all about you,' said Anne-Marie. 'Come on in Eric. I'll call Maman. She is out the back feeding the chickens' she said, trying to inject some normality into the proceedings before Hortense appeared.

'Please sit Monsieur,' suggested Henrietta, indicating the wooden, backless bench under the window.

'Thank you, but I would prefer to remain standing – my back is aching from the ride over here,' replied Eric.

'As you wish,' said Henrietta with considerable formality. 'Will you excuse me for a moment?' She was glad to escape into the rear garden where her mother and Anne-Marie were still attending to the chickens.

'Are you going to be out here for much longer?' said Henrietta. 'I don't know what to talk to Eric about.'

He was looking out of the window towards La Place when the three women came back in. Anne-Marie said:

'Maman, may I introduce my colleague and friend, Eric Farbres. Eric, my mother.'

'I am honoured and delighted to meet you at last, Madame Hubert,' said Eric, holding out his hand and bowing slightly from the waist. Hortense was a little taken aback by this display of formality. Nobody she had ever known had behaved like this and she held out her somewhat dirty, weather-beaten and gnarled hand to the young man, grasping his soft paw with an unexpectedly vicelike grip.

'I am very happy to meet you Monsieur – please take a seat.'

'That's very kind Madame but my back aches a little from the ride over here, so if you wouldn't mind I'll remain standing for the moment.'

'As you please, Monsieur Farbres.' They were all being very polite and struggling to find something to say which would not be seen as being too inquisitorial, although the purpose of his visit was to find out a little more about him at first hand. This was certainly Hortense's idea at least. Henrietta had been less than impressed with him from the word go and her attitude towards him was guarded and distant. Her antipathy towards him had been fixed firmly in place by hearing from her sister how he had avoided army service during the war and her own loss of her young husband. There was no way she would ever come to terms with that situation.

Hortense remained neutral though quietly optimistic about the outcome. Her attitude towards Eric was being swayed by her yearning for grandchildren – better still, male grandchildren. She still carried memories of her own childbearing past and her overwhelming sadness at losing a precious baby boy. She had begun to see this new development as a way of somehow putting to rights her own loss so many years before. Nothing would replace it entirely but she was prepared to give Eric Farbres a chance and for Anne-Marie to find some happiness.

This first meeting proved to be a challenging affair all round. It was obvious that Eric was uncomfortable finding himself in the company of three women, the youngest of whom he was now courting. It seemed to him that her sister was making it clear from the outset that she was not prepared to be friendly and was trying to distance herself as much as she could, within the confined surroundings of the little house. It must also have been a considerable shock for Eric to find himself in such cramped quarters because although his parents' house could not be described as palatial, it was very much larger in every dimension than this tiny space. Their house boasted a dining room, a salon and a kitchen while Hortense's house comprised a single living room on the ground floor which also was the kitchen. Nor did it offer much by way of comforts. The middle of the room was dominated by a long, solid, all-purpose refectory table. Beside it was a backless bench, matching the one under the window. A chimney made up most of one wall and was sufficiently large to accommodate two wooden chairs, one with arm rests and the other without. An iron grate stood in the middle of the chimney space where an all-purpose cooking pot hung. On the opposite wall and taking pride of place stood a waist-high wooden cupboard with four doors and an open shelf. It was blackened with age and although a simple unadorned affair it appeared to have been a cherished piece of furniture for a very long time, evidenced by the dull sheen of beeswax on its surfaces. The remaining wall facing the window comprised a curtained alcove, containing a bed and was the private domain of Hortense. A steep and narrow staircase to the floor above began beside the back door.

Hortense had insisted that Eric should sit in the chair with the armrests and it was moved from its place by the fire to the head of the table. She sat on the bench to his left and Anne-Marie to his right on the other bench, dragged over from under the window.

Henrietta perched herself on her sister's side but at the far end nearest the window.

Hortense wanted to know more about Eric and his family. There was something about the situation which she sensed had not yet been revealed and this was perhaps an ideal opportunity to get a little more information. She asked Eric:

'Has your family always lived down this way, Monsieur?'

'No. They came from Alsace originally and when my great-grandparents died my grandparents moved to Bourg-en-Bresse. Later, the family moved further south to Clermont where my grandfather worked in the Prefecture. When he retired they moved south again and bought a house in Petit Domvent. He helped my father get into the Prefecture.'

'So they came from Alsace originally. Was your great-grandfather a German by any chance? asked Hortense.

'No, although I'm told he spoke some German and Alsatian.'

'I'm relieved to hear it. It seems to me that your family has done rather well out of the Prefecture Monsieur! I am surprised you haven't maintained the family tradition.'

'Well, you see the war came along and it messed up a lot of plans.' It was about the worst thing he could have said. A badly misjudged and clumsy comment in view of the company he was in.

'It certainly did – Anne-Marie must have told you that her sister here lost her young husband and I too was widowed during the war. As you say, it messed up a lot of plans. If I may say so, you were extraordinarily lucky to have been kept out of it as you were.' Hortense stopped short of being pointedly rude to Eric but her comments were delivered with barely disguised sarcasm. She was now in no mood to keep up the pretence of belief in every word this young man uttered while Henrietta sat quietly fuming, not daring to speak for fear of being unable to restrain herself once she had started. Eric appeared to make no attempt to apologise for his clumsiness and was probably struggling to find an appropriate means to correct, what he realised was idiocy on his part.

An awkward silence followed for a little too long, and only broken when Hortense said, 'Could I offer you a glass of wine Monsieur?' It was meant to repair any damage she felt she may have inflicted on the relationship which was still only in its formative stage. It was also a gesture intended to lubricate the conversation which now showed signs of grinding to a complete standstill.

'That is very kind Madame. Will you and your lovely daughters join me?'

'Of course we will,' said Hortense.

'Not for me,' said Henrietta. 'I have a rather bad headache.'

This first encounter broke up shortly afterwards and Anne-Marie and Eric went off for a short tour of the village before Eric finally disappeared into the evening on his motor bike. Anne-Marie could barely wait to hear what impression he had made on her mother and sister.

'So what do you think of him?' asked Anne-Marie, addressing both Hortense and Henrietta after Eric had vanished up the road. 'Adorable isn't he!'

'He seems to be a very polite and well-bred young man although he obviously doesn't think that getting out of the war the way he did was anything to worry about. What he must have thought about us I cannot imagine.' said Hortense who was still trying to marshal her thoughts about him.

'Adorable?' said Henrietta. 'I don't think so. If you must know, there is a lot about him I don't like. It strikes me he thinks he's a bit superior to us and is only going along with it all simply because he wants you, Anne-Marie.'

'Well, thank you very much,' said Anne-Marie, whose eyes had already begun to fill with tears. Henrietta was clearly unable to see Eric Farbres in the same way that she did and it was deeply hurtful. It was to be a source of some considerable unhappiness between them for a while thereafter.

'You are being very unkind Henrietta,' said Hortense. 'Don't upset your sister like that. He seems to be a very nice young man and Anne-Marie is a lucky girl to be wanted by him – God knows there are precious few young men available now and we should all be grateful that he should have seen Anne-Marie as a possible partner. We all know well enough what it is that's getting at you, and we both understand how you must be feeling, but it does no good to blame him for your misfortune.'

'I know what you don't like about him,' said Anne-Marie angrily. 'You think he should have taken his chances in the mud during the war and maybe not come back in one piece or maybe not at all. Well I think he was damned lucky to have had a father who could pull strings for him. It might have been unfair but that's the way life is and I will not let you try to spoil my life because your Francois was killed.'

'It is not that Anne-Marie, but I simply can't take to him at the moment. I agree he is very polite and quite good looking and I daresay he sees us all as being a bit below his social standing, but I think he is inclined to be a bit bossy or something. I can't put my finger on it exactly.' She was doing her best to placate her sister, who was by now, tearful and very upset.

'For Heaven's sake stop bickering,' said Hortense. 'It does no one any good and we have enough problems to deal with without arguing between ourselves – so please stop it now.' A slightly sulky silence descended that evening but sisterly love was re-established a few days later, when Henrietta realised there was nothing she could say or do which would dissuade her sister from the course she had set for herself.

Four

During the year following Eric Farbres' first visit to Chalhac, the romance blossomed and early in 1920, he and Anne-Marie were married in the Marie at Domvent followed by a blessing in the little church in Chalhac. She became pregnant very soon after and within a year of their marriage Anne-Marie produced a baby girl. It was decided to name the child Isabelle after Eric's maternal grandmother and this was the cause of some friction between the families. Hortense had hoped, prayed and almost convinced herself that they would have a son and that Anne-Marie would insist upon the boy being named Albert, after her own late father. When it was announced that they had produced a girl, and that she was to be named after Eric's grandmother, it seemed to be a double slap in the face for Hortense. All was forgiven however when the new baby was presented to grandmother Hortense and Aunt Henrietta for the first time. The baby, though only a few days old, was exceedingly pretty.

'Can I hold her?' said Henrietta to her sister. Her maternal instincts were racing away at the sight of Isabelle snuggled against her sister's breast.

'Of course but don't drop her!' said Anne-Marie. Henrietta leaned over and tenderly gathered up the precious bundle, swathed in the shawl that had been used by Hortense some twenty five years earlier when Henrietta was a baby. She carefully pulled down the shawl from the infant's face and was immediately rewarded when her eyes opened to reveal two large brown orbs, which she tried to focus on Henrietta.

'She is very beautiful.' Henrietta's eyes began to fill with tears.

'Here, Maman! Hold your new grandchild!'

Hortense was itching for the chance to hold her one and only grandchild in her arms. She gently took hold of the bundle and peered into the shawl. There seemed to be some instant and magical connection between grandmother and baby because Isabelle appeared to smile directly at Hortense.

'I think she knows who I am because she is smiling at me! You do, don't you Darling!' she said looking down at the baby.

'She probably needs to lose some wind,' said the anxious mother. 'Let me have her Maman.'

A little reluctantly Hortense passed the child back to Anne-Marie who immediately began to gently pat the baby's back. Eric, the proud father had been standing watching the proceedings, from the opposite side of the bed. He too was quite naturally anxious that no harm should come to his infant daughter and was mildly relieved when the little bundle was back safely in its mother's arms.

'What do you think of our addition to the family, Grand-mère Hubert?'

'I think you must be very proud to be the father of such a lovely baby and I am exceedingly delighted and proud to be her Grand-mère. I know from experience something about the way you are feeling at this moment.' Hortense meant every word. The memories of giving birth to Henrietta and to Anne-Marie were still fresh in her mind and they had all come flooding back during the last several minutes.

'And what about you, Aunt Henrietta? Your thoughts?'

'I think she is delightful and will grow up to be a beautiful young woman. I like to think we will become friends as time passes. I am sure we will.'

* * * * *

When it had become known that Eric and Anne-Marie were to be married the question arose as to where the couple would make their home. The lodgings where Eric had been staying at Domvent could not accommodate a married couple but the problem was solved when Eric's father offered to rent them the house which had formerly belonged to his own long dead father. It had been bequeathed to Eric's father several years before and had remained empty ever since the old gentleman's demise. Eric and Anne-Marie were only too pleased to accept, and even more so since his father had suggested they could call it their own for a nominal rent for as long as they wished. Two months later they moved in. A great deal of renovation was required and it cost Eric rather more than he had anticipated to make the house viable after its long abandonment. Eric was still only in his late-twenties and possessed enough energy at the end of his working day to begin the task of patching, painting and mending items which were by then in urgent need of restoration. After nearly six months of hard physical work on his part, he and Anne-Marie were able to stand back and quietly admire their handiwork.

When Anne-Marie became pregnant, it was a matter of principle and pride that Eric insisted that she should cease working and this resulted in their income being substantially reduced. While the rent for the house payable to his father was less than might have been expected in the normal way of things, it was nevertheless still a strain on resources. He was an exceedingly proud man and was not prepared to admit to either Anne-Marie or to his parents that he was finding life financially hard going. There was also rather more than mere pride to Eric's personality, for he was also very ambitious and impatient. It was becoming increasingly clear to him that while the career he had embarked upon meant security of a very high order, it also meant that the promotional ladder was largely reliant upon colleagues either retiring or dropping out of the picture for some other reason.

These limitations to his job prospects became even more apparent when two former employees returned to work many months after the war ended. One had lost a leg and the other suffered terribly with his breathing, caused by exposure to poisoned gas. The director of operations in the licensing bureau had been obliged to take them back into employment despite their obvious physical defects. Neither of them ever made any direct comment about Eric Farbres, but when they eventually learned how he came to be working there, it was perfectly clear that they deeply resented his having been able to avoid the horrors of war they had endured and everything that he represented.

Eric was well aware of their attitude towards him and he sensed their almost palpable hostility. Even without taking them into account, it was abundantly clear that there were people well ahead of him in the queue for promotion, and he guessed that he would be sidestepped, regardless of qualifications or experience and despite any pressure that could be brought to bear by his father's cronies.

The more he pondered this dilemma the more he disliked what he saw. Privately, he held a strong conviction that he was somehow a cut above the general herd and those feelings did not sit comfortably with him being little more than a junior clerk. He had probably inherited this trait from his father who now saw himself as one of the elite, having landed his rather comfortable job in a branch office of the Prefecture. This was by no means a senior post but it carried a certain cachet, since he could 'name drop' and rub shoulders with men of some influence and power. It was therefore hardly surprising that his son should also have come to see himself as somewhat superior to his colleagues and a cut above the ordinary. This was a further reason why Eric found it increasingly difficult to contemplate the direction his current career seemed likely to take.

It was this self-regard that had made his first encounter with Anne-Marie's mother and sister, Henrietta, both awkward and difficult. They were essentially country people, living a mostly simple and often harsh, rural life in a very basic house in a small village. He could hardly have been unaware that this was the reality for most of the population within the area where he lived and worked, but until now, he had not really come face to face with it. He now had the responsibilities of a wife and baby, besides which he knew that he was considerably beholden to his parents for their house and that he was becoming trapped in a job that was looking increasingly like a dead end. He gave a great deal of thought to this situation during the following months. He felt unable to speak to Anne-Marie about it in case she worried unnecessarily, nor did he think it was the right time to raise the topic with his parents. He had never found it easy to make many friends and the few he had, tended to keep their distance from him, following their return from the battlefields. He could say nothing to his office acquaintances because their sympathies lay firmly with the two injured men, who were now bravely trying to cope with life. So he stayed quiet and waited for some as yet, unforeseen opportunity to arise.

Anne-Marie's old school friend Georgette continued to work in the same office and she had quietly witnessed the tensions increase almost daily between Eric and his fellow workers. She had not voiced her thoughts to anyone at work but occasionally appeared at

Anne-Marie's home. During one of these visits she made up her mind to speak to her friend about the matter.

'Does Eric ever discuss the office with you Anne?'

'Not very much. I think he probably feels I saw enough of it when I worked there.'

'Why?'

'Well, I probably shouldn't say this but he is not very popular right now.'

'Why? What has he done?'

'It is difficult to put into words, but really it is a case of what he didn't do.'

'What do you mean?'

'He wasn't a soldier.' The way she said it carried its own quiet condemnation of Eric. She had never before spoken to her friend about his exemption from the army or the way it had come about; it was a taboo subject and easier to ignore. Now it was out in the open. She began to wish she had said nothing as soon as the words were out of her mouth. Anne-Marie was still trying to grapple with this new piece of information.

'Eric has never breathed a word about this to me Georgette, are you sure you are not mistaken?'

'No Anne, there's no mistake. From almost the moment Michel and Thomas came back to work the tensions were there. When they realised that Eric had not even been in the army and had not had to put his life on the line, they both made it very clear that they were less than enchanted with the idea of having to share an office with him. You know how badly they had been injured so you could hardly blame them. I thought you would have noticed that something was going on.'

'I missed it somehow – how could I?'

'I can only think you were too taken up with the thought of marrying Eric and were blind to virtually everything else. Anyway, it is true enough and growing worse all the time.'

'I'll have to speak to him about it won't I?'

'It's up to you Anne. It may be better if you leave the subject alone and see what happens, but I cannot see how he can stay working where he is, with all this going on. I hope you will forgive me for telling you about it.'

'There is nothing to forgive Georgette – you are my best friend and I'm glad you told me.'

Five

Anne-Marie's marriage to Eric Farbres created a considerable gap in the lives of Hortense and Henrietta. The house on the square in Chalhac became quieter and emptier than it had ever been and both mother and daughter became acutely aware of her absence and of their comparative isolation. Her contribution to the family income was also greatly missed and so a period of self-imposed austerity ensued, which was uncomfortable and worrying for them. Both women received a small war widow's pension, which just about enabled them to survive but it was barely enough to live on. While Ann-Marie was still working and living at home they had managed to buy a cow, two goats and a few more chickens. The cow was kept on the grazing land on the other side of la Bache, made possible by an arrangement with the Mayor, Monsieur Bastien, whose land it was. It was agreed that he would receive a weekly supply of a few eggs - subject to weather conditions and the Hubert chickens' productivity. It was necessarily a flexible arrangement and there was no question of either party ever falling out over variations in the number of eggs actually supplied nor in the quality of the grazing on offer. The latter was always an unknown factor as it also relied upon the vagaries of the weather. As part of the agreement Monsieur Bastien would become the owner of any calves produced by their cow, until such time as she became too old and had to be slaughtered. When this occurred Hortense would be given the pick of any young animal for further milk production. The goats and the chickens were kept closer to home at the rear of Hortense's house and altogether these arrangements meant the two ladies managed to survive rather better than did many others.

Life had never been easy for the peasant farmer, particularly in this part of France, and in the aftermath of the Great War, huge hardship had to be endured, some of which was as a direct result of the war, in which so many men had perished. Many decided to give up the struggle for survival on the land altogether, sold up or abandoned their houses and moved to the towns, where industry was fast growing and where demand for labour meant there were plenty of jobs to be had. Henrietta had been seriously tempted by some of the opportunities that this situation presented and even voiced her thoughts to her mother that perhaps she could find a job in one of the fast expanding towns, such as Aurillac or even Toulouse or Clermont Ferrand.

Hortense was less than enthusiastic about the idea.

'And what am I supposed to do by myself here in Chalhac if you go off? How am I going to look after the animals, the house and everything?' Henrietta was rather taken aback by her mother's instant antipathy to the suggestion.

'Well, I just thought that I could earn some money and save enough for us to move.'

'I don't think that is a very good idea at all. In any case, I don't want to move from here. We have always lived here and your grandparents and your great grand parents lived here. I can't see any reason why we should just leave everything and everybody we know, simply to earn more money. No Henrietta, I am sure you are wrong to think that way.' As an afterthought she said, 'And what about me – what would I do in Toulouse?'

Whether consciously or not, Henrietta may have thought that by moving to a town there might be a better chance of finding a husband and maybe start her own family. In Chalhac the chances of finding a husband were almost certainly nil and she could see the years slipping by. Her sister Anne-Marie had made her move and had now been rewarded with her baby daughter Isabelle, whom Henrietta adored. The child dearly loved her in turn, but she was a constant reminder of her own situation and widowhood. Her mother's opposition meant that Henrietta was obliged to shelve the idea so she remained in Chalhac, milked the cow and fed the chickens. Imperceptibly she began to take on a different persona, becoming an ever more nosey, bored, frustrated and embittered widow.

* * * * *

Not long after Georgette's revelations to Anne-Marie that Eric was becoming a pariah at the licensing bureau, Eric finally decided he would speak to his father about his current predicament and its effect on his future career prospects. So far, he had not breathed a word to Anne-Marie about any of it as he felt unable to present her with any viable alternative plans for the future. She in turn, had said nothing to him, partly to protect her friend Georgette, who then might be blamed for stirring up trouble and in any case she felt it might put unnecessary pressure on Eric.

One Saturday afternoon he turned up at his parents' house on his motor bike. Madame Farbres was busy in the kitchen preparing food for a meal later that evening. After the welcoming preliminaries, he was told his father was dozing in the shade of the chestnut tree in the garden, having enjoyed the best part of a bottle of red wine with his lunch. He only stirred when Eric advanced upon him and said 'Good afternoon Papa!'

'What . . . Ah! Eric my dear boy – what a pleasure!' said his father, struggling briefly to gather himself. It had been a few weeks since they had seen anything of Eric, Anne-Marie or little Isabelle. 'And how is the young Farbres family these days?'

'Not bad Papa, not bad.' He could perhaps have qualified his answer with something about the situation at work, but just for the moment chose not to.

'Anne-Marie – how is she? And our beautiful granddaughter?'

'They are both very well. Isabelle is coming up to her first birthday in two weeks' time!'

'It seems barely possible.'

'It's true enough.'

'So to what do we owe this unexpected pleasure may I ask?'

Eric knew he could hold out no longer.

'I need your advice Papa.'

'Oh?' Suddenly his father was fully awake.

'I have been considering my future at the bureau and to be frank with you, I feel it will be a long time before I make any serious progress. I just wanted to get your view about it all Papa.' Farbres senior remained silent for a moment or two while he digested this information.

'What do you want me to say? – resign immediately?'

'Certainly not, although the situation has become quite difficult since two people came back after the war. They were both seriously hurt during the fighting and they will clearly take precedence over me where any promotion is concerned. In any event there is already a number of people ahead of me without taking either of them into account, and I am not sure that I want to wait that long.' He was careful to omit any reference to the bad feelings, now being overtly expressed. 'Besides, I have to admit that the work I am doing is hardly exciting and I am fast becoming bored with the whole thing. Of course I realise that it is a secure career – pension and so on, and I fully understand and appreciate your part in getting me into the job in the first place, but I cannot see my staying there for evermore.'

His father said nothing at first but looked directly at his son for what seemed to Eric, a lifetime. Finally he spoke:

'I see. Have you spoken to the director about any of this?'

'No. I have not even spoken to Anne-Marie – lest she should worry.'

'Probably for the best. Though I don't think you are right about your career prospects and you never know, the situation could change for the better sooner than you think.' Farbres clearly had in mind that he could again further enhance his son's career by some judicious lobbying of one or two contacts.

'If you have in mind what I think you do, I don't really want to go down that road. It could cause endless difficulties if it were seen that I had somehow got to the front of the queue.' He was careful to avoid saying anything to his father about the real reasons for wanting to abandon his present course and anyway it could do untold damage to his father's position at the Prefecture, upset some of his contacts, and lead to even more problems at Eric's place of work.

'I wouldn't worry about that – there are plenty of people who have received a little help in their careers through personal contacts. However, if you are of the opinion that you are running into a brick wall then it may be for the best that you make a move while you are young enough to become established in something you want to do, rather than kick your heels in a job you dislike for the rest of your life.' Old Farbres was being surprisingly pragmatic given that he had received no early clues from his son about his doubts.

'I am glad you can see it that way Papa. I would not have been able to forgive myself if you had taken the view that your efforts on my behalf had been a waste of time. I have learned quite a lot about people and administration in the time I have been down there, so it hasn't been entirely wasted. I have tried to be realistic about my promotion prospects though, and I really cannot see much happening for a long time – and I want to move up the ladder for all our sakes.'

'Yes, I can quite see that,' said his father, who had himself been frustrated earlier in his career within local administrative affairs for years, before finally landing a comfortable position which satisfied his own self-image as well as providing sufficient earnings to make life a comparatively easy ride. Besides which his own job also carried the very real advantage of a State guaranteed pension.

'I'll give it thought and perhaps we can come up with something which will fit the bill. I take it you don't have any ideas that could be considered?'

'Not at the moment, but now I have spoken to you I feel rather easier about it. Thanks for your understanding and help Papa.'

It was a huge relief for Eric to be able to unburden his thoughts upon his father, and that he had taken it so calmly. For the time being he decided to remain quiet about the matter with Anne-Marie – totally unaware that she had already been given most of the story by Georgette Vidal.

* * * * *

Three weeks later, a letter arrived for Eric from his father expressing his wish to see his son on a matter of some urgency and which might very well be of interest to him, and that they should get together for a discussion. It was fairly clear to Eric that his father had come up with something concerning his future and he sent a reply by return post, saying he would be glad to come over to their house on the following Saturday. When he arrived he was ushered into their salon, where his father offered him a glass of wine, which Eric gladly accepted. They both settled themselves, his father in an upholstered rocking chair and Eric in a rather ornate armchair.

'Now my boy, I have been speaking to one of my colleagues about your future and he is very sympathetic. I was of course careful not to disclose too much about your particular circumstances but he nevertheless understands that there is a certain urgency in the matter in view of your age, and that there is therefore no time to be lost. As it happens a cousin on his mother's side, is in the recruitment office at the Ecole de Gendarmerie in le Puy-en-Massenet. It seems they are keen to take on new recruits to replace some of the numbers lost to the force during the war. It has proved to be more difficult than expected because so many young and suitable men were lost or injured as you know. If you were able to consider this as a possible option, there should be no problem getting you into the school. Your academic qualifications as a young man and subsequent experience in local governmental affairs would ensure that you would be trained for the slightly upper echelons of the service – it is unfortunate that you were unable to gain entry to a university, as this would have ensured you would have been considered for the top layers but that is now past history. So what do you think?' Old Farbres took a large swig of wine and waited for a response.

This was a totally different direction to anything Eric had expected and he had not even remotely considered becoming a policeman. He carefully bit his lip, gazing at his father as he examined the possibilities. At first he questioned the thought of becoming any sort of policeman and the idea did not appeal very much. He immediately envisaged standing about in a cloak in all weathers directing traffic or lost people late at night, and early morning starts. When it came down to it he realised he had not the faintest idea what the Gendarmerie actually did.

'Well?' said his father. 'What do you think?'

'I'll give it some thought Papa. I must admit it has surprised me a little that you would think I might do such a job, or think of it as a long term career move.'

'There are worse directions you could take, I assure you. It would offer security, respectability, good chances of promotion, and a decent enough pension. What else do you need? I think you should seriously consider the idea. It might even help to redress any feelings of guilt you may or may not have about missing the fighting in the north a few years ago. I imagine you must have come up against people or friends who might now regard you as someone who was somehow able to dodge the war and remain unscathed.' Old Farbres had obviously given a lot of thought to some of the wider consequences that might have resulted from his manipulations. Even though Eric had not spelled out the details, he had begun to suspect that his son's apparent disenchantment with his job in the licensing office had a lot more to do with the return of the two battle-scarred colleagues than he had owned up to. His own career path was strewn with the wreckage of a number of lost and damaged friendships, resulting from his own ambitious strivings for advancement. It had meant that although he had now arrived in a comfortable professional position he had probably made more enemies than friends, while the friendships he had managed to retain were largely with people who in turn, regarded him as possibly a useful tool in their own struggle to the top of the pile. He increasingly recognised that his son displayed similar ambitious traits to those he himself possessed and as such, it would have done no good to attempt to deflect him from his path. Better to help than to hinder in these circumstances!

'Give it some thought Eric - I think this could be a very significant move if you choose to go in that direction. I will of course do whatever I can to help your advancement, should help be needed.'

'I am grateful to you Papa, for your efforts and this idea. I will give it serious consideration I promise. I will have to discuss it with Anne-Marie of course - she knows nothing about any of this as you know.'

Anne-Marie knew a good deal more about Eric's problems in his present job than he could possibly have guessed. Georgette had kept her fully informed about everything as it happened, so it came as no surprise that he now proposed to resign from the Licensing Bureau. She was however taken aback to hear that he was considering becoming a Gendarme. It sounded to her like an act of desperation and she was doubtful about the whole idea.

'What on earth prompted you to think along these lines Eric?'

'Well, I have been thinking about my present position for some time now, and it is perfectly obvious to me that it is going to take a lifetime to get anywhere above where I am at the moment. I have spoken to my father about it and he understands the limitations of what I am doing at the present time and promised to examine a few ideas on my behalf. He came up with the gendarme proposal.'

'So it was his idea then?'

'Yes.'

'There must surely be something else you could do Eric – must it be the gendarmerie?'

'Not necessarily but there is a shortage of men at the moment and if I get in now there is a good prospect of promotion fairly quickly. I have no intention of remaining a traffic policeman all my life, I assure you, Anne.'

'No, I wouldn't expect you to.' She had become increasingly aware of her husband's ambitious leanings, added to which Georgette's on-going commentary on life in the office, meant that it came as no great surprise that he would eventually decide to resign. That he was now seriously considering becoming some sort of policeman was difficult for her to take on board; it was something that had never been discussed, or even mentioned, at any time in the past. Moreover, it irritated her to think that her father-in-law should have been responsible for putting the scheme into his head and she thought it almost a certainty that he would again try to further manipulate the situation from there on in.

*　*　*　*　*

Within two months Eric Farbres had enrolled as a full time student at the Ecole de Gendarmerie in le Puy-en-Massenet. It took him nearly an hour on his motor bike to get to and from the school at weekends, so he slept in the barracks during the week. The training régime was quite tough, involving harsh physical exercise in the very early morning with more of the same in the afternoon. In between there were lectures on French law, geography, history, criminology, firearms and a host of other subjects deemed necessary by the authorities, as being essential for the satisfactory functioning of a gendarme. Eric quickly became a good deal more physically fit than he had ever been and soon picked up the rudiments of law, history and how the gendarmerie slotted into the national structure. Two years later he passed his final exams and was assigned to a divisional unit near Mauriac with a rank of junior officer.

Anne-Marie had avoided telling Henrietta or her mother about Georgette's on-going commentary on events at the licensing office. Although she wrote fairly regularly to her sister and mother with updates on Isabelle's progress and life in general, she had been careful to sidestep anything that could be used by Henrietta and exacerbate her sister's continuing antipathy towards Eric. She felt it would only invite more questions about his character and motives, which Anne-Marie was either unwilling or unable to discuss. As for Hortense, Anne-Marie did not want to give her mother any reason for concern about Eric or their futures. Life for Hortense and Henrietta was difficult enough without adding further worries and it had seemed best to remain quiet about any difficulties in which he may have become embroiled.

When Henrietta and Hortense finally learned from Anne-Marie that Eric intended joining the Gendarmerie and was working out the last few days at the licensing office, the news was greeted with very mixed reactions. Henrietta was the first to hear about this unexpected change of direction when Anne-Marie made a rare visit to Chalhac on the 'bus.' Eric's mother was going to look after Isabelle for a few hours and it would allow Anne-Marie to get out of the house for a change. Henrietta's immediate question to her sister was, 'Why?'

'Because Eric was becoming anxious about his job prospects, he can't see much chance of promotion for the foreseeable future and has been thinking about making a move for some time now.'

'Really?' It was hardly a question – more a sarcastic comment.

'I would have thought it was a very comfortable job to have landed. He was more than lucky to have had a father able to wangle him out of the fighting as well as getting him into such a quiet little number. Isn't it good enough for him?' Henrietta was quickly getting into her stride about Eric which would have precipitated another argument with her sister had it not been for Hortense's return at that precise moment:

'Anne-Marie! How lovely to see you Darling!'

'Hello Maman – How are you?'

'We are both fine, aren't we Henrietta? And how is my granddaughter – staying well I hope? – and Eric?'

'Yes. They are both well. I have been telling Henrietta about Eric. He is changing his job.'

'Promotion?'

'No. He is leaving the Licensing Bureau and is going to become a gendarme.'

'Whatever for? Are you serious?'

'Absolutely serious, Maman.'

'Rather sudden isn't it? Has he been sacked?'

'Of course not Maman.'

'Then why?'

'Well he has felt for some time now that it will take an awful long time to get anywhere near any promotion. There are people in front of him who will almost certainly get preference and he feels he can't leave it any longer.'

'What people?'

'There are two who came back after the war and who had both been injured; one lost a leg and the other was gassed and that messed up his breathing. They are both still quite young and Eric thinks they will be given preference over him whatever happens.' Hortense considered the situation for a few moments:

'I suppose that might be expected.' She could not quite believe this account of why there was this sudden change of direction and was deeply suspicious.

'Have either these young men ever spoken to Eric about any of this, I wonder? Do they know how it was that Eric managed to stay out of the fighting?'

'Eric has not said so although they would be sure to have rather strong feelings about the subject.' Ann-Marie was beginning to feel rather uncomfortable at being quizzed to this extent by her mother, who had until now, appeared to have rather favoured her son-in-law. Some doubts were seemingly creeping into her mother's mind and this was a new turn of events. It was even more difficult at this precise moment because Henrietta was witness to everything her mother had said. Henrietta added, 'I bet those two men were less than charmed when they got to know about Eric. Imagine how you would feel if you'd had your leg blown off or had your lungs wrecked, having come back to where you had been working before and then discovered that someone had taken over your job, and that he hadn't a scratch because he had dodged the war? I bet they have had a lot more to say to Eric than he has told you Anne, and who could blame them?'

'You might be right,' conceded Anne-Marie. She immediately felt guilty that she should be seen siding with her sister and mother against her own husband.

'Of course you have always had it in for Eric haven't you Henrietta? I imagine you have been waiting for something like this to happen so you could gloat about how right you were in the first place?'

'Not at all. I just felt that Eric was a bit big for his boots and felt very superior to us in our little house, tending chickens and a cow, and having no money. It was written all over him. His new motor bike and his gloves and his over polite way of getting round us; it was all too obvious what he was about. I suppose his damned father bought him the motor bike?'

Anne-Marie could stand it no longer:

'For God's sake Henrietta, shut up about it. I'm sick to death of the whole subject. You don't know him at all; he is a lovely man. He is kind, he's a good father to Isabelle and he wants to make his way in the world – not sit on his backside and hope for the best. The world doesn't work like that. I am sorry, but that is how I feel.'

'Stop it now, you two,' said Hortense, who could barely get a word in while the two sisters were crossing verbal swords. She was already having serious misgivings about Eric, and had begun to question her own earlier judgments of him. It could be that Henrietta might have a point concerning Eric's self-regard and thinking he was a cut or two above the common herd.

<u>Six</u>

Henrietta had taken a job as a part-time governess to the children of minor aristocrats Monsieur Henri and Madame Juliette, le Comte and la Comtesse de Villebarde, who lived in a small chateau a little way out of Chalhac. The house had seen better times and had once been a rather splendid affair, but had now taken on a shabby and careworn appearance. The Comte and Comtesse and their two children were the remnants of a once powerful family, originally allies of one of the Louis' in pre-revolutionary France. Comte Henri's ancestor had been a high official in the Treasury and a trusted supporter of the king. He had been rewarded with land and money, which he had used to build and furnish the original large house, where Henrietta was now to be found in charge of two slightly superior young children.

Money was always short for Henrietta and Hortense and it had been a big help to have a regular income, even though her wages were hardly generous. She had heard about the job vacancy for a governess at the chateau when one of the villagers was speaking to Hortense on market day. Pierre Brun worked at the chateau as a forester and general maintenance man and was aware of Henrietta's and Hortense's straightened circumstances. He promised, given a suitable opportunity, to speak to the chatelaine with the idea of arranging an interview, always assuming that Henrietta would be interested. She was indeed interested - not only did the thought of having an income appeal, but her frustrated maternal instincts made the job an even more attractive proposition.

The Comte and Comtesse interviewed Henrietta a few days later and it was agreed that she would be employed initially for a trial period of three months, to see how she got on with their offspring. If everything went well she would have a permanent job, at least until the children became older, when the position would be reviewed. Henrietta had been greatly impressed with the whole thing and recounted to her mother some of the details about the chateau and Madame la Comtesse.

'The chateau is not quite as splendid as you might imagine – it's all looking a bit shabby and run down now, but it must have been quite something when it was first built. Perhaps they don't see it any more as they have lived with it for all these years although Madame herself is very particular about her personal appearance. She was wearing a very expensive looking dress and her hair was all coiffed most beautifully, and her perfume! She must buy the very best when they go off on their trips to Paris – she told me that they go up there several times a year to visit friends, which is partly the reason for needing someone to keep an eye on the children when they are away.'

'What about le Comte, what's he like?'

'He did not say very much and left most of it to her, but he seems to be pleasant enough. I think it might work out quite well.'

A week later Henrietta began working at the chateau. She quickly got into her stride with the way she was to run things regarding her new charges. They were a brother and sister – Richard, aged eight and Sophie, six. Both were formal and very polite to Henrietta though she sensed they had clearly been drilled by their parents into seeing themselves as members of the upper classes. They were aware that their new governess came from the village just a few kilometres down the road and that she was obviously quite poor. Her clothes alone bore evidence of her impoverished circumstances and Sophie had made reference to the fact to her mother:

'Madame Suau is very poor isn't she Maman?'

'Yes, she is not very well off – very few of the villagers have any money. It must be hard for them to make ends meet sometimes.'

Comtesse de Villebarde was vaguely aware that in the world beyond the comparative comfort of their chateau, there existed an almost infinite number of ordinary people, living a hand to mouth existence which allowed for nothing beyond survival. For them, clothes were simply the means to keep out the cold in winter and to remain within the bounds of common decency.

Henrietta's duties included so far as possible, the application of basic disciplines upon the children, to get them up in the morning and ensure they were ready for bed in the early evening. She also had to supervise them at lunch, when it was not unusual for their parents to be absent, visiting friends or out pursuing other activities.

In addition she was expected to read to them from an extensive library. Unfortunately, most of the shelves contained massive tomes of heavy political dialogues, biographies and obscure philosophical treatises, translated from original Greek. Monsieur le Comte had inherited the chateau along with the contents of the library from his great uncle. He had been obliged to accept it as a whole with good grace as well as being obliged to express his enormous pleasure at his uncle's generosity and kindness. Most of the books were totally unsuitable as reading matter for Henrietta, let alone the children, and this imposed considerable difficulties for her. Her own instincts gravitated in the direction of rather less intellectually challenging books, partly to sustain some semblance of interest by her young charges and also to be able to get her own head around some of the writing. It was therefore with some relief that Henrietta uncovered a small section devoted to more readily digestible books and she drew upon this most of the time. For the most part even these were not entirely suitable reading matter for children of their age and Henrietta had to delete and concoct new passages, in long established tales which she felt would be more easily accepted by her young audience.

The working day that Henrietta was expected to put in at the chateau was long and less than convenient. She had to wake the children, get them both dressed and ready to present themselves at the breakfast table with their parents. In the evening, it was necessary to be there to oversee their supper before getting them ready for bed. Once there, and depending upon how weary they were, there was the obligatory reading to them, and this was something of a burden. The régime meant that Henrietta had to leave Chalhac on her bicycle quite early every day, in order to meet the demands put upon her by her employers and by her young charges. It also meant she was rarely able to get home before the early evening. She had tentatively suggested sleeping at the chateau during the week but was turned down by the Comtesse – probably because it would have entailed restoring a bedroom to a suitably civilized level to accommodate her – something she was not prepared to do for a number of reasons, not least being the cost involved. Although she and the Comte were ostensibly well off, the reality was a little different, as they were saddled with heavy running costs at the chateau. When Henrietta told her mother that she had approached the Comtesse about it, Hortense was less than pleased and was considerably relieved when she learned the idea had been turned down. Hortense had never lived alone in the house at any time during her life and since Anne-Marie had married, she had become even more reliant upon Henrietta for company and ordinary day to day affairs, so at least her daughter would be at home in the evenings and at night.

There were other considerations for Henrietta. She saw less of Isabelle than she would have liked and as Isabelle was now nearly ten years old she had missed too many of her niece's formative years for her liking. When she did see Isabelle their affection for one and other was immediate and obvious. Henrietta's bicycle had made it a little easier to get to her sister's home and to gain more access to Isabelle, but it was still difficult to find the time in view of her work at the chateau. Anne-Marie was always pleased to see her sister as Eric spent an ever increasing amount of time away from home. He had risen in rank and was now in charge of a small divisional unit near Clermont-Ferrand. From there to their home in Petit Domvent entailed a two-hour train journey followed by a further hour on his motor bike, which he kept near the railway station. Because Eric was away more than he was at home, Anne-Marie was often isolated for days on end. Eric's parents did what they could by way of moral support and came to see their daughter-in-law and granddaughter as often as possible. Farbres senior had an ancient motor car. He felt partly responsible by encouraging his son to join the Gendarmerie in the first place so he felt that visiting Anne-Marie would go some way go towards redressing the balance. Isabelle had shown a real fondness for her grandfather – more so in fact than for her father. Eric's ability to demonstrate affection was not something that came easily to him. His young daughter felt instinctively that she was being deprived or somehow excluded from his attention. It resulted in Isabelle drawing further and further away from her father, almost to the point of disliking him and being unable to relate to him. In contrast to this, Farbres Senior always looked forward to seeing both his daughter-in-law and Isabelle, and they both reciprocated warmly to the old man. Madame Farbres did not see quite as much of them as she already had a circle of friends with whom she spent much of her time. This was hardly accidental, because the road from St. Loup-des-Granges was narrow and very rudimentary, and her husband's driving abilities were equally basic, and were not helped by the motor car itself, which was extremely uncomfortable and unmanageable.

Anne-Marie's longtime friend, Georgette had been unable to find a husband and was resigned to the fact that she would probably have to remain a spinster. The effect of so many men losing their lives in the war meant that a disproportionate number of women were now likely to remain in a state of spinsterhood. She still worked at the Licensing Office in Domvent and had now risen in seniority to a fairly comfortable level. Her salary had increased and she had been able to buy a small house on the outskirts of the town. She now owned a small motor car as well - not new but serviceable which had opened up a whole new range of possibilities for visits to other towns and relatives. Among these activities was her habit of collecting Anne-Marie and Isabelle from their home and taking them down to Chalhac, giving Hortense the chance to see her daughter and granddaughter – something which would have been a rare occurrence but for Georgette's kindness.

It was during one of these visits that Isabelle decided she would like to explore the village by herself. She had been taken around with her mother a few years earlier, but was too young at the time to take much notice – and in any case there was not a great deal to be seen in Chalhac. On this particular afternoon Isabelle had become bored with the conversation between her mother and grandmother, with occasional interjections by Georgette. Her 'Tantetta'- the contraction conjured by the child several years earlier when she was unable get her tongue around 'Tante Henrietta', was not yet home from her duties at the chateau. There was nothing new added to the discussion about her grandfather's death in the Great War, or the tragic loss of Henrietta's young husband shortly afterwards. Isabelle had heard the same topics raked over endlessly and although she had no wish to be disrespectful to her grandmother, or to upset anyone for any other reason, she began to fidget. It was in these circumstances that she made her excuses to go for a walk around the village by herself.

During a brief lull in the conversation, she announced:

'Would you mind very much if I went out for a walk? – I'd like to see the village again. I don't really know anything or anybody here and it might be interesting.'

'Well, I suppose it is alright darling, but don't go too far because when Aunt Henrietta gets back and we have said hello to her, we will have to make our way home. Is it alright with you Maman?' added Anne-Marie to her mother.

'Of course it's alright,' said Hortense. 'The child must be bored to death with all this grown up talk.'

Isabelle needed no further encouragement. She had made her excuses as elegantly as she could manage, then let herself out and wandered across the little square, past the church and down the road towards the watermill. There was nothing happening, nor any indication that the mill might even still be lived in. Beyond this point there were no further signs of human habitation so she retraced her steps back into the shadow of the church and paused briefly at the little war memorial at the edge of the square. On the plinth below the small column, were the wilting remains of cut flowers, drooping now in the heat of the afternoon. Among the inscribed names were Albert Hubert and a little further down, François Suau. Isabelle paused for a few moments as she pondered what these two men had been like and was a little saddened to think that now she would never know her grand-père Hubert or her oncle François. It was impossible for the child to begin to grasp the enormity of the tragic events that had given rise to the little memorial, but it did register upon her that her family had been deeply involved, and continued to discuss the matter – as they were doing yet again this very afternoon.

She crossed the road and walked past the bakery. There was nothing to be seen as Monsieur Bonnet had shut for the afternoon, closed the shutters and was having a well-deserved sleep in the darkened room at the back. She had left the square behind her and began to walk along the road in the direction of Domvent. On the right a house came into view, one she must have passed several times when visiting her grandmother in Georgette's motor car. It was not very distinguished and looked as though it needed straightening up as it appeared to be leaning slightly, to one side. As she approached it she became aware that there was some sort of activity in the patch of ground beside the house. She stopped and surreptitiously peered between the branches of a large hibiscus bush which formed a partial boundary between the road and the house. A boy of about twelve was sitting on a rudimentary swing, hung from a tree. He was twisting the seat around several times, raising his feet, allowing the swing to spin him around in the opposite direction as it unraveled. He repeated this two or three times before realising that he was being watched. He got off the swing and sauntered over to the hibiscus tree, through which he could see the vague shape of Isabelle.

'Have you been watching me?' he asked the hibiscus.

Isabelle emerged from behind the bush so she would be in a better position to conduct a conversation. She felt slightly embarrassed, if not a little guilty, for having been caught out spying on him.

'Yes I was. I hope you don't mind – I wasn't being nosey. I just thought that what you were doing looked quite interesting. I haven't got a swing,' she added, hoping that this might placate him should he have taken offence.

'I don't mind at all,' said the boy. 'Would you like to have a go?'

'Yes please!' said Isabelle enthusiastically. She was only too pleased for the chance to somehow brighten up her afternoon. He ushered her across the few metres of tufty grass to the swing, which was still twisting and untwisting slightly. He steadied the seat for her as she sat down. Her feet only just reached the ground but were close enough at first to be able to wind up the ropes two or three turns, after which her feet were unable to gain any further purchase against the grass.

'Let me wind it round a bit more for you, otherwise it's not a lot of fun.' He began to rotate the swing gently round and round a few times. As he did so they came face to face at each rotation and he was considerably taken with what he saw. Isabelle was now a very pretty child almost ten years old, with large brown eyes, a well-shaped mouth and a big crop of frizzy dark brown hair. She was olive skinned.

'Hold on tight!' he said. 'I'm letting you go now.'

Isabelle shrieked with delight as the swing rapidly unwound.

'Can I have another go?'

'Yes, of course. Hold on.' He began the winding process again. 'I don't know your name.' he said, as he twisted her around.

'Isabelle - Isabelle Farbres.'

'That's a pretty name. I haven't seen you before – do you live near the village?'

'No. In Petit Domvent. I am here visiting my grandmother and Tantetta.'

'Where do they live?'

'On La Place. My grandmother is Madame Hubert.'

'Who is Tantetta?'

'My aunt, Henrietta Suau. I used to call her Tantetta when I was little girl, and it has rather stuck.' She felt rather silly having to admit to her babyish mispronunciation. She no longer saw herself as the little girl she had once been and this was an indication that she suddenly felt quite grown up, speaking to this young man.

'Yes of course I know them. Madame Suau must be your mother's sister?' He guessed right. 'Hold on again, I'm letting you go!' By the time she got off the swing Isabelle was quite giddy and had to hold on to one of the ropes.

'You'll be alright in a moment or two,' said the boy. 'I am Guy – Guy Gaillard. My father works at the quarry. It's not what he really wants to do,' he added, 'because he is a stonemason and makes things out of stone and builds things like walls, for houses and castles.'

Isabelle's eyes opened wider at this. 'Have you lived here long?' she asked.

'Absolutely ages.'

'How long?'

'About eight years. We all lived in Russia before we came here. My father lived in Chinon when he was young and then my grandfather went to Russia to find work. He was a stonemason too. When my Papa grew up, he met my Mama, when they were both working at the same chateau. Then the revolution began and it was terrible. Everybody was killing one another. My mother is a Jew and she was very frightened because some of her family had been murdered. Then my father had a letter one day saying he had been left this house in France by his cousin. My parents decided to leave Russia and come back to France. They had no money or anything, so we had to walk from Russia. My mother is Russian!' he added proudly.

It had been a rapid outpouring of the family's recent and not so recent, history. Isabelle could not quite take it all in at first.

'You walked from Russia?' she said incredulously.

'Yes we did. It is a very long way. We were all very glad to get here in the end.' He regaled her with a résumé of their journey from Russia, or what little he could remember – he had been a very small boy when they began their trek. Isabelle was quite spellbound by this tale and felt even more grown up to be the confidante of someone she considered to be a very mature young man – mature at least to her. Guy was not quite thirteen at that time.

'So the three of you came back to live in Chalhac?'

'Four of us,' corrected Guy, 'there's my brother Marcel as well. He is fifteen and he helps my father over at the quarry. Papa says he's not really strong enough for that sort of work yet, but he wants to teach him about stone working and things like that.'

Isabelle was hugely impressed with this whole story and quite excited to think that she now knew someone whose father was a stonemason or some sort of sculptor and she imagined, he made carved statues and things to adorn chateaux. She found the whole story absolutely thrilling. As if that were not enough, this boy had actually walked with his brother and his parents all the way from Russia. Although she had very little idea how far away Russia was, nor could barely grasp what it must have meant to walk that far, she was nonetheless suitably astounded.

'What about your parents?' asked Guy. 'What does your papa do?'

'He is an officer in the Gendarmerie.'

'Is he?' joked the boy. 'So you are a policeman's daughter! We will have to watch our step!'

'Yes, I suppose I am,' said Isabelle. There was a great deal more she wanted to ask Guy but she was becoming anxious about the time she had been out and felt the need to get back to her grandmother's house. In any case she did not want to be told off by her mother for disappearing for so long.

'Well I must go now, because they will begin to worry about me. Can I come and see you when we are back in Chalhac again?'

'Of course! I'll be here somewhere.'

'Lovely!' said the girl and politely shook his hand. 'Au revoir.'

She could hardly wait to get back to tell her mother about her encounter with Guy. She felt very grown up at having struck up a conversation with someone she had not known existed until half an hour before. She was greeted with a mixture of relief and pleasure by Hortense, Anne-Marie, Georgette and Henrietta, who had just arrived back from the chateau. Henrietta hugged the child to her breast.

'Darling! And what have you be doing this afternoon – I hear you were going to explore the village by yourself?'

'Yes Tantetta – I did and it's been very interesting.'

'Really?' said Anne-Marie, smiling at the others. 'There must be rather more to Chalhac than we have been able to uncover so far! Where did you get to then?'

Isabelle quickly recounted her short tour of the village, ending with her finding Guy Gaillard in his parents' garden. She excitedly told them about his parents' flight from Russia and that both his grandparents had been murdered, that the family had walked all the way from Russia when he and his brother were little boys. She recounted how poor they had been and that his papa had been left the house where they now lived, by his cousin. She added finally,

'Guy's mother is a Jew.'

'Well, he certainly opened up his heart to you Isabelle,' said Henrietta. 'It took me about three years to find out even less than you have been told in the space of half an hour!'

'Is this young man polite?' asked Hortense.

'Yes Mamie. He is very polite and quite nice. He let me have a go on his swing.'

'Well that's alright then.'

A short lull in the conversation followed as all four women digested the information supplied so unexpectedly by young Isabelle. Hortense said,

'They seem to be a good family. Gaillard works at the quarry, as does his son. It must be very heavy work. Madame Gaillard seems to be a nice enough person. She's Jewish of course,' she added.

'Russian Jewish,' said Henrietta.

'That's right. Monsieur Gaillard must have been very taken with her when he was working over there. I expect the poor man felt lonely and if, as Isabelle has been told, his parents were killed, he probably needed some company; she came along and he fell for her. Et voila! I wonder what her parents would have had to say about it – a mixed marriage and so on but they were probably already dead when he appeared. They were all caught up in the riots before the revolution so I expect they were killed or captured and maybe executed. I spoke to Madame Gaillard about it once and she was very cagey about it all – I fancy she was not eager for me to know about her Jewish ancestry especially as she had married a non - Jew, it must have been fairly difficult for her in a number of ways. Then of course she produced her two sons – half Jewish, so there were even more complications.'

'Personally,' said Henrietta, 'I don't feel very strongly about any of that. They have their sons – both seem to be polite and well behaved. The older one works with his father at the quarry so I suppose they need the money'

'You must have been talking to the younger one Isabelle,' said Anne-Marie.

'Yes. His name is Guy. He doesn't know yet what he wants to do when he leaves school but I think he is too clever to work in the quarry like his brother.'

This was very perceptive for a ten year old child. It was clear that during the course of their first encounter, Isabelle had managed to extract a great deal of background information about Guy, his brother Marcel and their parents, all in the space of less than half an hour. Georgette had been listening quietly to the interrogation and discussion about Isabelle's afternoon adventure. During a lull in the conversations she spoke: 'If I were you Isabelle, I would be careful not to say too much to your papa about Guy. Better still, I wouldn't say anything to him about today.'

'Why?' asked the child.

'Well, I happen to know that your papa is not very well disposed towards Jewish people.'

'What do you mean – disposed?'

'I mean that he does not like them very much. I know this because I worked with him in the same office for a few years – even before you were born, and I happen to know that he has no time for Jewish people. So if I were you Isabelle, I would keep it to yourself. It could cause a great deal of unpleasantness if he finds out that you have made a friend of someone who is Jewish.'

Georgette looked around the little room at the three other women, who were a little startled to hear her unexpectedly express her views so bluntly. That she should have done so to a ten year old child had been even more surprising. She now looked for their approval. 'Surely you must have been aware of Eric's thoughts about Jews, Anne-Marie?' she added.

'I don't think we have ever spoken about Jews or whether he liked or disliked them. There are not a lot of Jews around here anyway, so what's all the fuss about?'

'Believe me Anne, he has no time for them, and it is only my opinion of course, but Isabelle would be well advised to stay quiet about it all.'

A silence followed, broken only by Isabelle's small voice:

'Well I think he is very nice. In any case it's only his mother who's Jewish, so I can't see why anyone should get upset.'

'It's not quite that easy Darling,' said Georgette. 'The trouble is that children of Jews become Jewish if their mother is Jewish, which means that Guy and his brother are Jews. It does not matter that their papa is a Roman Catholic Frenchman or anything else. It is their mama's religion that counts.'

'Well I think it is silly,' said Isabelle, who was by now becoming increasingly angry. She began to think it would have been better had she kept her meeting Guy to herself and not said anything to anyone. It would have been her secret. Why was it that grown-ups made such a song and dance about things? They always seemed to want to spoil everything. Her news about Guy and his family had now been effectively doused with cold water and not only that, but she had somehow been made to feel guilty.

Henrietta sensed her young niece's disappointment at the way her family had undone what had obviously been a happy episode for her.

'Don't take any notice of us Isabelle. We are all a lot of old miseries. I'm sure Guy and his family are all very nice people and I, for one, am happy that you have made a good friend in Chalhac. Perhaps you can see him again when you are visiting Mamie?'

'I have already told him that I will call by next time we are here. Is that alright Maman?'

'Of course it is Darling!' said Anne-Marie, who had only just noticed that Henrietta was signaling to her with her eyes, that they should modify their comments a little for the child's sake.

'Did you say he has a swing in the garden? Perhaps you could ask Papi to fix one up for you – or if he can't, then maybe grand-père would do it if you ask him nicely.'

Seven

During the following five or six years, Isabelle and Guy Gaillard's relationship had gradually changed from being a mere childhood friendship, strong though that had been. By 1939 Guy was nineteen and Isabelle a very attractive seventeen. She still possessed her large brown eyes and dark hair though it was less frizzy now than a few years earlier and it was cut shorter with a small fringe. She was blessed with an attractively shaped mouth and, for a seventeen year old, a full figure. Without being able to imagine what might transpire as a result, their respective parents had bought their offspring bicycles, both coincidently for their thirteenth birthdays. Anne-Marie had suggested to Eric that it would be a good way for Isabelle to be able to get to see her grandmother in Chalhac as well as giving the child some healthy exercise. So when her thirteenth birthday arrived a new bicycle was produced, extravagantly wrapped in fancy paper and adorned with a large paper bow. The wrapping barely disguised the unmistakable outlines of its contents and Isabelle was thrilled more than she had ever been in her young life. Earlier in 1933, Guy's parents had also bought a bicycle for their son as a Bar Mitzvah present when he had attained the significant age of thirteen. While realising that there was little prospect of a big ceremony to celebrate his becoming a man with its attendant responsibilities, Sarah still felt it would be good to try to keep alive what remained of his ancestral background. Jules Gaillard went along with the idea of not wishing to destroy Sarah's cultural background altogether by denying their sons' half-Jewish ancestry. He was happy enough to be able to buy a bicycle for Guy as he had already done for Marcel, when he too had achieved thirteen, two years earlier. Guy had been immensely grateful to his parents, with a deep understanding even at thirteen, that life was anything but easy for them and that buying a bike represented a considerable portion of his father's income.

Isabelle was now in the habit of visiting her grandmother Hortense, and her aunt Henrietta - whom she still referred to as 'Tantetta' - on a fairly regular weekly basis. She could comfortably cycle to Chalhac from the family home in Petit Domvent, a trip she had done over the last six years on her birthday bicycle, and which had resulted in strong legs and good lungs.

Henrietta still had her job at the chateau, although she was now unsure just long it would last. By now the two children were twelve and ten years old respectively and there had been talk of their being sent to a private school for more formal education. In addition, she had noticed that other changes had occurred in the lives of the Comte and Comtesse which may or may not have been significant. Their car, a somewhat flamboyant Hispano-Suiza, had not been used for a number of months and according to the general handyman Pierre, to whom Henrietta occasionally spoke, it had broken down on one of their forays to Paris – something to do with the gearbox. It was his opinion that the Comte was unable or unwilling to pay the costs of a repair. Until then Henrietta had assumed that the vehicle was simply not being used, but the truth of the matter was that it was languishing in a garage somewhere near Bourges. She had seen them driving out of the chateau in a much less impressive machine and she began to wonder whether the family's finances were perhaps more precarious than she had previously imagined. The remnants of the French aristocracy were holding on as far as possible, to their land and property and trying to keep up appearances and standards. Their position however was becoming more eroded as time went by, due to the inexorable rise in the power of the trade unions and a steady drift away from the land towards the cities where the wages were better and prospects rather more promising.

Isabelle's weekly visits to Chalhac were no longer spent exclusively with her grandmother or aunt and, after a carefully judged and diplomatically gauged period of time with them, she would escape to the Gaillards' house. She had become more and more devoted to Guy Gaillard and this was affectionately reciprocated by the young man. Strangely, it seemed not to have occurred to either Isabelle or Guy that they might actually fall in love. Until now their relationship had been much more like that of brother and sister and neither of them had felt or needed anything more from their friendship. Her visits to Chalhac invariably included calling in at the Gaillards' house, where she was now a familiar figure. Both Sarah and Jules Gaillard had taken a strong liking to the girl and regarded her almost as a daughter. She was always warmly welcomed and this had indirectly led to the family being more generally accepted by the villagers. Sarah Gaillard's origins were no longer a matter of speculation and her Jewish background had become no more than a slight oddity. Why Jules Gaillard should have married her in the first place was occasionally a topic for speculation for some. Indeed in view of the lack of any solid facts surrounding their circumstances at the time, it was generally assumed that when Jules' parents died he had found himself stranded and lonely in a foreign land needing someone to care for him. The general consensus was that he had discovered Sarah to be in much the same situation as himself and they had fallen for one another. It was generally recognised that their two sons were turning out to be good hardworking people. Marcel was now nearly twenty-two, a strong young man and a real asset to his father at the quarry. He showed great potential as a stone mason as well as displaying some talent as a sculptor. In his spare time he had produced a recognisable bust of his mother which she had viewed with a certain degree of parental criticism, tempered by maternal pride.

'Do I really look like that?' asked Sarah when she first caught sight of his sculptural efforts.

'It's how I see you Maman. It may not be quite right yet – I may go back to it and see if I can improve it.'

'No, no Darling. Don't do that. I think it is lovely as it is. In any case you might spoil it if you mess about with it. What do you think Jules?'

'I have been watching him working on it for several weeks now and I think he shows great promise. I only wish I had the same degree of talent!'

'Don't put yourself down Papa – your skills are greatly admired. Let's face it, some of the aristocracy in Russia obviously thought well enough of your abilities to employ you as a full time restorer and repairer in their palaces. You would have been out on the street long ago if you hadn't been any good at your job.'

'It came to the same thing in the end, didn't it?' said Jules ruefully.

'Perhaps – but that was not your fault.' So Sarah's new stone image was set in a place of honour above the fireplace in the living room.

Isabelle had not been privy to this conversation and when she called by on the following Saturday, Sarah's stone bust was installed for all to see. She was ushered into the living room and was not immediately aware of the new stone item adorning the mantelshelf. Jules signaled to her with his eyes towards it and she followed his gaze up to the shelf.

'Oh. Mama Sarah! How wonderful! Marcel's handiwork no doubt?'

'Indeed it is,' said Sarah with enormous pride. After the initial shock of seeing herself presented in this way, she had begun to appreciate the artistry and hard work it involved.

'Your brother is very clever, Guy. I hope you appreciate him.'

'I do, I do, I promise!'

Guy regarded his brother's abilities with stone very highly, although, as is so often the case, he rarely voiced his admiration to any of the family, least of all his brother. It was all taken for granted that Marcel would join his father in working in some capacity in stone, quarrying or even becoming a sculptor. The latter option was not really considered a serious possibility, largely because the family had no useful connections in the art world, nor did they mix with people of that social background. He was thus destined to remain a quarryman for the foreseeable future, a prospect which he regarded entirely philosophically. He saw his occasional efforts at sculpture as a relaxation rather than having any monetary value. His mother took a different view and she had frequently discussed with Jules the potential earning power that her son's abilities might represent. Jules' response only reiterated what they all knew: that they simply did not move in the right circles to be able to take any advantage of their son's God given natural talents.

Meanwhile, Guy was moving in an entirely different direction. He had achieved good results in his final exams at senior school, and managed to get a place on a teacher training course. It was due to start with the autumn term, but it would involve living near the college in Clermont-Ferrand. They were out on their bikes when Guy told Isabelle about his good fortune in getting a place on the course. They were up in the hills behind the village – one of their favoured spots when she realised what was entailed and Isabelle could barely grasp at first its full implications.

'You'll be in Clermont I suppose, from Monday to Friday then?' she had asked.

'Worse than that Isabelle – Monday to Sunday.'

'You mean you will not be home at all?'

'That's about it, yes. The train fares would make it a virtual impossibility to get back every weekend, so I'll be stuck there most of the time. Of course if I can raise the cash I'll make it back as much as I can, but I expect I'll be too poor to manage it very often. Sorry!' he added.

'Sorry! What am I supposed to do if you're not here?' Her eyes started to fill with tears. She was beginning to realise just how much she relied on Guy being around and how big a part he now played in her life. She began to imagine life without him, without their conversations, their travelling around the hills and mountains on their bikes together. Her life would have to be re-ordered and would probably again become a boring round of obligatory visits to her aged grandparents on the outskirts of Domvent, punctuated with weekly visits to Chalhac to see 'Tantetta' and her maternal grandmother. The future looked distinctly bleak.

Until then, Guy had not really considered the effect that this might have upon Isabelle. He thought of her more as a sister and like his brother, took her presence for granted. Isabelle's view of him was rather different.

'Please don't upset yourself Isabelle. I'll come back as often as I can, but it will be important that I study at weekends and even if I did get home I don't suppose I'd be able to do any of the usual things. I'm sure you can see the problem.'

'Yes. I can see that of course, but the thought of not seeing you for what may be weeks is hard for me to take in just now. Where are you going to live up there?'

'There's a fellow I have got to know, Simon Wojakovski. His parents live on the outskirts of Clermont and they have agreed to put me up during term time. They are quite nice people – from Poland originally. So at least I'll have a bed to sleep in!'

'Well I'm glad you can see the funny side of it. I don't think it is a bit funny. I thought you might have given me some thought when you were offered a place on the course. You haven't said much about it to me and now it looks like you are committed to Clermont for the next two or three years and I am supposed to wait for you here while you achieve great things and get diplomas and all the rest of it.' Isabelle was getting into her stride and becoming more and more angry as she spoke. She did not know it but there were echoes of her aunt Henrietta in her reactions and her anger was building into something like a row.

Guy was somewhat taken aback by this very uncharacteristic outburst from Isabelle. His brotherly view of her was quite suddenly thrown into some disarray.

'Hang on Isabelle – I think I must have missed something here. Am I really so important to you that you are going to get all upset by my plans?'

'Good God Guy! You really are incredibly stupid sometimes. Can't you see how much I care for you? I thought you felt the same way about me, but I was obviously mistaken. I love you Guy – can't you see that?'

Guy was momentarily speechless – not to say stunned by this declaration by Isabelle. It really had not occurred to him that she regarded him so totally differently to how he saw her, which was simply as an affectionate sister. In his eyes she was obviously a very attractive creature, one he would defend to the death, but it had not struck him that she might see him as a sexual partner, any more than he might have seen a sister. He found his voice eventually:

'Oh God! Isabelle Darling! Please forgive me if you can. How could I have been so stupid and not seen what must have been blindingly clear to everyone except me. I will simply cancel my place on the course and do something else – how about that!'

'You will do no such thing! I will not let you wreck your plans for silly old me. I would never be able to forgive myself if you did that. It's just that somehow I had imagined that your course would be in St. Flour or even Domvent. I never dreamt it would be necessary for you to be so far away.'

'God! What a mess I have made of it. We will have to think hard how we can get around the problem.'

'Yes. Maybe we can think of something.'

She turned to look at Guy who had suddenly been thrown into total confusion. He was still trying to gather his thoughts as he gazed into the middle distance, towards Chalhac and beyond where the hills and distant mountains were becoming a hazy blue in the early evening light. Her eyes were still slightly tearful from her earlier outburst and Guy turned and saw for the first time a different girl to the one who until that moment he had taken for granted and been such a normal part of his life. He gently pulled her closer, kissed her still damp eyes and then found her mouth. This kiss was no longer a fraternal peck, but full blooded, passionate and long lasting. Isabelle knew that from that moment that theirs was to be a real love affair, not just a question of brotherly affection.

Eight

There had been an unspoken understanding by Isabelle's family that her association with Guy and his family would remain hidden from her father, Eric Farbres. When, several years earlier she had first excitedly told her mother, grandmother, Tantetta and Georgette Vidal that she had made friends with Guy Gaillard, the child's news had been greeted with a certain degree of caution – not to say wariness. Georgette in particular, had urged Isabelle that it might be wise if she kept her friendship with Guy from her father. She had worked for a few years in the close company of Eric and in their office he had made no attempt to hide his dislike of Jews. Her motives in suggesting to the child that it might be the clever thing to keep it all out of her father's line of sight had been kind and sensible. She could understand the child's excitement at finding such a new and interesting friend and anything she could do at this early stage to prevent the association from being destroyed by her father's intolerance was, in her view, worthwhile. At the time it had been difficult for Isabelle to understand but as she grew older she gradually came to see the sense in Georgette's advice. It had therefore become an established habit that Guy and the rest of the Gaillard family were never mentioned in Eric's presence. As Eric was more away from home than the other way about, it had not been unduly difficult to maintain this subterfuge. So far as he was concerned, Isabelle's visits to Chalhac were no more than a dutiful token of her love for her aunt Henrietta and grandmother Hubert. His animosity and sensitivities towards the Jewish community in France had more recently been aired to Anne-Marie and to his ageing father. Isabelle had been privy to some of his anti-Semitic rants, and now she could clearly see how her friendship with Guy would play, were it to be uncovered. Georgette Vidal's cautions had been fully justified.

The relationship with her father had never really become anything more than distant. Sometimes he seemed little more than a stranger to her, whereas she had nearly always related well to her Grandpa Farbres. Her grandfather had grown to love the girl over the years and this was almost certainly the result of his feeling that his son had been unable to fulfill the role of loving father properly because of his police career – something for which he had been largely instrumental in the first place. Old Farbres had instinctively felt the need to compensate somehow for that state of affairs. Eric's absences during so much of his daughter's childhood had resulted in this odd and rather sad situation and his parental instincts had never developed much beyond being a formality. When Eric did get home, which was mostly at the weekends – he tried to demonstrate his parental concerns and responsibilities to both Anne-Marie and his parents. Farbres senior was fully aware of Eric's professional commitments and some of the pressures he was under.

One such weekend, the two men were sitting in old Farbres' garden. They had been discussing some of the problems resulting from the influx of various refugees from the Spanish civil war. Eric had been ordered to oversee the setting up of a camp, which lay to the south beyond Toulouse, and would house and process some of these people. It had meant his continued absence from home for several weeks and Anne-Marie was showing signs of considerable impatience with the way things were moving. Added to this, Isabelle was still digesting Guy's imminent departure for Clermont Ferrand. She had said very little to her mother about it as she did not want to alert her to anything that might point to a more serious relationship with Guy than her mother imagined – so Isabelle too, was less than happy at this time.

'I can't see there's much alternative to what I am doing at the moment Papa,' said Eric. 'Anne-Marie is fed up. I don't get to see Isabelle as much as I would wish and I can see it will end in a row.'

'It's a difficult position for you to be in my boy – I can see that very clearly. Has young Isabelle spoken about any of it at home?'

'Not to me.'

'Then maybe to her mother? Do you think the child is unhappy with the present state of affairs?'

'She hasn't said so directly to me, although Anne-Marie has said she thinks something is up.'

'Perhaps she is just becoming bored. Have you given thought to her future: a job or a career? Let's face it, she is seventeen now – nearly eighteen. She really ought to be earning her keep. Perhaps you could get her into the police service in some capacity? It would not be difficult for you to get her in somewhere I'm sure.'

'Possibly – although I am not sure how enthusiastic she would be. I am afraid I am not exactly the ideal role model and I think she would probably imagine it would involve spending endless weeks away from home like her father.'

'Yes of course but I'm sure she would enjoy meeting a lot of new people as well as being paid for doing it. She could do worse.'

Eric was suddenly aware that the conversation was becoming almost a re-run of the one he had had with his father almost fifteen years before. Old Farbres had been instrumental in persuading Eric to join the Gendarmerie and it had paid off in career terms at least, although the downside was the detrimental effect it was having on his private life.

'I'll sound her out about it Papa – she might go for the idea.'

'Yes – why don't you?'

The following day, Eric, Anne-Marie and Isabelle were having lunch together. It had not been a particularly merry occasion – Isabelle appeared to be sulking about something and Anne-Marie was using mono-syllabic replies to Eric's attempts to make conversation.

'Well it makes a change to be at home for once doesn't it?' offered Eric as an opening gambit. It was becoming difficult for him to find anything to talk about now he was home. He had spent the last several weeks doing his best to organise the latest refugee camp and it had been less than easy. He had shown little sympathy for most of the arrivals and he was becoming increasingly bad-tempered. Now he was back home again he was finding it a problem trying to pick up on the mundane aspects of family life. He had grown so far from Anne-Marie and his daughter that he hardly knew where to start.

'Yes it does make a nice change to see you home again,' said Anne-Marie with barely disguised sarcasm. 'When are you likely to appear again?'

'I'm hoping it will not be long. I have a conference to attend next weekend in Clermont, so that will make it impossible. I'm afraid we are going through a difficult time right now – there are hundreds, if not thousands, of people coming out of Spain and we are doing our best to keep some sort of control of the situation. We don't need them here in any event. They are a mixed bunch I can tell you: Trade Unionists, Communists, Jews, foreign sympathisers of all sorts as well as their own. When it all quietens down again we will have to decide what to do about them – they will not be able to stay here, that's for sure. Paris will have to decide.'

Isabelle made no comment on any of this. She was tempted to say something in defense of Jews but was wise enough to let the moment pass. She had been well aware of her father's views from the day she first discovered Guy on his homemade swing in his garden and how her mother, grandmother, aunt and Georgette had reacted. Their warnings at that time that she should say nothing about the friendship, had been taken on board and for the subsequent six or more years, had been maintained – amazingly so. How Eric Farbres would have reacted had never been put to the test although it raised questions about the way the situation might develop at some future time.

'So Isabelle, how do you spend your time these days? It must be pretty boring with nothing very much to do during the day. .Have you considered starting work somewhere?' It was a clumsy and abrupt introduction to the topic. 'We could probably get you into a worthwhile job in government somewhere or other. The wages are not bad and you could have your own money to spend, as well as helping out with the bills.'

He managed a smile of encouragement – something he rarely practised these days.

Isabelle responded with 'Mmm.' Her thoughts were several kilometres away in Chalhac, where Guy was packing his clothes and books before leaving for Clermont the next day.

'Well?' asked Eric.

Isabelle was at that moment recalling the last time she and Guy had wandered on their bicycles around the plateau above Chalhac. It was a wild area with rocky hillocks, shallow caves, and small valleys – the remnants of volcanic activity long since extinct. The only inhabitants were goats and lizards where buzzards slowly circled high above. To Guy and Isabelle it represented total freedom from parental control. They had found a cave – deeper than some, offering total privacy and quiet, where they had explored each other's bodies and made love.

'Isabelle! Your Papa is asking you a question.' said Anne-Marie.

'I can see you're in no mood to discuss your future,' said Eric, who had privately concluded that his daughter was probably in the throes of one of her 'off' days.

'I'm sorry Papa. You were saying?' asked the girl who was now desperately trying to catch up with the conversation, which had evidently been taking place while she was in her own quiet reverie.

'If you're back with us now Isabelle, I was suggesting that perhaps you might consider getting a job – even starting a career: local government or something. Your grandfather made a successful life for himself in that area and never regretted it and I'm sure between us we could find a place for you in some sort of administrative role. You would need training of course, but I cannot think you would find that particularly onerous.'

'Maybe, Papa. I'll think about it.'

It was hardly an enthusiastic response but for a brief moment she had felt some affection for him, something she had rarely managed. She had recognised his concern about her and added:

'It is kind of you to give time to worrying about me when you are obviously so busy. Thank you Papa dear.'

Eric was a little taken aback by this unexpected response from his daughter and found it difficult to make any further comment which would not upset the delicate state of equilibrium so far achieved.

'Good! Give it some thought Cherie: it could be a very good thing for you and all of us if you were able to make your mind up to do something of the sort.'

Isabelle had already begun to draw the conclusion that getting a job somewhere, earning money and gaining some independence might be the clever thing to do. Since it looked as though Guy would no longer be accessible for the foreseeable future, her days could prove to be very boring. She was also aware that both her father and grandfather had made some success of becoming public servants in their own particular spheres, so there seemed to be no real reason why she should not do the same. She guessed that they could bring to bear considerable influence upon the sort of job she might land.

She was not yet eighteen but she had already begun to display some instinct for the manipulation of her future.

Nine

David Markovich, his two sisters and their ageing parents had fled Russia following the 1917 Revolution, when the Bolsheviks were making life even more precarious and dangerous for Jews than ever before. David and his father Moishe ran a small tailoring business in one of the poorer districts of Petrograd and were obliged to work long hours in order to make ends meet. Moishe had been glad to pass on to his son his tailoring skills as had his father before him, so the family tradition was being well maintained. All of their work was done by hand and the resulting quality was very much better than average and highly regarded by those customers who were lucky enough to have been pointed in their direction.

However the family had become increasingly anxious about their future prospects in the light of deportations, beatings and indiscriminate punishments being handed out by the new administration. Some of their friends and one or two relatives had already become innocent victims to the random viciousness now let loose. The sheer unpredictability of the situation was too much to leave to chance, so after much soul searching they decided to abandon Russia altogether, the country that had been their base for several generations, and to try to make a new start in France.

They headed for Paris where they had friends already established and whom it was hoped, would be able to help them find somewhere to live and to set up shop once again. It worked out fairly well for them and within two years of leaving Russia, they found a diminutive apartment above a small shop in the Left Bank. It was not a particularly salubrious area and the apartment was extremely cramped but it was fairly secure and they were once again able to resume tailoring. They invested in a small commercial sewing machine which removed much of the laborious handwork and life became reasonably tolerable for several years. It would have continued in much the same way, had it not been for Moishe Markovich suffering a massive and fatal heart attack. His loss was severely felt by all the family, not least by his widow who, very sadly, died within a year of losing her husband.

David continued to run the business single-handedly but found it impossible to maintain the same level of quality and quantity he and his father had been able to achieve. Within a year of arriving in Paris both his sisters had married and moved away from the city, which meant that he could not look to them for any help in the shop or to perform any essential domestic tasks, which left him with considerable problems. He pondered the matter for a long time, considering a number of possible moves, and finally decided to sell up the business, move out of Paris altogether and set up once again elsewhere.

He had heard there were empty shops in Rouen which might suit the scale of the tailoring business he had in mind. So one weekend he took the train to Rouen to investigate the situation. There were indeed a number of shops available and he found likely looking premises within sight and sound of the cathedral. It was positively diminutive but had a small shop window which looked out onto a narrow pedestrian lane. Above was a single room which served as living space, bedroom and kitchen. At the back was a small walled area where in one corner stood an evil smelling privy with a half door – a gesture towards ventilation. The whole package suited David well enough and he searched out the landlord, agreed a rental – which was less than half he had been paying in Paris – and by spring of 1935 he had moved in.

Things went fairly well for him during the next three or four years, until Germany's invasion of France in 1940. Following Hitler's rise to power in 1933, David had become increasingly anxious about the way events were unfolding in Germany and elsewhere. The Nazi régime was already openly persecuting Jews and anyone else perceived as non-Aryan. There had been a steady influx of Jewish refugees into France from Germany, Poland, Russia, and the Balkans throughout the 1930s. Some chose to escape to England and even more went to America, but there were many with relatives who had long since established themselves in France and had settled down into a relatively peaceful existence. They were obliged to accept that while they were mostly tolerated within the indigenous French populace a good deal of anti-Semitic feeling existed, together with an underlying resentment about 'foreigners' in general. David could partly understand how his French hosts felt about his presence but he was prepared to put that aside when it came to earning a living, and he respected his customers and they in turn respected him with his self-evident tailoring skills.

His considered view concerning Hitler's ambitions was that his armies would be unlikely to halt at the French border, so by the time Germany actually walked into France he had already made some preparations for a further uprooting. He had organised his escape plans so far as he could, although as yet, he was undecided about a final destination. Germany had already walked into the Low Countries, Austria, Poland and Czechoslovakia and had now arrived in France. It was beginning to look as though England would also be overrun, so there were not many options left open to him. Despite this, and long before the German army actually arrived in northern France, he began to prepare for his inevitable departure which included making a small trailer from some old perambulator wheels with a wooden box perched on top. It was big enough to accommodate his precious sewing machine, a few bolts of cloth and other tailoring accessories, plus one or two essentials like a kettle and a frying pan. There was sufficient space for some clothes, a pair of shoes and a few personal possessions including a faded brown photograph of his parents on their wedding day in Petrograd. He already owned a very secondhand bicycle and had a tow bar made which fitted just below the bicycle's saddle. On top of the contraption was a piece of tarpaulin to keep out the weather. After a dummy run to see how much luggage it would carry - which above all, had to include the cloth and sewing machine – he found it was heavier to tow than he imagined and not very stable, but he decided it would have to do.

* * * * *

On the third of June the Luftwaffe bombed Paris signaling the beginning of the exodus of a large part of the population from the north. By the middle of 1940 it seemed that all of northern France was moving southwards. The German military had moved quickly along the Channel coastal area and were heading towards Rouen. By the sixth of June the sounds of gunfire and bombing were getting closer and it was then that David together with thousands of his fellow citizens decided that enough was enough and that he would leave before the invaders arrived. In the early hours of June the seventh he locked up the little shop, pushed his bicycle and trailer through the side door into the alleyway and joined the tidal wave of confused and frightened Frenchmen and their families, now already on the road and heading south, hoping to escape the clutches of the fast advancing German army.

He was probably better prepared than many, although he quickly realised that it was not going to be easy. The roads were jammed with panicking people, some with suitcases, shopping bags, and sacks and others with young children in their arms. People pushed prams filled with babies and belongings and cars were overfilled with families, their roofs piled high with as many possessions as possible. There were hand carts, wheelbarrows and bicycles – anything with wheels that could be pushed or pulled through the streets. Most shops had closed days before, having sold the last vestiges of food and drink. Their owners had pulled down the shutters and joined the stampede with the rest. There had been a few trains at first but most had been commandeered by the military and the few that remained were overfilled with humanity and luggage. The main railway station presented scenes of total confusion: no one had any idea if any more trains would run and would be passengers were left with no answers and no hope of ever getting onto a train going in any direction. David had seen the crowds of people milling about around the railway station as he slowly wound his way out of the city and he quietly congratulated himself for his foresight in making the preparations he had. Even so he had to practically pick his way forwards at first because there were so many people on the roads and in his path. Once he was beyond the confines of the city it became marginally better although there was still a mass of scared humanity to be negotiated. Stationary cars were left at the side of the road having broken down or run out of petrol. Desperate owners stood at the roadside with their immovable family car, children, elderly parents and their belongings.

He was not making for any particular town and in any event his knowledge of the roads beyond Paris, was to say the least, sketchy. His first concern was to put as many kilometres between himself and the invaders as quickly as possible and his instincts were to stay with the crowd, hoping that there would be some with a clearer idea about where they were heading. As far as the eye could see, there was a slow moving procession of terrified and despairing people trudging along. He began to suspect that very few had any real notion about their destination but all were driven by their instinct for self-preservation and the need to escape southwards. There were numerous small villages and townships on the way where locals had already left their homes and joined the flight. Others had stayed on and apparently made the conscious decision to take whatever advantage of the situation they could by selling or bargaining with the passing masses. By sheer necessity, many were prepared to pay the outrageous prices being demanded by their fellow countrymen. Bread, eggs, milk, or butter – everything had become scarce and it was only those who were prepared to pay who were able to eat. Many sought overnight accommodation for their elderly parents who were mostly in no fit state to spend nights in ditches, in fields or under trees, so rented rooms also became a valuable source of income for their owners who, together with their shop keeper or farming neighbours, were just as ruthlessly exploitative. Anything with a roof was on offer, be it a shed, a barn or a pig sty.

David had imagined that the further away from the north he travelled, the quieter the roads would become but this did not happen for a few days. At one point he noticed a road sign pointing to Chartres which also showed the distance to Paris. He found this very worrying because he had gleaned enough about its relative proximity to know that he must still be too close to the German army for comfort. He looked up at the sun to get a rough directional fix and veered to the right at the next road junction and temporarily left most of the crowd behind, only to rejoin it again at the next main road crossing. After two or three days he was within range of Le Mans and needed to rest for a while; he was already stiff and tired from the unaccustomed exercise and the strain was beginning to tell on him. He was rapidly running out of food and needed to replenish his meagre stock but as he entered the city it became clear that most of the inhabitants had already moved out and David wondered how far he would have to go before being a safe distance from the German invaders. He looked in vain for an open bakers' shop but they had all closed. Those that did not sport shutters over their windows had obviously been emptied of everything edible so he began to make his way across the town's centre, hoping at first that he might spot a source of food and perhaps find somewhere to sleep for the night. There were already enough bedraggled looking families wandering about, pushing laden prams and handcarts to persuade him that he was probably too late even now in his quest for food and lodging so his initial optimism was fading fast. He eventually found a little shaded square with stone seats beneath the trees. One or two had already been taken by exhausted refugees, who were doing their best to create some sense of order for a brief few hours before they set off again into the unknown.

He leant his bicycle and trailer against the back of one of the few remaining seats. Within minutes he was joined by an elderly and extremely frail female dressed in widows black. She carried no possessions other than a walking stick. Creakingly, she sat down at the other end of the bench and emitted a sigh of relief as she did so.

'Good afternoon Madame,' ventured David, in as friendly a manner as he could muster.

'Not very good I'm afraid,' she replied.

'No . . . I agree the news is not what we could wish for. Do you live locally?' He had already noted the fact that she was not encumbered with anything other than her walking stick.

'I do. Just down the road over there,' she said, pointing with her stick which wobbled as she held it up vaguely horizontally.

'Do you have a family Madame?' he asked, optimistically hoping that if she did, they might perhaps have a spare room on offer.

'Ha! I do have a family, at least I did have a family until yesterday, but they have left me here alone to manage the best I can, while they have run away with the rest of them.'

'If you don't mind my saying so, that sounds very unkind, not to say cruel,' said David. 'Why would they abandon you like that?'

'It's very simple Monsieur. They felt I would be unable to keep up with them. My legs are not very good and they thought they might have to run for it in order to escape. Run indeed!' she added scornfully.

He was too diplomatic to say so but he could imagine the family's dilemma the situation posed. He had witnessed her arrival at the seat and the obvious difficulty she had walking there from her nearby home finally relieved at being able to sit down. Her family would have known only too well what this would have meant for their attempt to get away and they probably hoped that in the event of their home town being overrun, any civilized beings would be unlikely to treat an elderly lady too badly.

'It would have been a most difficult decision for anyone to have to make and an even more difficult position for you to accept Madame.' David was doing his best to sound conciliatory. It struck him that in the course of a few minutes he had become quite involved in a family problem now probably being enacted thousands of times, right across the country at this very moment. David was not one to beat about the bush. He asked:

'Is their house now unoccupied?'

'It's not their house. It's my house if you must know and the family live with me.'

'I see,' said David who had very rapidly picked up on the lady's situation and was trying to devise of a way of delicately inviting himself into what was now presumably, a much emptier house than it had been forty-eight hours before. 'Is it possible you might perhaps consider renting me a room for the night? As you have probably guessed I have been running away like the rest of them and I am desperately tired and in need of rest.'

Her eyes narrowed slightly as she gave him an intensely hard look. His clothes, his beret, his shoes and his bicycle and trailer, leaning against the back of the bench, were all carefully scrutinised.

'How far have you come, Monsieur?'

'From Rouen, Madame.'

'Had the Boche arrived by the time you left?'

'No, but they were on their way.' He noticed she called the Germans 'the Boche.'

'Would you have been in any special danger had you stayed on?'

'Very possibly. You see, I am Jewish.'

Her eyes opened a little wider and her eyebrows went up.

'I must say you don't look very Jewish. You are not dressed like a Jew and you don't have a beard or a big hat. What do you do for a living?'

David inwardly smiled at her preconceived notions about how a Jew should look.

'I am a tailor. I make gentlemen's clothes. My father and my grandfather did the same. We lived in Russia until the Revolution but we decided that it was becoming too dangerous for us to remain so we got out while we still had our skins intact. I am ashamed to say that we were never a very orthodox family – religiously speaking, but we were, and I still am, Jewish. I am sad to say, the Nazi régime in Germany has been the cause of much grief and cruelty to Jews already, as you will no doubt be aware. I could not risk staying in Rouen in the hope that I would be overlooked.'

'No indeed,' said the lady. 'How long would you need to stay?' she asked.

'Only tonight, if that's acceptable Madame. I would be greatly obliged to you if you were able to accommodate me.' In his desperation to secure a bed for the night, and in the face of a great deal of competition from elsewhere, David had become overly formal in his attitude towards the good lady. He almost bowed to her.

'In the circumstances I will be very pleased to offer you a bed Monsieur – Monsieur what?'

'Markovich Madame, David Markovich.'

'How could you be anything but a Jew with a name like that!' said the lady with a twinkle in her eye. So David had a good night's sleep for once. His saviour and hostess, Madame Baudet provided him with a breakfast of sorts in the morning and sold him a loaf and some eggs to keep him going. He was extremely grateful and was eager to repay her kindness for taking him in for the night.

'What do I owe you for the bed Madame?'

'I have no idea Monsieur. Let's forget about it!'

'Oh no, Madame. I cannot possibly accept that. It would be quite wrong.' He had a small bundle of francs in his hand and began to count some of them out onto her table. She protested that she did not want his money and was glad to have had his company in what would again become an empty house. In spite of her objections he made her accept what he hoped would be considered fair and left some money on the table, thanked her again for her kindness, wished her good luck and finally bade her farewell.

A fair way beyond the city some sort of aerial activity was going on. He was not close enough to see what was happening but there seemed to be several planes flying about, some muffled explosions and then comparative silence. Four or five kilometres further on he found huddles of terrified people, some standing in the road, others crouching in the ditch at the side – too frightened to move. A hundred metres further on he came across what at first looked to be the results of a small battle. The road was cratered near the middle and there were the unmistakable human remains of more than one person in the road. The crater was still smoldering and emitting the acrid smell of explosives. To the side and scattered about were the remnants of household items: a bent perambulator on its side was spilling out clothing. At the road's edge, small groups of people were gathered – some badly hurt and unable to stand, others doing their best to comfort the injured. David asked one of the survivors what had happened. The man trembled with fear and shock.

'They came straight in over us, turned back and dropped bombs from their infernal planes. What have we done to deserve this?' He sobbed hysterically as he spoke, and waved his arms in the direction of the carnage.

'Is there a doctor among you by any chance?'

'Not that I've seen – we're doing what we can, but some are not going to make it, that's for sure.'

David was horrified as he surveyed the scene, and felt totally helpless. He said:

'There's not much I can do to help but if I can find a doctor of some sort down the road I'll tell him what has happened here. I must leave you now.'

He was wracked with guilt at having to leave them and to cycle away from the scene, knowing perfectly well there was little he could have done that would have been of any value. As he said it, he knew that the chances of discovering a doctor among the slow moving throng or anywhere else were virtually nil. Several kilometres down the road his anger was starting to subside and his spirits began to lift a little. His thoughts turned to the kindness shown by the elderly Madame Baudet in Le Mans the previous day. Indeed contrary to what he had become to expect, she had been perfectly happy to invite him into her house, regardless of having learned he was Jewish. It had helped to restore some of his belief in humanity's basic goodness despite the evidence to the contrary that he had witnessed earlier that day. As he cycled along, he considered the vile wickedness that Man was prepared to inflict upon his fellow creatures. It was then, that David swore that somehow he would redress the balance and if that meant taking some sort of revenge, so be it; the thought spurred him on as he pedalled his bike and trailer along the road. At that moment he had no idea what form his vengeance might take, but he knew deep down that he was going to settle one or two moral debts. These included a 'thank you' to Madame Baudet and taking a swipe at the régime which had the effrontery to walk into France, the country to which he owed so much.

The following day he arrived in the northern outskirts of Tours. Moving closer to the centre he was not very surprised to find the city looking uncannily deserted – shops and banks were closed and the streets were littered with the signs of the hurried departure of its inhabitants. No one thought it would become necessary to evacuate and there had been little or no forward planning. As a result there were cars, small trucks and vans out of petrol, abandoned wherever they had come to a standstill. David could imagine the state of mind of their owners finding their means of escape frustrated, because not only were there few petrol stations, but those that did exist, were either empty or closed. Their owners had decided to get out while they could, locked up and left people sitting at the side of the road with their precious and essential belongings at their side, hoping that someone or something would miraculously appear to pluck them out of danger.

There was some sort of hold up on the bridge across the river caused, so far as he could see, by an ancient horse drawn van. The elderly horse had evidently collapsed and died through hunger or exhaustion or both - and its owner and a number of helpers were trying to manhandle the poor creature's remains to the side of the road. The van also had to be moved out of the way, but without any motive power, it would have to remain where it was. The owner's wife, his children and an old man, together with bedclothes, a mattress, a chair and general household items were all in or tied on to the van which was now hopelessly stranded three quarters of the way across the bridge. David wished he could have helped in some way or maybe sympathise with their predicament, but he knew he would only get in their way if he stopped, so he pedalled by and into the city centre. The closer to the middle he penetrated, the more deteriorated the situation became and he was glad to find his way through the confusion to emerge on the outskirts and into the countryside again. The roads were becoming a little less crowded although every so often he would catch up with small groups of people trudging along, exhausted and hungry.

His own food supplies were again now reaching a critical level. The bread and eggs that the good Madame Baudet had given him, were now mostly exhausted and the physical effort required to propel his bicycle and rather heavy trailer, had begun to tell on him. He was no stranger to hunger having endured some terrible times in Russia after the Revolution, but his situation now was rather different. It was imperative to keep going southwards. He felt compelled to put as much distance between himself and the German army as he could, and as quickly as he could. He passed through endless villages and a few small towns until he reached the point where he barely took any interest in where he was exactly, his only concern being finding someone prepared to sell him something to eat.

The next day he was in the general area of the Limousin. He had seen a sign pointing to Limoges but decided it would be too far from his intended direction and he had already discovered to his cost that most of the bigger towns were openly exploiting weary refugees or had already sold out, so he went on. Eventually he came upon a small community – not a town at all. He had been on the road since before dawn and had barely slept. The village was just beginning to stir and as he slowly cycled through he was suddenly aware of the smell of baking bread. It caressed his nostrils like a magic potion, attracting him like a giant magnet, which pulled him towards the source of the wonderful aroma. It emanated from the centre of the village where a house with an extension at the back contained a diminutive bakery. When David arrived at the doorway the baker was busily removing loaves from an ancient oven and stacking them on their ends on to a wooden shelf. It was uncomfortably hot in the little building but the baker was apparently oblivious to both the heat and to David.

'Good morning,' said David, trying to sound as normal as possible and not wishing to look or sound as though he could be easily blackmailed into paying an inflated price. Until that moment the baker had not seen or heard the stranger arrive and was a little startled to see a scruffy little man leaning on a bicycle outside his door.

'And Good morning to you,' said the baker. 'What can I do for you?'

'Is it too early to buy some bread?'

'There's some here that's been out for a bit,' said the baker. 'The rest needs to stand for a while – it will be too hot to touch, let alone eat.'

'Can you spare me a couple of baguettes?' said David. He did not want to appear too greedy at what he recognized was a difficult time for so many people.

'Of course Monsieur – will two be enough?'

David was a little taken aback by the baker's question: 'Will two be enough?' He could hardly believe his ears and for the briefest of moments wondered if it was just a bad dream he had been having during the last week or so.

'Well, if you are sure Monsieur, I'll take three then.' He was intrigued to know how it was that the baker could appear to be so generous with his bread, so he followed up by asking, 'How are you finding things at the present time for our country? Have you seen many refugees from the North?'

'No – It's been very quiet here although my brother lives on the main road in Tulle, and he says he has seen a steady stream of people heading south.'

This explained quite a lot. Evidently the little road that David had elected to take had not been noticed or chosen by the southbound horde and the village baker was still able to satisfy his local customers' normal demands.

'Do you know how far the Germans have got? I left Rouen about ten days ago and they were a little too close for comfort then and I've seen them bombing people on the roads running southwards. I know this for a fact because I only just missed being caught up in one of their raids.'

'You are a little out of touch my friend. Do you know that Maréchal Pétain will probably become Premier? The government has left Paris and they say they tried to set up in Tours but the Boche was already there, so they tried again in Bordeaux. For all I know the Boche may have beaten them to it so they could be anywhere by now.'

David realised how close he had come to being overtaken and wondered how the good Madame Baudet in Le Mans was managing, to say nothing of the poor souls with their dead horse on the bridge in Tours! He also guessed that if the Germans had made it to Bordeaux they probably intended to take the coastal areas to the West, rather than running directly southwards.

'Good God,' said David. 'So it's come to this?'

'It has indeed. Where are you making for?'

David still had not got as far as deciding on a firm destination in his plans and decided that it would be better to tell a slight fib than own up to not having the faintest idea:

'My sister lives near Aurillac and I am heading there.'

'You should be safe enough there.' It was a qualified reply that did not entirely inspire confidence and carried a distinct tinge of doubt. 'How are you off for food – apart from bread that is?'

'To tell the truth, not very well.'

In the short time since his arrival in his doorway the baker had taken a liking to David and felt some sympathy engendered partly by his now ravaged, facial appearance. He had become drawn with lack of proper food and sleep and by the unaccustomed exercise – something David had never taken before. The baker also realised that his visitor wanted to be as far away as possible from the German army.

'Give me a moment – I'll ask my wife what we can spare.' He disappeared through a door at the side of the bakery and re-emerged a few minutes later with a small basket containing some apples, a piece of sausage, a lump of cheese and bottle of red wine.

'Can you make use of this stuff?'

He was almost speechless. The generosity of this man and his wife was something he had rarely encountered and he found the experience extremely humbling. When he recovered his voice, he replied, 'Can I not! I can't thank you enough Monsieur. I am more grateful than I can possibly say. How much do I owe you?'

'Pay me for the bread and you can have these bits.'

'No, no, no. I will not hear of it. You must not do that. Now - how much?'

'Well if you insist, but it is my way of lending a helping hand to just one poor devil against the damned Germans – there's not much more I can do.'

'If they were all like you Monsieur, the world would be a much better place. Sadly, and in my experience, it seems it is not always the case.' As he spoke he produced some francs from his money belt and placed some into the baker's hand.

'Will that cover it?' he said.

'It's more than enough my friend but I really don't want to take it from you. Do I take it you have seen some hard times in the past then? How far have you come?'

'From Rouen and I believe I only got out just in time. They could have made life very difficult for me if I'd stayed there. Being a Jew makes life difficult enough without being pushed about by the Nazis.'

The baker hesitated for just a little too long before he asked, 'You're Jewish?'

'Yes – and a Russian Jew at that!'

'Well I wondered about your dialect. I must say you don't look very Jewish and you are obviously a gentleman.'

The comment made David aware that even in the depths of the Limousin countryside the same biases and preconceptions existed and despite himself, the baker had said more than enough to indicate clearly where his habits lay. Were Jews not expected to behave like gentlemen? he wondered. Evidently not!

Although David had not reacted to his remark, the baker made a belated attempt at trying to undo what clearly might have been interpreted as being quite offensive, despite telling David he was obviously a gentleman:

'Please forgive me Monsieur. I had no right to say such a thing to you. I am afraid it has so often become our habit to be rude and intolerant of our Jewish countrymen and it is too easy to become tainted.'

'Think no more about it – you are not alone and I can quite see how easy it is to fall into a trap sometimes. We can all be stupid occasionally.'

'You are very generous and understanding Monsieur. You were not born in Rouen I suppose?'

'No. My parents and grandparents were born in Russia and my two sisters and I were born there as well. The family left there shortly after the Revolution when a great deal of violence was being meted out by the Bolsheviks against Jews - and sometimes by Jews themselves - and we left for Paris, thinking life would be safer in France – and indeed it was for a number of years. We had friends living in the city already and they found us somewhere to live and eventually we were able to restart our lives and business again.'

'What business were you into?'

'We were tailors – and I still am. Sadly, as a result of the German invasion I decided that the risk of being picked up if they discovered I was Jewish, was too high – even though I may not look very 'Jewish.' Knowing how they have been treating Jews in Germany and elsewhere it would have been difficult, if not impossible, to stay hidden so when they reached Paris I decided they were too close for comfort. I had left Paris already by 1935 - not long after my parents died, and moved to Rouen into a smaller shop. However when they bombed Paris I left Rouen and headed south. It was obvious to me that the Germans were not going to stop at Paris or even Rouen for very long and they very nearly caught up with me.'

'I can understand your anxieties,' said the baker. 'So you will live with your sister in Aurillac I imagine?'

Having begun the fib about his sister's supposed home in Aurillac he was obliged to pursue the same line: 'I hope so, yes.' The reality was that he had not the remotest idea where either of his sisters now lived, having lost contact with both of them years before. He knew that Aurillac was somewhere to the southwest and it was one of the few places he could give a name to when he had been asked.

'Well Monsieur, I wish you well on your journey and that you are blessed with a peaceful life from now on. You will forgive me if I get on with my work now as I will begin to see my customers arriving before long. Perhaps when all this is over you will be able to call in again and we can continue our discussion?'

'I would enjoy that and if I can I'll make a point of it. Thank you again for the provisions – you are too generous. Au revoir, Monsieur.'

They shook hands and David stowed his loaves, an egg, cheese, sausage and wine into his trailer and restarted his journey.

* * * * *

The landscape was changing all the time now. There were many more hills and he had to dismount and walk, pushing his bike slowly up steep gradients and then getting back on for as long as possible, freewheeling down the other side with the little trailer bouncing dangerously behind. This seemed to be the pattern for a long time and eventually he coasted into the outskirts of a small town. There had been a sign giving it a name but by the time he reached the centre he had forgotten it. The place had a rather deserted look to it and there were very few people about. He needed somewhere to sleep and it all looked very unpromising so he made his way through the main street and out of the other side where he came upon a small derelict factory. There was nothing to stop him from going inside the crumbling building and after a short exploration he found what had probably been a manager's office. The windows had been smashed leaving broken glass everywhere and there was a hole in the roof at one side, but apart from that it seemed a likely place to park himself for the night. He was not worried about its state and simply wanted to put his head down and sleep. It was devoid of any comfort but was quiet and reasonably secure so in no time at all he had fallen deeply asleep, dreaming of Paris, his parents and their tailoring shop. He awoke early and apart from being stiff and aching, the result of lying on a damp cement floor all night, he felt better for the rest. He made a breakfast of sorts from a chunk of bread with a raw egg broken over it. He would have preferred a boiled egg but he had used the last of his matches so was obliged to make the best of it.

Another day loomed and the going was very slow. He was sick of pushing the bike up steep inclines and he was becoming saddle sore, so that even downward slopes were uncomfortable, besides which he was becoming considerably undernourished and weak. He found he was in the middle of very hilly country and to his left he could see mountains and what appeared to be the top of volcanoes. Volcanoes? He thought. France does not have volcanoes does it? Eventually he reached a bigger road with a sign pointing to Mauriac.

He found he had once again caught up with a few more refugees from the north or elsewhere. They were trudging along pushing handcarts, perambulators and barrows – anything in fact with wheels. One family was leading an overladen donkey, its back piled high with their possessions while they walked slowly beside it. They all looked at least as weary as he felt and he longed to stop and rest for a while, but was driven on by what was now, habit and fear. He had no idea how close the pursuing army was and imagined that if he stopped for too long, he would be overtaken. He found an old barn on the outskirts of Mauriac that had already been discovered and occupied by a family from Chartres. They were friendly people and, like David, were still in a state of fear. He established that they were not Jewish but terrified about their future if the invaders caught up with them. He remained quiet about his Jewish origins as it seemed to him that they might somehow feel he could be held responsible for their plight.

Morning came and he bid them good luck and a safe journey and set out again. He was undecided which road to take now and took pot luck. Beyond Mauriac there was a sign pointing to Aurillac but he felt compelled to steer clear of larger towns. His overnight companions had told him that Aurillac was a much bigger town than Mauriac – and they seemed better informed about it than he was. He took a rough bearing from the sun and began to head vaguely eastwards and away from Mauriac and almost immediately encountered steep gradients, and became involved in yet more walking. He carried on in roughly the same direction for the rest of that day and eventually found a small clearing within a wooded area. He had no tent or cover and had found that nights in the open were distinctly chilly, even in June. In order to stay warm and get any sort of rest, it was necessary to lie down on a heap of leaves and to cover himself with even more.

By the morning he was beginning to have serious doubts about the wisdom of taking on this enterprise in the first place. Would he really have been discovered by the German invaders if he had stayed on in Rouen? After all, even in the short time he had been on this escapade, he had been told twice he did not look Jewish, so perhaps he could have passed as a native. He spoke good French, good enough to fool any German and get away with it. In any event, if he managed to settle somewhere fairly safe, what was he going to do for a living? There did not seem to be any larger towns that would be likely to provide enough demand for the sort of tailoring that he was trained for. Suppose the Germans did make it to the southernmost areas and he was still found out, what then? He realised that he had been arguing with himself for some time and had not drawn any firm conclusions from his meanderings. Had he been talking to himself? He wondered. If he had passed anyone as he trundled by, they would probably have concluded he was some sort of deranged tramp. He smiled briefly to himself at the thought.

He stopped for a while to take stock of his situation and eat the remains of his food. It had now become critical and he found he was in a wilderness of rough roads – little more than farm tracks, all of which seemed to disappear in the direction of yet more hills and beyond that, mountains. The prospects of finding anywhere to obtain any nourishment seemed remote.

At dawn the following day he took the first road that turned away from the hills and pushed on. Quite suddenly he realized he was passing alongside a substantial stone wall. It obviously belonged to some sort of estate and continued for at least half a kilometre before abruptly turning away to the right and vanishing into more wooded land. It was still very early in the morning and the sun was barely above the horizon. The wall held promise of nearby civilization and he was heartened by the thought; a little further on, a gap in the trees revealed the bell tower of a church. Minutes later he found he was running into a small village with a little square and a shop. At the top of the square he could see a middle aged woman sweeping her doorstep. She stopped what she was doing when he appeared, and stared in his direction before going back inside and closing the door. He was desperately tired and he propped his bike and trailer against the single tree growing in the middle of the little square. It would provide something to lean against and rest.

David had arrived in Chalhac-sur-Bache.

<u>Ten</u>

He had been dreaming he was in a forest being chased by a pack of mad dogs or wolves and someone was shouting to him to jump up into a tree. They were calling to him, saying, 'Monsieur, Monsieur, you must get up.' The dogs had almost caught up with him when he awoke with a start to find he had six or seven people staring down at him as he sat propped against the tree. Someone in his audience murmured 'He'll be alright now he's awake.'

One of them asked 'Are you OK Monsieur? Do you need help? I'm afraid you can't stay here because this is market day and you are in the middle of La Place. Madame Meral will arrive shortly and she always puts her table here under the tree. She will be very unhappy if she discovers you in her space.' David was still struggling to gather himself and was sleepy and confused and had barely taken in anything being said to him. All he had managed to grasp was that he had to move and that someone was going to get upset if he didn't. He managed to get to his feet. He felt rather giddy and ached all over. His backside felt numb and he was terribly thirsty. He checked to see if his bicycle and trailer were still leaning against the other side of the tree and was relieved to see everything was still where he had left it two hours before. He said;

'Of course, Monsieur. Please forgive my intrusion. May I ask where this is?

'This is Chalhac-sur-Bache Monsieur. Can I ask where you are from?'

'From Rouen in the north.'

'Really! So you have come all this way on your bicycle? To escape the Boche I suppose?'

'Correct,' croaked David who had no intention of pursuing the matter any further as his mouth was as dry as a bone. 'Where can I get something to drink?' He probably sounded abrupt but he was desperate for something to slake his thirst.

'Over there is Monsieur Fournier's bar. He will be glad to help I'm sure.' He pointed to where Jacques Fournier was already outside carefully unwinding his patriotically coloured awning and arranging two or three metal chairs. He was anticipating there would be thirsty customers from the market as it would be another hot day. David thanked his interrogator, pushed his bike and trailer between the small bunch of curious locals surrounding him and made his way over to the little bar.

'Good morning Monsieur. Am I too early to get a drink?' he said hopefully.

'It's never too early in my bar Monsieur. What would you like?'

'Anything wet will do right now – I'm parched.'

'Beer?'

'Wonderful! Is there anywhere here where I can get something to eat?'

'My wife could make you some breakfast or something a little more substantial if you are prepared to wait a while longer.'

'That sounds very good to me. I'll wait if I may.'

'Excellent! I'll bring you a beer if you would like to set yourself down here or in the bar,' said Fournier and disappeared inside. A minute or two passed and he reappeared with a litre jug of beer and a glass. David could hardly wait and drank deeply and greedily.

'I could manage another one of those,' he said. Twenty minutes or so later Fournier's wife appeared with a tray piled with the first substantial meal he had seen for what seemed a lifetime. She had conjured a mixture from the remains of their meal the previous day, comprised mostly of stewed pork and beans, covered in a rich cheese and garlic sauce. It was accompanied by a complete and still warm baguette and large jug of red wine. David thanked her warmly for her efforts at such short notice. She smiled and lightly shrugged her shoulders as if to say 'It's nothing Monsieur – this happens all the time.' In truth they rarely provided food for their customers and were only geared to liquid refreshment in the form of beer or Fournier's own wine made from grapes from the small vineyard down the road from Chalhac. Jacques also made a particularly strong marc, mostly for their own consumption but produced on special occasions or when he or Marie were ailing and required something stronger and warming.

He was left alone to quietly devour his meal. Eventually Fournier re-emerged from the back of the bar and sat down opposite him as he was finishing a third glass of wine. Life had magically begun to take on a different hue since eating – together with the effect of the beer and wine. He produced a quietly appreciative belch.

'Forgive me Monsieur – my digestive system has become unused to taking proper food for a few weeks now. That was truly excellent. Will you join me with a glass?'

'Thank you but not right now – I have an entire day to survive and I try to remain sober for as long as possible – you will understand, I'm sure.' He had no idea who this stranger was, where he had come from, what he was doing here or where he was going. He had asked Marie when they were out of earshot, if he had given her any clues about his mysterious arrival overnight. She was unable to help as she had barely said anything to him. 'I'll ask him what he is doing here – why Chalhac of all places?' wondered Jacques.

'So where are you making for Monsieur?' he ventured.

'Making for? Anywhere the Boche aren't going to be. Where are they now?' he asked, as an afterthought.

'In Bordeaux and all along the west coast.'

'Are they coming this way?'

'I don't think so – You know we have just surrendered to the Germans? There is some sort of plan agreed for le Maréchal Pétain to set up a new separate government which will look after the southern part of the country, and the Boche will run the rest of it from Paris. Of course they're bound to grab all the ports and industries in the north. I don't think they're much interested in our part of the world.'

'Surrendered? Good God. So do you think you're safe here then?'

'So far as we can see, yes. You are obviously very concerned that you should get as far away from the Germans as you can Monsieur - may I ask why? – You seem to be particularly anxious.'

David again quickly recounted his life story starting in Russia, that they were Jews and threatened by the Bolsheviks during and after the revolution, their time in Paris and finally his departure from Rouen. 'Wouldn't anybody be anxious? I can tell you Monsieur, that in the two or three weeks I have been travelling from Rouen, I have seen some terrible cruelty being meted out - perfectly innocent people running for their lives with young families and elderly relatives while the swine were bombing and machine gunning them from the air. That's why I may seem to be a little anxious to get as far away from them as possible – I am sure you can understand,' said David sarcastically.

His rapid outpourings about what he had seen over the last week or two could hardly be contained and his anger had been reignited once more as he relived it all over again. He had almost been able to put some of it to the back of his mind until then, but his fury still bubbled to the surface. He was faintly surprised that Jacques Fournier should question his reasons for being anxious to escape the clutches of the invaders, and found it almost ludicrous. Was this man so out of touch with the real world that the possibility of being overrun by Germans in his quiet little village was beyond his understanding? Was he unable to imagine what that might come to mean?

Fournier was a little taken aback by David's barely disguised angry outburst and for a moment or two was at a loss to say much in response. It had registered on him that his new customer was a Jew and an ex-patriot Russian. He had listened to what had tumbled from the mouth of the man sitting opposite him, but it took some time for the full implications of this to sink in.

'Forgive me Monsieur. It was stupid and clumsy of me to even question your motives for getting away from the north. You must realise that although we have heard the news about thousands of people leaving the northern areas of our country, it is impossible to imagine the terror being felt by all these good folk, to say nothing of the vile way the invaders are inflicting mindless cruelty. Obviously we are not being told the whole truth on the wireless. Forgive my idiocy – it was not meant to be anything more than an attempt to get to know a little more about you. If you don't mind my saying so, you don't look very Jewish!' he added.

'So I have been told many times.'

'So what do you plan to do now?'

'I am not sure.' His anger was beginning to subside a little following Jacques' apology and he was obliged for the first time since his arrival to consider his situation. He had not got as far as making any particular plans for his future – beyond saving his own skin. He had virtually no family left – he had lost all contact with his two sisters, years before when they were still in Paris. His parents were dead, so to that extent at least he was a free agent. His ambitions extended no further than being left alone to make a reasonable living for himself; something he had been quietly achieving, until being rudely interrupted by the intrusion of the Nazis.

At that precise moment he would have preferred not to have been quizzed by Jacques Fournier and was quite suddenly overtaken by his need to sleep. He had been rudely awakened from his slumbers only an hour or so before and had only managed to grab a couple of hours anyway - his meal, beer and wine were now making their effects felt: 'The first thing I plan to do is to get some sleep - is there anyone in the village who might be able to put me up for a day or two? I could really do with getting my head down – I haven't had much sleep for days now and I only arrived here a few hours ago when the sun was barely up. I was well away when they woke me – I could have slept for hours.'

Jacques Fournier nodded sympathetically. 'Stay there for a moment or two while I check something out.' He limped away and vanished into the middle of a bunch of people at one of the market stalls, re-appearing a minute or two later accompanied by Sarah, the Jewish wife of Jules Gaillard.

'Madame Gaillard, this is a fellow countryman of yours. Monsieur' . . . He realised he did not know David's name, 'forgive me, Monsieur, I didn't catch your name!'

'Markovich, David Markovich.'

'Monsieur Markovich,' repeated Jacques to Sarah.

'I am delighted to meet you Monsieur. I am Sarah Gaillard. You are from Russia?'

'Enchanté Madame. Yes, my family and I were in Russia until 1919 and we got out when things were getting difficult. You know Russia well?'

'Yes. I know Russia very well – I was born there and I am Jewish. I take it that you are Jewish as well? Markovich could be nothing other than Jewish!'

'My family can be traced back at least a hundred and fifty years in Russia and before that in Poland. So Yes, I am Jewish . . . Shalom Madame Gaillard!'

'Shalom indeed! Your name – Gaillard is French, not Jewish?'

'Correct. I married out before we left Russia. My husband Jules Gaillard is a stonemason. His late cousin left him his house here in Chalhac and this is where we now live.'

In turn, David gave Sarah a potted version of his recent history, and not so recent history, in Paris and in Rouen. Jacques Fournier had been privy to this conversation and had listened intently to both tales. During a brief pause in their stories he said,

'Monsieur Markovich asked me if I knew of anyone who might be able to offer him a bed for the night. It struck me that while your son Guy is away in Clermont, it's possible you could allow him to take his place for the night?'

'Why not?' said Sarah, with a beaming smile. 'It will be a pleasure to have you with us Monsieur. When I have packed up my table in the market I will come over and we can walk around to our house.'

David was overjoyed at the prospect of having a bed to sleep in for once. He had last slept in a bed in the home of the elderly Madame Baudet in Le Mans.

'That is incredibly kind of you Madame, and of you Monsieur to think of asking Madame Gaillard if she could help. I will forever be in your debt.'

'This is a difficult time for many people Monsieur and it could become more difficult in the future. It is only right that we should try to help those who are not as lucky as ourselves, whenever we can. Wait for me here,' she said, and vanished once again into the small crowd on La Place.

Sarah re-appeared an hour or two later to collect David. He was so tired that he had fallen asleep again at the little table with his head on his arms. She gently tapped his shoulder and said 'Monsieur Markovich!' He tried to gather himself but was confused and appeared to be frightened. He had been dreaming again, this time that he was in his little shop in Rouen where a German soldier had ordered a suit which had to be ready by the next day. If he failed to deliver he would be shot. When David finally came back to reality he found he was soaked in perspiration and was considerably relieved to find himself sitting under the awning of Jacques Fournier's bar. The little market was fast closing down and there were fewer people about. Some had gathered inside the bar and had been able to observe the sleeping stranger at the table outside. In truth there was not much to be seen other than a scruffy little man with greying hair, several days growth of beard and a sun burned complexion. Jacques had briefed them on who he was and where he had come from, so by the time Sarah returned to escort him to her house, a good part of Chalhac's populace already had a fairly good idea who the newcomer was. There was a lot of conjecture about what he might do and where he would go after he left the Gaillard's house. They were also intrigued by the fact that here in their midst was someone who had actually seen and witnessed the way the invading armies were behaving. Fournier had repeated to his assembled audience some of David's account as told to him and again to Sarah two or three hours before. Some shook their heads sadly and others nodded and shrugged their shoulders, as if to say, 'what could you expect from those savages?'

Sarah said 'If you are ready now to make a move Monsieur we will walk round to our house – it's just around the corner and a short way up the hill. Is this your bicycle and trailer?'

'Yes. I am ready when you are - lead the way!' Before he left he put his head around the bar's open doorway and called over to Jacques, 'My grateful thanks Monsieur – perhaps I will see you tomorrow?'

'I look forward to it' said Jacques.

David and Sarah made their way out of La Place and up the road. His bike and trailer felt heavier now that the immediate pressure was off. He had somehow managed to muster some inner strength in his effort to escape but was now sapped of energy and resolve, besides which, he was just a little drunk. He did not care very much at that moment because in a vague way he began to feel the curious sensation of having arrived at the destination he had been aiming for all along. It was not yet very clearly defined – and was probably the result of the kindness he had received from Jacques Fournier, and now Sarah Gaillard.

'So your son is away at the moment Madame? I hope he won't object to my taking his bed?'

'I don't think he'd mind at all – in any event he is not expected home for a few weeks yet, so you don't need to bother yourself about it too much. You will have to share the room with my other son, but he will not mind, if you don't.'

'You have two sons?'

Sarah nodded and explained that Marcel was the older of her two sons and worked with his father at the local quarry and that Guy had recently started training to be a teacher at college in Clermont-Ferrand. She was clearly very proud of them both.

He leant his bicycle against the wall of the house and Sarah ushered David inside. The 'salon', as Jules liked to call it was simply furnished with some secondhand items, some of which looked very used indeed. They had arrived from Russia with nothing and were obliged to find a few essentials. There had been the remnants of late cousin Maurice's furniture lying about when they first arrived, but it was hard to imagine it had ever been used. Most of it had been infested with woodworm and they had used it as fuel for the fire. Jules had quickly constructed a large bed of sorts and Sarah had made up a paillasse of coarse linen. It was filled with straw, partly cadged from Monsieur Bastien and partly from negotiation by Jules who had agreed to rebuild a couple of walls for Bastien in part payment.

The bed was sufficiently large to accommodate Sarah, Jules and both their sons in the early days and since the floor upstairs looked unsafe in Jules' opinion, the bed remained in the salon on the stone floor. After a year or two it was decided that for everyone's sake, the boys needed a room and beds they could call their own. By that time Jules had largely rebuilt the floors above and since he had become established at the quarry and earned a regular wage, he had been able to buy new wood and the necessary supplies. He constructed two new beds for the boys' exclusive use. Marcel and Guy were thrilled at the prospect of having their own beds for the first time in their lives while Jules and Sarah also enjoyed a degree of privacy they had not had since before the boys were born.

Sarah ushered David up the stairs to the upper floor and opened the door to the boys' room. One bed stood against the wall beside the door, the other under the window, which looked out onto a small patch of grassy land at the back of the house. Beyond that the ground fell away to the river - la Bache. A large ornate wardrobe with a spotted and barely reflective mirror on its middle door, took up most of one wall. Some of its ornamentation was missing but it was one of the few items remaining from cousin Maurice's possessions, which had not been used as fuel for the fire. It was still useable and served perfectly well for their sons' clothes, such as they were. Against the other wall opposite the window was a small table on which stood a wash basin and a water jug. Nothing matched and both pieces were chipped and crazed. Beside the table was a simple wooden chair.

'This is Marcel and Guys' room - you can sleep in Guy's bed here,' she said indicating the bed by the door. 'Marcel prefers the bed beneath the window. I hope that will be acceptable.'

'To be honest Madame, I could sleep anywhere right now. Over the last two weeks or so I have had to do just that, so this is absolute Heaven by comparison.'

'Well I am happy to be able to help you get over what must have been a difficult time for you. Jules and I know very well how cruel life can be and I know he will be only too pleased to help out at the present time. As you know we lived in Russia for many years and decided we could no longer tolerate the treatment being handed out by the new régime after the Revolution. It was grim enough under the Czars but it became even worse afterwards. But then you know all this, don't you!'

'I certainly do Madame.'

'Now, do you need to get in your possessions from your trailer?'

David had momentarily forgotten about his bike, trailer with its precious cargo – even his sewing machine. 'Yes, perhaps I will bring some of that in if you have no objection.'

'Why would I object Monsieur? I know what it must mean to you.'

'I'm sure you do Madame.'

So the trailer was unloaded and the sewing machine and two bolts of cloth were brought in and stood against the wall near the foot of the stairs. The bicycle and trailer were wheeled around to the back and left under a small porch that Jules had recently built. David carried everything else up the bedroom and made a small heap of his things on the floor beside the bed. Ten minutes later Sarah tapped gently on his door to enquire if there was anything he needed. There was no reply and she crept silently into the room, but he was already dead to the world, still fully dressed and gently snoring. She retreated quietly – or as quietly as she could down the creaking stairs.

Jules and Marcel came home from the quarry later that afternoon unaware of David's arrival. Sarah had to quickly explain what had occurred, from the time he was discovered under the tree on La Place, his meal hastily conjured by Marie Fournier at the bar, the stir it had created in the market and finally, in the light of his dire straits, her invitation to put him up for the night.

'So where is he now?' asked Jules.

'Asleep in Guy's bed. I hope you don't mind Marcel – the poor man was exhausted and had nowhere to sleep so I thought it would be alright with you. It is only for the night anyway.' Her fingers were crossed behind her back as she said it. Whether or not she wondered if Marcel would object, or hoped that David would not become a permanent fixture was uncertain. Either way neither Marcel nor his father was inclined to begin an argument about it and David was left undisturbed for the rest of the day. He eventually woke up in the early hours of the next morning to the sound of Marcel's snoring, and lay there considering his next move. He was still unsure about developments with regard to the German invasion or how far away they were. For that matter he had not the remotest idea where Chalhac actually was or whether the invaders were likely to suddenly appear.

Marcel awoke at 6.30 and looked over towards Guy's bed. David was wide awake and gazing up at the ceiling.

'Good morning Monsieur! You slept well I hope?' said Marcel.

'Good morning! You must be Marcel? Yes, I slept like a log all night – did I snore?'

'A bit, but don't we all?'

'Probably,' said David. Marcel's obviously friendly enquiry was an encouraging start. 'I hope your mother has explained how I come to be sharing your bedroom with you. She assured me you wouldn't mind. I'm not sure how your brother would feel about it if he knew I had taken his bed!'

'Don't worry about that. He is up in Clermont in digs with a friend, so he has probably taken somebody else's bed himself, so he shouldn't complain.'

They talked continuously as they dressed. Marcel wanted to know more about the stranger and what had happened to him during the last few weeks while David wanted to catch up on events during that same period. He had only the barest outlines of what had been happening and he was still anxious to know if he was likely to be safe where he was. Marcel had been able to glean a certain amount of information that emanated from Jacques Fournier's wireless. He however had thought that some of the reports had begun to show all the signs of pure propaganda and sounded a little too optimistic about where the country was heading in the future. He said that what they had been told conflicted with David's version and in any case there was no news about what had happened to the French army. He said the local miller, Malet, had two sons who were both in the army and he hadn't heard a word from them since the north was overrun by the invaders and that this was causing a great deal of anxiety for Malet.

'You know that Maréchal Pétain is now in charge of the unoccupied part of the country?' said Marcel.

'Yes, I gathered that much from the bar owner yesterday. What do people think about that here? Do they think he'll make much of a job of it?'

'At the moment we are all waiting to see what will happen, but my parents are now fretting a bit because we had a letter from my brother who has started a teaching course in Clermont. He has heard rumours that Pétain is saying he will stop Jews from becoming teachers. It isn't official yet but it has obviously been discussed or suggested somewhere up there. We will have to wait and see if any of it is true.'

'I wouldn't be surprised. Old Pétain has never been much in favour of us – it's probably one of the reasons why he was put up for the job in Vichy in the first place. I don't like the sound of it. Do you think we are safe here?' David was beginning to feel just a little uncomfortable all over again. Although the Nazi invaders probably had as much of the country as they wanted or needed, or could reasonably control, the fact that some distinctly right-wing people had been appointed to run the remainder, left him wondering about the future.

'Safe? Have Jews ever been safe? My parents had enough of it in Russia and I'm sure yours did. My father is not a Jew as it happens but my mother is, so my brother and I are technically Jews and judged by what we've heard over the last few years, the Nazis would be only too pleased to label us for their own purposes. We are just hoping for the best and will try to keep our heads down. What Pétain will do about any of it is open to question, especially as he now has a lot of Fascists backing him in his new 'administration.' Then there is the little matter of the refugees arriving from Spain, plus the left-wing agitators in the cities and elsewhere. We cannot see at the moment what the new government will do about all of them. The Communists have already stirred things up in industry and called strikes, so it all looks a bit dangerous. Fascists against Communists! Pétain is bound to try to stamp on them.'

'Have any Spanish showed up here in Chalhac?'

'An old truck came through here a week or two ago with some pretty tired looking folk in the back waving flags – they didn't stop but we think they were from Spain. We don't know where they were going or anything about them, but I wouldn't be surprised if a few more appear.'

'What do the locals here in the village think about Jews? Or should I say, think about you and your family?'

'So far as I can tell they seem to regard us as being fairly normal people! The fact that my Papa is French and non-Jewish has probably helped. His cousin left him this house when he died a few years ago, which is how we came to be here in the first place. I gather that Papa's old cousin Maurice lived here all his life so when we appeared it was more or less accepted that we were continuing where he left off. Some of the villagers were a bit doubtful about Mama as she had a funny dialect when she arrived and when they discovered she was Russian and Jewish, that probably took a bit of digesting – you know what country people are like!'

'It is the same all over I'm afraid although I have to say I've come across some very kind and understanding people during this last couple of weeks. Perhaps it has something to do with the fact that the country has been invaded by the Hun and thinks that Gentiles and Jews should all stand shoulder to shoulder to fight them off.'

'Maybe,' said Marcel, but he sounded less than convinced.

David and Marcel arrived at the breakfast table together. Sarah said 'Ah! There you are! This is Monsieur Markovich from Rouen, Jules. Monsieur Markovich, this is my husband Jules.'

'It's a pleasure to meet you my friend. You got some sleep I hope - Marcel snores like a pig!'

'I slept like the dead – it would have taken more than a bit of snoring to wake me I can tell you. I want to say how grateful I am for allowing me to stay in your house at short notice. Your good wife took pity on me yesterday and I will be forever in debt to you both for your kindness.'

'I didn't have much say in the matter. Sarah told me all about you when I got home yesterday afternoon and I didn't have the heart to throw you out again!' said Jules with a chuckle.

They settled down to eat their breakfast, such as it was. Sarah had made some coffee washed down a few hunks of bread accompanied by cheese. They all began to talk together as soon as they finished eating. Jules was first off the mark:

'So what will you do now Monsieur – do you have any plans?'

'None right now. All I've wanted to do was to get as far away as I could from the damned Boche but it sounds to me that they are not going to be very much interested in this part of our country - I hope not at least. Now they've got old Pétain to run it for them perhaps they will leave us alone. If this is how it is going to be then I might stay where I am – I don't mean by that that I would expect to stay in your house for evermore of course!' he added hastily. 'I'll have to look around for somewhere to live and set up my business again, but I have to think carefully about it before I make any decisions.'

'So perhaps you would like to stay here for a day or two - at least until you have had time to recover yourself a little. Looking at you now, I can see you have had a hell of a journey to get this far. You could do with some regular meals and a good rest for a day or two. What do you say Sarah – could we put him up for a few more days?'

'Of course we can. I'm afraid the food isn't going to be up to much but you can have whatever we have.'

David could barely believe his luck. The generosity and kindness these people were showing him had completely thrown him and he was lost for words.

'I don't know what to say,' he stammered. 'You know hardly anything about me and here you are offering me a bed and food and a chance to gather myself. Are you sure you want to do this?'

'My friend, we know what it is means to be hungry, being chased about and being bullied. We have first-hand knowledge of all that and such was the reason we left Russia, as you and your family did a few years ago, so I know that Sarah feels much the same way. You have only to say yes and we will go along with your decision – O.K?'

David needed no further encouragement. He had been accepted into their family – at least temporarily and for once in a very long time he felt he belonged.

'Your other son – Guy? What happens when he comes home?'

'We'll think about that when he gets here,' said Jules.

Eleven

Following Eric Farbres' attempt to persuade Isabelle to get a job, he was true to his word and put some feelers out to see what might be available in local government. He mentioned the problem to his father who took an immediate interest in the matter:

'I'll be glad to help of course. Does she have any ideas herself I wonder?'

'Not that she's said. Anne-Marie might know but we'd hardly spoken about it until a few weeks ago. I don't get as much time as I would like at home and I must admit I don't really know what she's up to most of the time.'

'How old is she now?

'She'll be eighteen next birthday.'

'High time she was earning some money of her own then.'

'I agree.'

'Give me time to ask around – I'll see what I can do.'

The conversation drifted towards the more pressing issues associated with the Armistice recently signed with Germany. The remnants of the earlier French administration had now arrived in the spa town of Vichy and hotels and other buildings had been commandeered to serve as government offices. Eric had been sent down beyond Toulouse to oversee the organisation of another 'internment' camp for ex -patriot Spanish, Communists and Jews, who were being picked up as they emerged from Spain following the civil war. They were a motley crowd and had to be provided with identity papers showing ethnicity and country of origin, marital status, age and a host of other details, some of which seemed a little unnecessary. It was all very time consuming but the authorities insisted, so it had to be done. Not all of the people emerging from Spain were gathered up by the French authorities. Many had crossed the frontier via the Pyrenees using very unofficial crossing points and considerable numbers simply vanished into the French countryside. None of this had done much to moderate Eric's anti-Semitic views and he blamed the arrival of hundreds of Jews from Spain for his inability to get home at weekends. In Eric's case it meant that apart from imposing considerable strains on his marriage, his absences had resulted in his becoming almost a stranger to his daughter.

Old Farbres did not manage to make much progress in his attempts to find a likely starting point to a career for his granddaughter but had remained very interested in her future. During one of Eric's very occasional weekends off, he and Eric were again discussing possible moves.

'There must surely be some vacancies in the police service Eric – have you made enquiries in that direction?'

'Of course, but they are looking for graduates and unfortunately Isabelle can't conjure up degrees she doesn't have – so this puts her out of the running before she even gets an interview. I'm not sure where we go from here. I would like to think she could get into local government in some sort of capacity but of course they are pretty fussy who they take on as well. At this rate I can see her becoming a hotel worker doing some menial task, with no future prospects at all.'

'I agree it is all very difficult,' said his father. 'We mustn't let it drift on though – I am sure something will turn up.'

'I hope you're right.'

* * * * *

In the second week of July the National Assembly convened in Vichy. Pétain, aided and abetted by Pierre Laval, announced that the Third Republic was henceforth abolished and would be replaced by a new 'French State.' Furthermore, it had been decided that the old and cherished cry, 'Liberté, Egalité, Fraternité' would be replaced with 'Travail, Famille, Patrie.' Concluding his address, Pétain said 'I make a gift of my person to the country.'

In Chalhac, Fournier's bar was filled with some of the villagers who were sufficiently interested or worried about the direction in which the country might be taken in the future. No one expressed any pleasure at what had just been announced over the wireless though one or two wavered slightly when they heard Pétain announce his apparently patriotic dedication of his person to the country. In the bar his declaration was mostly seen as a transparent effort to fool what was left of the French nation into blindly accepting him, the new régime and its principles.

'I don't like the sound of any of that. It sounds to me as if old Pétain is either going a bit barmy or he has been told by his lord and masters in Berlin what to say,' said Bonnet the baker. 'Probably both,' he added. The majority agreed with Bonnet's sentiments and a sense of gloom descended once more upon the little gathering.

'It has all the marks of a madman to me. If he thinks he can curry favours from Hitler and his crowd by wrecking what's left of France, he must be more simple than we thought,' said Fournier. 'As for making a gift of his person to us – I don't know whether to laugh or cry!' This was greeted with barely suppressed laughter.

'What in God's name does he think he's doing? What's wrong with Liberté, Egalité and Fraternité anyway?' added Malet.

David Markovich had been standing just outside the doorway of the little bar during the broadcast and managed to hear most of it. He had also heard the subsequent comments voiced by the villagers and finally left them to it. He felt a mixture of foreboding and excitement at some of their responses and this began to sow the vague notion that if this sort of reaction were to be replicated elsewhere in the country then it might be possible to settle one or two scores - something he had promised himself on his journey southwards. He decided to discuss what he had just heard with Jules Gaillard.

Jules and Marcel arrived back from the quarry later that afternoon and David was waiting for them in the salon. 'You missed an interesting speech this afternoon by Pétain,' he announced.

'Oh yes? And what did the gentleman have to say?' said Jules.

David gave him so far as he could, a verbatim account of the old man's pronouncements including the abandonment of the Third Republic and its replacement, together with the dismissal of the long established 'Liberté, Egalité and Fraternité in favour of 'Travail, Famille, Patrie.'

'He's a poor old fool,' was Jules' immediate reaction. 'It's as clear as the nose on your face that he has been spoofed into all this by that Fascist gang in Berlin not to mention a good number of our own countrymen including Laval and his pal Darlan. I'll be interested to see what will happen over the next few weeks when people begin to fall in.'

'I'm with you entirely Jules.' David had long since begun to call his temporary landlord by his first name. His presence in the Gaillard house had become almost semi- permanent since nothing very suitable had appeared by way of alternative accommodation so it had become almost accepted by the family that he would live there for the time being. No pressure was being brought to bear on him and the arrangement suited David very well indeed.

'What do you think Marcel?' asked David.

'It certainly doesn't sound like good news. Why change everything like this – cancelling the Republic and so on. It must mean that Pétain is under orders and simply wants to save his own skin and keep Hitler and his friends on his side. We all know le Maréchal is a Fascist and is probably an egotist as well, so for the Nazis it was an obvious move to have this part of our country governed by someone like him who didn't need much persuasion in the first place. Not only that, but the old man is still seen by millions of people as a hero from the last war so he was their best bet, as someone to win the rest of us over. That's what I think anyway.'

'It seems to me you've got it about right Marcel,' said Jules. 'Until we get an idea what's really going to happen there is not much we can do – even if we want to.'

Sarah had been listening to this conversation and eventually said, 'Well I think we should all be very careful from now on. We already have a pretty good idea about the way the Germans are behaving where they have occupied – David here has seen some of it with his own eyes – and if Pétain is under orders to run it their way, then it might become very tricky, not to say dangerous. Not only that, but remember that apart from Jules, in this house we are all Jews. Our elderly leader is already anti-Jewish as well as anti-communist, anti-trade unions, anti-freemasons, anti-gypsies and anti-just about everything else – so we could easily find ourselves in the firing line and he won't need much encouragement from Berlin or wherever the orders are coming from.'

'Yes – you're right Cherie,' said Jules. 'We could all be very vulnerable if Pétain is ordered to turn the pressure up, so we must think about this very carefully. Not everyone in the village will be against him of course and we must be wary about who we speak to in future. When Guy gets back from Clermont next month we will have to warn him about it all because he could find himself in real danger – particularly if they discover he is technically Jewish. Lucky for him our Gaillard name has served to keep him out of harm's way so far, but you never know.'

'What about Isabelle?' said David, who had been told about her father being a policeman and the fact that he had been kept in the dark for years about her relationship with Guy.

'Isabelle can be trusted. I'm quite certain she'd never risk wrecking her friendship with Guy under any circumstances,' said Sarah. 'But she'll have to be very careful, especially as her father is a Jew hater. Heaven knows what he would do if he ever finds out the truth about the pair of them – and even her mother Ann-Marie, doesn't really know the whole story – Isabelle has told me virtually everything and her mother might be very surprised to hear how far things have gone. You may not realise it, but Isabelle and I have become very close over the years and she talks to me a lot more than she does to her own Mama.'

'Well I'm going to speak to Jacques Fournier tomorrow,' said Jules. 'He can be trusted I know. I'll ask him to sound out some of his customers to see which way they're thinking. We can't be sure how others will see any of this and some might simply sit tight and hope for the best but I can't quite believe that we're the only ones to want to change things.'

* * * * *

The telephone rang on Eric Farbres' desk.

'Farbres – is that you?' demanded the voice on the other end.

'Speaking. Who's calling please?' Eric Farbres knew perfectly well the voice at the other end as that of his boss, Colonel Roger Boudeau in Clermont-Ferrand. He had taken a dislike to Boudeau almost from the moment he encountered him the first time, two or three years before and his opinion of him had not changed very much since then. He saw him and continued to see him as short tempered, irritable and a bully. Eric could do little about it other than to make the occasional pretence not to know his voice when he made abrupt demands on Eric by the phone and when he invariably assumed that his voice would be instantly recognised. The only effect this had on Boudeau was to irritate the man more than ever. They were very small victories for Eric but they yielded a certain satisfaction. Despite these fairly frequent encounters Boudeau had not learned much about simple manners that would have made for a better working relationship. His view of Eric Farbres had been tainted when he discovered that Eric's entry into the Gendarmerie and his subsequent and rapid rise from the ranks to become a member of the officer elite had been engineered by his father who had pulled strings, if not actually bribed, one or two influential friends in the Prefecture. It continued to madden Boudeau that Eric had been able to take considerable shortcuts whereas he had been obliged to gain a degree at university, before he was even considered for entry into the officer corps. Nothing was ever voiced about the matter for fear that Eric might drop a mischievous word to his father resulting in damage to his own career, so the grudge remained.

'You know very well who this is Farbres. I have new orders from my superiors here in Clermont which directly concern you. They have been instructed by Vichy that we must set up a more intensive system that will monitor the civilian population for any signs of dissent that might appear against the régime. We have been given instructions that, in order to facilitate this, we are to take certain measures including setting up a number of strategically placed units, where it is considered trouble could arise. As you are aware, difficulties are arising as a result of the Civil War in Spain, and are creating a great deal of extra work for everyone. Some of the people coming across are not all to be welcomed and it is possible that trouble could be stirred up. Vichy wants anything of this nature firmly stamped on. My colleagues and I have taken a hard look at the geography and despite voicing my own doubts they have drawn the conclusion that Domvent would be a suitable choice as one of the locations in which to place a local unit. As you are familiar with the town and the surrounding area, they appear to think that you would be a sensible choice to lead it. Your own views about this would be useful. I should reiterate that it is only because you are likely to be familiar with the local populace that you have been chosen as its head.' It was a begrudging and unnecessary remark but Eric was hardly surprised.

Although Domvent had been selected as a likely location for the new unit Boudeau was less than enthusiastic about its choice. He knew that Farbres lived fairly close by and was therefore the most obvious choice as the person to command it. There was no way he could advance any objection that would make sense to his fellow officers, so he was obliged to go along with their decision. The fact that Eric Farbres was likely to be put in command of a small police unit was doubly irritating to Boudeau, but he was powerless to do anything about it.

'So Farbres, you will shortly be given some guidelines and instructions covering the whole issue. I should add that we will allocate personnel from other units – we think about twenty will be sufficient for the moment – and you will have authority to hire one or two civilian staff for certain administrative posts. I imagine you will recruit locally? That's all for now – you will hear more from me shortly. Goodbye.' The phone was put down before Eric could make any response.

The call left Eric excited and a little befuddled. There were a lot of questions that needed answering but the general drift was clear enough and from his standpoint looked to be good news. He immediately wrote a brief note to Anne-Marie giving her the outlines of what had just transpired, and another to his father explaining the latest development. He had already thought that if, as Boudeau had said, he could hire civilian staff locally, there would be nothing to prevent him from recruiting Isabelle for the role of clerical assistant in the office.

He was home for the weekend a day or two later. He and Anne-Marie drank to the future which had suddenly begun to look a great deal rosier.

'So will it mean you'll be home at the weekends now?' asked Anne-Marie.

'I imagine so. I daresay there will be times when I will need to be in the unit, but generally speaking it should make things a lot easier.'

'Wonderful!' she said. The strain on their marriage had been difficult to handle and there had seemed no way out of the situation. It now began to look as if it was all about to change and with little effort on their part. It seemed too good to be true.

'Have you spoken to Isabelle about any of this yet and that there might be a chance of a job for her in the offing?'

'Well I told her that you might be moving back to Domvent shortly – but I thought it would be better if you told her what you had in mind. I hope I did right?'

'Absolutely. Where is she?'

'At Chalhac visiting her grandmother.' She was careful to avoid saying anything about their daughter calling on Jules and Sarah Gaillard. Hiding Isabelle's romance with Guy had only been possible because of Eric's frequent absence from home and it had already occurred to Anne-Marie that it might become more difficult, if Eric was going to be based at Domvent in the future.

'When can we expect her back?'

'Later this afternoon I would think. It takes her less than an hour on her bike and she usually leaves Chalhac in the mid-afternoon.'

'Good. We'll tell her all about it then.'

Isabelle had left her grandmother's house after finishing a bowl of unidentifiable vegetable soup and a chunk of bread which Hortense had insisted she ate. Isabelle had been hungry and she thanked Hortense warmly for her kindness. It was something that had become a sort of a tradition. Most weekends Isabelle would cycle over to Chalhac on Saturday morning, unless the weather was bad, and pay her respects to Hortense and her aunt Henrietta if she happened to be home. Her 'Tantetta' was frequently obliged to work at the chateau and then Isabelle did not see her at all. This weekend was one of those, so after a respectable time, she politely made her excuses to Hortense, and cycled across La Place, past the bar, around the corner and up the road to the Gaillard's home. She always looked forward to seeing them and hearing the latest news on Guy's progress in Clermont.

She had been introduced to David Markovich two or three weeks before. He had quickly become a more or less permanent feature in the household. He had fully recovered from his arduous journey from Rouen and was now in the process of trying to find somewhere small and cheap enough, where he could resume his tailoring business. It had proved impossible so far but Jules and Sarah were very sympathetic and allowed him, together with his sewing machine and possessions to remain in their house for the time being.

He was unable to repay them for their kindness but swore that one day he would somehow make up for it.

'No luck I suppose with your search for a shop then, Monsieur Markovich?' asked Isabelle. She had not known David quite long enough to be able to address him less formerly. David was comfortable with her polite formality and he had not yet suggested that it was alright by him if she called him by his first name.

'Not yet I'm afraid – but I live in hope. Someone, somewhere, must own a small place that they would be happy to earn a little rental on, but I haven't found anyone up to now.'

'I am sorry. That must be very difficult for you. What will happen when Guy comes home later next month? Three of you can't share that bedroom surely?'

'No. We won't have to! Monsieur Gaillard has made a sort of bedroom for me in the roof. When Guy gets back I will have to retreat up there. It means using a ladder to get in there but it will serve its purpose if I am still here. He has also made a little bed for me, so it will be quite cosy.' "Cosy" barely described it. The roof space was intensely hot and stuffy and when the sun came up the heat was almost unbearable, but David was in no position to complain. He was a non-paying guest of the Gaillard family after all and he still thanked his lucky stars that he had been pointed in their direction at the outset. Although he did not pay rent to the Gaillards he made an effort to try to make it up in other ways. He was the first to volunteer for any household chores and helped Sarah with the preparation of food such as it was, but while he had managed to salt away a small amount of cash during his time in Rouen, it hardly allowed for a regular payment of rent. He felt guilty about this and occasionally handed over token amounts of cash to help with household expenses, little though they were.

Isabelle eventually arrived home in the late afternoon. The route back was mostly uphill as Chalhac lay about halfway down the valley. The Farbres house in Petit Domvent was about twenty kilometres from Chalhac but Isabelle's legs were strong and she enjoyed the freewheeling down from her home as well as the effort of the uphill climb back. When she returned that afternoon she was flushed with the effort but otherwise relaxed. She hadn't expected her father to be home and expressed her pleasure at the sight of him in the salon with her mother.

'Papa! How lovely to see you! They have given you some time off for once?' As she said it she was already preparing her story about how and where she had spent her day. 'It does make a change doesn't it?' Eric felt relieved that his daughter had reacted so warmly to his sudden appearance. 'As a matter of fact I had some important news to tell you and your mother, so I asked to be let out for once.'

'It must be very important then,' said Isabelle. 'Are you going to tell us about it?'

'Yes of course. 'The main thing is that I am getting some promotion. Not only that, but I have been instructed to set up a new small unit in Domvent. I will be its head in addition to which they want me to recruit one or two civilian personnel for the office, which could be an ideal opportunity for you Isabelle. Sorry to spring it on you like this, but do you think it is something you would consider?'

Isabelle was a little taken aback by this sudden announcement. Anne-Marie had told her that her father was likely to be moved back closer to home before long, but that was about all. It had never crossed her mind that she could find herself working for him and it took a little time to digest the idea. She imagined that working with her father and being within his close proximity would impose new restrictions upon her. It required careful thinking about and she wanted to play for a little more time.

'What sort of job would it be Papa? I mean, would I be in the office and working for you directly, or for somebody else, or what?'

'At the moment Cherie I don't have all the details and until we begin to set it all up I can't be certain how many personnel will be needed, but if you are interested you can be sure there will be a job for you because I will make all the decisions about who we employ.'

'Would I need to type and that sort of thing?'

'Probably, but you would quickly find your way around a typewriter. In any case your Mama can type and she could give you a few lessons if I borrow a machine from the office. To be honest I can't believe you would find the work particularly difficult. Tell me what you decide as soon as you can, because we will need to be up and running fairly quickly.'

Isabelle was somewhat unnerved by the prospect of working for the police, although she could see it might mean a short cut into what could prove to be an interesting change of direction.

'Can you give me a day or so to think about it Papa? I think it's very kind of you to look on me as a prospective colleague! I am flattered that you are prepared to put so much trust in me. Suppose I messed things up and made you look an idiot – then what?'

'I don't think that's very likely Cherie and even if you did, it would be me who would have the job of telling you off! So you can hardly lose. Let me know by next weekend if you want to do it because I have to answer to my boss shortly how things are progressing.'

'It sounds a real opportunity for you Isabelle,' said Ann-Marie. 'If I were you I would take up the offer. These sort of jobs don't come up that often in places like Domvent and those that do, usually want people with all sorts of qualifications, which would probably count against you in the normal way of things.'

'I am sure you are right Maman and it could be a good move I suppose but I'll need a little time to think it over.'

'I understand that Isabelle,' said Eric 'but there's not a lot of time to play with, so give me your answer as soon as you can.'

'I promise I will Papa dear and thank you for thinking I might be right for the job.'

Twelve

Isabelle wrote to Guy the same evening to tell him what had transpired that afternoon when her father had offered her a job in the gendarmerie office and that he would be her boss as well as being head of the unit. She had already thought through some of its implications and was anxious to tell Guy that they would have to be extra careful in future since her Papa would now be based in Domvent and might therefore be spending more time at home. She received a reply from Guy a day or two later saying that he had taken her warnings on board and would take every care necessary. He also said that rumours continued to circulate that the new régime was planning moves against Jews, communists, gypsies and freemasons. As yet he had been unable to discover how much of this had any foundation of truth, but it was unsettling to say the very least. He agreed with her that in the circumstances they would both need to be extremely cautious. He added that if she did decide to take up the job offer she might be able to verify what was going on in Clermont and Vichy, 'but you would have to be very careful Cherie – and not take any unnecessary risks.'

On Monday she wrote to her father saying that she had carefully considered the job on offer and that she would like to accept and looked forward to discussing the details with him as soon as things were settled in Domvent.

Eric wrote back and said that suitable new premises had been found for the unit - previously a school - now disused, since a new and larger school had come into being. He thought it might take a week or two to make any necessary alterations, but she could expect to be working there by sometime in August. His letter was couched in a certain clinical and official style and lacked any sign of affection as a copy would have to be sent to his boss in Clermont and it was therefore a little cold, but Isabelle could understand his reasons.

By the first week of August, Isabelle found herself behind a desk in the new police office. Originally an all-purpose schoolroom in the main building, it had now been divided into two pairs of smaller rooms, one of which would be taken up with her father's office and the remaining three rooms including her own, were to be allocated to whatever clerical staff became necessary. There was no sign of Eric when she first arrived and the whole place seemed very bleak and empty. She was welcomed by one Lieutenant Michel Boyer, a polite and formal young man, whom Isabelle guessed was not long out of an officer training academy and that this was probably his first official posting as assistant and second-in-command to her father, Major Eric Farbres.

Her arrival was expected and Boyer had been briefed by Eric about the family relationship. The young man had left a small bunch of wild flowers in a jam jar on her desk as a gesture of friendly welcome. It may also have been an effort to curry favour with her father but whatever the reason, Isabelle appreciated the thought.

'Welcome to our unit Mademoiselle Farbres – I am afraid your father has been called away this morning and will not be back before fourteen hundred. Can I offer you a coffee?'

'That's very kind Lieutenant – thank you!'

There were few comforts in her office which contained only a government issue wooden desk upon which stood a very used-looking typewriter, an empty filing tray and the flowers. A wooden typist's chair, a filing cabinet and brown linoleum on the floor completed the ensemble. A tall single window looked out onto what she assumed had once been a children's play area, separated from the road outside by a stone wall with a pair of ornamental cast iron gates to allow access. It was a dispiriting start to her working life and she hoped that as time went by, things would improve. There were no signs of any other personnel and she asked Boyer when the rest of the staff was likely to appear.

'We expect them later tomorrow afternoon; they will be arriving from Clermont in our own transport. There should be about twenty of them altogether plus two NCOs to keep them in order. They will live on the other side of the wall in a new building designed specifically for this sort of purpose. They will eat and sleep there so you won't see much of them as a rule. We will have a small lorry, a car and a motorcycle at our disposal and there's a telephone which will live on Major Farbres' desk. I imagine that when we have settled in properly, a few improvements could be made.'

It did not take long for young Boyer to detect an aura of gloom surrounding Isabelle as she sat at her empty desk, her eyes vaguely focused on the newly constructed wooden partition wall, a part of the conversion from school to military use. He felt a little responsible for Isabelle's unspoken dismay.

'We can hope so Lieutenant because right now it strikes me as being pretty grim.'

'I am sure it will get better in the fullness of time,' said Boyer.

Isabelle thanked Boyer for the coffee and he retired to Eric Farbres' office on the other side of the partition. There was nothing to be done by either of them until Eric returned in the afternoon, so they were obliged to spend several boring hours considering their respective careers.

Eric Farbres arrived back at the unit he warmly welcomed Isabelle and congratulated her on her wisdom in choosing to start her career in the way she had. He thanked her for her prompt decision. He explained to Isabelle one of the reasons for setting up the new unit was that the new administration in Vichy was concerned that dissent among the populace might be generated as a result of some of the measures now being actively considered and being put in place. This had been mostly happening he said, since the recent ending of the civil war in Spain. It had meant that a considerable number of Spanish and Jewish anti-Franco fighters were now turning up in France – many of whom disappeared into the French countryside and were almost impossible to trace. There was a fear that some of these people could forge links with communist agitators and Jews and cause a lot of trouble. It was therefore beholden on the French to try to help stamp out this sort of activity.

Isabelle listened to her father's lecture and managed to remain silent even when his undisguised antipathy towards the Jews came up. Despite her anger she nodded in agreement with him but she was churning inside with fury that her own father could be so obsessed and apparently sold on the ideas he was now expressing. She would have dearly loved to tell him about David Markovich's experiences and that he had witnessed the inhuman bombing of innocent refugees on the road near Le Mans and then to have challenged him to justify the new Pétain-led espousal of the German inspired 'government' in Vichy. But she remained quiet knowing full well that were she to let anything drop concerning Jews in general, or the Gaillard family in particular, including her love affair with Guy and the conspiracy of silence that had surrounded the whole subject for so many years, there was no telling where the ramifications might end.

Her first day in the new unit in Domvent eventually came to an end. It had hardly come up to expectations and had been even more boring than anticipated. There had been nothing for her to do apart from laboriously typing two letters from her father to his superiors in Clermont, which had simply confirmed that progress within the unit was running to the agreed plan and that he had now recruited a new civilian employee.   The day had seemed interminably long and she was glad to escape on her bicycle for home in Petit Domvent. Ann Marie was anxious to know how it had gone for her daughter and Isabelle had regaled her with her first, and not very enthusiastic, impressions. Her mother said:

'Well I suppose it is too early for you to make any sort of judgment at the moment but I daresay when the rest of the men turn up and begin their proper duties there will be more work for you. Did you have any typing to do?' Although Ann Marie had been a self-taught typist/clerk years before, she had been given the job of attempting to instill a few basics about typing into Isabelle. Eric had put forward the idea, knowing that Ann Marie had eventually become an adequate typist at the licensing office. His expectation that she would be able to teach their daughter how to become a fully-fledged typist within the space of two or three weeks was clearly a little optimistic, but Isabelle had slavishly produced the two letters for Eric's signature and he seemed satisfied with the results, or if it were not the case, he did not say so.

The following days proved a little more interesting. On Tuesday afternoon the remainder of the personnel arrived in the back of a lorry followed by a motorcycle and a small van. Isabelle caught sight of one or two of them but they were mostly busy settling themselves into their new quarters on the other side of the wall. She did see a senior Non Commissioned Officer when he came into her office by mistake and was directed into Eric's next door. She could hear various discussions about training and risks concerning riots, but was unable to learn all the details through the partition wall.

Eventually she was asked to type out a list of all the personnel now making up the unit and another list of people assigned for 'special responsibilities.' What the special responsibilities were to be was unspecified. The week passed uneventfully and Isabelle began to get into some sort of routine. Eric seemed fairly relaxed with the way things were going and the little unit began to function as a recognizable gendarmerie.

On Saturday morning Isabelle told her mother she would go down to Chalhac to see her grand-mère as usual and would look in on Sarah and Jules Gaillard in the afternoon. She arrived before midday and received her usual warm greeting by Hortense and her aunt.

'So how is the job progressing?' asked Henrietta – they both knew she had started to work for her father and were intrigued to hear how it had gone.

'It's been OK but I have to remember not to mention the Gaillards or Guy. I'm not used to having Papa on the other side of the wall all day or to see him at home so much, but I think it will be alright in the end.' She crossed her fingers as she said it.

'We've had some excitement here Isabelle: a little pamphlet was put under the door of Jacques Fournier's bar sometime on Wednesday night headed, "Fight for your Freedom". It urged everyone to rise up and make life as difficult as possible for the Germans and their Vichy "puppets" as it called them. It was written by someone who is clearly an educated person, probably a communist - and is trying to gather support for his ideas. The pamphlet has been duplicated and had obviously been doing the rounds because it was looking a bit tatty. Its last words said "Pass this on to as many people as you think will agree with the sentiments expressed". Jacques called a meeting in his bar yesterday and let everyone see it and to get an idea how people hereabouts might react. I'm not sure how your grand-mère or I can be expected to contribute much, but it must mean there's enough folk unhappy with what's going on. Even the people who admire Pétain for his adventures in the last war are beginning to have doubts about what he's doing, to say nothing about his cosying up to the Germans, so I don't know how it will pan out.'

Isabelle stayed at her grandmother's house until mid-afternoon. Hortense had provided a simple meal of soup and eggs. They discussed immediate topics, including what Eric thought about Pétain and the new régime and the health of her mother and paternal grandparents. She finally left for the Gaillard house where Jules and Sarah were waiting for her in the 'salon' and where she was greeted with intense affection. David Markovich and Marcel were over in Fournier's bar discussing the pamphlet.

Jules said, 'Your aunt and grand-mère will have told you about the pamphlet Isabelle and it raises some very interesting questions involving us – you included. Marcel and David are down at the bar talking about it with Jacques and I'm sure they won't be the only ones down there. It will be interesting to know what he has been hearing this morning. There've been some rumours going around in Bordeaux that the Germans have already executed someone for cutting a telephone line and now people are being ordered to guard phone lines all day and night. They also say that they've been rounding people up – mostly Jewish I might add – and they're taking them away in buses. I don't know how much to believe but if it's true we must be thankful that we are in Chalhac and not in Bordeaux. Let's hope they don't change their minds about Pétain and take over all the country.'

'Has your father had much to say about the new government, Isabelle?' asked Sarah.

'Not a lot, but I know he will be more or less in favour because of his attitude towards Jews. Everybody knows that Pétain is anti-Semitic and more or less on the side of the Nazis. I can't imagine what he thinks he can gain from backing Hitler – you've only to look at what they are doing up in the north to see that they are going to steal everything they can from us and take it all back to Germany. I think it's terrible. To think that my dear Papa is happy to go along with it gives me nightmares.'

'It must be very difficult for you Isabelle and for your mother. Have you been in touch with Guy? He wrote last week telling us again that the government might prevent Jews from being teachers. It's only a rumour but if it is true, it would be a terrible blow for Guy – he has set his heart so much on the idea of becoming a teacher and if he's stopped now because of new rules being invented by Pétain, I don't know what he will do. You know he is due home next week don't you?'

'Yes, he replied to my letter telling him that I had started working in the next room to Papa. I warned him to be extra careful now as Papa was spending more time at home and in Domvent and he's taken on board my warnings. He also mentioned the rumours coming out of Vichy about Jewish teachers and that if any of it is true we'll all be in serious trouble, because you can be certain it won't stop there. He told me he was coming home next week and looked forward to seeing us. It seems like a lifetime since he was here – I wonder if he's changed?' Although it was only a few weeks since he left for Clermont, it seemed like a lifetime to Isabelle.

* * * * *

She had been working in the Gendarmerie for over a week now. Eric had kept her reasonably busy, mostly with typing lists, standing orders and duty rosters. One morning he appeared in her doorway and said:

'Isabelle, I have received new orders from Clermont. Colonel Boudeau has been instructed by Vichy that gendarmeries across the French State must, in future, take active measures against possible dissent. From now on we are to examine the post and if we suspect that a letter contains any sign of anti-government sentiment, it must be opened carefully, the contents read and if necessary decisions will be made regarding punishment for crimes against the State. This goes for all letters going out and coming in to Domvent and the surrounding area. Personally, I am not altogether in favour of this sort of action but we are obliged to obey orders. We are authorised to collect letters from post offices before they are sorted for delivery. I am appointing you and as many uniformed officers as might be required, to look after this task. The officers will report to you if they think they have uncovered anything of this nature and you in turn must tell me, or in my absence, Lieutenant Boyer, what evidence you or they have discovered. Where letters have been unnecessarily opened and are found to be innocent, they must be resealed and stamped to indicate that their opening had been officially sanctioned. Is that quite clear?'

Isabelle was quietly horrified. She managed to control her innermost thoughts however and said, 'Perfectly clear Papa. Don't you think all this is a little extreme though? After all, there hasn't been any reason to suspect there is any real dissent – as you call it – down here in the south, has there?'

'Not very much as yet, I agree, but there are certain measures to be announced shortly which could change the picture. I am unable to give you details at the moment because they are not yet approved by the new Assembly and it would be inappropriate for me to spread rumours even to you.'

'And how are we supposed to recognise suspicious letters – will they be written in blood?' said Isabelle sarcastically. 'And when does this start Papa?'

Eric ignored his daughter's sarcasm. 'Letters addressed to people with foreign sounding names might be regarded as possibly suspect. There are plenty of Spaniards and Jews in the country, who might be tempted to revolt against the new administration and it is those we need to weed out. As to when we begin, it starts with immediate effect – it's too late today to do anything but I have been in contact with the postal people to explain the position and they will co-operate, so we start tomorrow.'

The following day, several bags of letters were delivered to the unit from the main post office in Domvent. Isabelle had no idea how many letters they contained but it was a substantial number and she quickly realised that it would be almost impossible to examine and try to decide if any might be suspect. She hoped that as she was going to be in charge of the operation, she would be in a good position to remove any of her own personal letters, or those to or from Guy and his family from scrutiny by overzealous gendarmerie spies. It was however very unsettling to know that the régime was prepared to counter any opposition to their ideas so ruthlessly. She also knew that although she might be able to exclude particular mail passing through her hands, it would be almost impossible to prevent her gendarme assistants from opening any letters which she would prefer were not opened.

She tackled her father the next morning about exempting their own personal letters.

'Well I don't see our family as being a likely hotbed of internal strife Isabelle, do you?' said Eric with a smile, 'but if you feel uncomfortable about any of this I will ensure our family letters are excluded and are to be considered innocent. I'll issue instructions to Lieutenant Boyer to tell the men to put our own mail aside. We will have to arrange our own special mark that our examining team can recognize.'

'How about a small green dot on the corner of envelopes? I'm sure we can find some green ink that we could use. We'll know then that our letters – if we have to write to anyone, will stay private. Does that sound too complicated?'

'That sounds like an excellent idea Cherie – good work!'

It was a relief to know that her father approved of her idea so whole heartedly, because it meant that he still had not the remotest idea about what was going on under his nose. She was faintly amazed to think that nothing had been said by anyone in Chalhac over the years that could easily have alerted him to what he would doubtless have considered treachery within his own family. Eric regarded his family as being above suspicion and Isabelle was grateful beyond words – but she could hardly tell him so.

That weekend she cycled down to Chalhac, made her dutiful visit to her grandmother and Henrietta and in the afternoon called in on the Gaillards. Guy had only been back from Clermont for an hour when she appeared and there was a sense of celebration in the air when she arrived. Isabelle was almost overcome with pleasure at seeing Guy again – and they both felt distinctly awkward, not quite knowing how or where to start again in front of the family. Guy felt clumsy and embarrassed with a need to embrace Isabelle as passionately as he would have liked and Isabelle was well aware of the difficulty this presented and said,

'Guy Darling, let's get out on our bikes for a breath of fresh air. There's a lot to talk about at the moment and we can both catch up with the family here over the next few days.'

'Good idea. Would you mind very much if we disappear for a while Mama? Papa?'

'Of course not. Go out and get to know one another again! – It must seem like ages for you both,' said Sarah.

Isabelle and Guy left the assembled family group and vanished on their bikes into the afternoon sunshine, out of Chalhac and up onto the plateau. In a shady and secluded spot they had discovered several months before, they made love, tenderly but with some urgency as if time itself were beginning to run out for them.

* * * * *

There was much to discuss, not just for Guy and Isabelle but for Sarah, Jules, Marcel and David Markovich as well. When the 'pamphlet' arrived, delivered by an unseen hand, it had brought into focus that there were like-minded people in the country who were anything but happy with the direction in which things were moving. Its content was a real call to arms and for its readers to be prepared to fight, if necessary to the death, for the sake of their beloved France. Its purpose was to sow the seeds of the idea in as many minds as possible, that there was perhaps still a chance of overcoming the catastrophe in which the country now found itself embroiled. It called, not for massive military attacks – which were out of the question in any event – but for the steady erosion of the will of those attempting to change the country into something different. It said:

'France has no wish to become another colony of Germany and if you, as a citizen, wish to remain essentially French, then you must be prepared to do whatever is necessary to achieve that end.'

It concluded with the words:

'Finally, trust no one because these are dangerous times and our enemies will watch for any sign of discontent and will be ruthless in their determination to take complete control of our country. Vive la France!'

The sole topic of conversation in Jacques Fournier's bar was how a village such as Chalhac could be expected to make much of a contribution to the sentiments expressed, admirable though they were. Jacques' single leg, the other lost in the Great War, was a constant reminder of his own limitations and his bitterness at being prevented from continuing with a career as a joiner and he still felt helpless and angry. The arrival of the pamphlet had re-awakened his sense of injustice and he was now trying to maintain a sense of patriotic unity within his little domain:

'Now gentlemen, we must not allow the Boche to crush our spirits. These are early days yet and there will be much to do if we decide we will work for the greater good. I think we should take very seriously the warning in the pamphlet that we should trust no one, unless of course we are certain that the people we speak to are thinking the same way as ourselves. Madame Hubert's granddaughter Isabelle has told us that in future our letters are at risk of being opened by the gendarmeries. As you know, she now works in the new unit in Domvent - headed by her father, but she disagrees with everything he is doing or has said. She is in a delicate, but advantageous, situation. She will do her best to ensure that letters to or from us are kept from the prying eyes of these nasty people – but you must still be careful that when you write to your friends or relations that you say nothing that might give them an excuse to pick on you.'

The miller Malet was keen to help. He had still heard nothing from either of his sons and he had to assume they had been taken prisoner when Rouen was overrun and were now presumably behind barbed wire somewhere in Germany. Anything he could do, to get them back safe and sound, was worth doing and he said he would do his damnedest to achieve that end.

'I'm glad to hear you take that view Malet. You have good reason to feel proud of your sons. We are all proud to know they have served our country so well.' It was a brave if slightly over-stated attempt by Jacques to keep alive the momentum so far achieved. Some of those present were not altogether convinced that there was very much that could be done about any of it and were inclined to try to make the best of a bad job, but Jacques would have none it:

'We all know that the future is very uncertain at the present time and of course we don't know the whole story yet. Old Pétain and his friends in Vichy and Berlin seem to be prepared to lick the arse of Hitler for their own reasons, but he's an old man and it seems to me he is going a bit daft. Hitler and his friends see him as a stupid old fool I'm sure, and that anything they tell him to do, he'll do, just to keep in with them. He obviously thinks that if he plays along with them, they'll see France alright in the end, but judging by the way Hitler has behaved in the countries he's walked into so far, we are likely to come out the losers like the rest of them. The old idiot doesn't seem to realise that he means nothing to the 'Führer'- other than his being the means to an end. For all our sakes, we must try to save our country from these savages and from Pétain's stupidity and not just go belly up in front of them – that would be too easy.'

'So what do you think we can do about it?' asked Bonnet the baker. 'So far as I can see we are pretty helpless down here. We don't have any guns or bombs or anything that we could use to fight with, so what are we expected to do that will have any sort of effect on the people in Vichy or Berlin?'

'I don't think that our anonymous pamphlet writer is really suggesting that sort of thing but there has to be a lot we can do that will mess up or slow down their plans, so we need to get down to thinking about possible moves. Whatever we decide to do, we'll have to be careful not to be seen as the villains of the piece, because they'll jump on us hard if they think we're at the back of it. If you need convincing about any of this, you should speak to Monsieur Markovich. We've all heard about his getting out of Rouen and his trip on his bike down here. He has seen with his own eyes just what they are capable of – machine gunning and bombing civilians on the road – and it wasn't by accident that they were doing it. The latest we hear now is that people are being shot and arrested in Bordeaux and taken away, so do we just sit around and hope it won't happen here? I don't think so.'

With that rallying cry from Fournier, the dozen or so jammed in the bar began to disperse. Bonnet needed to get his afternoon sleep, having been bread baking since the early hours and Malet hadn't eaten since breakfast and urgently required feeding. Monsieur Bastien had to attend to one of his cows and the rest were expected by their wives and families to be home at a respectable hour. When the last of them left, Jacques poured a beer, sat down outside under his awning and put his feet up on one of the metal chairs. He was soon asleep.

Thirteen

The following weeks went by far too quickly for Isabelle and Guy, while at the same time her days at work dragged painfully slowly, marooned in her office in Domvent. Days were mostly spent in the brain numbing task of examining hundreds of envelopes for potential suspected dissidents. It was at best thankless as she had absolutely no intention of obeying the 'rules', and was only going through the motions of doing the job asked of her. She had been allocated a young gendarme to help with the work, but it was clear that his heart was not in it either and he too was bored out of his mind. When Eric was safely out of range and Lieutenant Boyer was involved elsewhere in the unit they spent most of the day chatting. Her young gendarme helper had joined the service in the expectation of being a member of a physically active crime fighting unit – and not in an office sifting through heaps of letters. The only redeeming feature for the young man was in having a very attractive young woman on the opposite side of the table - it helped, but not a lot. Isabelle thought she had better make it appear that they had uncovered possible wrongdoing and so opened one or two randomly chosen and perfectly innocent letters, and then resealed them with sticky labels and stamped them as instructed. There were some which might just have been a little suspect but there was no way that Isabelle was going to interfere with them and they were ignored.

By four o'clock she was more than ready to escape the gendarmerie and as soon as she heard the town clock strike the hour she was on her bike and out of the gate and heading for Chalhac. She could make the village in less than thirty minutes, but she and Guy had a pre-arranged place on the road to meet, which lay half way between the village and Domvent, so they were in one anothers' arms most days, fifteen minutes after she finished work.

Anne-Marie had long since guessed what was going on between Isabelle and Guy and was extremely happy for them and was prepared to make excuses for her daughter's late arrival on the odd occasion when Eric actually did come home on time – which even now was rare. So, for the time being Isabelle and Guy were able to spend a good deal of time together. They had been discussing their future together one afternoon and Guy said:

'It looks like the régime in Vichy is getting more and more extreme. The rumours going around in Clermont about Jewish teachers can't just be empty rumours. My pal Simon's family are in touch with someone in the know in Vichy and whoever it is has seen or overheard something. Until now I haven't told you everything I've heard, but it's not just teachers affected because it now seems they might be planning to put a stop to Jews becoming doctors, or being allowed to practise, or lawyers working within the Judiciary - and I suppose this means legal advisors, and a lot of other things. They reckon they'll ban the Communist Party and the freemasons and if it turns out that our sources are even half accurate, it looks as though we are all going to be heading for a rough time before long. I haven't told my parents everything I've heard because I couldn't be sure it was based on fact and it is unfair to frighten them unnecessarily too soon. But you and I Isabelle have to make some plans for the future and be ready to fight for our ideas even if it is dangerous.'

Isabelle visibly blanched at this new outpouring from Guy. He had been careful to avoid putting any of this in his letters in case they were intercepted. He had anticipated that letters might be opened and was not in the least surprised when Isabelle told him that it had now become official policy. He had been a little aghast to hear that his own lovely Isabelle had been appointed by her father to systematically examine the post. When she told him how she was dealing with it, he relaxed a little and was quite amused to think that her dear papa had entrusted her with the task.

'So, what do we do Guy? Until we really know what they are plotting in Vichy I can't see how we can make any serious moves that will make any sense.'

'Well you are doing your bit already Cherie. Sabotaging the letter opening is a good start but you have to be very careful because sooner or later your father or someone else is bound to ask questions about the lack of results. It won't show yet for a while but if things begin to develop as I think they might, there could be a lot of so called illegal letter writing going on. If that happens we might have to deliver our own post by hand.'

By the end of September Guy had to go back to Clermont to resume his teaching course. There were some passionate 'au revoirs' between them and they strung out their precious time together until the last possible moment. Guy took his bike with him this time anticipating that it could be useful if things became difficult in Clermont and was obliged to abandon everything at short notice. He had not said so to Isabelle but he fully expected to find that he and Simon Wojakovski, could find themselves off the course and probably put to work in some sort of factory. He could barely imagine how the future might develop but stories were slowly percolating down the line from the north describing how all manner of people – mostly Jews - were being rounded up and taken away in buses and on trains. He could not be sure how much of this was pure invention on the part of bored or politically mischievous people but if it was true then he might have to get away from Clermont quickly. He wrote to Isabelle as soon as he arrived back at the Wojakovski house, having established that nothing more dramatic had occurred while he was away, but the stories emerging from further north were bad enough. He told Isabelle that people were being arrested for attempting to get across the new demarcation line and in at least one instance, shot by an overzealous French policeman for failing to stop. Isabelle intercepted Guy's letter when it was brought in with hundreds more from the Domvent post office for checking. She thanked her lucky stars that she had been given the tedious job of inspection by her father and was now keenly aware about just how much power she wielded in her little office. After her last meeting with Guy, she felt she should tell Guy's family as much as she knew about the way the situation seemed to be developing and had made up her mind to it.

The following weekend she was down in Chalhac again and made her way first of all to her grand-mère Hortense's house on La Place. Her aunt 'Tantetta' was home from the chateau as it happened, so she was doubly pleased to be there. She was not always able to catch up with Henrietta as much as she would have liked because her aunt's duties at the chateau took precedence over most other things. After the usual pleasantries Isabelle asked Henrietta:

'How's life at the chateau these days Tantetta? What do Monsieur le Comte and la Comtesse have to say about the current situation?'

'You may well ask Isabelle. La Comtesse told me yesterday that they are planning to move to Switzerland. Their friends and one or two distant relatives in Paris have already got out because they couldn't stand the sight of the Germans strutting about in the city as if they owned it. She said that she and le Comte planned to send the children to Switzerland anyway, so they have decided to go with them. Someone they know has a big house on the edge of Lac Léman, which they can rent for the time being, so they are going to go while they still can.'

'Lucky for them!' said Isabelle. 'So, what's going to happen to you and your job – is that the end of it?'

'Not altogether. They have said that if I like I could remain at the chateau as a sort of housekeeper – to keep an eye on it while they are away. It would mean I'd have to look after the place on the inside and Pierre would keep his job looking after the grounds. It won't be as time consuming as it is now because there will not be the children to worry about and I will be free to go up the chateau more or less when I please. They are going to give me the keys so I can get in and out and I am going to take them up on their offer.'

'Well that sounds very good to me Tantetta – what do you think Grand-mère?'

Hortense was beaming with pleasure.

'I think it is wonderful Isabelle. It seems your aunt has fallen on her feet once more. We have many reasons to thank Monsieur le Comte and Madame la Comtesse.'

'They obviously trust you enough Tantetta to allow you to have the run of the place. Did they employ a cook while you were there – I've never thought to ask before?'

'Yes, when I first started there they did have a cook and a maid, but I think they began to run out of money and they got rid of them. It was only because they had to have someone to take charge of the children when they went off to Paris, that they didn't get rid of me as well. I'm sure they would have done so otherwise. Now, of course, things have changed and they've got the wind up and want to get out of the country altogether. They want to hang on to the chateau and not have it fall into rack and ruin while they are away, so without anyone else to ask they've given me the job of looking after it. I am perfectly happy to do it if they keep on paying me, so that's what I'm going to do.'

'When are they leaving – do you know?' asked Isabelle.

'Any day now I should think. They haven't told me exactly but la Comtesse has been folding clothes and fussing around, so I think they'll be off shortly.'

'You'll have the place to yourself for the foreseeable future, then won't you? Does that worry you Tantetta, to be alone in a great big house like that?'

'No, not a bit. I've been there by myself quite a lot in any case, so I'm used to it. When the fire is alight in the salon it is quite cosy – a bit draughty sometimes when the winds are blowing but otherwise it's OK. Perhaps you could come and visit me one day and I'll show you around. It must have been lovely when it was new but I'm afraid it's got a bit tatty over the years. Some of it is nearly falling down at one end and nobody is allowed to go in there because they think it's too dangerous – it's such a shame to have allowed the place to get into that state.'

'I'd love to do that Tantetta – I could pretend you are la Comtesse!

'That's about as close as I'll ever get to becoming a Comtesse!' said Henrietta. 'I'll let you know when they have left and I'll give you a tour.'

An hour or so later Isabelle made her way over to the Gaillard house. Apart from Guy, they were all there in the salon. She was given her usual warm welcome and polite enquiries were made about her mother and father.

'Your mother is well I hope?' said Sarah. 'And your Papa – is he just as busy?'

'Yes, they are both well and Papa is very taken up with dealing with what Vichy sees as potential threats to the new régime. We don't see that much of him even though he is based in Domvent now. I think Maman is a bit disappointed to think he's not able to get home at a civilized hour all the time, but his hours have improved so she's happier than she has been for a while.'

'And how is your letter opening task progressing Isabelle? asked Jules. 'Have you discovered any 'wicked wrongdoers' yet?'

'What do you think? I've had to open one or two perfectly innocent letters just to let them think that we are doing the job. Papa and his superiors in Clermont and Vichy will begin to think there is something fishy going on if we don't come up with some suspect letters. Don't forget that if you write to Guy or to anyone else, you must be careful not say anything that could be seen as anti-government. Unfortunately I can't control the post once it leaves our office, so it could still end up in the wrong hands and we could all be in a lot of trouble. Remember it's not just me opening the mail in our office because I've had to accept help from one of the junior gendarmes. He's a nice enough man but he might become a little too inquisitive before I could stop him opening something incriminating and there's no way I could do anything about it. So be warned.' She explained the scheme for putting a green dot on the corner of envelopes when letters containing anything private needed to be protected from prying eyes and that her father had approved the idea without the slightest suspicion that it could be exploited by the very people he would like to identify. They were all amused by the idea but still anxious.

She told the family and David about the continuing rumours circulating in Vichy and Clermont and that Guy had not wanted to worry them unduly when he was home but it all had a ring of truth about it. They had not heard about the shooting of someone trying to cross the demarcation line between the occupied north and the Vichy controlled south and were horrified.

'Do you mean to tell me that one of our police actually shot his fellow countryman for trying to get across the line? That's terrible if it's true,' said Sarah.

'That's what Guy's friend Simon Wojakovski's family has heard – they know someone in Vichy and the story is doing the rounds there.'

'Is the policeman going to be arrested I wonder? asked Jules.

'I'd be very surprised if he is. No . . . they are all under orders from Paris – or very likely from Berlin, and they are backing up our wonderful new régime in Vichy. I think this is what we can expect in future – or worse,' said Isabelle.

'I'm afraid you might be right Isabelle,' said David. 'Pétain and his crew in Vichy are obviously going along with the Germans.

What the Germans want is what they tend to get. Now having put old Pétain in charge with his pals Laval, Darlan and the rest of them, the door is wide open for their rules to be applied to the rest of us, whether we like it or not, and Pétain isn't going to argue with Berlin. He obviously thinks that by agreeing with it all, he'll get favours from them in the long run and that in some mysterious way, France will come out stronger and more powerful than it's ever been. Not a chance!' he said with a shake of his head. 'Not a chance!'

A silence fell upon the little gathering in the Gaillard salon while they mulled over what had just been said. David's pronouncement rang true and it had been delivered with real fervour.

Finally, Jules said:

'We've just got to come up with a few ideas to try to counter all of this. I don't know what we can do immediately, although Isabelle here is doing her bit already and we are extremely grateful Isabelle. It's difficult for you knowing that your father is part of the problem so we are doubly grateful Isabelle! You have warned us to be wary – and you in turn must be very careful because I don't like to think what might happen if your papa discovered you are sabotaging some of his best efforts.'

'Don't worry about me Papa Jules! Over the last few weeks I have become pretty cunning in covering my tracks. Even Maman is managing to make excuses for me while Guy was home. I was getting back late when we met after I left the office in the evenings.' Isabelle had taken to calling Jules 'Papa Jules' as a form of loving familiarity in the same way she now called Sarah, 'Mama Sarah.' They both looked upon Isabelle almost as an adopted child. Although neither of them had actually said so, they had both secretly wished they had produced a daughter as well as their two sons. Isabelle had unknowingly filled the gap quite nicely for them.

'Just take care, child,' said Jules.

Marcel had sat quietly listening to the discussion and so far, had not voiced his own thoughts about the present situation. He had been digesting everything that had been said, and finally said:

'I've been thinking. If, as you say Papa, we must dream up some ideas to try to fight back, then don't forget that you and I have access to some quite useful ammunition – I mean the dynamite we use at the quarry.'

'It sounds a bit drastic Marcel,' said his father who was a little taken aback by his son's apparent willingness to resort to open violence. 'I don't think we should go too far down that road just yet – although it's impossible to say what might happen in the future. Perhaps we should keep that under wraps for the time being?'

'I was not suggesting we should go about blowing things up of course, but there are some serious things going on – maybe not here in Chalhac or anywhere very close but people are being executed right now by Germans in Bordeaux and in la Rochelle, for daring to fight back, literally and sometimes just answering back. If they were ever to move this way then we may be forced to take more drastic measures. Let's face it, where in Heaven's name would we get weapons of any sort if that were to happen? I think we should quietly salt away some of our explosives and detonators right now before someone in Vichy decides to check up on likely sources of that sort of thing and confiscates anything that might look like a risk to them.'

'I think the boy's right,' said David. 'I bet there are people up in Vichy right now wondering about who has got access to what. I wouldn't be the least bit surprised if you get a visit from some official or gendarme asking for a list of explosives currently held by the quarry and how securely they're held and so on. If that happened, it would be too late then to do anything so I think we should get some of it out and hidden away somewhere while we've got the chance.'

Jules said 'Maybe you're right David. OK, tomorrow Marcel and I will raid our store shed and bring some of it home. We'll have to find a spot to hide it away but we can think about that later.'

'I know just the place,' said Isabelle. 'There's a little cave Guy and I discovered a while ago up on the plateau. It's dry and completely hidden. You would have to know where to look to spot it. I could take the stuff up there on my bike and hide it away – I know it would be safe.'

Marcel said, 'I could come up there with you Isabelle so that we would both know where it is. If anything happened to you we'd never find it if it's as well hidden as you say. What do you say?'

'OK – Let's do that.'

The following weekend Isabelle and Marcel cycled up into the hills behind Chalhac. Isabelle's bicycle had always had a basket on the handlebars and it now contained eight sticks of dynamite individually sealed in their original waxed paper coverings together with a small metal box containing ten detonators. Her father could have scarcely foreseen that his birthday gift to Isabelle years before would later become the means of the illicit transportation of dynamite. On top of this deadly cargo lay some bread, a chunk of cheese and a bottle of water. It was all covered with a small cloth, tucked in around the dynamite. Up on the plateau a gentle breeze wafted the fragrance of wild herbs and flowers. Much of the route to Isabelle's secret cave was now a barely visible path trodden over the years by goats and their herdsmen, but was now largely overgrown and had all but disappeared. At a particular point Isabelle said, 'I think we need to cut across about here, towards that little escarpment over there Marcel – follow me, I hope I can find it again!'

She seemed a little vague as she approached the slopes of the escarpment and stopped to get her bearings, looking around her. In the distance she spotted a large and very bent, dead olive tree which immediately registered on her and she said to Marcel,

'That's where it is – up beyond that tree over there!'

They made their way through the scrub towards the old tree and Isabelle leant her bike against it and disappeared on foot into the undergrowth growing on the sloping ground. Beyond the slope the ground became a near vertical cliff strewn at its foot with broken eroded rock from the cliff face. Marcel could hear and occasionally caught a glimpse of her as she made her way through the dried and tangled vegetation.

'Come on Marcel, I've found it!' He caught up with her, following the sound of her voice as she expressed her enthusiasm for the cave again. Not many weeks before, she and Guy had made love inside its dim interior and it held special memories for her – but this was hardly an aspect of its attraction she could repeat to his brother, although Marcel had already guessed that this had probably been the case in any event. She stood just inside the entrance and greeted him as if she was showing off a new home he was visiting for the first time. She waved him in with a sweep of her arm.

'This is it – what do you think?' her voice echoed around the inside of the cave.

'Let me take a look for myself. Have we got a torch?'

She handed Marcel her torch, something she had remembered at the last moment and together they carefully inspected the interior of the cave. Isabelle and Guy had never previously ventured quite so far inside as they had not carried a torch with them. The darkness as they progressed inwards became intense and the space between the side walls began to narrow quite suddenly. Eventually, Marcel said that he did not see any point in trying to go any further, as is looked like it would end up as no more than a crack in the rock; so they turned around and retraced their steps back towards the entrance. Both felt a distinct sense of relief at seeing the strong sunlight again after the blackness, although neither of them said so.

'It certainly looks to be ideal Isabelle – perfect for this stuff. It's as dry as a bone and it looks to me as though it's never been any different. Sometimes caves have dripping roofs and everything stays damp, but not this one. I think we can safely say this will do quite nicely. There's a good place just over there' – he pointed over his shoulder a short way back into the gloom to where a natural ledge projected just above head height.

'That should be a good spot for it – out of sight of any casual visitors, although it might be a very long time before anybody else calls by!'

So the dynamite and the box of detonators were unloaded from Isabelle's bike and carefully carried into the cave and placed on the ledge. They were both relieved to know they could not now be challenged or caught with the deadly load they had been carrying since earlier that morning. 'Let's have something to eat – I'm starving,' said Isabelle.

They sat down in the cave entrance and the girl laid the cloth on the dusty ground and they began to eat the small picnic she had brought with her.

'I'm sorry it's not more,' said Isabelle, 'but it will have to do.'

'No need to apologise Isabelle. It will keep us going until we get back.'

It seemed a good opportunity to talk to Marcel without the need to dilute some of the more difficult questions for the benefit of his family or David. She said:

'Tell me honestly Marcel, has Guy ever let on to you how he feels about what's happening at the present time? I mean, what does he think about being on the teaching course and how safe or otherwise he might be? He's said quite a lot to me but I think he might still be holding back some of his innermost thoughts, even to me.'

'Good question Isabelle. Well he has told me that he is extremely anxious at the present time because he knows for sure that the stories coming out of Vichy are authentic. Simon Wojakovski's parents - where Guy lodges, have a cousin in Vichy. He is the source of the information, so you can be sure that everything being told to us is authentic – not just hearsay. He works in the local government offices there, but since the new régime has taken over, a lot of the department has vanished. The cousin was one of the luckier ones and has kept his job – not quite the same, but still within earshot of much that's going on. He caught sight of a memo on a desk which clearly stated, so far as he could remember, that "measures will be put in place to ensure the elimination of Jews, Communists, and foreigners in the main established professions including medicine, education and the law". He didn't get a chance to see who had signed it, as he only had time for a brief look before they came back to the desk, but he had seen enough to be able to remember most of it and that's how Guy got to hear about it. So that's the story.'

'Oh God. Did Guy say what he will do if it does all fall to pieces? He's always wanted to become a teacher since we were children - it would break his heart if he were to be stopped now through no fault of his own.'

'I know. Not only that but if it does happen he will be very angry. One of the reasons he took his bike back with him this time was because he really does think it will all blow up and he may have to get out before he is picked up and forcibly made to work in a factory or something. He's heard that is exactly what's been happening to a lot of people already and the idea doesn't exactly appeal, as you can imagine. He hasn't decided what he'll do but my guess is he'll make it back here on his bike and think about it then.'

'What about you Marcel? Could they force you into doing something other than quarrying?'

'They could of course but so far as I can see they've lost track of me and no one seems to know I exist. When we came back from Russia my mother had to register her presence in the Marie in Domvent, as did my Papa, but somehow Guy and I were left out of the system and they haven't caught up with me yet. They obviously know about Guy because he had loads of application forms to fill in before they accepted him for the teaching course, so they must know all about him, which is a bit worrying for the family as you can imagine.'

'So, do you think that you and the family could be in danger because of Guy? He's done nothing to be ashamed of after all.'

'Of course, he hasn't, but you might be just a little too optimistic about the way things are developing in the country. The so-called new 'French State' with Pétain and his friends, are turning the country into something very nasty indeed. Guy has gleaned quite a lot of information about the way things are moving and it's not good, believe me. It hasn't taken long for the Germans in the north to dish out absolutely vicious penalties for all sorts of fairly minor 'infringements.' People are being shot, tortured or thrown into prison for simply demonstrating. Students in Paris and elsewhere have been beaten up simply because they were in the wrong place at the wrong time. As for our fellow Jews, it is all bad news. Jewish families are being rounded up in Paris and then shoved onto trains heading east. It's not certain where they are ending up but it's thought they are being made to work in German factories. If, and it is a big "if", they decided to take over down here, then we could expect to be treated in much the same way, which is the best reason to try to stop them somehow. We'll need a lot more sticks of dynamite than we've tucked away today.'

Isabelle was lost for words as she tried to digest Marcel's outpourings. Guy had clearly been privy to quite a lot of what was supposed to be confidential information but because he did not want to frighten her or his family, had decided to hold much of it back. He had told his brother as much as he knew and Marcel had also decided it would be better to stay quiet for the time being. However, now that Isabelle knew most of it she decided that the time had come to let her nearest and dearest into the secrets and to tell them just how much danger they could all face.

* * * * *

The same morning that Isabelle and Marcel were hiding the dynamite, a meeting was taking place in a third-floor room of what had, until a few weeks before, been the Hotel du Parc in Vichy. The hotel had been commandeered by the new authority and had now become the seat of government of the 'French State.' The meeting was in the office of Maréchal Phillipe Pétain. There were three others around the table: ex-newspaper magnate Pierre Laval - a strong supporter of Hitler, Admiral François Darlan and retired military officer Maxime Weygand. Pétain wore his military uniform adorned with an array of medals, Laval was dressed in a formal striped business suit, Darlan wore his admiral's uniform and Weygand was in his army uniform – a little moth-eaten, but serviceable.

'Gentlemen and fellow officers,' began Pétain somewhat portentously, 'I have called this meeting today to bring you fully up to date with the present position in our region and to confirm again the measures agreed with a view to improving French racial purity and the necessity to take firm action now and in the future. Laval here has instigated the printing of information about the subject for the benefit of the education authorities and this has now been distributed to schools, colleges and training establishments. All are required to follow the guidelines as laid down in new legislation. As you will recall, further measures will be needed, but for the moment, we should proceed cautiously. You will doubtless be aware that since the armistice with Germany and the consequent establishment of the new French State, things have been beginning to improve in our beloved country. Certain undesirables have been picked up already and where necessary are being interrogated with the intention of identifying other individuals or groups who represent a threat to law and order. We have a suitable location for these purposes: namely the Hotel Algeria here in Vichy. It will house our new Commissariat Général for Jewish Affairs and will I hope be headed by Xavier Vallat. Monsieur Vallat will be familiar to most of you and his credentials ideally reflect political attitudes in line with our own.' This elicited a slightly restrained cough from Weygand.

The Maréchal continued, 'Of course we must expect some reaction from sections of the population for whom one or two traditions are necessarily being dropped or modified. It is perhaps fortunate, and I say this with the greatest humility, that it was decided to name me as Head of State. I am certain that my appointment came about, as a result of my popularity with a substantial part of the populace, which regards me with some respect and affection, remembering me for my service in the Great War. This provides us with the best opportunity to put in place a number of what might perhaps be considered 'contentious' measures, without too much opposition. Our new allies in Berlin and Paris are very supportive of our attitudes and we can expect their full co-operation should we require any help with enforcement. We are on very good terms with Herr Hitler and his high command and this bodes well for France's future. Our collaboration with Germany will, in my view, yield the best outcome for our country and my entire strategy has been focused upon our future wellbeing and strength. To this end I have publicly dedicated my person as a gift to our country.' This had the effect of producing the hint of a smile from one or two of those at the table and had Pétain not been there, it may have induced laughter. The smiles were hidden behind hands but the old man had not seen anything anyway. He continued,

'This, I believe has helped reinforce our position and we should build upon this over the next several months. My discussions with you individually and corporately during these last few weeks will, I anticipate, begin to bear fruit. I have also authorised certain other professional bodies to be alerted to changes in the pipeline, in so far as their new responsibilities towards their members are concerned. I have in mind such organisations as the Confédération des Syndicats Médicaux Français, and the Judiciary.

As we are all aware, the infiltration by Jews into so much of French society, has understandably and justifiably created a great deal of resentment, not to say racial hatred. It has long been my view that this situation can no longer be tolerated. It is perhaps fortunate that with the help of our German friends who regard this matter in much the same way as we do ourselves, that we should reverse this trend. I intend to broadcast to the people on the wireless shortly to reinforce this message. I have outlined the main points we will be putting in place and these are spelled out in the memorandum in front of you today – I don't think there will be any surprises as you have all been privy to our discussions over the last month or more. Do you have any problems or comments you wish to raise before we go public?'

Laval spoke:

'I note that there is no specific mention made of the communists and their stranglehold on the unions, nor how we should deal with left-wing Spanish and Jewish refugees and gypsies who still appear to be arriving in not inconsiderable numbers after General Franco's success. There are also the questions surrounding freemasonry and its influence across society. They alone could prove to be a dangerous opponent with their secrecy and numbers.'

'Yes – indeed. I think you will find that I will be taking a strong line against all these people in the fullness of time. For the time being we should concentrate our efforts towards the dismantling of the 'Israelites' known spheres of influence – and there are many. Are there any further comments?'

There was some gentle head shaking in response.

'No? Very well gentlemen. We will proceed then as planned.'

Fourteen

Two virtually identical letters arrived for Guy Gaillard and Simon Wojakovski on Saturday morning the fifth of October. They were from the Ministry of Education newly situated in the former Plaza Hotel on the far side of Vichy's Parc des Sources. Both letters announced with brutal politeness that "Revised conditions agreed by the new administration require that specific guidelines are adhered to regarding admissibility of certain racial groups to particular professions, which in this instance include teaching. Having re-examined your application for inclusion to the introductory phase of the teaching course we have to inform you that in the light of your Jewish background your participation in the said course is now terminated with immediate effect. Please arrange for your personal effects, books, papers etc. to be removed from the college premises within 72 hours of receiving this letter".

Guy was first to read the letter and went back to the beginning and read it again. His first reaction was 'Shit! The bastards have done it.'

Simon quickly tore open his letter which, apart from his name at the top was virtually the same.

'Oh no! What do we do now Guy?' Their minds were spinning around with the enormity of what they had both been obliged to read. It was too early for either of them to take it all in and impossible to grasp the full implications of what looked like mindless vindictiveness.

'We have to think about this very carefully,' said Guy. 'First of all it means that you and I and our families are at considerable risk now; something I've feared for a long time. I think we should tell our people that they must stay calm but also prepare plans to move out – God knows where to, but it's suddenly looking very dangerous for all of us. After that we will have to think out a plan of action for ourselves. We obviously can't change the damned government but I'm sure there must be enough of us affected by this sort of idiocy who will want to do something. We'd better grab our stuff from the college as soon as we can – we don't want to give them an excuse for making more trouble for us – it's difficult enough.'

Early on Monday morning Guy and Simon cycled over to the teacher training college on the other side of town to collect their belongings, at present in lockers outside their usual lecture room. On the way Guy posted a quickly scribbled note to Isabelle, telling her what had happened and that he expected to be back in Chalhac sometime on Tuesday. They had only been in the college a few moments when the door of the lecture room opened and their tutor Michel Blanc appeared. There was no one else about but his whole manner was distinctly furtive.

'Good morning gentlemen,' he began.

'Good morning,' they choroused, both nervous at being discovered on the school premises that early in the morning. For a moment Guy thought perhaps they had walked into an elaborate government trap.

'Could I ask you to step inside for a moment,' said Blanc, indicating the lecture room. They did as bidden and he carefully closed the door behind them and turned the key in the lock. 'I can understand your reasons for arriving so early this morning because the staff here have all been notified about "certain measures" as they describe them, being put in place. I just want to say how much I regret that you are being obliged to leave us and to assure you that none of this is any of my doing. On the contrary, I have been impressed with your performance so far and it is disgraceful that the authorities see fit to waste obvious talents and enthusiasms such as yours, because of political and racialist prejudice. I hope you will understand that I am totally against what is being done at the present time and sooner or later some of us here on the college staff are likely to come in for very similar treatment. My membership of the Communist Party and the Teaching Union will almost certainly become an issue and I fully expect to be dismissed as a result. So gentlemen, we are looking in a similar direction in this matter. You are possibly aware or perhaps have guessed, that groups are already being established with the intent of fighting back and restoring France to its previously happier times. We all acknowledge that not everything has been perfect for several years, but the new situation now is intolerable. The Maréchal and his friends are fools if they imagine the French people will go along with everything they are proposing, for much longer.'

Guy was the first to speak:

'We can hope you are right but what do you suggest we do now? – I feel very exposed and helpless and I am certain that Simon here feels much the same.'

'Well for a start Monsieur Gaillard, I happen to know someone living not far from your family's home. He is in Domvent and already has a small circle of likeminded people who live down there. If you were to contact him you would recognise him to be someone you could trust with your life, as well as being sympathetic and in tune with our views. I suggest you contact him as soon as possible.'

'How do I find him?'

'He is a doctor of medicine – name Miklos Lovas – Hungarian. We became friends at university here in Clermont and have remained friends ever since. He lives and practises in Domvent and you'll find him at 7, rue du Cantal. It is essential that you use an agreed introductory password. If you don't, he will deny all knowledge of me and everything we jointly support and you will be wasting your time if you so much as knock on his door. You must commit it to memory and not write it down. You will hardly need reminding that we are all on very dangerous ground here and you must take great care to ensure that the safety of our group is not in any way compromised. If and when you call on Doctor Lovas, you must open your conversation with, "It's a brighter day over the mountains". He will know then that you have been introduced by someone who knows you well enough to be trusted.'

'That's very encouraging Monsieur Blanc and I'm most grateful. I assure you I won't forget the words! What advice can you offer my friend? As you probably know he lives here in Clermont with his parents. They are Polish Jews, so it seems to me that they are all at serious risk as well.'

Blanc turned to Simon and said, 'Yes you do have a problem, along with so many others. I'm unable to offer any very useful advice, other than suggesting that you and your family could try to get out of the country altogether and as quickly as possible. I realise of course that this is virtually impossible, without having very substantial funds to bribe border guards and so on – and even then it is very risky. Do you have anyone who could keep you hidden away for a while?'

'I don't think so,' said Simon, 'although I'll speak to my parents about it. But I don't feel like running away and hiding – I want to fight our corner on this and I bet my parents feel the same way. Are you in contact with any similar groups in Clermont who might need a recruit? If there is someone I could get in touch with, that would be a good start.'

'If you're really prepared to risk all and have had enough time to consider the implications of becoming involved in this sort of enterprise, I suggest you buy a beer down at the Café Metropol on rue Bellon. Ask for cousin Nicole – that is enough to get you started – but be very careful because here in Clermont there are many ears listening out for possible dissent and you could find yourself being picked up for suspicious behaviour and interrogated – something I wouldn't recommend. Beyond that I can't say a lot to either of you which might be of much value. It is possible we will meet up again before long – let's hope it will be in happier circumstances.'

They both began to speak at the same time and then Guy said:

'Simon and I will be forever in your debt Monsieur. Your encouragement and friendship is something I doubt we will ever be able to repay, so thank you. I'd also like to say how much we have both enjoyed your lectures – I know I speak for Simon in this respect and perhaps one day we will be able to continue where we have left off – we can hope so.'

'That's very kind of you to say so. We must assume that the current situation will go on for a while yet so it may be some time before we can begin again. Unfortunately there are some, even in this college who naïvely believe that Pétain is doing a good job and would be prepared to shop their colleagues or their own grandmother were they to step out of line. That's why I locked the door after you and why I urge you again to be very careful in the future. I bid you au revoir for the moment and wish you both bonne chance!'

He unlocked the lecture room door and peered warily out into the corridor.

'All clear – go now.'

* * * * *

On Tuesday morning Guy took the train to Domvent. He had his bicycle with him, a few clothes and his books, all crammed into the saddlebag on the bike. Some emotional farewells were said to Simon's parents, who in the short time he had stayed there, had become very attached to Guy and had begun to regard him almost as an adopted son. He had also said a difficult goodbye to Simon, with whom he had become a strong and devoted friend. They both vowed to stay in contact so far as possible and reminded each other yet again to be careful.

He decided against calling on Doctor Lovas immediately as he had yet to tell his parents and Isabelle what had been going on since Saturday, when the fateful letters were delivered. So he cycled down to Chalhac, arriving in the mid-afternoon. Sarah was a little shocked to see him appear since there had been no warning by letter. She guessed that something was up and that it had been enough to precipitate his unexpected appearance. He quickly explained what had happened regarding both his own and Simon's dismissal from the course and that they had discovered their tutor to be a fellow conspirator. She was deeply saddened to learn how his hopes had now been so abruptly dashed and after a few minutes began to feel not just pity for her son, but also a deep anger towards the new régime.

'How can they dare do this to you Guy? It is outrageous to ruin your life at the stroke of a pen like this. It's like Russia all over again before we left and I thought we would be living for good in a civilized country when we got here – it seems we were mistaken.'

'I know Maman – and I am extremely angry as well. I can't imagine what Isabelle will say – although thinking about it, she may have slightly mixed feelings – she was quite upset when she thought I would be away for a couple of years.'

'Your tutor at the college sounds like a good man – when are you going to call on the doctor in Domvent?'

'I need to speak to Isabelle, Papa and Marcel first. It means that if we decide to become more deeply involved, we must agree on how far we want to go with it all because it will almost certainly become extremely perilous. Where's David at the moment? He will have to be brought into this as well!'

'In his room.'

'I'll speak to him now.' Guy called him from the top of the stairs. 'Are you there David?'

After a moment David's face appeared. 'Are you O.K.?'

'Yes, I'm alright, but I'm off the course.'

'They've done it then. Just a moment – I'll come down.' The homemade rope ladder with wooden rungs was dropped down from the roof space and David carefully made his way down to the landing below.

'When was this Guy?'

He described everything that had occurred starting with the arrival of the letters on Saturday. David sat there slowly nodding his head as the tale unfolded.

'This is terrible – it just goes to show where it is all heading. I think you should talk to your doctor friend and find out how he sees things. There are obviously many more people besides us who are prepared to do more than just sit tight and hope for the best. I daresay there are plenty who will prefer to do nothing, and the sad thing about that attitude is that they will wake up to the situation when it is too late to do anything about it.'

'I'm not sure whether we can do much anyway David, but at least we are aware of the dangers and are ready to have a go rather than sit on our hands.'

'What about your friend Simon and his family – what are they going to do?'

'Simon has been given a contact name in Clermont and I imagine he won't hang around too long before he talks to him. I don't know much more than that.'

'Well, we will have to discuss all this with your papa and maybe Jacques Fournier – he'll want to know we're not alone. We'll wait until Marcel and your Papa get home and then talk it through.'

Jules and Marcel arrived later and were both surprised and delighted to find Guy there, but they quickly realised that his appearance meant things were not as they should be. After Guy explained what had happened, he said he needed to contact Isabelle, because she would have received his scribbled note by now and he needed to fill her in with the details.

'Of course you must,' said Jules, who was beginning to grasp what it would mean for Guy and Isabelle.

'I'm going to head back towards Domvent right now,' said Guy. 'There's a good chance she'll be coming down from work, so I'll probably meet her on the road.'

Guy had not gone very far out of the village when Isabelle appeared, heading at full speed down the hill. She saw him on the other side of the road, heading for Domvent. She slowed to a standstill, leant her bike against the grassy roadside and flung her arms around him, sobbing loudly.

'Oh God Guy, what are we going to do?' she managed to say between sobs.

'It will be alright Cherie - we mustn't panic. There's a lot to do and to talk about now but we must make plans and this will mean speaking to people we can trust and who think the same way we do.' He said they should go on down to Chalhac and that for a start he would speak to Jacques Fournier and that he aimed to call on Doctor Lovas in Domvent in the morning. He had explained to Isabelle about the doctor and the secret phrase that he had to use when he introduced himself. It all sounded a little 'cloak and dagger' to have to resort to that, but in view of the awful things already being perpetrated by the new régime, it made sense.

'I agree completely,' said Isabelle.

They continued down the hill back into the village, talking all their time and finally arrived back at the Gaillard house. Isabelle had regained her composure a little and they all sat around the table looking glumly across at each other, trying to read minds. It was hardly a happy occasion despite their all being together again.

Jules said, 'Well I'm going over to the bar and tell Jacques what's happened. He'll naturally want to know and he might have a few ideas by now, about what we should be doing. It seems to me we are going around like headless chickens at the moment and don't know what to do next. This doctor in Domvent might be able to advise some course of action but let's see what Jacques thinks. Who's coming over with me?'

The men decided to join Jules at the bar and Isabelle said she would take the opportunity to call on her grandmother and Tantetta. She would not be able to stay there long because the light was fading fast and it would be difficult on the road back to Petit Domvent. Sarah said she would stay behind and make something to eat for them when they got back from the bar.

Jacques Fournier was very sympathetic to hear about Guy's abrupt dismissal from the teaching course and was quick to see the dangers that Guy and his family could now face.

'It seems to me that if they have got as far as identifying Guy as Jewish or partly Jewish and are sufficiently twisted in their thinking that they have seen fit to chuck him off the course, then it means they are capable of anything. So I think all of you, including David, must prepare to disappear at short notice. Don't ask me where to – I haven't had time to think about that, but I'm sure you are aware of the terrible danger to which you are all exposed.' He paused for a moment and followed up by saying, 'And it raises questions about Isabelle and where she's working. She will have to be very wary in the future because if her dear Papa gets wind of her links with you Guy, there will be all hell to pay.'

'I assure you Jacques, she knows exactly what the score is, and so does her mother. Neither of them agrees with being involved in all this letter opening and so on. Although they can't say so, they don't think Eric Farbres should have worked for Pétain's set up in the first place. However he does and even if he wanted to get out, I doubt if he could do so without becoming a suspect himself. In any case I'm sure he quite enjoys being the little dictator, so I don't see him doing an about turn.'

They were all sitting or standing in the privacy of Jacques' little salon behind the bar. His wife Marie stayed in the front to serve any customers who might appear, although at this time of day there seemed little chance of a sudden rush. The atmosphere was gloomy and only broken when Jacques said, 'Would any of you like to join me in a glass of something? I feel we need to cheer ourselves up.'

The mood lifted after this and Jacques called to Marie to bring a bottle or two of his marc and some glasses. It was a master stroke by Jacques who sensed that they were all in a grim state of mind as they contemplated the future. When their glasses were filled, he said 'Gentlemen, . . . to the future and to our ability to defeat our enemies whoever and wherever they are!'

'I'll drink to that,' said David Markovich.

Guy told them briefly about his lecturer Jean Blanc, and that he was clearly an ally. He described Blanc's nervousness when telling Guy and Simon about his fears for his own future and about the doctor in Domvent. Jacques listened intently to everything he had to say and when he finished he said:

'Well I think we can all take heart from this. We are sorry of course about Guy's despicable treatment, but it means that there are plenty of people who think the same way we do. We must also remember that there are probably many people who might disagree with us and are prepared to sit tight, believing there is nothing we can do. It is those people who could very easily become our enemies and might even turn against us and report what they might hear. I know I've said it before but we must be doubly certain when we are speaking to neighbours and casual friends, that we know for sure where their sympathies lay. This situation is extremely dangerous for us all and we must not take any chances – to do so could prove fatal – and I mean fatal. We are hearing about some of the terrible things going on elsewhere in the country and it's not a pretty picture.'

The little bunch of conspirators silently nodded their agreement.

'When will you introduce yourself to the good doctor, Guy?' asked Jacques.

'I'm going up there tomorrow – I'll be interested to hear what he has to say. It should be an instructive meeting.'

'Indeed,' said Jacques.

Meanwhile on the other side of La Place, Isabelle had been speaking to her aunt 'Tantetta.' Henrietta and Hortense were startled to have seen her arrive unannounced on a weekday. She explained what had transpired regarding Guy and gave them a brief account of his meeting his lecturer the previous morning. The two ladies were horrified to hear about the perfunctory dismissal from his teaching course and the fears expressed by Jean Blanc. Isabelle explained that Guy planned to meet up with the doctor in Domvent and to see what he advised.

'What are Guy's parents going to do?' asked Henrietta. 'It is going to be a dangerous situation for them now, surely. Have they somewhere to hide or go to should they need to? And what about poor Monsieur Markovich – his situation is even more dangerous I would have thought.'

'There are many questions coming out of all this Tantetta and we don't know yet how things will develop. We must wait and see before we go jumping in the wrong direction.'

'Has Monsieur Markovich found anywhere yet for his tailoring business?' asked her grandmother. She had been kept up to date with his efforts to find somewhere and was intrigued to know how he was getting by. 'What on earth is he living on if he's not working?'

'He helps out at the Gaillard house as much as he can and pays them a little rent from his savings as well, but it cannot be easy for him – or for them.'

'Did you know that the Comte and Comtesse have finally left for Switzerland?' said Henrietta. 'They have some friends with a big house near lac Léman and have agreed to rent it to them until things settle down again here. They seem pretty confident that everything will get better before long - I wish I could share their optimism. They have left me in charge of the chateau while they are away – there's not much I can do other than to light the fires occasionally and keep the place tidy. Pierre is staying on to look after the grounds, which might mean we can have some vegetables and fruit in future. He is already keeping his relatives supplied as it is and he sells some of the produce at the market! With the Comte out of the way we can hope we will come in for more of the same. You must visit me Isabelle and I'll show you round – it's quite an interesting old place. What about next weekend?'

'I'd love to Tantetta – I'll look forward to it.'

With that, Isabelle made her farewells until the following weekend and left for home in Petit Domvent. She arrived back in the early evening. It was only just light enough for her to make the journey safely, and Ann-Marie had begun to get a little anxious. Eric Farbres was still down near Toulouse and not expected back in Domvent until later in the week. Isabelle recounted the details of the day's happenings to her mother, who was also horrified to hear about Guy's dismissal from the course. She outlined what had been discussed with Guy, his parents and David Markovich. She had not been in on the meeting in Jacques Fournier's bar but guessed it had covered much the same ground. She thought it best not to mention Doctor Lovas to her mother for the time being, not because she distrusted her but felt that it would only need a slip of the tongue to alert her dear papa that something was going on between them. She had seen the orders from Clermont and Vichy telling them to be doubly alert to any signs of dissent among the populace and Isabelle was playing safe for now.

* * * * *

The following morning Guy cycled up to Domvent, making a slight detour past the gendarmerie, in the faint hope of catching a glimpse of Isabelle at her desk. The ornate cast iron gates at the front of the building were no more than three or four metres wide, bordered on each side by a substantial stone wall. It proved to be a wasted effort to have gone that way as there had been no opportunity in the moment it took to cycle past, to see anything on the other side of the gates. He still felt it was worthwhile if only to get some idea of where she now spent her working days. He continued down through the town, and found rue du Cantal easily enough and identified number seven, which lay near the far end of the road.

He leant his bike against the wall. Beside the front door an engraved brass plate identified the doctor and listed his various impressive sounding qualifications. Guy gave the door two firm bangs with its brass knocker. A moment or two passed and then the door opened slowly, emitting a protesting creak as it did. A stockily built man in his fifties stood there. He had deep set grey eyes, a sallow complexion and the remains of what had once been fair but was now greying curly hair at the sides of his head. He regarded Guy sternly as if to say, 'There's not much wrong with you young man – why are you wasting my precious time?'

Guy almost read his mind by saying 'Good morning Doctor Lovas! It's a brighter day over the mountains. My name is Guy Gaillard.'

The doctor's eyes visibly widened for a moment. 'Come in my friend.' His demeanor towards Guy was instantly changed. He held out his hand to his young visitor. They shook hands as though they had known each other for a lifetime and not just for the last few moments. 'You and I have some common ground and a few of the same friends. May I ask who is your contact in this connection?'

'Jean Blanc in Clermont.'

'Ah yes! Jean and I have been good friends for many years – we met at university in Clermont. He was studying history and languages and I was studying medicine. How is Jean these days?'

Guy told the doctor about the conversation he and Simon had had with Jean Blanc and the circumstances which had prompted it. 'He seems well enough but he is fearful for his job since his membership of the Communist Party and the union might be seen by the new administration as being a means to pollute the innocent minds of his students. Now that we have had a taste of the 'French State's mindset', his concerns for his future are probably justified.' This elicited a nod of agreement from Lovas. Guy went on to tell him about Isabelle and her employment by the gendarmerie in Domvent. He explained that her father commanded the unit and was a committed fascist. He described the letter opening task that she was obliged to perform and her loathing for it.

'What is Isabelle to you exactly?'

Guy gave Lovas the whole story from when he first spotted Isabelle behind the hibiscus tree at his parents' house in Chalhac, right up to the present time. He also told him that more recently they had become lovers. Lovas smiled and nodded sympathetically and followed up by saying, 'You are absolutely sure Isabelle can be trusted? She is, after all her father's daughter and her instincts for self-preservation might override her fondness for you. Remember that blood is thicker than water.'

'It's quite natural that you might take that view Doctor Lovas but I must tell you that our feelings in the matter run very deep. She and I have a massive understanding and knowledge of each other. We met as children and became friends almost immediately. Her relatives in Chalhac warned her from the start that she should be wary about saying anything to her father about any of it, knowing that he was an anti-Semite and were he to get to know about it, the consequences would be dire. As a child she had little idea about the complications that might emerge as a result of becoming involved with anyone other than a Roman Catholic Christian. As children we grew to regard each other more as brother and sister and, to my shame, I missed the glaringly obvious fact that as time passed, she had fallen for me. I had taken her for granted over the years and it was only when I was about to take up my place on the teaching course and would be mostly away for the best part of two years, that she made it perfectly clear how she felt about me. So I can assure you doctor that she can be totally trusted!'

'Good. I am convinced! I must fill you in with some of the details about how things stand here – in and around Domvent. You will have gathered that we have formed a group of people, resistant to events now unfolding under the new régime. We are dedicated to the eventual overthrow of the so-called 'French State' and its leaders. I am sure you and I both regard Pétain as a near senile old fool, who has been manipulated into the position he now holds. He has some very nasty and extremely Fascist friends and they see Hitler as an ally and a means to regaining France's former glory. If it weren't such a serious matter, it would be almost comical. Pétain seems extraordinarily naïve for someone with his experience of politics and the military that he must have gained over his lifetime. He seems to have been unable to recognise that he has walked into a trap set by the Nazis – it's almost beyond belief. Hitler clearly only sees France as a means to his own ends, namely the domination of Europe, and has already begun to take everything from our country. We are told that coal and iron ore are already being shipped out by train to Germany from the north and you can be sure that's only the start of it. At the present time we can think of ourselves as being rather fortunate in that we are not being ruled directly from Berlin. Our fellow countrymen in the north and west are already faring a good deal worse and the German military machine and policing have moved very quickly to establish a stranglehold. Following the Armistice, and according to Pétain, we are now their allies. I very much doubt if many of our fellow countrymen in those parts now take the same view of the situation, so we must be vigilant here and ready for anything.'

He continued, 'If it comes to it, it might be possible to cause some minor irritations to the Nazi régime here in the south, but realistically we have very little clout. Eventually we might even be able to inflict some serious damage on the new set up, but we are thinly spread and there is virtually no co-ordination between groups. That man de Gaulle, over there in England, keeps making speeches about keeping the flame of resistance alight, but to be honest I don't think that sort of thing will do much good. I imagine he sees himself as some sort of knight in shining armour with a plan to ride in on his white charger when it's all over and to take all the glory. I think perhaps the British might have it right with their broadcasts on the BBC which give us a great deal of encouragement. They are very good and people with wireless sets listen in as much as they can. I believe that Churchill probably tells the BBC what to send out over the air. Do you or anyone else in the village have access to a wireless? It is quite important to try to stay in touch with events as much as possible.'

Guy told him that the local bar proprietor had one and that they all listened as much as they could to the BBC, despite the jamming now taking place.

He had listened intently to what the doctor had been saying and it gave him considerable heart. 'I am with you Doctor Lovas and I am sure when I tell my family about you and one or two others in the village that I can really trust, they will be keen to help. By the way, did I tell you there was a pamphlet left in the local bar a week or two ago. It was stirring stuff and it will have gone around the whole village by now.'

'Yes – I know all about the pamphlet because we wrote it. We only made about thirty copies and they were all distributed around the area. You approved I hope?'

'Very much so, but do you think that something like that might alert the authorities to the fact that there is some sort of organisation established within the immediate vicinity. Isn't that just a little dangerous right now? Knowing how the people in Vichy and elsewhere are carrying on, I imagine they will move heaven and earth in order to find the instigators.'

'I daresay you're right but we have taken the view that anything that will use up some of their resources and time, can only be to our advantage in the long run. It is true that they will probably become more inquisitive and unpleasant but we have to put up with those consequences if we are going to win. You will agree I hope?'

Guy was not altogether convinced at first but, after a long conversation with the doctor, his persuasive powers and obvious sincerity won him over completely.

'I will pass on everything we have discussed this morning with my family and friends in Chalhac, Doctor Lovas. I know they will react favourably. When you next plan a get together with your, and our colleagues, let me know. Don't use the post because it is not to be trusted now, or the telephone. Hand delivery seems to be the only sensible and safe way to make contact. I'll ask Isabelle if she would be willing to collect any messages directly from you, bring them to us in Chalhac, and when necessary she can deliver any messages back to you.'

'That seems absolutely sound to me,' said Lovas. 'But she must be made to understand the risks she be would be taking, because it could be very dangerous. It has been a pleasure meeting you Guy and I look forward to seeing you again before long.' They shook hands and Guy finally left. He cycled past the Gendarmerie on the way back hoping to get a glimpse of Isabelle but was still unlucky; he arrived back at the village half an hour later.

Sarah and David were given a brief rundown of his meeting with the doctor which they both approved and applauded. Jules and Marcel were not yet home from the quarry, so Guy walked over to the bar to let Jacques know how things had gone. He too was happy with what Guy had to say and greatly encouraged to know that there was already another group in Domvent. Guy told him that the mysterious pamphlet originated from them, so there were no doubts about their sincerity. He also told Jacques about the possibility of enrolling Isabelle into becoming their unpaid postman. She would have to agree to the idea of course and there were obviously huge risks to her if she took it on, but he felt sure she would want to do it. He said he would put it to her as soon as possible, which could be the next day – if not, then at the weekend.

Fifteen

On Saturday Isabelle cycled down to Chalhac for her usual visit to her grandmother and Tantetta, as well as seeing Guy and the rest of the Gaillard family. It would have been too dangerous for her to go down any sooner, as Eric was expected back from Toulouse earlier than planned and it would have proved difficult for her mother to explain away her absence had he suddenly appeared. As it turned out he still did not get home until late on Friday evening so all seemed entirely normal and in order.

She called first on Guy and his family. Having hugged and passionately kissed her, he quickly outlined his meeting with Doctor Lovas. He told her he had tried to spot her at her desk in the gendarmerie when he cycled past the gates and Isabelle smiled at this and gently shook her head as if to say, 'You really are a little daft Guy.'

He explained, 'We discussed the difficulties about staying in touch with his group in Domvent because of the letter opening and the possible dangers in telephoning. I told him that Bonnet had the only phone in the village and although he would no doubt like to help, it would be asking too much of the man to expect him to take seditious calls. The operators could begin to smell a rat and report odd goings-on. I don't think we should put him in that sort of position. So what would you say to the idea of becoming our unofficial postman Cherie? It would mean a certain amount of cycling to and fro and it could become even more risky if your papa or his bosses in Clermont and Vichy begin to turn up the pressure. Even your presence in the gendarmerie's letter opening operation can't safeguard every letter that gets into the system because you're not the only one opening the mail, but if you were to agree, some of the problems could be solved. What do you think?'

Isabelle chewed gently on her lip as she considered the proposition and finally said,

'The main problem is that I can't be certain to be available at the drop of a hat. Papa's presence at home and at the gendarmerie might get in the way of things. He does go away of course and then there wouldn't be any difficulty, but if he is about, then I would have to dream up an excuse for getting out of the office or for arriving home late. He's bound to catch on eventually. Apart from that, yes, I'll do it.'

'That's wonderful Cherie! I could meet you on the road sometimes and you could turn around and head back. I'm sure we can work something out.'

'O.K. – take it that I'll do it. My bike will have to do a few more kilometres in the future!' She explained she had not called on her grandmother or Tantetta yet and they would be looking out for her, so she would have to leave. 'If I have enough time, I'll call by again on the way home.' She cycled down the road and around the corner, past the bar and took her little diagonal shortcut across La Place towards Hortense and Henrietta's house where they were waiting for her.

After the usual preamble covering the health and welfare of Isabelle's mama and papa and polite enquiries about grand-père and grand-mère Farbres, they gravitated towards the ongoing political concerns that were engulfing the country.

'What do Le Comte and La Comtesse have to say about it all, Tantetta?' asked Isabelle.

'They left for Switzerland on Monday. They were a bit guarded about it when we spoke but I think they are slightly in favour of Pétain, if not Hitler and his pals. They didn't actually say so, but they have never once voiced anything critical about any of it. Now of course, they have cleared off altogether and I suppose they'll sit tight in Switzerland and come back when it all settles down again – and that might take longer than they imagine.'

'So you are going to be a temporary châtelaine then Tantetta?'

'Something like that although I don't suppose la Comtesse de Villebarde would see it quite that way!'

'No, I'm sure she wouldn't. When am I going to get a tour of the chateau - is that still on?'

'Of course, Cherie! We could go up there now if you would like to – I've got the keys. Do you have enough time to spare this afternoon to take a quick look?'

'Yes of course – would you mind grand-mère if we disappear for a while? It seems too good an opportunity to miss.'

'I don't mind in the least child, I've plenty to do here,' said Hortense.

So Henrietta and Isabelle cycled up the hill out of the village and in through the big wrought iron gates that guarded the chateau. The main door to the building was still very impressive despite signs of neglect over the years. It was solid oak, studded with oversize iron bolts holding massive hinges in place. Henrietta inserted a giant iron key into an equally large keyhole and slowly turned the key. The old lock mechanism crunched a little but seemed to work remarkably well, all things considered, and she pushed open the door with her shoulder. The door protested a little as it was opened, emitting a deep moaning creak as they walked in. At first sight the entrance hall with its stone floor seemed rather gloomy but after a moment or two, Isabelle's eyes became accustomed to the dim interior after the strong afternoon sunlight outside.   Facing the front door a broad stone staircase divided at the top and led onto a landing. Several oil paintings of le Comte's ancestors adorned the walls on either side of the staircase, the men mostly in military uniforms and one or two stern looking women.

'Mind how you go Isabelle, the floor is a bit uneven here and there. This is the salon,' said Henrietta, as she opened a pair of tall elegant doors decorated with gilt beading. Entering thc big room Isabelle was immediately aware of a distinctly musty smell – an amalgam of damp books, dusty fabric and general disuse. At one time this would have been the last word in luxurious surroundings but the ravages of time and a degree of neglect had reduced the room to a shadow of its former glory.

'This must have been wonderful a few years ago,' said Isabelle.

'You're right Isabelle - it must have been quite something in its heyday. I think le Comte and la Comtesse have lost sight of it all now and don't see it anymore. It's such a shame.'

Isabelle tried to take it all in – the great marble over mantle with its massive iron fire back. On the wall above hung a huge gilt-framed painting depicting a hunting scene and there were more family portraits on the walls on either side. The furniture did not strike Isabelle as looking particularly comfortable – and several armchairs and two chaises longues revealed bits of their horsehair interiors which poked through the brocade surfaces. Around the walls were a variety of pot - bellied commodes and ornate glass fronted cabinets, some containing antique silverware and china. Above their heads were enormous black carved wooden beams supporting the floors above.

'I can see what you mean about the place being draughty when it's windy – you would definitely need to keep the fires well-lit or you would probably freeze to death in here. What are the bedrooms like? They must be pretty cold in the winter.'

'I'll show you, come on.' Henrietta led the girl out of the salon and up the staircase to a number of bedrooms, some of which were obviously unused, while others served as the children's bedrooms and a nursery. Isabelle quickly put her head around the doorways of some of them and Henrietta said, 'and this is the main bedroom.' She ushered Isabelle into an ornate room where in the centre stood two identical massive four poster beds sporting canopies above with yellowing fine mesh curtains to keep out flying insects. The beds had been stripped of all of their bedding apart from their deep mattresses. Against one wall a pretty tiled fireplace was about the only item that struck Isabelle as being of normal human proportions. There was some sort of dressing room and toilet out to one side. The room overlooked the overgrown grounds and vegetable garden at the back, which in turn backed on to the forest. In the distance were the mountains.

Isabelle was greatly impressed with the whole thing as she had never been inside anywhere as large or luxurious as this. She turned to her aunt,

'It must be rather strange for you Tantetta to be working in a place like this during the day and then having to go home to the house in Chalhac at night.'

'Yes it was at first but you get used to these things in the end. I'm already missing the family being here and they've only been gone a few days, but I daresay that will pass.'

'Nobody knows when all this will be over – it can't go on forever like this. I suppose le Comte and his family will come back again then?'

'Almost certainly,' said Henrietta. 'Meanwhile Pierre and I have the run of the place. Pierre never comes inside as he has said he feels he doesn't belong in here, so he spends most of his time out in the park and vegetable garden.'

'I've just been thinking – is there anyone else likely to come to the chateau while they are away – friends or relations? If not, then there's this big empty house practically begging to have people living in it. I wonder if David Markovich would be interested because he has been trying to find somewhere to start up his tailoring business again. Would there be anything to stop him moving into one of the smaller rooms with his sewing machine – I know he would be a perfect tenant and it would solve his immediate problem as well as getting him out of Jules and Sarah's hair!'

Henrietta considered the idea for a moment or two and said,

'That is quite a thought Isabelle – it had never even occurred to me. What do you think David would say?'

'We'll soon find out – I'll ask him when we get back.'

* * * * *

David was washing the floor in the kitchen in the Gaillard house.

'David,' she said 'I think I've found you a workshop - a very big workshop!' Isabelle told him about her afternoon at the chateau and that there seemed to be no reason why he could not quietly move in with his sewing machine and belongings. She explained that Henrietta was now effectively in charge, that le Comte and la Comtesse were now safely tucked away in Switzerland so there would no point in saying anything to them about it. Nor would there be any rent to pay. 'While the cat's away the mice will play!'

David looked stunned for a moment. 'You mean I could have somewhere in the chateau to set up again? Wouldn't that be trespassing without Le Comte's permission?'

'Who's going to tell him? Tantetta has the run of the place – the front door key included. Pierre won't care either way and you could call it your own for a while – at least until they come back from Switzerland and God knows when that will be. So what do you think?'

'When could I go over there to take a look? I'd like to see what sort of space I might have. Have they got electricity in the house because my machine needs some power?' David had quickly begun

155

to picture himself in a work room again and was warming to the idea by the minute.

Isabelle assured him that there was some electricity laid on – not in every room she thought, but she remembered that Henrietta had turned lights on here and there during her tour earlier.

'You will have to arrange the details with Tantetta about going over there but I can't see any problems with that.'

The next day David made an inspection and decided upon a small room which had been the children's playroom when they were very young. It was on the floor above the main bedroom high up in the house, looking out over the park. Two days later he packed his trailer with the sewing machine and some cloth, re-attached it to his bicycle and made his way out of the village. He left in the evening to avoid drawing too much attention to his move as he did not want to have to explain the circumstances in which he was to become a new tenant at the chateau. Questions might be asked and it could even arouse ill-feeling in the village. So far as he was aware, no one saw him leave and Henrietta was waiting for him outside the gates when he arrived. The Gaillard family had waved him 'au revoir' as he left and wished him good luck with his move. Sarah was quite tearful to see him disappear down the road and David felt a little sad to leave them.

It took several days for him to become organised and he was obliged to go back to the Gaillard house once or twice to collect the few things he had gathered while he was there. The family was full of questions for him about it all: 'Are you going to be comfortable in that draughty old place? What will you do about food?' and so on. David had to play it all by ear, but the issue at the forefront of his mind was where he would find some customers. He had already decided that it would be out of the question to have customers visiting him at the chateau. It meant he would have to call on them instead in order to collect work, make adjustments to work in progress and then make deliveries. He also had to establish some sort of supply chain for raw materials, which could present real problems. Fabrics and cotton thread were now strictly rationed – if they were to be found at all, so he would need to find likely sources, legal or illegal - David was not fussy.

He had long since realised that the opportunities for making high quality suits were probably nil - this was not Paris or Rouen. In this part of the world clothes were essentially working garments to keep out the cold and not a fashion accessory. After much thought, he decided that he would become a self-styled repairer of clothes instead. He let it be known via Jules and Jacques Fournier that he was able to take in work again and put it to Jacques that perhaps the bar could become some sort of collection point. Jacques said he would be happy to go along with the idea since it might provide him with a few more customers as a side effect. There were no immediate takers when the news was out, but David had not expected much to happen very quickly in any case, although eventually one or two people did appear in Jacques' bar clutching a variety of tatty clothes, some of which were probably beyond repair. David did his best to restore most of the items that came his way and their owners seemed satisfied enough with the results and he was able to make sufficient money to keep himself in food and drink.

* * * * *

The telephone rang: it was Colonel Boudeau demanding to speak to Eric Farbres. Lieutenant Boyer had been left in charge of the unit as Eric was out of the town on official business for the day, and so Boyer had taken the call.

'May I ask who is calling please?' said young Boyer.

'Tell him his superior in Clermont Ferrand needs to speak to him – he knows very well who that is,' said Boudeau. 'Tell him to be quick about it.' The phone went dead.

When he arrived back in his office later that afternoon Boyer told Eric about the call. He knew immediately who the caller was when he was told him how it had gone.

'That was the renowned Colonel Boudeau in Clermont,' said Eric. He had told young Lieutenant Boyer about Boudeau and warned him that he was not the easiest man to deal with. He had been careful to omit telling Boyer about his own history within the gendarmerie lest it might generate any bad feelings towards him; it remained a sensitive issue for Eric despite the passing of so many years.

157

'He didn't give me a chance to respond in a polite way – he simply banged the phone down before I was able to say anything.'

'That was definitely Boudeau - true to form. I'll call him right away. Thank you Lieutenant.' Eric rang Boudeau's office and was answered by the man with an abrupt 'Yes?'

'I understand you wish to speak to me sir. How can I help?' Eric adopted a faintly deferential style for once.

'Farbres. I have been given instructions by my superiors in Vichy that we must tighten up security down there. They seem to think that there is evidence of growing unrest in our area, probably as a result of the Spanish situation. They also believe that here in Clermont there exist a number of dissident groups emerging. We have uncovered one group already and heard rumours of others, but as yet we have discovered little firm evidence. Our informers continue to function very well but it means we have to wait until something provides us with a reason to act. I take it that in your territory around Domvent things are quiet? I notice there have been no reports from you following the mail examining – I am quite surprised that nothing has so far emerged from that operation. Are you sure this is being pursued with due diligence?'

'I assure you sir that my staff are following the rules to the letter – if you will forgive the pun.' The humourless Boudeau made no response to this unintentional joke. Eric continued:

'A number of questionable letters have been opened which were thought to be suspect but upon examination were found to be completely innocent. I think we can conclude from this that if dissident activity does exist in this area, it is at a very low level. Of course we are all alert to any signs which might indicate increasing illegal activity of any description and I can assure you that you'd be the first to know if the position were to change.'

'Good,' said Boudeau. 'There is another issue I wish to address and upon which our superiors require us to act as quickly as possible. This is the matter of explosives used in quarrying businesses. It has occurred to Vichy that there must exist amounts of this material lying about in quarries and elsewhere, which could present a threat to the peace were any of it to fall into the wrong hands. I want you to examine all records held by local quarry operators in and around your area, with a view to confiscating any material of this nature. I have no idea how many locations are involved, so I cannot offer any advice or information which might help, but there is some urgency in this matter so you must give this your immediate attention, understood?'

'Completely.'

'Keep me informed on progress in this matter Farbres. I am under a certain amount of pressure here.' The phone was put down without any further comment or polite niceties.

Isabelle had been standing just inside her office listening intently to his responses on the phone and from what she had managed to glean Boudeau was questioning her father about the letter opening operation. She had been unable to hear anything about quarries or explosives. Eric called to Isabelle through his open office door:

'Could you come in Isabelle, I have some new orders which will require your attention.' He told her what she had already overheard about Boudeau's concerns about letter opening and went on to outline the latest orders from Vichy regarding explosives kept in quarries and elsewhere. Isabelle inwardly smiled at this. She thought how clever Marcel had been to anticipate the very thing now being contemplated by Vichy as well as making their timely trip to the cave to hide the dynamite and detonators.

'I will be writing to the concerns running these operations, to tell them that we will be checking quantities of this sort of material, the security arrangements surrounding them and so on. I think we can assume that we will be confiscating most or all of it in any event, just to be on the safe side. There will be a number of letters to be typed as a result and I would like you to give this your attention just as soon as I have drafted suitable letters.'

'Of course Papa,' replied his dutiful daughter. 'Will you be home on time this evening or do you have other work to complete?' asked Isabelle.

'No. I'm afraid I'll be a little late. I have these letters to write and I've other matters to address. You can tell your Maman to expect me sometime before twenty hundred.' Even to his daughter he had adopted his habitual and semi-official mode of speech.

As soon as she could without arousing suspicions, Isabelle headed out of Domvent and down the valley towards Chalhac. Guy was waiting for her at their pre-arranged spot on the road and she quickly told him about the proposed moves against quarries and that her father was writing to all the quarry owners to give them notice of the government's latest requirement.

'Marcel was right then wasn't he? We'll have to warn as many of them as we can because if there is pressure from Vichy it must mean they will be crawling all over the quarrying businesses including where papa and Marcel work, and they're bound to start quite soon. If there is still a lot of this stuff left at the quarry at the moment, we'll have to shift it out of harm's way before they turn up – it will be too late then. I'm going back now and you had better be sure to be home before your dear papa gets back.' Isabelle nodded her agreement and they kissed and reluctantly parted, Isabelle making her way back up the hill towards Domvent and Guy towards Chalhac.

'It's what we expected isn't it,' said Marcel when he was told. 'I think tomorrow we should grab as much as we can and hide it as quickly as possible.'

'Hold on Marcel!' said Jules, ' I think we should leave a bit for them to take away or they are bound to think it strange for a quarry to be without explosives or detonators around - it could look very fishy. They could easily put two and two together and begin to wonder if there is a security leak somewhere in their system. It could even point a finger at Isabelle, since she and her father were the only ones to know what they were planning.' They both agreed that it would have been a mistake and just showed how easily they could have unwittingly fallen into a trap.

It was agreed that the following morning Marcel and Jules would take most of the dynamite stock and detonators out of the stone shed at the quarry. The stock book would have to be suitably modified, and some careful alterations made, involving the removal of pages and writing up new details on fresh pages. They hoped no one would look too carefully at the entries. Marcel said,

'Do we have some way of warning other quarry operators what's likely to happen? Even if they don't want to become involved some might want to preserve their stocks for ordinary use. Without explosives a lot of rock will not budge, which could make their lives very difficult.'

Jules said he knew one or two people in nearby quarrying businesses and would let them know as soon as he could that they were likely to be inspected by the gendarmerie shortly. Next morning Jules and Marcel began to move most of the contents of the store to the temporary safety of a large fissure high up in the rock face at the back of the quarry in case a sudden inspection was sprung on them. Guy was to transport it back to his parents' home in the village and he thought Isabelle would be happy to make a further visit with him to 'their' cave at the weekend to hide it. Guy said he would cycle up to Domvent in the morning and call on Doctor Lovas to update him and that he would call by the quarry later to take the explosive material back to Chalhac.

As planned Guy made a visit to Doctor Lovas. The door opened to him and Guy said,

'It's a brighter day over the mountains Doctor.' On his first encounter with Lovas they had agreed that if there was anything that might present a risk to his calling, then the passwords would either not be said at all or if it was, and went unacknowledged, it would mean that danger existed in or near the surgery. This morning nothing was amiss and Lovas said,

'Good morning to you, please come in.' Guy was led into the doctor's salon at the back of the house. It was comfortably furnished in an unmistakably mid-European style.

'Anything to report?' asked the doctor.

Guy gave him a detailed account of what had transpired the previous day in the gendarmerie and that his father and brother were at that very moment removing most, but not all, the dynamite and detonators from the quarry's store. He told him that he and Isabelle planned to take all of it up to their hiding place beneath the escarpment at the weekend. He also told him about David Markovich's newly founded tailoring premises in the chateau. He explained that le Comte and la Comtesse were now in Switzerland and had left Isabelle's Aunt Henrietta in charge of the building. The doctor smiled at the thought of a poor Jewish tailor taking up residence in a chateau – free of charge at that.

'I imagine there's little chance of his being disturbed there if questions are asked in the future?'

'That's how we saw it,' said Guy.

Lovas sat back for a moment, scratching his chin as he pondered the news from Guy.

'It's obvious that the gang in Vichy is intent on squashing any dissent before it gets going, but luckily for us we are already a couple of steps ahead of them and reasonably organised. They are still trying to plug some of the gaps they have not even thought about, including the quarries and explosives. I need hardly say that your father and brother must tread very carefully when they turn up to inspect the books. By the way, how old is your brother? It occurs to me that if he looks like a healthy young man, they are likely to ask difficult questions as to why he is not in the army. If, as you say they appear to have lost track of him altogether then it could present a further risk for all of you if they begin to look into the records. I imagine that your father's family name has meant that suspicions about your Jewish connections through your mother have so far been missed, but it might be safer if your brother Marcel can somehow be kept out of sight.'

'Yes, Marcel is two years older than me and very aware that his existence has not been recorded anywhere, or if it was then it has been lost. It has meant that he has been unable to claim food rations – not that it has been a huge problem so far, as we have access to a variety of sources of food in the surrounding area. Marcel is not the only one to have become a non-person: David Markovich the tailor also needs to remain invisible for obvious reasons, but this has hardly been a problem for him. His move into the chateau should provide him with enough food from the chateau's vegetable garden in future, and I daresay the groundsman Pierre will be happy to provide him with anything he needs. Pierre already has a nice little sideline in the market as it is, so there should be no big problems in that direction.'

'Good,' said Lovas. 'Now I must ask you to leave because I expect a patient to appear at any moment and it is best if you are not seen here too often as we can never be sure who is on our side – better safe than sorry.'

Guy took the point and left almost immediately, quickly cycling back to the quarry three kilometres from Chalhac. By the time he arrived, his brother and father had moved nearly all of the dynamite and detonators out of the store shed and hidden it in the fissure high in the rock face. Without a ladder it would be impossible to see and they had hidden the ladder behind some rubbish, so they were fairly relaxed with the situation. Jules was busily making the necessary alterations to the record book when Guy appeared. He quickly told them that the doctor approved of their moves so far and that he had suggested Marcel was best kept out of sight in view of his age and physique which Guy described as excellent. They both agreed that it would be the best bet and that for a day or two Marcel would absent himself from the quarry until the inspection had taken place. Guy added that it might be possible for Isabelle to find out which quarries were to be visited and when, but he could not promise anything.

Guy had a small satchel over his shoulders used for carrying oddments to and from his lectures in Clermont. It was now loaded with some of the dynamite to be taken straight back to Chalhac to be hidden temporarily under a pile of wood behind the house.

On Saturday Isabelle was back in Chalhac, partly to visit her Grand-mère and 'Tantetta', and to see Guy and his family. This was followed by a further visit to the cave and this time with Guy to hide the remainder of the dynamite. The basket on her bicycle was filled again with several of the waxed parcels – more than on her previous visit with Marcel. Guy had to carry the remainder in his satchel together with some detonators. It was now early October and a cool breeze was blowing across the plateau, signaling the approach of winter and although the cave itself was now partly in shadow, the summer's heat had warmed the rocky entrance and its immediate surroundings so it was comparatively warm inside. Isabelle told Guy that when she and Marcel had made their earlier visit, they had picnicked outside in the sunshine. This time it was quite different and after they had placed their deadly loads on the shelf with the first consignment, Isabelle said,

'I think it will be best if we have our lunch just inside, to get out of the wind.'

'Good idea Cherie. What have we got?'

'Nothing very exciting but we will not starve.' She unwrapped a loaf, some sausage, two apples and a bottle of wine.

'Why the wine?'

'I just thought we need to celebrate being together again – we might not get too many chances in the future. You never know how things are going to work out.'

'You sound a bit gloomy Cherie. What's brought that on?'

'Nothing in particular but there seems to be so many things happening over which we have no control. It's probably working in the gendarmerie that's having its effect on me. Don't take any notice of silly old me.'

'I know what you mean. To be thrown off the teaching course has been a real blow for me and it worries me to think that they seem to be doing as they like in Vichy and ordering people about without even thinking about it. I suppose they are simply following instructions from Berlin or somewhere, and blindly agreeing to it in the name of racial purity, as well as trying to hold onto their jobs. The trouble is that old Pétain is being driven along by people like Laval who is very chummy with Hitler and the whole bunch of them in Paris. He doesn't give a damn about us. It seems to me that all he is interested in, is holding on to his money, as well as staying at the top of the pile. So far as he is concerned, the country can go to hell. He's obviously made the conscious decision to back Hitler, who he thinks will be able to grab France in any event and will then turn it into a satellite of Germany and then suck it dry. Of course poor old Pétain fondly imagines that he is in control and can manipulate the situation in such a way that the country will come out stronger and more vital than ever. If he really believes that, he needs his head examining. I've discussed this endlessly with Doctor Lovas and he has some good, reliable contacts and gets a lot of information about what's actually happening. He has some friends in high places and they can see every day the way things are going, so we have a good ally in him.'

'Yes, we are lucky to have him on our side. More wine?' She was becoming sick of the subject of Laval and Pétain's machinations and wanted to forget about it all for a while. Guy poured more wine into a large mug which they shared. They had finished the food while he was airing his views to Isabelle. They now gazed at each thoughtfully.

'You know what I want to do Guy? I want to make love to you, right now!'

Guy had been thinking along the same lines and needed no further encouragement. He had been considering the matter since leaving the village an hour or so earlier, but had wondered whether Isabelle might see love making in the cave as being an inappropriate end to their task of delivering explosives: somehow the two did not mix - he need not have worried. She was smiling at him, eyebrows raised questioningly. 'Well?' she asked.

Just inside the cave entrance, still warmed by the remains of the lowering sun, they made tender love on the dusty and uneven floor. The cave echoed slightly with the sounds of Isabelle's cries of pleasure.

Sixteen

Eric Farbres appeared in the doorway of Isabelle's office, with some hand-written sheets of paper. He explained that he had drafted a list of addresses and a sheet of orders together with a schedule detailing the anticipated timetable for the inspection of quarries in the area. 'I would like you to get these out as soon as you can Isabelle and let me know when they are finished. Colonel Boudeau in Clermont is anxious to get this underway and we need to comply quickly.'

Isabelle's heart quickened slightly when she realized that this was exactly what she had been waiting for and that she could now warn Jules and Marcel about the imminent arrival of a gendarmerie inspection team. When she examined the paperwork she saw that the 'teams' would probably comprise three gendarmes with either her father or more probably Lieutenant Boyer in charge. The orders were to 'search stores for explosives, making sure the general area within a quarry's perimeter contains no undisclosed materials and examine paperwork and records of deliveries and usage of explosive materials. Where appropriate, materials must be confiscated.'

The forward thinking by Jules and Marcel had been fully justified. The letters were addressed to the quarry operators. These were not necessarily the people who actually ran the quarries. Jules was the only official employee at his quarry but there was a small group of quarry owners in the immediate area who would not, in the normal way of things, have received any early warning of the proposed inspections. It was fortunate that Isabelle and her fellow conspirators were to a degree, in a position to alert other operators close by. Marcel did not appear as an employee since he did not officially exist. It struck her again, reading the hand written material from her father, that there was no telling how many quarry owners or operators, would be for or against the Vichy inspired orders. It was perfectly possible that some might approve of Pétain and the new administration. It could be dangerous for her, Guy, Jules, Marcel and everybody else if the assumption was made that they were all on the same side. She resolved to speak to Jules about it before he made too many moves.

She typed out the lists and timetable and made extra carbon copies for Jules and for Doctor Lovas, carefully hiding the extra copies in her desk drawer. She then took the top and second copy into Eric Farbres for his approval and signature. He looked through them and said 'Excellent! Your typing skills are obviously improving Isabelle. You really are becoming a real asset to the unit.'

'Thank you Papa – I'm glad you think so.' She wondered what his opinion of her would have been had he known the unvarnished truth. It did not bear thinking about and she quickly dismissed the idea. 'Are you home this evening Papa?' she asked as casually as she could.

'Eventually – yes, but probably a little late.'

'I'll warn Mama. If there is nothing else I'll be off now Papa. OK?'

'Yes of course. I expect I'll see you later.'

Isabelle quickly put the illicit copies into her bag, grabbed her bike and was out of the gate before he could change his mind. She had arranged to meet Guy at their usual spot on the road and he was waiting for her when she arrived. She could hardly wait to give him the copies of the inspection schedule and quickly outlined the main points while he scanned through them. They had a few days before anything was due to happen because the quarry owners had to be informed by letter. It meant that Jules and Marcel would have enough time to check that nothing suspicious remained of their recent removal of dynamite stocks and alterations to the stock book. She also told Guy her thoughts about what could be safely said to other quarry people, in case some might not agree with their small group's actions and inform the authorities – something now being urged upon the general public as being their duty as good citizens.

'So as long as we are careful there shouldn't be a problem. Remember that Marcel will have to stay out of sight while they are poking about. We don't want them asking any questions about him.' She explained that she could not wait around for long this evening as her papa would be home – later perhaps, but definitely home. They embraced and finally parted, she towards Domvent and he to the village.

Guy was back in Chalhac within ten minutes of leaving Isabelle, and Jules and Marcel were already home. They registered considerable satisfaction with Marcel's foresight in removing the dynamite and the speed with which Isabelle had got the information to them about the inspection schedule. It gave Jules time to double check that the quarry was all in order, so for the moment the panic was over. Guy told them that Isabelle had made another spare copy of the schedule which he planned to take up to the doctor in the morning because he would want to be kept up to date. He repeated Isabelle's latest thoughts concerning what they might say to others in the quarrying business, when alerting them to the prospect of inspection by the gendarmerie.

'That's quite a thought. Isabelle is a clever girl,' said Jules. 'We don't really know how other people regard all this and it can be very dangerous now to even ask someone for their views because it means that you might be questioning the whole issue.'

* * * * *

A week went by and on the following Tuesday Lieutenant Boyer accompanied by two gendarmes arrived at the gate of Jules' quarry. Boyer sat in the front of the small truck beside the driver and the two gendarmes stood in the back. Jules had received notice from the quarry owners to expect an inspection team to arrive – something he was well and truly prepared for – and he saw the truck arrive. He sauntered over to the gate and let them in. Boyer and the two gendarmes got out of the truck and the young Lieutenant produced his authorising letter and identification for Jules, who went through the motions of examining them.

Boyer had adopted his official mode and was not prepared to take any nonsense from Jules.

'I would like to see your secure storage arrangements Monsieur Gaillard and all documents regarding explosive materials being used here.' He looked about him and pointed to the stone built store that now contained rather less dynamite than it had a little over a week before. 'That is your secure store I imagine?'

'Correct sir. Would you like to take a look?'

'I would and while we are about it, I'd like to see your record of stocks held at the present time and any other relevant documents.'

'Of course,' said Jules. 'My office is in the hut over there and if you care to accompany me, I'll get out the books and you can check up on the store. There is not a huge amount of explosives for you to see at the present time as I was about to put in an order for fresh supplies later this week, but you are welcome to see what we are carrying at the moment.' Boyer nodded his agreement and went through the pages of the record book – now a little thinner than it had previously been, having had several pages removed and new, much modified dates and quantities inserted. He seemed satisfied with what he was shown and they walked a few yards over to the stone store shed. Jules made a show of removing padlocks and undoing heavy locks on the door.

'You can see we are very careful about security here Lieutenant. We don't take any chances with this stuff.'

'No. I can see you take your responsibilities seriously Monsieur.'

Inside the store it was quite dark and it was necessary to use a torch to see anything. There was an ancient steel cupboard at the far end and this too had an elaborate padlock and two built-in locks. Inside were a few waxed packages containing dynamite together with two or three boxes of detonators and a coil of wire. Beside the cupboard stood a black painted metal spark generator with two wire terminals and a 'T' shaped plunger on the top. Jules prayed that the generator would not be regarded as a possible threat to law and order and be confiscated; it was something he had not considered until then. Boyer ignored it, probably because he did not recognise its significance, or perhaps he thought that without explosives, it served no purpose anyway.

Boyer peered at the notes he had taken when examining the record books. He counted the packs of dynamite and boxes of detonators. 'Well it all appears to be in order Monsieur. Now I have to tell you that I am under orders to confiscate all explosive material in quarries across the area. This is not in any way intended to be a punitive measure, rather more a preventative action. The authorities are anxious to prevent the illegal use of this type of material by dissident groups who may be tempted to make some sort of violent protest. We hope you will see this in that light.'

Jules knew that this was going to occur but was obliged to register surprise and anger. 'I can see how that might worry the authorities but how do they expect me and others like me, to be able to work? This is hard work anyway, but if I am expected to get stone down from the rock face without explosives, they don't know what they are talking about.'

'I will pass on your thoughts on the matter Monsieur and I can see that you may have a problem in the future, but we must all obey the law.' Michel Boyer was basically a polite young man and felt some sympathy for Jules, who he could see was no longer young and realised that the task of dislodging large pieces of rock from the natural wall of the quarry, would become more arduous from now on.

In the meantime the two gendarmes had been examining the rock face, the piles of stone stacked in the yard and undergrowth nearby. They discovered the ladder which had been partly hidden beneath some greenery behind the office hut. One of them quietly said something to Boyer about the ladder, who then turned to Jules and said, 'It seems there is a ladder partly hidden over there Monsieur. Why is it hidden like that?'

Jules explained that it was not used very much anyway and he did not want it used unlawfully by anyone managing to get into the quarry area, or to steal it altogether. As he could see, there was no large shed or storage facility for anything of that size so he thought the best thing he could do was to hide it somehow. It seemed to satisfy Boyer, who began to give orders to his gendarme helpers to remove the materials from the store.

'We must leave you now Monsieur Gaillard. Thank you for making this task tolerable.' He gave Jules a receipt for the small heap of materials now reposing in the back of the lorry and they drove out of the gate. Jules breathed again at the sight of them disappearing down the road. It had gone better than he hoped and they had been unable to find anything that could be regarded as suspect.

* * * * *

In Clermont Ferrand Colonel Boudeau had been enthusiastically carrying out orders from Vichy, which were rapidly becoming more extreme. A network of pro-régime sympathisers had been recruited as spies whose task was to listen out for and if possible, to overhear any conversation which might be interpreted as dissident. They spent most of their days, evenings and sometimes nights, listening for any activity which they considered might fit this category. Two such people had been drinking coffee at the Café Metropol in Clermont, trying to give the impression they were just two ordinary businessmen taking a little time away from their desks for a while. The clientele in the Metropol was generally a mix of professionals, students and office workers, taking their lunch or a coffee break. The same faces appeared most days, occasionally punctuated by travelling salesmen touting for business, or simply taking a break from their labours. One morning a student arrived, who the two 'businessmen' noted was evidently not a regular customer, as the counter staff's greeting was just a little too formal and not casually friendly. One of them happened to overhear the words 'cousin Nicole.' In view of what, until then had seemed to be a less than familiar relationship, it was odd that the student should be saying something about a cousin. It was stranger still that the man behind the counter nodded and a few minutes later, came out to the table where the student was now sitting. The young man then followed him through a beaded curtain into the back of the premises.

This was enough for the 'businessmen', who concluded these were grounds for further investigation. They left the Metropol shortly afterwards, one walking briskly to the post office to book a call on the telephone to Boudeau's office and the other waited within sight of the Metropol for the student to re-appear. Half an hour later the young man emerged, and walked up the road, followed at a discreet distance by the remaining 'spy.' Boudeau registered satisfaction with their efforts in his own particular fashion –'just about polite' would best describe it – Boudeau did not do pleasure.

The same evening a contingent of gendarmes surrounded the Metropol and everyone inside was ordered out, loaded into a closed van and taken to Boudeau's headquarters. The lone student had been followed to what was assumed to be where he lived and was later arrested for behaviour suspected of plotting against the State.

Seventeen

Guy had called on Doctor Lovas to enquire if he had any information concerning the rumours circulating about round-ups of French and non-French Jews. According to the Chalhac grapevine and in nearby villages, endless stories circulated about whole families being taken away in buses in the middle of the night. It was said this was happening across ever increasing areas in the 'unoccupied' zone. So far the immediate area around Domvent had not been affected, but Guy and his family were becoming increasingly concerned lest they were to be targeted. The stories were obviously based on real happenings and although most of the local population were not yet very excited about the matter, nor even particularly anti-Semitic in its attitude, a degree of unease began to take effect and sides were being taken. Some people were quietly horrified to think that individuals and entire families they knew had been simply swept up, herded into buses and driven off into the unknown. It was said that no notice had been given and people were just disappearing, leaving houses and their possessions and businesses behind. Very ordinary and long-established families were suddenly being gathered up and taken away without any prior warning. It was not known where they were being taken to or even why, although guesses were being made. Some more accurate than others.

Some locals chose to turn a blind eye to this state of affairs and even silently applauded Vichy's Nazi inspired actions. Scores were being settled for grudges held by some who went even further, by telephoning or writing to the authorities to say they thought 'undesirables' were living or working nearby and this may have accounted for some of what was now taking place.

Isabelle had been unable to overhear any relevant telephone conversations her father may have had in this connection. Farbres' office door was not always open enough for her to gather any useful information, but as she was the sole typist she had access to written orders coming in from Clermont and Farbres' orders going out to the unit's staff. She was therefore in a strong position to give any early warnings that might be relevant. Guy had quizzed her from time to time, in the light of the continuing rumours, but she was unable to add very much to what was already known.

'I think I'll speak to the doctor about it again – he may have heard something from his pals in Vichy. They keep their ears to the ground and so far, the bits of news they have given him have been pretty accurate.'

* * * * *

Lovas had welcomed him warmly that morning and followed up by saying,

'I have some seriously bad news. It seems a café-based group in Clermont has been uncovered and a lot of arrests have been made. I take it you didn't know.'

'No, I've heard nothing from that direction. Do we know which café? There has been a silence from Simon for a little while but I assumed he was being extra careful and not taking any chances by writing unnecessarily.'

'Very wise, but somehow their cover has been blown. I don't have any details of names at the moment and I have asked my contacts for more information, but only if it is possible to get it without arousing suspicions. It is pretty clear that the pressure is being turned up and if they begin interrogating suspects in order to uncover more groups or individuals, we can expect something of the sort down here eventually. It doesn't bode well for the future. I suggest you remind your family, your friends and anyone else, to be very careful and not trust anyone, unless they are certain where they stand.'

'The family is very aware of the situation, I assure you but I agree they must be kept on their toes all the time. If we or they become careless, the results could be disastrous. Is there any other way we could find out more about the arrests in Clermont? It would be a setback if the café in question turns out to be the Metropol, hopefully my pal Simon wasn't there at the time. It might also mean that Jean Blanc could be at risk, if they connect him with a group.'

'I agree, but it was Jean who passed on the news to me, so we have to assume that right now he hasn't been picked up. He said that he may have to disappear very soon because the whole situation was very dangerous up there. He was unable to say much over the phone because of the chances of operators listening in to our conversation. What he did say was cloaked in vague references about his health and the need to 'take a holiday in the country.' I think we may lose a source of information if he goes into hiding, which will be unhelpful, but he can't take any chances.'

'We don't really know if Simon has been arrested do we? We don't even know for sure whether it was the Metropol café they raided, so it's possible we are being unduly pessimistic.'

'No, we don't know for certain, but if Jean has got the wind up and was prepared to ring me to say as he was obliged to vanish, I think we can take it things aren't exactly very healthy. Do you think that your Isabelle could find out more from her father – without arousing suspicions of course?

'She is an obvious source of information, but she is also extremely wary. Most of the tips she has managed to supply have been as a result of listening to his telephone calls, or discussions with his second in command, Lieutenant Boyer. She also types the orders and letters, so if there is anything important, she learns about it as soon as it appears. Of course, if we slipped up and acted on information which could only have come from Farbres' office, or via Isabelle, then she would be in very serious trouble and so would we. She has to trust that we too, don't make any mistakes.'

'Of course but she seems to be well up to it. I take it the inspection of quarries went off reasonably well, thanks to Isabelle's early warning.'

'It seems so. Boyer and two of his henchmen poked around my Papa's place but were unable to discover any discrepancies in the way it was being run. They took away what remained of the explosives, detonators and a coil of wire, but left behind the spark generator, so we can consider it a small victory. It's a pity about the wire but it should be possible to get more if it becomes necessary.'

'Excellent! I have already indicated to some of our group that some good work is going on here and they are very grateful. They have also suggested that it may be an idea to give Isabelle a coded identity which might give her a degree of protection against accidental discovery. What do you think?'

'Good idea. Would you like me to talk to her about it, after all she is the one in the hot seat and I imagine she would approve, if it gives her some protection.'

'Do that. Now I must ask you to go as I am expecting a patient any time soon. Stay in touch and be careful. By the way, did you by any chance hear Winston Churchill on the wireless a day or two ago? He was saying that England is ready and waiting for the German invasion – and followed up by saying "So are the fishes" – very droll!'

'No, I'm sorry I missed it, I hear it went down well. I hope for their sake that the English don't have to come face to face with the Germans. Their sense of humour might be severely tested.'

* * * * *

Coincidently, a day or so later, Isabelle was at her seat facing a small pile of mail on her desk awaiting her examination. There were no green dots on any of the corners of the envelopes and she about to put them back into the post office bag for collection by the post office van later, when Eric Farbres put his head around the doorway and said,

'Could you spare me a moment or two Isabelle? I've something important to discuss with you.' The tone of his voice seemed to indicate there was something serious he was about to say and Isabelle was immediately on her guard. Had he stumbled across something?

'Of course, Papa.'

'Isabelle, you are probably more familiar with many of the inhabitants in Chalhac than I am. Your grandmother and aunt have lived there all their lives and they would have a good idea if anything illegal was going on I'm sure.'

'I am sure they would Papa – so what are you saying?'

'We have had an anonymous letter from someone in or near the village, which seems to hint that we should take a look at the chateau. Your aunt Henrietta works there doesn't she? Surely she would know if there was something illegal being hatched wouldn't she?'

'I'm quite sure she would.'

175

'Well I feel obliged to send a small inspection team over there anyway to take a look in the next day or so. We need to be alert to anything happening which might create an unwanted situation for the administration. There are still a number of undesirables coming into the country from Spain and elsewhere and unless we pick them up, they have the potential to stir up unnecessary trouble. I can hardly believe the chateau is a hotbed of revolutionaries or Israelites, but you never know! It might be best if you avoid mentioning any of this to your aunt in case it alerts anyone who could be up to no good.'

'Of course, Papa.' Isabelle was quietly horrified at this news and it was nearly impossible for her to appear normal. She had visibly blanched as her father told what he planned to do but he seemed oblivious to his daughter's complexion. She said 'How many people are you planning to send over Papa –there's quite a lot of it to inspect.'

'I thought five or six including Lieutenant Boyer. I'll aim to get them down there by next Wednesday. It will be necessary to brief Boyer on the best way to go about it – I doubt if he has had to make an official inspection of any sort of chateau before and he will need to be extra courteous and careful.'

Isabelle had managed to extract some essential details from her father without appearing too inquisitive. It was now urgent to warn David Markovich and Henrietta what was likely to occur in the next few days. She and Guy had long since found a suitable 'message box' a little way out of Domvent – a hollow log a few metres from the road. They agreed on a signal provided by a particular tree at the roadside which could be bent to an 'N' for Non, if no messages had been left in the log. If the tree stood upright then there could be some sort of message. She quickly scribbled a note to Guy outlining the planned visit by the gendarmerie on Wednesday and during her lunch break cycled down to the 'box' and tucked it inside the log. She was back in Domvent within minutes. Guy had spotted the upright tree and collected the hidden note and was on his way back to Chalhac before two o'clock. Henrietta opened the big door to him and he quickly explained his sudden appearance.

'We must warn David as soon as possible that the chateau will be examined for hidden 'Israelites' and that someone in the village has written a note to the gendarmerie and has managed to stir things up for everyone.' David was called from his upstairs room and told the details. He took the news surprisingly calmly:

'I've already made plans for just such a situation occurring.'

'What are you going to do then?' asked Guy.

'I plan to become Monsieur le Comte for the duration of the visit.'

'It sounds a bit risky to me David – suppose one of Farbres' men recognises you as not being the real thing, what then?'

'It's a chance I'll have to take, but I spoke to Isabelle about the people in the gendarmerie and she said that none of them are locals – and even Farbres doesn't know much about the village here, so it's unlikely they would know what the le Comte or la Comtesse look like.'

'What would you wear David – your wardrobe can't be exactly overflowing with clothes.'

'No, mine isn't but Monsieur le Comte left a lot of his clothes here when they left for Switzerland whereas la Comtesse took nearly all of hers – as Henrietta can confirm! I've already made some changes to his smoking jacket - it has been a fairly simple matter for me to make alterations to some of his things and they are all ready to be put on – and though I say so myself, I was quite impressed when I looked in the mirror to check the effect! The main problem was that he takes a smaller size in shoes than me and I had a job getting into them – I hope the planned inspection doesn't take too long because I'll end up crippled if I have to wear his shoes for any length of time! I've spoken to our groundsman, Pierre and he has agreed to act as a gatekeeper when they show up. It might lend a sense of normality to the chateau, if it appears to be properly staffed.'

'Looks like you have given some thought to the situation here David – I hope to God you can pull it off. If it all goes wrong, we are all in trouble.'

'I understand that Guy, but sometimes we must take a few chances in this life. I think the odds are in our favour on this occasion.'

* * * * *

On Wednesday morning a small truck with six gendarmes on board plus Lieutenant Boyer arrived at the locked gates to the chateau. Pierre Brun, in his role of gatekeeper emerged from the now long defunct sentry box beside the gates. He addressed Boyer from inside the gates, as he was about to climb down from the truck.

'Good morning Sir! How can I help you?'

'I am authorised to make an inspection of the chateau and grounds,' said Boyer.

'Are you expected, Lieutenant?'

'No. There has been no opportunity to give any notice about this. Will you please unlock the gates now?' Boyer had adopted his best authoritative voice partly with the intent of setting the tone for this visit from the start. He felt that it would go towards demonstrating to the gendarmes in his charge who were privy to this first encounter, how best to exert their own authority upon any other people within the chateau.

'One moment please.' Pierre made great play of fetching the oversize and rather rusty looking key, from the little guard box. He had been carefully briefed by Henrietta and David about his role in the pantomime about to be enacted. He managed to unlock the long since disused lock on the gates and pulled them creakily open.

'Will you please follow me and park your lorry near the front door.'

Boyer climbed back beside the driver and began to slowly follow Pierre along the uneven gravel road to the front of the chateau.

'Wait here please,' said Pierre before climbing the steps to the old front door where he gave a purposeful tug on an iron ring at the end of a chain suspended beside the door. From within came a dull, unmusical 'clonk' from a cracked bell. After a minute or two the door slowly opened revealing Henrietta who feigned surprise at seeing Pierre on the door step.

'Pierre! What's the trouble?'

'No trouble Madame Suau, but the gendarmerie has orders to inspect the chateau. Is Monsieur le Comte available? He may wish to be present.'

'Wait there Pierre while I speak to Monsieur le Comte.' She carefully closed the door on him and on Boyer, who was standing at the foot of the steps. A minute or two passed before the door opened again. Henrietta addressed Boyer over Pierre's shoulder,

'Will you follow me Lieutenant? Monsieur le Comte will see you now. Come this way please.'

Boyer turned to face the lorry and said, 'Remain where you are for the moment.' He followed Henrietta into the dim hallway, passing the staircase and paused at the door of the salon. Henrietta gently tapped on the door.

'In!' responded David Markovich.

The Lieutenant was ushered in to face the bogus Count. David was dressed in a heavily embroidered smoking jacket, a silk shirt and cravat and corduroy trousers. He rose from one of the high-backed chairs to greet the visitor. Henrietta formerly announced Boyer's arrival:

'May I present Lieutenant Boyer of the Gendarmerie unit in Domvent Monsieur? Lieutenant Boyer, this is Monsieur le Comte de Villebarde.'

David gave a formal nod of welcome as he stubbed out a cigarette. He held out his hand to Boyer and followed up saying,

'So, what's all this about Lieutenant?

Boyer explained as politely as he could the circumstances which had led to the visit and that with the Count's permission he would like to look around the chateau, both inside and out, with a view to uncovering any suspicious signs of political dissent or other activities which could be interpreted as anti the régime. David smiled broadly at the young man.

'Are you seriously suggesting Lieutenant that my home is harbouring a group of criminals? Where ever did this idea spring from?'

'I am not permitted to say precisely Monsieur but we received an anonymous note from someone in the area which suggested that some sort of illegal activity was taking place here. It was my superior's duty to look into the matter. I imagine that you would be aware of anything of the sort occurring if that were the case?'

'Of course,' offered David. 'Please feel free to examine the house and surrounding park if you must, but I feel you'll be wasting your valuable time.'

'Thank you Monsieur. In the course of our duties, we are obliged to waste quite a lot of time on fruitless enquiries - it goes with the job. With your permission I will instruct my men to carry out a search immediately.'

'Very well – carry on. My groundsman Pierre, whom you have already met, will be pleased to give your men a guided tour around the park and grounds. Madame Suau will be pleased to show you and your men around the house. You may examine everything. I have no wish to remain suspected of any wrongdoing.'

Henrietta remained standing to one side during this interview and was quietly impressed with David's performance. After they had made their polite exit from David's presence, she accompanied Boyer and two of his men up the staircase to the floors above. Cupboards and doors were opened, revealing a few of the la Comtesse's clothes, left behind when they left for Switzerland. They eventually came to David's room containing his sewing machine.

'A sewing machine – whose is this?' queried Boyer.

'That is Madame la Comtesse's hobby. She likes to make clothes for the children and sometimes even for herself. Of course when they left for Switzerland the machine and some of her clothes had to be left behind. I expect she will go back to it when they return.'

'Did Le Comte not go with them to Switzerland then?'

'Oh yes. They all went, but Monsieur le Comte has a number of business interests here and he is anxious to remain in touch with the situation as well as keeping an eye on the house. It entails a lot of documentation and so on to make it across the border in both directions, but he feels it is worthwhile to make it back occasionally.'

'He evidently places a good deal of trust in you Madame and presumably has discussed some of his private business affairs with you. That is a little unusual isn't it?'

'Perhaps, but I have worked here since the mid-thirties. I was employed as the children's governess originally. They are now at a proper school in Geneva – I don't expect I'll recognize them when they finally return. They all regard me as part of the family now and trust me absolutely.'

'I notice le Comte has a curious accent doesn't he? I wonder where he picked that up?'

Henrietta's heart skipped one or two beats. Up until now the encounter with the gendarmerie had gone fairly smoothly. While David Markovich's French was entirely fluent, it still carried traces of his Russian background. It was something that all those who knew him simply did not notice anymore and no preparation had been made to answer any questions in that direction. Henrietta had to think very quickly.

'I believe as a boy, he and his parents lived in Alsace for a number of years – perhaps that's what you are hearing Lieutenant.' She prayed that Boyer was not familiar with the Alsatian dialect.

'Yes. That's probably it.'

Henrietta's blood pressure and heart rate began to subside to somewhere near normal.

'Do you know where the 'anonymous' letter came from Lieutenant, or is that a state secret?

'I'm afraid I'm unable to say anything else about it Madame – it is as you call it, "a state secret".'

'Well you know what I think – someone in the village is jealous that our groundsman Pierre is able to sell vegetables from the chateau in the market and is making money out of it for himself. Whoever it is that sent that letter imagines that Monsieur le Comte is unaware of what's going on and wants to stir up trouble for Picrrc.' I can assure you Lieutenant that Monsieur le Comte knows all about it and couldn't give a damn. There are plenty of vegetables here anyway and le Comte will probably go back to Switzerland before long so he won't need any of it. After all, should Pierre allow the stuff to rot in the ground?'

'I will make a point of mentioning it to Major Farbres when I submit my report, Madame Suau.

Henrietta felt she had done as much as she dare to reinforce what she hoped would be a clean bill of health for the chateau and that they would be left alone from here on. Just as Boyer was about to leave, David appeared in the doorway of the salon and said,

'You are leaving us now Lieutenant – I trust you feel a little easier about the situation here?'

'Yes, thank you Sir - I am satisfied that everything seems to be in order.'

'Excellent.' He turned to Henrietta and said 'Madame Suau, will you fetch a couple of bottles of my better red wine from the cellar as a small reward for wasting the officer's time.'

'That's very generous of you Monsieur – and quite unnecessary, but thank you.'

Shortly afterwards he and his men left the chateau and were let out of the gates by Pierre, who ceremonially locked up behind them. There were sighs of relief all round as the lorry pulled away from the chateau gates. A minute or two later Pierre appeared at the front door, smiling broadly.

'That's over Monsieur Markovich! They didn't arrest you then?'

'No Pierre. Thanks for playing your part so well. I think we can help ourselves to another bottle of Monsieur le Comte's wine, don't you? Will you join us in a glass?'

Pierre hesitated for a moment or two but then reluctantly agreed. He was ushered into the salon by David while Henrietta went down the cellar again for more wine. Until that moment Pierre had never seen the inside of the house, let alone the salon.

'My word! This is very beautiful.' He could not find the words to describe his sense of wonder as he walked in. Its shabbiness went by him entirely so he was hugely impressed. To be invited inside and to imbibe some of the Monsieur le Comte's wine were two actions he had never in his wildest dreams imagined would ever happen. 'Thank you Monsieur Markovich – it's very kind of you.'

'Don't thank me Pierre, I'm just taking liberties with Monsieur le Comte's trusting nature while he is happily away from all this in Switzerland. He might have quite a lot to say if he were ever to find out we have been raiding his wine collection. Let alone discovering that his smoking jacket and trousers are shorter than he remembered and don't fit him anymore. Of course, if he is a true patriot, he might feel that a bottle of wine here and there was a price worth paying as his contribution towards our fight against the Nazis. I can tell you I won't lose any sleep over the matter, and neither should you!'

'I hadn't thought of it like that – I reckon you're right.'

Henrietta appeared carrying two bottles of a very expensive Bordeaux red. She hoped Monsieur le Comte did not keep a very exact tally of the wines in the cellar. 'A glass for you Pierre?'

'Thank you Madame Suau, yes.'
'Here's to our success today and in the future!' said David.

* * * * *

The following morning Eric Farbres called Isabelle into his office.

'I have Lieutenant Boyer's report on the inspection of the chateau at Chalhac and as far as he could see, there was nothing amiss. Your aunt and le Comte were very accommodating, I understand, and I am mildly relieved to know, that there was nothing going on there which could have resulted in a difficult situation for all concerned – not least your aunt, who is of course also my sister-in-law. The family connections could prove to be a considerable embarrassment, should any improprieties be discovered. I believe your aunt suggested to Boyer that she thought the anonymous note could have simply been a bit of mischief aimed at the groundsman, who she says makes a small profit from selling some of the produce from the vegetable garden at the chateau. This sounds very believable to me and I think we can safely dismiss the matter as being an irrelevance. I will write to le Comte today expressing my thanks for his co-operation in the matter and perhaps you can indicate to your aunt my personal thanks.'

'Of course Papa. Would it help if I delivered your letter to the chateau personally as I will almost certainly visit grand-mère Hubert on Saturday?'

'Yes, why not? It would be a measure of our respect for le Comte's position if we are seen to be responding quickly to his hospitality.'

Isabelle could barely suppress her amusement and relief at the way Boyer had been taken in by David Markovich and Tantetta's masquerade, and his evidently favourable report back to her father. There had been no opportunity to hear anything directly from Chalhac about how things had gone the previous day, but it sounded like good news all round. It also struck her just how far her aunt Henrietta had now become embroiled in the whole situation. If David's true identity were to be uncovered as a Jewish imposter, with his impersonation of le Comte de Villebarde as well as living in the count's chateau free of charge, the real count would be certain to rush back to discover what had been going on in his absence. The ramifications following his re-appearance were impossible to imagine. She quickly dismissed the thought.

Eric Farbres wrote a cringingly polite letter of thanks to 'le Comte', aka David Markovich, expressing his apologies for the unforgivable intrusion. He also warmly thanked le Comte for his generosity regarding the wine since Boyer had been obliged to tell Farbres that le Comte had been kind enough to make a gift of two bottles of what he assumed was a better than average Bordeaux red.

On Saturday morning Isabelle cycled down to Chalhac and made first for her grandmother's house where she guessed Henrietta would be. There was still a sense of excitement in the air when she arrived and both were anxious to hear from Isabelle how her father had responded to Lieutenant Boyer's inspection report. She smiled broadly as she handed the letter to her aunt, typed the previous day in which her father had expressed his undying devotion to Monsieur le Comte, Madame la Comtesse and their children's wellbeing, as well as thanking him for his co-operation, understanding and forbearance in permitting the unexpected intrusion and inspection of his home. He was delighted to be able to inform Monsieur le Comte that no further invasion of his privacy would be necessary as nothing had been uncovered that might point to any illegal or suspicious activity – not that for one moment had he seriously imagined anything of the sort would be found. He added that his house keeper Madame Suau should be praised for her willingness to help during the inspection. He noted that he and le Comte had some common links with Alsace, through their forebears and that it might be interesting if an opportunity could be found to meet up sometime in the future. It was a transparent attempt by Eric Farbres to ingratiate himself with le Comte, a move inherited from his father, namely his instinct to find possible allies in the furtherance of his career.

Henrietta laughed out loud as she read the letter and knew how David would enjoy it. 'We really fooled them didn't we? Just imagine, what he would do if he got to know how big a fool he had been made to look.'

'I've already considered that Tantetta and it doesn't bear thinking about. Quite apart from the consequences for his future, our own positions would be, to say the least precarious. Not just us either – half the people in the village would come under suspicion – it could end up very messily.'

'Well I think we should quietly carry on as before. David's situation seems to be fairly safe now – although we still don't know who it was in the village who wrote that nasty little note. Do you think it would be possible to dig it out from your Papa's filing system Isabelle? Whoever it was might be tempted to stir things up again and become more specific about what they think is going on. If they know for sure that Monsieur le Comte has remained in Switzerland since leaving with his family and that David has been living and working at the chateau in his absence, it could become very complicated for all of us.'

'There's also the little matter of David's supposed origins in Alsace, which you had to invent on the spur of the moment Tantetta. I don't really know if Papa has any idea how his forebears spoke, or if he would recognize that David's dialect carried a Russian influence or was in any way different to Alsatian French. You were pretty safe saying it to Lieutenant Boyer because he was unlikely to have had much contact with that part of the country. As for Papa's suggestion that he and le Comte might have some common ground worth exploring at some future date, we'll just have to hope that it doesn't go any further.'

Henrietta said she would pass the letter to David in the morning, so Isabelle departed, leaving them to ponder the latest situation while she went over to Guy and his family to tell them all about it. She gave them a verbatim report about Eric's letter to 'le Comte' and how Lieutenant Boyer and her father had been totally taken in by David, Henrietta and Pierre. The only remaining problems were the identity of the anonymous writer of the note to the gendarmerie and what action could be taken to stop any further trouble making. The dangers posed by any unexpected visit by le Comte who was at present safely tucked away in Switzerland, also needed to be thought about.

Guy was hugely impressed with the way the chateau inspection had been handled and the apparently calm way that both David and Henrietta had dealt with what could easily have turned into a disaster. Instead, a breathing space had been made for everyone involved as well as putting the anonymous note writer in his or her place. Isabelle and Guy were able to get some private time together before she was obliged to leave for home. They went for a short trip on their bikes up to the surrounding forest and eventually Isabelle said she would have to leave in case her Papa wondered how long she normally spent with her grandmother and aunt. She did not want any suspicions aroused unnecessarily regarding her regular absences from the family home on Saturdays – it could be too easy to fall into some sort of unintentional trap. Guy agreed and before they parted he said he would go up to Domvent on Monday and tell the doctor how things had gone at the chateau.' He added 'I meant to say I've been thinking about a pseudo name for you, what about "Giraffe"?'

'I don't know whether to be flattered or insulted! – are you suggesting my neck is too long or something?'

'No! I think you have a lovely neck – and everything else besides. No Cherie, I simply wanted to give you a name that doesn't seem to have any connection with you at all.'

'I suppose you're right – if I was called "typist" or something like that, it would immediately point to someone in an office, so it does make sense. OK, I'll be "Giraffe" from now on. You might find kissing me a problem in future – I hope you will be tall enough!'

'I'm sure we'll manage!'

* * * * *

On Monday morning Guy made for Doctor Lovas' house in Domvent. Lovas opened the door to him and Guy recited the security phrase.

'Come in my friend. It is good to see you! There is someone here anxious to see you again. Come through to the salon.'

There was a moment of anxiety for Guy as the doctor ushered him into his inner sanctum. Standing with his back to the unlit fire was Simon Wojakovski, smiling broadly at Guy whose face lit up on seeing his friend was safe, having imagined that he might have been one of those picked up at the Metropol in Clermont. To see him looking so fit and well was a tremendous relief. They hugged one another and immediately began to question what had been happening over the last several weeks, when the risks in making any sort of contact were such that they had both implicitly understood the need to keep their heads down. Guy wanted to know more about the raid on the Metropol café, who had been arrested, and how he managed to avoid being picked up. Simon said that he had simply been lucky in that he had not paid his usual visit that day. When he heard about the police raid he made what he hoped would look like a casual bicycle trip along the road passing the café.

'There were gendarmes posted at each end of the road and one was standing outside, waiting I suppose to pounce on anyone who showed any interest in the place. I kept my eyes straight ahead as I went past and I wasn't followed, but I could see enough to confirm what had been going on. It's been boarded up ever since and the owner and most of the customers that day are still being held and questioned. The fellow the police spies followed, was taken off somewhere else – I can't say where exactly, but rumour has it that there is an interrogation unit in Vichy, and that's hardly likely to be a picnic. I don't know who the person is, but someone has been a little careless or perhaps over confident. Clermont is a dangerous place these days Guy, and you and I must be grateful that we have such good friends as the doctor here.'

'What about your parents Simon?'

'At the moment they are staying put and I have tried to persuade them to leave and hide up somewhere, but they are very reluctant to abandon their house. I have told them how dangerous it is now, but they are very stubborn and won't be told. It's a terribly worrying situation. I told them that I was going to get out of Clermont in case my friends at the Metropol were bullied into naming people like me and they came looking for me. This is another reason for trying to get my parents to move away because if they get to know who I am or what I was up to, they'll be certain to go to my parents' house looking for me.'

'You managed to remember our coded introduction for the doctor here? – Was he word perfect Doctor?'

'He was – and it was as well he was because if he had stumbled over the words I would not have let him in. It's my golden rule.' Lovas went on to say that he had invited Simon to stay with him for a few days while he decided on his future moves.

Guy said he might persuade his own parents to put him up in the roof space in their house in Chalhac which had recently become vacant when David Markovich moved to the chateau. 'I can't speak for them of course but I will be surprised if they turned the idea down.'

Lovas had clearly been considering possible options open to Simon, which might offer him a degree of security for the time being. It was with some relief and gratitude that they heard Guy's initial response to the matter. Lovas said that while he was very sympathetic to Simon's position, he felt it would be chancy to allow him to stay in his house any longer than necessary, because sooner or later he could be spotted by one of his patients or even by a sharp-eyed gendarme. Guy's proposal for him to be hidden in Chalhac made a lot of sense. He went on to ask,

'And what about Wednesday at the chateau Guy? I take it they managed to pull it off? I gave Simon the outlines about what was being planned by the gendarmerie and how David Markovich and Henrietta Suau planned to deal with it.'

Guy gave them both an account of how it had gone and that Lieutenant Boyer had been completely taken in by the charade. He also added the slightly unforeseen complication regarding David's accent which still carried traces of Russian. He added that Henrietta had been obliged to offer as an explanation for what Boyer had described as a 'curious accent', that this was perhaps the result of his living as a boy for several years in Alsace. Boyer had mentioned the matter in his report to Eric Farbres. They all hoped that Farbres would not be too familiar with the Alsatian accent, despite his fairly recent ancestry, and that his grandparents originated from that part of the country. Farbres' letter to 'le Comte' had hinted at the prospect of meeting up with him some time to share their common background. The doctor and Simon both smiled broadly at this.

'He should know!' said Simon.

'Let's hope he never gets the chance to meet the real Monsieur le Comte,' said Guy.

Eighteen

Chalhac's little church on La Place held a secret. With very few exceptions, the only people to whom it had ever been revealed were the successive Roman Catholic priests, most of whom remained in place until they retired, died or very occasionally moved away to another post. It was an established tradition that when a new incumbent took up the post in Chalhac he would be given, amongst others, the details concerning the history of the church, how it came to be destroyed and then rebuilt in the early seventeenth century. It was well known in the village that during the 'Wars of Religion' a group of anti-Papist Huguenots had ransacked and set alight everything inside the little building and had done their best to pull down the old stone walls. Not much had remained. The priest at the time, Père Jean-Paul had only just managed to escape with his life, but it had been a close-run thing. When things settled down a little following the Edict of Nantes, he returned to Chalhac and made it his personal mission to oversee the rebuilding process. He also had it in mind to exploit, if he could, a curiosity about the building. It had originally been built above a small underground stream. The stream ran from the hills above the village and emptied finally into the river 'la Bache.' It was only just below the surface and the builders must have been unaware of its presence until they began to rebuild some of the foundations. They must also have decided to carry on with the building process as more problems would probably have been encountered, had they decided to start all over again elsewhere.

The rebuilt church had sprouted a small, barely noticeable buttress on one of the outside walls. Père Jean-Paul, had been watching the stonemasons as they worked and had suddenly become aware that the ground close to the wall had begun to fall in, revealing a narrow opening leading he imagined, quite correctly, to the underground stream below. Having barely escaped with his skin a few years before, he decided that an opportunity existed to build an escape route from the church to the outside, should circumstances in the future demand it. With a modest financial incentive, he persuaded one of the masons to make the opening wide enough for an inspection to be made of what lay below the surface. He was lowered on a rope into the hole and discovered that there was indeed a small stream running through a natural fissure beneath the surface, which was wide enough for a man to stand up in. It was arranged that a false 'buttress' be built around and above the hole and a suitable opening made in the church wall which would lead to the inside of the church. The outside would lend the appearance of a strengthening buttress. A new confessional was made on the inside wall and it would disguise the secret opening behind it. The builders were sworn to secrecy during this whole process and so far as is known, the truth was never revealed. The church was re-named 'Sainte Barbara' in honour of the stonemasons.

Nearly three hundred years later Père Patrick Mulligan, an Irish born man from Londonderry, became the local priest, looking after his flock in Chalhac and in two nearby communities. He shared his time between the three churches which he reached on the ancient bicycle inherited from his immediate predecessor. He had been encouraged by his parents in the 1920s to make the church his career and had been coerced into becoming a choirboy and slowly progressed through the local church hierarchy, into becoming an altar boy. His advance through the Catholic priesthood process was slow, involving a seminary in Northern Italy and culminating in France during the inter-war years. He did not much like what he saw going on in Germany and Italy and vowed he would try to help people being bullied and displaced by the Nazis as much as he could. When Germany invaded France in 1940 it spurred him on to consider how he could best help to fight some of the iniquities from which the local populations were suffering. He had almost forgotten the church's secret escape hatch behind the confessional and it struck him that there might come a time when it could be used to good effect. He realised that he would have to take someone into his confidence within the village about the secret panel and who might know likely potential users. He had imagined circumstances could arise where a person or persons might come under the suspicious gaze of the authorities in Domvent, Clermont or even Vichy, and who had to be quickly hidden or made to disappear. He considered telling Monsieur Bastien, the Mayor, but decided against him since he might have remained a little too close to the authorities. In the end he decided to speak to Jacques Fournier in the bar opposite his church.

He was a little nervous at first about approaching Fournier about his proposal to let on about the church's secret. It had, after all remained a closely guarded secret for nearly three hundred years, but he felt strongly that the circumstances now prevailing in the country demanded extreme measures. He hoped the Good Lord would forgive him. One afternoon he appeared in the doorway of the bar. Jacques greeted him as warmly as he could.

'Good Morning, Père Mulligan! To what do we owe your presence in our humble premises?' Jacques was neither a church-goer nor was he a believer. He had seen sufficient misery inflicted on fellow human beings in the First World War to convince him that if there really had been an all-seeing Almighty, then none of it would have happened and moreover, he would still have both of his legs. He was too polite to voice any of this to Père Mulligan but his attitude towards him remained a shade guarded. As it happened there were no customers in the bar when he arrived so this made it a little easier for the good cleric to speak in confidence.

'And a good morning to you Monsieur Fournier! Why the visit? Well I would like to take you into my confidence on a matter of some importance. What I have to tell you must be kept under your hat. Can I have your assurance that nothing I tell you will go beyond these four walls?' Jacques was mystified at this sudden and unexpected approach by Mulligan. Was it some scandal Mulligan had uncovered?

'Of course, Père Mulligan. You have my solemn word. What's the problem?'

'First of all could I ask you how you view the new régime in our country and your opinion of our new leaders?'

'Before I answer your question, dare I ask what your view is? This is after all an important and delicate matter.' Jacques had to be sure of his ground before he became too involved in whatever Mulligan had to say. If he discovered that his sympathies lay with Pétain and the Vichy régime in general, then he would have to tread very carefully. So far as he knew, no one had been privy to Mulligan's political opinions. The way the question had been put to him appeared to indicate that the Père wanted to get something off his chest.

'It is delicate as you put it,' said Mulligan. 'I must tell you that I am, to put it mildly, a little uneasy about the way things are shaping up at the moment.'

'Can I take it this means you don't like it very much, or would that be overstating it?'

'No. It is certainly not overstating it. To be frank with you, I think what's going on at the present time is loathsome. I am of the opinion that le Maréchal is becoming senile. He is obviously prepared to obey instructions from Vichy, Paris or Berlin or wherever the orders are coming from and nobody dares to speak against him.' It was too late now for Mulligan to retract this outburst and he knew it. 'Of course it is only my personal view at the present time – it may improve when things settle down.' Mulligan tried to gently backtrack now in an attempt to leave space for manœuvre should it become necessary.

'I am pleased to tell you that we are very much on the same side Père Mulligan. I am delighted to know that we are allies in this matter and it is good to know there exists someone of your stature prepared to stand firm. But tell me Père, does this mean you are out of step with most of your fellows in the church? From what I hear, it sounds as though the Roman church is prepared to accept moves by Vichy to get rid of the Jews in our country. How do you stand on that?'

'I am afraid you are right Monsieur and I don't like it at all. I am very substantially out-numbered in the matter and there is little I can do other than say openly what I think in the churches here. My views are not always greeted with much enthusiasm but I believe my thinking is right and I will continue to say so.'

'You are to be admired Père – not everyone can claim the same courage of his convictions. There is already a small group of us in the village dedicated to fighting for our freedoms with whatever means are available to us. I will not tell you everything right now about how we are progressing but you can take it that we do what we can. Was there another matter you wanted to raise?'

'Indeed there is. My church over there has a little secret. No one, other than my predecessors or me has ever broken our promise to keep the secret. That I am about to break my promise now is an indication of how much I care about our country. I know I am a foreigner in the strictest sense, but most of my life has been spent here and I will do everything in my power to protect it against foreign invaders – even if it means breaking a vow. Do you think you could come over to the church right now, because it will be much better if I show you what all this is about? I think you will find it of considerable interest.'

'I'll be glad to Père - I am intrigued.'

Together they walked across La Place to the church. There was no one inside and it felt very cool and quiet.

'Come over here to the confessional Monsieur. This contains our secret.'

Jacques made his way to the ornately carved confessional box, with its heavily embroidered curtains. Père Mulligan said:

'Sit yourself down in the box Monsieur. I don't intend to extract any confession from you today!'

'I'm glad to hear it! So what happens now?' asked Jacques as he settled himself on the wooden seat behind the curtain.

'You'll see in just a moment. I'll get myself into my side' said Patrick Mulligan, pulling over the curtain in front of him. Jacques could hear Mulligan as he stretched to reach behind his back and could vaguely see him through the carved separating screen in the confessional. 'Now then' announced Mulligan. Jacques was aware of a sound behind him like a small wooden plank being scraped across a floor. He turned in his seat to see the back panel of the confessional had slid open sideways to reveal a darkened space. The opening was less than a metre high and no more than half a metre wide. He realised it was the inside of the buttress. How clever of someone he thought.

'That is our little secret Monsieur Fournier. If you were to turn around and climb through the gap you would find yourself beside a narrow shaft leading down to the underground stream that passes beneath the church. One way goes nowhere but the other way leads down to the river, to just below Monsieur Malet's mill. It is possible to get from this end of what might be termed a tunnel, by walking in the stream, half crouching until the opening at the river end, where the tunnel becomes much lower and it is necessary to go on hands and knees. At this time of the year the stream is not much more than a trickle but after the snows melt higher up, it becomes a veritable torrent. You can hear it quite clearly from inside the confessional, even with the panel shut. There are iron rungs on the side of the shaft which allow anyone wishing to get down there, to climb down without much difficulty.'

Jacques sat for a moment where he was, as he tried to grasp some of the implications that this revelation held for their resisting group, or anyone else trying to escape the law.

'This is amazing Père. I can imagine that if it came to it, this would be a Godsend – forgive me! It's wonderful that you should offer to help in this way. I take that this is what you have in mind?'

'Of course – and I forgive you for taking the Good Lord's name in vain.'

Jacques wanted to know how secure the opening mechanism was. Mulligan showed him the precise piece of carving on his side of the screen that it was necessary to release in order to allow the panel to slide open. There was also a simple catch so that a fugitive could lock the panel in place from the tunnel side. He could hardly wait to impart this news to the small gang of trusted supporters in his bar.

'Now remember what I say Monsieur Fournier: You must not spread any of these details around. It is our secret and you must respect the nature of what I have shown you. If it helps in your fight against the current political setup, then I will feel I have been able to contribute something useful. You will understand that my position in the village and the church means that I must be seen as unbiased, whatever transpires in the future. Meanwhile I wish you and your supporters good luck and every success. I will stay in touch now and then, but I must be careful – as must you,' he added. As he saw Jacques out of the church he said,

'Can I expect you to join in one of our services one day? You know you would be very welcome.

'It is kind Père of you to invite me but I'm sorry to have to disappoint you. I am not a believer.'

Mulligan did not even blink by Jacques' response. 'You might change your mind one day – the invitation remains.'

* * * * *

It took Jacques a great deal of self-control to wait until the regular gang appeared later that afternoon. Jules Gaillard and Marcel were the first to arrive, followed shortly after by Bonnet, the baker. Jacques could barely suppress his excitement.

Bonnet said with a smile, 'My wife saw you and Père Mulligan going over to the church earlier. Does this mean he has persuaded you to become a convert at last?'

'There's not much chance of that my friend. No – but he is on our side in the matters that concern us. Not only that, but he has let me in on a big secret inside the building: There is a tunnel leading out!' He proceeded to recount his conversation with Mulligan and the Père's revealing the secret tunnel entrance behind the confessional. He added that Mulligan had sworn him to secrecy and that he had entrusted him with the secret, which has been kept for nearly three hundred years. He went on to say,

'I hope Père Mulligan understands that for his secret to have any value for us, it was necessary to tell you and other members of our group about it. We must all be very careful not to tell the wrong people about it – I would remind you that there is someone in the village who has already tried to stir up trouble at the chateau. We are lucky that 'Giraffe' was able to alert us about the Gendarmerie's inspection. If that same person got to know about the escape tunnel and told the gendarmes about it, not only would it become worthless but it would be a disaster for both the Père and us. So for everybody's sake I suggest you speak to no one about it apart from our own immediate circle.'

The others were thrilled and excited by what they had been told. They understood very well the dangers of inadvertently mentioning something about it which could be picked up by the wrong person.

'Let's hope it's never necessary to use it,' said Marcel. They all nodded in agreement.

'This calls for a glass of wine all round I think!' said Jacques. They were all happy to go along with his suggestion and drank solemnly to the future.

Nineteen

Chalhac's Mayor Robert Bastien was beginning to feel uneasy about his village and its inhabitants. He took his responsibilities very seriously and it was necessary to stay in touch with local opinions, arguments and events in order to maintain a peaceful community. A small village like Chalhac would occasionally have some issue that required a firm hand. He was capable of resolving matters before they became significant and had to keep his ear to the ground in order to get a measure of what was going on. The village had put him there in the first place because he was trusted by the majority to make wise decisions on matters which might arise. Now however, he felt he was being shut out. The new administration headed by le Maréchal Pétain had initially met with a mixed public response, but a year or so later there were very few people prepared to voice any opinion - publicly at least, about the direction in which the country seemed to be heading. People were becoming increasingly nervous, following reports from across the country of severe punishments being handed out for minor infringements of new laws and regulations. It was in response to this that people were prompted to stay out of the line of fire by saying nothing except in private. Robert Bastien in his official position of Mayor was basically the ground level connection between the village and the prefectural system that France embraced and he was ultimately answerable to the system. In France there had long been an instinctive distrust in government and officialdom – and the Vichy version was no exception. Chalhac's Mayor became the focus for that distrust and he was seen to be the embodiment of government, by the local populace.

At first he could not quite put his finger on where he was going wrong. He went into Jacques Fournier's bar one morning, ostensibly for a beer. It seemed to be a good place to sound out what was going on.

'Good morning Jacques,' he said, 'I could do with a beer if you have some. Will you join me?'

'It's a bit early for me but thanks for the thought.'

'How are you making out these days Jacques?' said Bastien as he settled himself on a chair in the corner by the bar counter.

'Is your trade holding up?' He hoped it would illicit some comment, from one professional to another.

'It could be better but I suppose it is the same wherever you choose to go, isn't it?'

'Probably'. That gambit had achieved nothing. Bastien took a long slow drink from his glass, gazing at some point in the middle of the floor as he did so. He tried another approach:

'How is Madame Fournier dealing with the various shortages these days? It looks to me that it might get worse before it gets better – what do you think?'

'You might be right,' said Jacques. 'We muddle through somehow but it's very difficult sometimes. I managed to get a decent piece of bacon last week but I doubt if that will occur again, so we'll have to eat smaller portions for a while. You are in a better position in that respect. If the worst came to the worst you could always kill one of your cows.' The last comment was delivered half joking and half seriously.

'It would be an act of desperation before I resort to killing off my herd.' It was almost as if Bastien had never given any thought to last resorts of that nature. It pulled him up with a start. Jacques continued,

'I hear the Germans are taking livestock back to Germany from farms in the north. Not just livestock either – animal feed and cereals are all being shipped out. The locals up there are having a thin time of it.' Jacques was now considering Bastien's motives. He rarely came into the bar during the week and not very often at the weekend so he had to conclude that the Mayor wanted to know something. He decided that the best course of action would be to turn the situation around and gently quiz Bastien about his views on the new régime. He continued,

'We can hope the Nazis don't become interested in this part of the country. If they ever did, we can expect to be treated in a similar way. Or perhaps you see the future differently? 'He was on dangerous ground here and not sure that he had been wise to ask outright about the Mayor's attitudes.' Bastien in turn would have preferred not to have to answer direct questions which in themselves had already given a clear indication about his interrogator's position. He could somehow incriminate himself if he were a little careless with his answers.

'Personally I don't believe it could ever come to that.'

'Are you really so sure Monsieur Bastien? Hitler's army has already walked into most of the European countries without even thinking about it. He has most of the Mediterranean coast as well. It would mean taking complete control of all this part of the country. Le Maréchal would be eager to help no doubt.'

'You must understand Jacques that for better or worse, I am still the Mayor here. As such, I am in a rather delicate position because I represent the government, albeit at a low level. Whatever my personal views, I am answerable to the Prefecture. I do my best to keep the village at peace with itself as well, so I am wearing two hats – and that's not always easy.'

It was a startling admission by Bastien that he was caught up in his own dilemma. Fournier was amazed at the Mayor's willingness to speak so openly, and it was something that required careful consideration by his bunch of conspirators. The Mayor had not actually spelled out his opinions of the present administration or of its leaders, so care needed to be taken not to make any incriminating comments to him. Much now rested on whether Robert Bastien acted differently from now on. He must have realised that Jacques would discuss with him the bar's customers hoping perhaps to revive his flagging popularity. On the other hand, he may have had different motives.

'I can see where you are coming from on these matters,' said Jacques, 'and you do have some difficulties to contend with. Perhaps you and I should talk this through one evening. Our village cannot be the only one struggling to make sense of things at the present time.'

'Good idea Jacques – we'll do that. I must be off now, I've plenty to do.'

'Before you go, there is a little matter that came to my ears a few weeks ago. You might be able to throw some light on it: Madame Henrietta Suau who works for le Comte has let it be known that the whole chateau was searched by the gendarmerie after someone sent an anonymous note suggesting some illegal activity was going on.

Henrietta was quite upset about it, but she said le Comte was quite amused to learn the chateau might be thought to be hiding a lot of criminals.'

The Mayor smiled broadly at this. He said, 'My dear Mama was partly responsible for all that. She and her lifelong friend Marie-Louise Dumas have little else to do these days but to observe the passing scene, such as it is. Mama is now confined to her chair downstairs and can see out onto La Place. Madame Dumas usually has a stall on Wednesday, to sell some of her garden produce. When her husband was alive they did quite well with their vegetables. She has had to cut back on quantity these days – she is in her mid-eighties I think – but she is still proud of the quality of her stuff and it is reflected in her prices. Then she discovered le Comte and his family had moved to Switzerland and left Pierre Brun, his groundsman and Henrietta Suau in charge of the chateau. It didn't take Pierre long to realise he could make some money out of the chateau's vegetables since the family were not going to need them. He began to sell some of the stuff at silly prices. It did Marie-Louise no good at all. She and Mama put their heads together and wrote a note addressed to the gendarmerie suggesting there was something illegal going on at the chateau. She did this hoping that once they'd investigated, they would issue some sort of warning to Pierre saying he could be charged with stealing le Comte's onions and carrots.'

So that was it. Henrietta's quick response to Lieutenant Boyer's evasions regarding the source of the trouble-making note, was almost exactly right. Madame Dumas would have hardly believed how close she had innocently come to putting so many people's futures at risk. Jacques had to register mild curiosity about the matter:

'So why were the Gendarmerie searching the entire chateau if all they were investigating was le Comte's vegetable garden?'

'I would think that the gendarmes have been told to keep a look out for any signs of dissent and therefore they are inclined to overreact. Whether they really imagined the chateau was harbouring loads of Spanish, communists or Jewish refugees, is hard to say. They must have been slightly disappointed at finding no one other than le Comte, Henrietta and Pierre Brun!'

'Has Pierre stopped selling vegetables now or is it just the same?'

'Mama seems to think that Madame Dumas has scored a small moral victory. Perhaps Henrietta has had a quiet word in Pierre's ear saying that although le Comte does not mind what happens to his vegetables when he is away, maybe he should show just a little more respect for the chateau's resources.'

'Well Monsieur', Jacques said, 'it has been a pleasure talking to you and I will not delay you longer. We'll get together one evening or whenever is convenient, and have a long discussion about things.'

'We must do that Jacques. Until the next time. Good bye.'

Jacques Fournier could hardly contain himself. It was now close to midday and no one had been into the bar apart from the Mayor. Eventually Jules appeared followed closely by Marcel.

'Before anybody else comes in, I have some intriguing news for you. Robert Bastien came by this morning and he clearly wanted to pump me about the village. He did not say so, but I think he has suddenly become aware that he is being kept out of things. I had to be careful not to say too much but I got the impression that he is beginning to see the light in regard to the new Pétain régime. I think I managed to sow the seeds of doubt when I reminded him that in the north, farmers were having their cattle and animal feed confiscated and that it was all being sent over to Germany. Either he knew what was going on before I reminded him, or he didn't. I told him if they ever got down here they'd probably pinch his cattle as well. All he said was that he was in a difficult position because of his Mayoral duties.' Jacques told Jules and Marcel about the rest of their conversation and finished by reiterating his warnings about talking too openly to people outside of their little group. He was already having his own slight misgivings about some of the things he had said to Bastien, and hoped he hadn't fallen into a deliberate trap. He said there was much to discuss about the day's chat and maybe they should all get together in the evening.

* * * * *

That evening Jacques gave the conspirators an account of the morning's conversation with Bastien. It raised a number of questions about the Mayor and his views on the current political situation. As far as Jacques was concerned the first thing that sprang to mind was whether Monsieur Bastien could really be trusted in the light of his responsibilities as Mayor. What did they think?

There were furrowed brows and lip chewing for a while in Fournier's back room before Marcel broke the silence.

'Is there some way we could lay a small trap for him which would give us a good idea which way he is pointing? It would have to be something we could leave for him which he wouldn't think was specifically meant for him. If he began to suspect there was some sort of plot being hatched, it would wreck the whole thing. He could change whatever direction he was pointing in at the moment, just like that and he might come down in favour of the wrong side. You must remember that as a group we do not exist so far as he is concerned. He has only spoken to Jacques and that would not have proved anything very much for him. Does anyone have any other ideas?' No one did apparently.

'Suppose you fill in Guy about all this – he might be able to come up with some ideas,' said Jacques.

The little gathering stayed for a while and tried to dream up other ideas but more time was needed for them to digest this new information about the Mayor. Over several months now they had all avoided speaking to him and turned the other way when he was headed in their direction, so they were all aware that the Mayor might have been upset by what had now become an established habit by many of the villagers. Some felt a degree of sympathy for him – he had after all been chosen as Mayor nearly twenty years before because he was trusted and popular. It was only since the Vichy government had been established that he had suddenly become an unknown quantity. As such and with no evidence to the contrary, he had to be regarded as a possible supporter of the hated régime. If that were proven to be the case, then he would be exceedingly dangerous to know.

That evening Guy had spent some time talking to David Markovich and Pierre Brun in the salon at the chateau. Henrietta had gone home to the village leaving them in front of a comforting fire in the big fireplace. The evenings were cooler now and the chateau had not been warmed for several months. In the summer, the temperature within was livable, but rarely ever warm. In the depths of winter when the snow arrived, there was an ongoing battle to keep the building anything approaching cosy. Pierre was endlessly cutting up old trees in the grounds and bringing them round to the kitchen entrance when the family was in residence. Now, however, he was bringing the logs directly into the salon and stoking the big fire as necessary. David and Henrietta had made it clear to him that while le Comte was safely out of the way, he should use the chateau as his home and get some comfort from it.

They covered a lot of ground, much of it centred on le Comte and his family who, by any standards, would be regarded as wealthy. He had substantial industrial investments and a certain amount of farm land. The latter was insignificant compared with his holdings in industry, which produced a fairly comfortable standard of living. They owned an apartment in Paris and, until the Demarcation Line became established between the northern occupied and the southern free zones, they made frequent visits to the city where they had several friends. La Comtesse would go to a fashion show, visit her coiffeur, restock her perfume cabinet and buy some more clothes. He would meet his own friends, play some cards, drink some cognac and visit a shady club or two. Life was pretty good. It changed when the German army walked in and the line of Demarcation between the north and the south was set up and was being more and more vigorously policed. Le Comte found that despite generous bribes being on offer, without the correct permits, the doors had been closed. He and la Comtesse finally had become exasperated and had decided to move to Switzerland. A family friend had properties there and it was arranged that they could rent one of them which was a lovely house on the edge of lac Léman. They had long since planned to send their children to Switzerland for their education in any event so it made sense.

Le Comte could maintain his business interests from there and thought it would be possible to travel to and fro into France without much difficulty. Their chateau in Chalhac could be looked after by Madame Suau and Pierre Brun, so it seemed to them that life would be tolerable until the present problems were resolved. They had privately assumed that Hitler would eventually control most of Europe, including France, and had fallen for Pétain's line to support the new French State.

Guy, David and Pierre had covered most of this ground with Henrietta, who had become more knowledgeable about the family, its hopes and aspirations, than practically anyone else alive and it was a constant source of interest. During their ruminations this particular evening, the question arose regarding how le Comte would deal with the situation should Hitler's plans not come to fruition. Would he remain in Switzerland for evermore or come back to France? If it became clear that the Vichy régime was going to collapse, would he change sides and support the resistance? There was an infinite number of questions that even le Comte himself could not possibly answer.

When Guy got back to the village it was dark apart from the light in Jacques' bar. Guy put his face around the door and was greeted by Jacques and Marcel.

'Come in, come in,' said Jacques 'We missed you this evening – you won't know about this morning.' He proceeded to relate everything to Guy that had taken place earlier in the day and all that had been said and discussed in the evening. 'It's just possible we have a new recruit, Monsieur Bastien, but we are looking for a way to test him. If we decided he was safe then he could be a real asset.'

'I agree,' said Guy who followed up by saying that he and David together with Pierre had spent an hour or two discussing le Comte in the comfort of the salon of his chateau. 'Like you we couldn't get very far because much of it depends on the Germans and their moves. It would be a considerable plus for us were le Comte to come on our side, although I don't think that is likely. He is making more money than ever at the moment because the Nazis are buying all the machine tools he can make at his plant in Clermont. He also has money in the chemical industry and that is working at full stretch, so while it is in his interests that the invaders should win, he is hardly likely to want to back us.'

'What should we do about the Mayor, Guy?'

'I think we should speak to the doctor – he might have a few ideas. I'll go up there in the morning.'

The doctor welcomed Guy warmly as usual after the preliminaries and wanted to know what had brought him up to Domvent so early.

Guy rapidly explained, starting with Robert Bastien's visit the previous day.

'So we need some ideas about a way to establish for certain what our Mayor's position is, politically speaking. I need hardly say that we are all wary of asking him outright where he stands regarding Pétain. Jacques Fournier got quite close to doing so but drew back before he incriminated himself. He said to us later that he wondered if Bastien had picked up any clues to where Jacques stood. The pair of them behaved very warily towards each other. We all stand to risk everything if we make the wrong move.'

'What sort of trap did you have in mind?' asked Lovas.

'That's just the problem,' said Guy. 'It has to be something that he would respond to in some way which we could recognise, but which he would not even suspect was a trap.'

'Do you know if he ever had sight of our pamphlet? I imagine most people saw it before it finally fell to pieces.'

'I cannot be sure. It's possible he didn't because it landed in Jacques' bar first of all and he passed it round to people he knew could be trusted, and the Mayor wasn't one of them, so he may have missed it altogether.' I have already suggested to the rest of our group that it's about time we went into print again. I have not done much about it yet, but I feel we need to keep up the pressure if we can. It could be an opportunity to entrap our friend. We would have to be a little devious about it – not just its content but how we made sure he saw it, without his realising it had been planted for him to see. Just how we do that needs some careful thought.'

'And he would need to respond in a way that we could regard as a signal,' said Guy.

'Of course,' said Lovas.

Guy went on to tell the doctor about the discussion he had had with David Markovich and Pierre and that they had drawn the conclusion that le Comte was an unlikely prospect as a supporter of any resistant groupings. It was glaringly obvious that le Comte would choose to back the likely winner if it meant a more generous pay out in the end. Although they thought he was not a particularly political creature he would appear to be a pragmatist.

Twenty

When Guy next called on the doctor about two weeks later Lovas had a draft version of the next pamphlet for his comment. 'Something like this might be appropriate – what do you think?'

Guy carefully went through it. It read:

Are You a Patriot?

If you feel proud to be French do not be fooled, as our leaders in Vichy have been, into being persuaded that collaboration with the Nazis in Paris and Berlin will make for a stronger and happier France. Your fellow countrymen in the occupied north would tell you otherwise. They already know the Nazis are busily stealing our natural resources like coal, iron, basic foods and cattle plus manpower and transporting everything back to Germany. Our industries are now forced to work exclusively for the benefit of the 'Reich.'

The Vichy régime headed by our aging Maréchal Pétain was deluded into believing that if France agreed to Hitler's demands, and when the enlarged Reich had trampled on all other countries in Europe, France would remain a favoured ally to the German victors and rewarded accordingly.

This was never Hitler's plan. His sole and exclusive aim is to use every means possible to increase the size and strength of his Reich. The natural resources of all countries will be plundered and their manpower, skills and talents will be turned into forced labour. This has already been imposed upon prisoners of war in the occupied zone. We know this to be the case because we have trusted informants in Paris and Berlin, plus documentary evidence, to back it.

If you feel you have any influence within your community, pressure must be brought to bear on le Maréchal and his fascist cronies. They must be made to see that the course they are pursuing is terribly mistaken and will only end in disaster for our beloved country. Speak up now to your friends and contacts before it is too late and before all is lost.

* * * * *

'What do you think?' asked the doctor. 'Does this fit your plans for the Mayor? It is intended for general circulation in any event. We now have a sympathetic printer who has promised to produce as many copies as he can with the paper he has. I have no idea how many that might be.'

'It is very good and looks right to me,' said Guy. 'All we have to do now is to devise some way we can make sure he reads it and responds to it.'

'It must be fairly easy to ensure he sees it but more difficult to make sure he responds or even comments. A comment would be helpful in assessing his mindset.'

'I think I will have to simply discuss this with Jacques. His bar would seem to be the best place for this exercise but the Mayor is not usually a regular customer. It all needs consideration.' Guy left shortly afterwards for Chalhac.

He picked up a note from Isabella from their log on the way, opened it and it said, 'Need to talk.' He was not sure whether it was urgent or simply some heartfelt yearning as they had not seen one another for about two weeks. He decided it was the former and guessed she would appear later on her bicycle. Sure enough, her bike was propped up outside the Gaillard house when he arrived.

'Hello Cherie – got your note – everything OK?'

Isabelle put her arms around him and hugged him to her. 'Yes, everything is OK at the moment but I overheard some phone conversations this morning. I couldn't get it all but it sounds as though the bosses in Vichy are trying to tighten up yet again on Jews, freemasons, gypsies and communists. I heard the words "concentration camp construction - put in place – urgency – round-up – Clermont – Domvent" and many more besides. I thought you should know.'

'It sounds like the pressure is on again. Did your father have any more to say to you afterwards – he wouldn't have known you were outside his door listening?'

'No. He stayed in his office for the rest of the day. He must have been chewing over the latest orders I suppose. In the end he said I could go home early and that he would be late. I took the chance to get down here and tell you about it – I must not be too late getting back in case he changes his mind.'

Guy told her about the new leaflet being prepared and that he was going to talk to Jacques this evening about the Mayor. After that they made their fond farewells and she went briefly over to her grandmother's house on La Place, said hello, and left for home. It was already beginning to get dark. She had not been home for fifteen minutes when her father arrived.

'You planned to work late Papa – you changed your mind?' She realised how risky her visit to Chalhac had been. Had she spent more time in Chalhac some awkward questions would have been asked.

'Yes – I'd had enough for today. Vichy seems obsessed with making more demands on us. They don't understand how few of us there are here and how big an area we are expected to cover. Now they want to begin the construction of at least one other concentration camp and could I advise the best place to put it. How do I know?'

Farbres was obviously becoming a little desperate and was tired after several trips to both Toulouse and Clermont.

'Poor Papa. I hadn't realised it was getting the better of you. Perhaps things will quieten down again before long and you can take some leave.'

'It doesn't seem very likely right now, but you never know.'

Guy went directly to his parents' house in Chalhac and spent time with them and Simon Wojakovski, describing the new proposed leaflet. He had seen the proof copy but there was no easy means of making another copy other than a handwritten version. He had managed to make a scribbled edition whilst still at Doctor Lovas' house – it was barely readable but the essential points were there. Later in the afternoon Jules and Marcel arrived home from the quarry. It was becoming too dark to work safely, so they packed up their tools and left. Guy was obliged to repeat much of what had been said about the leaflet and they both agreed it struck the right note. Guy said they should discuss with Jacques the best way to ensure that Mayor Bastien read it, took on board its content and hopefully, made some indication as to whether he approved or disapproved. Sarah said they should eat before going over to Jacques as she had made a casserole of sorts and the suggestion met with general approval.

They all felt better for eating and Jules could easily have taken a quiet nap before going over to the bar, but resisted the temptation.

Jacques warmly welcomed them. 'I expected to see you earlier but I'm glad you are here now. Can I offer you a drink – on the house for a change?' They all settled in their favourite spots while he poured drinks for them.

'Now Guy, I would like to hear how you got on at Domvent today. Has the Doctor made any progress on the matter?'

'He has indeed,' replied Guy, who handed over his scribbled version of the proposed new pamphlet. It took time for Jacques to decipher some of it but at the end he said 'That just about sums up everything we are saying about the situation now, doesn't it?' He was clearly impressed. 'How do we get it printed?'

Guy explained that a printer had agreed to make as many as possible, but exact numbers were impossible to predict. Whatever happened there would be at least one for Mayor Bastien's attention. 'Which brings us to the question of, how we might persuade him into the bar here, without his suspecting some sort of ruse. We don't want him arriving already on his guard.'

Jacques said, 'That is an easy one Guy. He has already agreed with me that we have plenty to discuss and that we should get together sometime soon. I could call on him and invite him into our salon, then casually invite Marie to sit with us, if, indeed there were nothing much happening in the bar.'

'Sounds plausible to me,' said Guy. 'What do you think Marcel and you Papa?' They both nodded their agreement quite vigorously. 'And Simon, my good friend, what's your view?' He replied saying,

'It's OK as far as it goes, but if Bastien has already been got at and he has simply been waiting for an opportunity to blow our group apart, what then? Some of the people in Clermont are very nasty and will not hesitate to use every means possible to crush resistance to the régime. I can say this from bitter experience. The group I belonged to was crushed because there were listening spies waiting for any opportunity to pounce – and they did. I heard later that the fellow they picked up, speaking the coded introduction, was arrested and taken to an interrogation unit in Vichy. Someone we knew survived 'interrogation' but it was anything but funny. Had he yielded, he would have been shot. As it is, he got away with his life, but he will take a long time to recover from the ordeal. It is this sort of thing that we are facing and I'm not sure whether any of you realise how ruthless and brutal they are.'

For a moment or two there was a stunned silence.

Guy spoke first. 'I've known Simon and his parents for a while now and he is not one to exaggerate. Simon's parents have gone missing at the present time and we can only hope they got out of harm's way before they were swept up and taken off. I think Simon should be thanked for bringing a sense of reality back into what we are up against. Thanks Simon. Anyone want to comment?'

Jacques followed up saying, 'It is a timely intervention and thank you Simon for it. It is easy for us, who have been barely affected by what's going on elsewhere, to lay our plans as though the same extremes would not be applied against us. We have said it time and time again, to be careful who you speak to and what you say. The effects of this appear to have made their mark on our Mayor – which is why we are here this evening. You will have to trust that whatever I say to him will not give him reason to pull the plug on us. You must also hope that he will not suspect he has himself walked into some sort of trap. It is a tricky one altogether and much depends on how the conversation goes between us.' He continued by saying that if Marie remained in the salon with them it might make it less of a formal occasion – she could add her observations on shortages from a female point of view.

'Which leaves the problem about how the pamphlet can be introduced without arousing his suspicions.'

Marcel said, 'Could you leave it on a chair you offer him to sit on, and then quickly make a show of removing it before he sits down? He may get a glimpse of it as you take it away.'

'Sounds too chancey. If he didn't react, I couldn't try it again, so then what? You'll have to leave it to me to sort out – I'm sure I'll be able to deal with it.' Jacques had his fingers crossed as he said it.

Guy called on the doctor to give him the go ahead to get the pamphlet printed. Lovas was pleased that no changes had been made and said the printer had already begun to set most of it up, so they could expect it to be delivered within the next day or so. Guy said he would call by a day or so later to collect a few. Lovas had explained that the Domvent group had an organised delivery system in place and that they would ensure Chalhac had some delivered directly to the village. When he got back, Guy told Jacques what had been promised. He suggested that the tête-à-tête with Bastien could be arranged with luck, about four days later. Jacques said he would call on the Mayor and fix a date.

* * * * *

Jacques caught up with Mayor Bastien as he was emerging from his mother's house on La Place.

'Are you free one evening this week Monsieur Bastien? I thought we might have our chat over a drink. The drinks are on me!' he added.

'Yes. Why not? Any evening this week would be right for me.' It was arranged a day or so later.

Bastien appeared at the bar where Marie was presiding.

'Good evening Monsieur Bastien, it's good to see you. I'll call Jacques.' He emerged from their little salon and greeted Bastien with a smile and a handshake.

'Please come through to our salon,' invited Jacques. 'It's not very big but it suits us quite well. He was ushered through, via the bar, where Jacques had placed the most comfortable chair close to the fire. The other chair was littered with some paperwork on top of which lay a strategically placed copy of the pamphlet. 'Please make yourself comfortable,' said his host, indicating the chair by the fire. As Bastien bent to sit down his eyes fell immediately upon the pamphlet.

'I see you have received one of these,' said the Mayor, pointing to it. 'My Mama had one under her door during the night and I read it while I was over there this morning.'

For once Jacques was briefly lost for words. After a sleepless night rehearsing what he hoped would be believable responses to how Bastien would react on spotting the pamphlet on the armchair, it had suddenly become a waste of time. Gathering himself he managed to say 'Really? What do you make of it?'

'Well, despite my supposed neutrality in these matters, 1 have to say that whoever put that together knows what he is talking about.'

'Jacques was stunned. 'Let's have a drink – what can I get you? A beer, a marc or some red wine?' He was desperate for a drink now.

'I'll settle for a beer Jacques if I may. By the way isn't it high time we dropped all this formality, please call me Robert!'

'I'll join you ROBERT! This calls for a small celebration. It seems we are on the same side in this matter. I hope you will understand that I am obliged to speak for some similar thinking friends and they will be interested to learn that you may be in a position to lend us at least your moral support.' He called out to Marie who was still in the bar, serving three customers who just happened to be Jules Gaillard and his two sons, Guy and Marcel. They sat silently listening carefully to the conversation taking place a few metres away from them, in the Fournier salon. Marie had carefully left the door very slightly ajar. 'Two large beers please Marie!'

They sat talking to one another for over two hours, consuming more beer in the process. Finally, Jacques suggested a glass of marc. They covered a lot of ground during the evening, ranging from how Bastien saw his own position as Mayor to whether he thought he could be purged from local affairs if word got out that he was opposed to the Vichy régime. They also touched on his attitude to Jews.

'Well to be honest Jacques, I have had very little occasion to become directly involved with any Jews. When Monsieur Gaillard turned up here with his Jewish wife and their boys it didn't seem to be very significant. Gaillard's cousin had lived here all his life and his only surviving relative was Gaillard. I believe it took some time to track him to Russia, but when they arrived and settled down here, it all seemed quite natural that the family line, such as it was, would continue. They all seem to be respectable and hardworking and have never been a cause for concern. The only other Jewish person I have been aware of in the village is the gentleman who cycled here from

Rouen. I have yet to meet him – I believe he stays with the Gaillards and I'm told he plans to move on eventually. Live and let live is my motto!'

They discussed the Pétain régime and the way it had come about and they were largely in agreement about le Maréchal's mental condition. Eventually Jacques said, 'I think we should discuss all this and more. It is getting late and you and I will need to be up in the morning. Let's stop here and return to these issues another time. It's been very interesting talking to you.' He was desperately tired and needed to get some sleep having lost so much the previous night. Although he did not voice it, Robert Bastien felt much the same, so they were in total agreement and ready to finish. By the time they made it out to the bar the three Gaillards had already silently vanished into the night.

'I'll speak to you again quite soon Robert – it's been very worthwhile I feel.'

'Yes indeed. Good night Jacques!'

* * * * *

In the morning Guy made his way to the bar where Marie was the only one visible. Jacques was trying to catch up on the previous night's lack of sleep when he had been awake doing his best to rehearse possible questions and answers arising from the pamphlet's appearance. As it turned out, he had mercifully been let off the problem by Bastien. The late night that followed, together with more alcohol than he would normally consume in an evening, had knocked him out. Marie however, was wide awake and explained the problem.

'It went well last night,' said Guy. 'We were able to hear nearly everything that was said and I would think Jacques must be very happy with the result.'

'And relieved!' added Marie whose forbearance had been tested to the limits during the last few days by Jacques, who had been struggling with the responsibility placed on him by the pamphlet and its effects on the Mayor. Marie had been on the receiving end of his constant attempts to find a safe formula to deal with the endless ifs and buts.

'He has been quite difficult to live with during this past day or so. There will be plenty to talk about now.'

Jacques suddenly emerged from the salon looking the worse for wear. 'I could do with some coffee Cherie. Good morning Guy! God, I feel terrible right now.'

Guy murmured his sympathies to him, followed by general congratulations on the way it had gone the previous evening. He said 'I've a stiff neck this morning having spent two hours or more straining to hear what was going on. At least I don't have a hangover! Have you managed to give any thought to it all yet? Quite a lot was said and I only hope Monsieur Bastien will remember most of it. When we have all given our opinions on the results so far, I think it would be wise to remind him of what sounded to us like a firm rejection of the current governing set up. We should also remind him not go about the village blabbing openly to everyone about his political views. There must still be some in favour of Pétain and his government and they could stir things up for us and him, if they feel they are becoming outnumbered.'

Jacques had barely been listening to Guy since his arrival downstairs. He had finished the coffee rapidly warmed by Marie and would have dearly liked to go back to bed again, but duty called and he could see some people heading his way across La Place. He visibly straightened his back and turned on what he hoped was a welcoming smile. Guy could see this was not going to be the best time for any further discussion and left him to it. He was anxious to talk about it again with Doctor Lovas, who had been the main author of the pamphlet in the first place and would want to know how it had been received – especially by Chalhac's Mayor. He decided to cycle up to Domvent again to see the doctor. It was now Friday and it would be more difficult on Saturday to talk with him as he usually had more patients to see. Also Saturday was when he had time with Isabelle when she visited her grand-mère and his parents. When he announced he was going to Domvent his mother said, 'Do you think it might be better if you talk to the doctor on Monday after we have all had a chance to discuss it with everybody. They will all want to know about it and David hasn't been in on any of this: nor have Henrietta and Pierre.'

He could see the sense in his mother's suggestion and decided to leave it until after the weekend to see the doctor. Instead, he cycled up to the chateau to give David, Henrietta and Pierre an outline of what had been going on. All three were just a little guarded in their responses but could see that it might be useful to have the Mayor on their side. Their later meeting took place in Jacques' salon. Everyone had seen the pamphlet and awarded it full marks. Several had been delivered to the village and its immediate surrounding area so most people in Chalhac knew there was some sort of resistance organisation nearby and some were becoming more jittery as a result.

'So what do we do now?' asked David.

'I'm going up to talk to the doctor on Monday,' said Guy. 'He will want to know how all this has gone. I want to ask him how many pamphlets were delivered, both here in Chalhac and elsewhere. We need to know because we don't know how far the net has been cast and how much response there might be. We will have to decide among ourselves if Bastien can be really trusted, not to spill the beans about us. When Jacques talked to him, he was very careful not to say how many there were of us or who we were. So he is in the dark as much as we are. He might make a few guesses because he knows that the bar here is a popular meeting point for many people, but if no one has spoken to him over the last few months, then he will not have much idea what everyone has been saying, about him or the situation in general. If he really looks favourably on what was said in the pamphlet I would think he will set about trying to gain people's trust in him again. If he doesn't, perhaps we should think twice before we can look upon him as a friend.'

They all agreed that it would be wise to hold fire until the position looked more certain.

Saturday dawned and Isabelle announced her intention to cycle down to visit her grand-mère and Tantetta. Eric was going into his office in Domvent and would not be back before early afternoon. After a quick breakfast she kissed Anne-Marie and Eric on their cheeks and rode away in the direction of Chalhac. Hortense and Henrietta were both at home and they made a fuss of her.

'Have some coffee Cherie,' said her grand-mère, 'I've just made some.' The coffee was pretty terrible, being a concoction of chicory, dandelion leaves and other unidentifiable plants from nearby fields. There had been no real coffee for weeks and it had become necessary to invent something new and call it coffee. Isabelle was far too polite to tell her grand-mère what she really thought of it, but it was hot, wet and she was thirsty after a fairly rapid ride down to the village. While she drank her 'coffee' Henrietta said that Guy planned to see the doctor on Monday to get his advice.

'I hope he is careful because there is a lot of pressure coming from Vichy. I've seen some of the orders my father is supposed to obey and they all point to a rounding up of Jews, communists and suspected terrorists. Our little unit in Domvent can't possibly do what is being demanded of it and it's getting my Papa down. Not that I'm in favour of any of it of course, but I feel just a little sorry for him. He is looking quite tired at the moment and he told me he intends to go to Clermont on Monday to plead for reinforcements, which means he will be able to make more people unhappier than ever. My dear Papa still believes in the way le Maréchal is behaving and seems to believe that Hitler and his friends will do the right thing by France when they have conquered the rest of Europe, including England. I'd love to be able to persuade him to change his mind, but if I so much as hinted he could be wrong, he would quickly realise that I was thinking the other way and all trust in darling daughter would be lost for good. There's nothing to be done about it.'

'No – I'm afraid you are right,' said Henrietta. 'We'll see what Doctor Lovas has to say about it.'

Isabelle made her farewells and made her way over to La Place, around the corner to the Gaillard house. They were all there with the exception of David who was delivering some repaired clothes to their owners. She was given a warm and affectionate welcome by all and made herself comfortable in the one and only soft chair, usually occupied by Sarah. She was brought up to date with the situation as much as possible and Guy said he planned to call on the doctor on Monday to see what he had to say. There was much to discuss with him and in any case the doctor could not, or would not, act on his own without first talking to the rest of the group in and around Domvent. They all agreed that it was the best course of action for the moment. After some private time with Guy she made her way home.

* * * * *

On Monday morning Guy presented himself at Doctor Lovas' front door. Before he could utter the coded preamble, Lovas said 'Do you have an appointment?' Guy had to gather his wits together for a moment before answering 'No, I'm afraid not.'

Then I suggest you write to me and I will try to get you on my list. Good day young man.' He quietly closed the door on him. Something had happened or was happening when he called. Guy quickly looked around him before cycling away as normally as possible. Once on his bike he felt a little calmer and considered what to do next. Clearly there was something amiss and he suddenly felt very exposed. Had he been observed or watched over the last few weeks? Had anyone seen his meetings with Isabelle or found their 'post box' log? Did they know who he was or where he lived? Worse than that – did they know who Isabelle is? There had been no one hanging about near the doctor's house so far as he could see but that was not to say there were no spying eyes in the house opposite. He decided to take a slightly different route out of the town and up into the hills to throw off any followers. He knew the area very well and that he could get back to Chalhac without following his normal route. He eventually arrived home about two hours later. This was much later than expected and Sarah had become quite concerned about it. He quickly explained what had transpired at the doctor's front door.

'So far as I could see there was no one watching. Whether or not the doctor had someone in his house, asking questions, or maybe just an early patient needing attention I can't say. Either way it was deeply worrying and I realised how easy it is to slip up so I came the long way home. It was about an extra fifteen kilometres but I thought it was worth it if it meant I could shake off anyone trying to follow me.'

Sarah was deeply anxious now despite Guy's attempts to sound calm about it. Inside he was in a state of turmoil and was not sure what to do next.

'I think I'll go over to the bar and talk to Jacques about it. Perhaps he'll have some sensible suggestions.'

Sarah said she wanted him home when Jules and Marcel arrived for their lunch.

Jacques was slightly taken aback when told. Most of them had half expected something like this to happen sooner or later, but this was totally unexpected. They had believed that some sort of warning signs would emerge somehow, which would put them on their toes, but this hadn't happened.

Jacques said, 'It may be that the doctor simply had a patient with him and didn't want you to be seen by anyone in his surgery when it could not be easily explained.' Guy said he had already considered that, but there had been something about the doctor's attitude which had not seemed quite right. Jacques tried to be fairly encouraging but could see the dangers only too well.

'See what your Papa has to say and perhaps we can talk about it later,' suggested Jacques who had been rattled.

Guy followed his advice and told Jules and Marcel all about it while they ate their lunchtime meal. None of them could come up with any comforting answers and Guy said he was going to go back to Domvent to check out the situation so far as possible – even speak to the doctor if it were safe to do so.

'Don't take any chances Cheri,' said Sarah as he set off again.

He took the usual route to Domvent and the post box tree stood upright, indicating there was a message of some sort in the log. He stopped and took a hard look all around to ensure no trap had been set by their enemies and finally went to the hollow log. Inside was a scribbled note from Isabelle:

"Do not do as planned - DANGER lurks – letter explains later."

He needed nothing more for the moment. He turned the bike around and went like the wind back to Chalhac. Sarah greeted him with, 'What's happened?'

He showed her Isabelle's note.

'Whatever has occurred it does not sound like good news. She must be planning to leave another letter – this evening I suppose. I'll have to go up again later.'

Sarah expressed her concerns for Guy who would now have to travel up towards Domvent in the dark. It would be the third time that day he had made the journey – not very onerous, according to Isabelle and Guy, during daylight but could be difficult at night. Guy made light of it to his Mama: 'I know that road like the back of my hand,' he said. Jules and Marcel were home by late afternoon. The light was beginning to fade quite quickly and Jules decided they should shut up the quarry before it got dark. They read Isabelle's note.

Marcel said, 'She wasn't to know what time you were going to call on the doctor so I suppose she thought she would try to warn you as soon as she could about whatever was going on at the doctor's.'

'That's about it Marcel. Do you fancy a cycle ride this evening – I could use some company?'

'Try to stop me!' said his brother. 'I was already ahead of you.'

When they had eaten their evening meal, the brothers got back on their bikes and set off in the dark towards Domvent. The road was very familiar to Guy but less so for Marcel who struck many deep potholes as they went along. Guy did his best to warn him about some but the almost total darkness meant his warnings came a little too late sometimes. Guy realised that they must be approaching their signaling tree and almost went past it. It had been straightened up since Guy had picked up Isabelle's note, when he had bent it to an 'n.' He retrieved her letter which must have been left on her way home. It was simply too dark to read where they were so they turned tail and carefully rode back to the village. Sarah was waiting for them when they arrived and expressed her relief at seeing them looking normal and undamaged.

'How was that road?' she asked.

'What has she got to say?' said Jules.

'We haven't read it yet Papa. The light was too bad.'

'Well get on with it,' said Jules, who was becoming impatient to know the truth of the matter. He was not normally an impatient man, but the events that morning as recounted by Guy had made him aware all over again, how dangerous life was beginning to look. He was understandably anxious and more irritable because of it and he wanted to get some sort of explanation. Isabelle's letter might help he thought.

'I'll read it to you right now,' said Guy. 'She says:'

"Darling Guy, This morning, before I arrived in my office, my Papa had already arranged for four gendarmes to station themselves where they could observe a house in the town here. He had left for Clermont by the time I arrived so I had no opportunity to ask him about it. The Lieutenant was out with them as well so I asked one of the lower ranks what was going on. He said someone had written a letter to the gendarmerie reporting suspicious activity at a doctor's house at 7 rue du Cantal. I knew that you planned to call there today but did not know when. I had no way to warn you other than a note. I hoped I would be able to stop you before you became involved. Let me know what happened please. With fondest love."

There was silence for several moments when Guy finished reading the letter. Finally Marcel said, 'She did her best to save the situation – what else could she do?'

Guy added, 'Let's all stay calm about this. When I called on the doctor he must have known he was being watched. We have no way of telling how he knew, but he did and when I turned up at his door he had already prepared his response to me or anyone else he wanted to protect. His legitimate patients would be safe anyway so it was only the group members who presented any risk. The password introduction worked well, although he made sure I was unable to recite it today. It might mean someone from the gendarmerie was in the house and could have overheard any conversation at the front door. Yes! Of course Isabelle says the young Lieutenant Boyer had gone with the others. I bet he was there listening, when I called.'

'I don't know how long our luck will hold,' said Marcel, 'but if you are right Guy, then it could have been much worse. The Lieutenant is still very inexperienced according to Isabelle and clearly has not learned very much after inspecting the chateau and meeting our own special 'count.' Nor did he add much to his knowledge when he looked at Papa's quarry. Perhaps we should be grateful that he decided to make his presence known to Doctor Lovas, who would be able to run rings around him -assuming of course that it was him in the house when you knocked.'

Guy said there remained a number of questions to be answered. Isabelle would have most of the answers but in the meantime the doctor's house would have to stay off limits. He said that he could not be certain that he was not followed but there would have had to have been a car, a motorbike or someone fit enough to chase him on a bike. He doubted that any of that was the case, so he felt fairly relaxed about the whole thing for the moment.

Jules was less than convinced that they could relax. Until they heard the background to it from Isabelle, always assuming she would know, he felt they should all be very wary. This was the first time any of them had come almost face to face with a really dangerous situation. The moment appeared to have passed but no one knew how it would be reported back to Farbres. They had no idea how the doctor dealt with the matter. Everyone thought it had to be remembered that whatever Lieutenant Boyer had to say in his report, he didn't work in isolation and Farbres may not be happy to leave the subject alone.

'You're absolutely right Papa,' said Guy. 'We must be very wary at the present time because we know too little about any of this. With luck Isabelle will have the answers. It leaves us up in the air at the moment but we will have to wait until Saturday.'

Saturday dawned eventually and the Gaillard family plus Simon, David, Henrietta and Jacques Fournier were all gathered in their house, awaiting Isabelle's arrival. Jacques had left Marie in charge of the bar for once. There was an almost palpable sense of anticipation as they waited for Isabelle who they knew would call on her grandmother before she visited them. She made it her rule to see Hortense and Henrietta first on Saturdays and this one was no different. When she arrived Hortense told her that her Tantetta was over at the Gaillard house and that they were all there waiting for her.

'Can I offer you some coffee Cherie, before you go over there?' asked Hortense.

Isabelle politely declined saying she would prefer some water as she was quite thirsty. She did however accept some soup and a chunk of bread. They talked about her job and her father. Hortense enquired about Farbres Senior and her grandmother. Isabelle said that Eric's father was beginning to show his age. She added that Madame Farbres was a pleasant enough person and that they always made her feel at home when she visited. Hortense, having satisfied herself that her granddaughter was fairly happy in her job and life generally said,

'Well Cherie, I'll let you get over the road to see your other family and friends – they will be waiting for you. Be careful with all this going on at the present time, I realise you are involved in some of it and I worry about you. I hope to see you again next week.' With that, Isabelle made her farewell to Hortense and crossed La Place and went up to the Gaillard house.

She was welcomed as never before. There seemed to be so many people gathered and she was slightly overwhelmed.

'My Goodness! You are all here,' she said. 'Are we having a party?' She seemed genuinely puzzled.

'No Cherie, no party,' said Guy, 'we are all interested and anxious to learn what we can about my aborted visit to Doctor Lovas on Monday. We've been fretting about it ever since.'

'Oh! I see. Well there's not that much to tell really. When I arrived at the gendarmerie my Papa had already left for Clermont. He had arranged a few days ago to go there, so he was expected. He had his boss, Colonel Boudeau on the phone on Friday afternoon, telling him to tighten things up here, as he had received a letter from someone in Domvent saying that they thought the gendarmerie should investigate the Hungarian doctor in rue du Cantal. My father promised Boudeau he would send an appropriate team to look at the situation, headed by Lieutenant Boyer, who he felt was sufficiently experienced in making these sorts of enquiries to ensure we had some proper answers. I was there when Papa gave Boyer his instructions, which to me, seemed a little open ended. He told Boyer to take four gendarmes with him in the lorry. They should position themselves where they could observe the house while he, Boyer, should call on the doctor without warning, and make a thorough verbal investigation of the man; his qualifications, how long he had been a resident in France and so on. My father did not really believe there was much to it and that the letter to Boudeau was from someone who was aggrieved in some way by a foreign doctor – in this instance Lovas, a Hungarian. I saw and typed Boyer's report about it and it sounded as though Boyer came away full of admiration for Doctor Lovas. He said there had only been one unexpected caller while he was there – Guy of course – and the doctor had politely turned him away. The doctor had three other patients with appointments and they were dealt with quite quickly. The four gendarmes in the lorry saw Guy knock on the doctor's door and being turned away. He was on a bicycle and had vanished into the distance before they could give chase. His conclusion was that Doctor Lovas was a highly qualified and respectable professional. In his view there were no grounds for further investigation. My Papa has always taken a dim view of Colonel Boudeau and wished he could escape his clutches, but he has always been in the background. There is undisguised mutual contempt by both men so orders emanating from Boudeau, have never really been accepted gracefully by Papa. This has been a factor in this particular case I am certain. So that's the story!'

'Has your father made any unofficial comment to you about Boyer's conclusions?' asked Marcel.

'All he said to me was that it was just as he had expected.'

There was a mixture of broad smiles and slight frowns as her audience tried to digest this altogether welcome but unexpected twist to an incident that had earlier had all the makings of an imminent disaster.

A lot of breath had been held as Isabelle began her tale and when she finished it was possible to hear multiple exhalations as they began to relax once more and blood pressures began to subside.

Guy said, 'Thank you Isabelle Cherie – we are all grateful to you for giving us a straightforward report on how all this came about. We know what sort of risks you must be taking in various ways and all under the nose of your papa. We can expect similar incidents as time passes and we may not always have you in the background to help us or warn us. We must consider ourselves lucky to have you doing the job you do.'

Everyone started talking together at this point. Then David pointed out that nobody knew for certain what had actually prompted the letter writer to put pen to paper, or why he or she had written directly to the Gendarmerie headquarters in Clermont rather than to the local unit in Domvent. Nor did they know how Colonel Boudeau in Clermont would react when he received a report from Eric Farbres. Would he want to look further into it? There remained a number of unresolved questions which it would be wise not to ignore. Jules said that he had been thinking much the same way as David and that they must not lose sight of the fact that they were dealing with a bunch of very dangerous people, who literally had the power of life and death over them. These situations can quickly get out of hand. If young Boyer had stumbled across and reported any incriminating evidence at the doctor's, and if this had ended up with Lovas being arrested for plotting against the state, there would be no way of saving him from a firing squad. This had a sobering effect on the gathering as they all tried to imagine the scenario placed before them by Jules.

Jacques said, 'Well I must get back to the bar so I might see one or two of you later. Thank you, Jules and Sarah for your kind hospitality and thank you Isabelle for doing a grand job for us – we'll forever be in your debt.' Isabelle half shook and half nodded her head in acknowledgement as he departed.

David said to Guy, 'What do you plan to do now then – sit tight for a week or two and see if Boudeau and his friends in Clermont make any further moves, or try another visit to the doctor?'

Isabelle answered for him. 'No report has gone to Boudeau yet Guy so for the moment it would be fairly safe for you to talk to the doctor. We would like to hear his version of what went on, although Boyer was quite taken with him judging by his report to Papa.'

Guy said that he had drawn the same conclusions about a further visit and had made his mind up after she had given them her version earlier. He was anxious to know what the doctor's conclusions were, so he planned to go to Domvent on Monday morning.

Guy chose to go the long way round to Domvent on Monday as a precautionary measure and although it added fifteen or more kilometres he arrived in the town from a different direction. If there were any sort of watch being made for him on the Chalhac road, he would not have been spotted. It seemed to him from now on both he and Isabelle would be wise to avoid being seen together anywhere, and any way he could lessen the risks to her and anyone else seemed worthwhile. He arrived at the doctor's door having first made a dummy run past number seven to see if there was anything looking like a gendarmerie lorry parked nearby. There was nothing remotely like a transport vehicle to be seen nor anyone visible hanging about within range of the doctor's house. He cycled back again, and knocked on the door. Lovas appeared looking completely normal and relaxed.

'Good morning!' said Guy, followed up with, 'It's a brighter day over the mountains.' Lovas smiled broadly and said, 'Come in.' It was clearly safe. Lovas said, 'I wondered how long it would be before you showed up again.'

Guy recounted everything that had transpired since his previous abortive visit. He also gave him an account of Isabelle's report on how it came about that the gendarmerie had set up their surprise visit to him on Monday.

Lovas listened intently and said, 'I began to wonder if a leak in our set up had occurred, following the latest pamphlet. It must have been seen by more than a few villagers after all. When the young Lieutenant Boyer arrived looking all stern and official I was immediately on my guard. I needn't have worried however because he struck me as completely out of his depth and I could have told him a pack of lies and he would have swallowed everything. As it was I did not tell any lies although there were sins of omission. He seemed a pleasant enough young man, but he has a lot to learn about interrogation! So presumably Farbres will in turn write to his unpleasant superior-Boudeau, in Clermont giving us the all clear?' We will have to be wary of him I feel, because he might want to pursue the matter further as it was he who insisted Farbres look into it.'

Guy said they were all in agreement with his view. He had grasped the essentials very quickly and his thoughts about Boudeau lined up exactly with their own views expressed on Saturday evening. He reminded the doctor that Lieutenant Boyer had also been in charge of the chateau and the quarry inspections. Lovas laughed out loud. 'The Grand Inquisitor!'

Guy then turned his attention to the questions surrounding the Mayor in Chalhac, Monsieur Bastien. He and Lovas had already considered how best to trap Bastien into revealing his political leanings and that the pamphlet seemed to be the best way provided it were possible to ensure that he read it without suspecting he had been set up. When he told Lovas that Bastien's mother had received a copy and that he had spotted the implant in Jacques Fournier's salon, it had been completely accepted as an item to be discussed. He went on to describe how Jacques and Bastien had sat drinking while he and his brother Marcel listened carefully from the other side of the doorway. They had all drawn the conclusion that Bastien was basically on their side regarding the present political set up but that he was caught by his obligations as Mayor.

'Difficult that one', said the doctor, 'I would be careful for the time being. Give him time to think about it – perhaps he'll be a little more forthcoming given time. Does he have any idea about our group?'

'I doubt it, although he may wonder if there is any activity within the area. Jacques became quite close to saying as much but held back at the last moment. I didn't ask you how many pamphlets were printed and sent out in the end?'

'Just over three hundred. A few were put out here in Domvent but they were mostly sent out to the villages. Have you had much comment about them?'

'Very little. But people are still nervous about speaking up.'

Lovas said he thought they had covered it all for the time being and that he expected a patient to arrive shortly so he would have to stop there. He thanked Guy and asked him to express his appreciation to their group in Chalhac for their efforts and particularly to Isabelle. With that, Guy left for Chalhac. He took the normal route and the post box tree was upright! He stopped and removed a note from the log from Isabelle. It read: "I love you!"

225

Twenty-one

They were all relieved to see Guy appear back in the village. Sarah had been worried about him ever since Monday's episode and could not wait for him to return. He quickly outlined his conversation with the doctor and they both thought they were fairly safe for the time being. He then went over to the bar and went over the same ground again.

'That Boudeau man needs to be watched though, doesn't he?' said Jacques. 'He could make life difficult for us all if he really began to dig around.'

'Doctor Lovas said much the same. We must be on our guard over the next few weeks because if he feels he could get one over on Farbres by uncovering something that had been missed, he may very well set up his own investigation. Isabelle has told me about a sort of low level feud between the pair of them which has gone on for years apparently – so he could easily take the opportunity to damage Farbres' reputation. I feel a little sorry for young Boyer. He is obviously not the right man for the job and he would get it in the neck if Boudeau and his henchmen managed to uncover some wrong-doings that he had missed. I'll ask Isabelle to let us have a copy of her papa's report to Boudeau so we can better judge whether he might be tempted to have another go at the doctor or elsewhere. That's as much as we can do for the moment.'

* * * * *

On Monday morning Eric Farbres appeared in Isabelle's office doorway holding a few handwritten sheets of paper. He said, 'I have drafted a report to Colonel Boudeau on our interrogation of the Hungarian doctor in the town here last week. I really don't think there is much to worry about, but Boudeau seemed to think we should act quickly on the matter. As you know I did move quickly and set the thing up in order to keep him quiet. I wouldn't want him stirring up unnecessary trouble for us here. He and I have never really got on together and if he could damage my position, I think he would, given the right opportunity.' Isabelle inwardly smiled. She had voiced her father's thinking little more than three days ago in Chalhac. They were well ahead of him.

'Do you think he would do that Papa?' she asked.

'I doubt it but he is quite a vindictive man and might be tempted. I've been quite positive regarding our findings last Monday, so I hope he can be soothed sufficiently to ensure he doesn't feel it would be a worthwhile exercise.' He left Isabelle to get on with typing his handwritten effort. She had barely started on it when Boyer appeared.

He greeted her with 'Good morning Isabelle! How are things with you this morning?'

Isabelle replied that she was OK and indicated she had to get on with typing her Papa's report to Boudeau in Clermont.

'Of course. Don't let me delay you.' He then lowered his voice, 'I would like an opportunity to speak to you about that operation out of earshot of anyone else here.' He indicated her father's office with a tilt of his head.

'Yes Lieutenant. I'd welcome a cup of coffee. You are very kind.' There seemed to be some skull-duggery going on and she was prepared to go along with it for the moment. Her father was only the other side of a wooden partition wall and could easily have heard any conversation had he listened hard enough. He left her to her typing.

Farbres' report was framed in a semi-official language, which left little room for subtlety. Even if Eric had been able to find the words, it was doubtful whether Boudeau had the sort of mindset that could interpret their deeper meaning. So, it was all said in a version that left no opportunity for further discussion:

Dear Colonel Boudeau, herewith my findings following the raid and interrogation of the Hungarian doctor, Miklos Lovas at number 7, rue du Cantal in Domvent. My second in command, Lieutenant Boyer was in charge of the operation. He is a man of considerable experience in this type of operation and can be trusted to deeply interrogate persons of questionable origins or character to ensure that law and order are maintained. I personally set up a small contingent comprising four men with suitable transport to monitor any suspicious activity in the street outside. Boyer reports the following:

> *Doctor Lovas is a Hungarian gentile.*
> *Born in Hungary in 1890.*
> *He has lived and was educated in France since 1901.*
> *He attained his medical qualifications in Clermont Ferrand.*
> *He is highly intelligent in Lieutenant Boyer's opinion.*
> *He has no political affiliations.*
> *He is trusted and admired by all of his patients.*
> *His financial status gives no cause for concern or suspicion.*
> *There were no signs of any illegal activity or paper evidence to be seen.*
> *Three appointed patients called and were seen by him.*
> *All three had been pre-booked in his diary, which Boyer verified.*
> *There was only one other caller who had no appointment.*
> *Lovas sent him away suggesting he made an appointment.*
> *This last item was confirmed by my men. The caller arrived and left by bicycle.*
> *The caller left nothing at all and collected nothing from the premises.*
> *I discussed the operation at length with Lieutenant Boyer on Tuesday and he was of the opinion that Lovas is a highly qualified and professional person and that there is nothing to give us any concern. Boyer has a keen eye for detail and anything of a suspicious nature would have been questioned. Nothing of the sort came to light.*
>
> *Signed. Eric Farbres. Officer in Command. Gendarmerie Domvent sub unit.*

Isabelle carefully typed the report and made four carbon copies – one each for Eric and Boyer, one for the file and one for the group in Chalhac, which she hid carefully in her bag. She took the top copy and envelope addressed to Boudeau into her papa's room.

'Excellent Isabelle! Thank you for getting that out of the way so quickly. I wonder what our friend in Clermont will have to say?'

'Yes I wonder.' She could have added that she also wondered what her Papa would say if he knew half of what was going on in his family and now possibly in his own office. If Lieutenant Boyer's surreptitious approach to her, an hour or so ago before was anything to go by, he could be embroiled in something more complicated than he could possibly imagine.

'I have to go to Toulouse again tomorrow Isabelle and I will not be back before Thursday. Your Mama knows already. Should Boudeau call, which is possible in the circumstances, let Lieutenant Boyer deal with it. He will keep me in touch.'

Isabelle sympathised with her papa about his having to travel down to Toulouse yet again. However she was secretly pleased to have him out of the way for a few days. It would mean she would have time to find out what Boyer had to say, without fear of discovery.

The next day Isabelle arrived at the gendarmerie earlier than usual. Boyer was already sitting at his desk when she arrived and stood up when she came through the door.

'Good Morning Lieutenant!' she said breezily. 'How about some coffee? I'll make it.' She quickly produced the coffees and sat down behind her desk. Boyer perched on the corner of the desk. 'So what do you want to tell me about that you were evidently not keen for my father to hear?' she asked.

Boyer was uncertain whether to pursue the matter at all and was clearly struggling to make up his mind. His boss's daughter was sitting looking at him expecting him to say something and he still wasn't sure of his ground. 'Well,' he began, 'Your papa has a great deal of confidence in my abilities which I don't really share with him. He seems to think that because I went through Officer Training College and have been given the position I now hold, that I can interrogate and even bully suspects into yielding information that they may not even hold. That Doctor Lovas for instance is a very nice, honest, clean living man. He came from a decent family in Hungary and they settled here when he was just a boy. They put him through university and he eventually got his medical degree. He's obviously well respected here in Domvent. I quickly got the drift of conversations he had had with each of the patients who called while I was there, and while they were respectful, they were friendly and not contrived. However, your father seems to have taken the view that everyone outside of government circles should be regarded as suspect and that they are trying to bring down the régime. I shouldn't say this, but there is much I don't like about the present set up in Vichy and I got the impression that the doctor doesn't exactly approve either. Of course, I deliberately omitted mentioning any of that in my report as you will have now seen. There is a pamphlet doing the rounds in the town at the present time. I've seen it and it is quite persuasive. It gives a lot of very authentic information about what is going on in the north and it is not good. Germany is taking everything back to the fatherland. Prisoners of war are also being sent back there as slave labourers. It can't be right.'

Isabelle was transfixed by this outpouring of truths by Boyer and for a few moments was lost for words. What line should she take? If she offered her thoughts about the way Pétain's régime was functioning and Boyer even hinted to Farbres that his daughter was of the same opinion, he would probably throw a fit. She picked her words,

'These are difficult times Lieutenant and we must be wary of saying the wrong thing to the wrong person. In my grand-mère's village people are terrified to talk to one another for just that reason. No one trusts anyone else any more. This is very sad. We must also guard against injustices occurring and I am sure my Papa has told you enough about Colonel Boudeau's attitudes towards him and that if he could score points over my father by using an innocent third party, in this instance the doctor, he is ruthless enough to do it. We can hope that Boudeau decides against any further action in the doctor's direction. My Papa has said as strongly as he can, that he thinks you did a good job and were unable to uncover any suspect material or views, so we must wait and see how he responds.'

Isabelle could barely wait for the day to end in the gendarmerie. As soon as she could she left the confines of her office and made for the post box tree. She had scribbled a note to Guy at her desk earlier in the afternoon so she wasted no time in stopping for longer than necessary in case anyone came past. No one did and she got back on her bike and pedaled up the hill towards Domvent and out of the other side and on towards her parent's home village. Her mind was full of her conversation with Boyer that morning and she could not let the subject go. Had it been midsummer she would have continued down to Chalhac but the light was already fading and she would have faced the problem of cycling back up on a dry rutted lane in the dark. She would have dearly loved to tell Guy and the rest of them about Boyer's near confession that day. It would have to wait till Saturday.

Saturday duly arrived and Isabelle raced down to the village as quickly as the road would allow. She made for her grandmother's house first of all. Hortense was waiting for her to arrive and seemed excited about something. When Isabelle asked what had happened she said that Simon Wojakovski's parents had made contact with their son and were safe and well at a farm to the east of Clermont.

'Wonderful,' said Isabelle.

'Have some coffee Cherie,' said Hortense. There was no dodging the awful concoction that time. 'And some soup?' Isabelle gratefully declined saying quite truthfully, that she had eaten a good breakfast less than half an hour before. She drank the coffee, which her grand-mère appeared to enjoy but which made Isabelle wince. The usual topics were examined although she avoided any of the recent events and their possible repercussions.

'Where is Tantetta this morning?' asked Isabelle.

'At Gaillard's house with the rest of them.' The way she answered her granddaughter's perfectly normal inquiry contained just a slight edge. It seemed that she felt she was being left out of some of the gatherings and it was beginning to get to her. It was true that the little group of dissidents had no wish to allow an ageing lady relative to become involved in their plotting, but Hortense was unable to understand or to imagine how intricate some of this was becoming and simply felt left out.

Isabelle had picked up her Grand-mère's tone of voice and said, 'Much of their conversation these days can be a bit boring grand-mère. You won't be missing much I promise you.' She left Hortense shortly afterwards having tried to placate her a little more and felt uneasy about it, but there was not much she could do.

She went quickly over to the Gaillard house and found everyone there as her grand-mère had said. 'Tell Isabelle about your parents Simon!' said Guy. This was clearly the main purpose for the assembled gathering that morning. Simon described his anxieties surrounding the subject following round-ups of Jewish families in and around Clermont. His parents had stubbornly refused to leave their house, despite Simon and Guy telling them how dangerous it was to remain where they were. Their minds were suddenly changed when their friends and neighbours, Margot and Saul Kamzepolsky were suddenly arrested in the early hours of the morning, given five minutes to collect a few possessions and bundled into a bus. They had no idea where it went. The Wojakovskis were suddenly faced with a real situation which they previously had preferred not to acknowledge and they were terrified. Simon had reluctantly left them to it weeks before, having pleaded with them to find someone who might be prepared to keep them out of sight.

Their luck held when Simon's mother was stopped in the road near their home by another neighbour who wanted to know if Olga Wojakovski had any more news about the Kamzepolskys' fate. Olga had nothing new to tell her but asked the neighbour if she knew of anyone who might be prepared to hide herself and her husband for a week or two while the heat was on. She replied saying she might just be able to help and two or three days later she called on Olga to say that a distant cousin was prepared to help in any way possible. Within three days Olga and her husband had packed up as much as they could, loaded it onto a small horse-driven van and were transported to a farm twenty kilometres east of Clermont. The elderly owners were kindly and very concerned for people like the Wojakovskis and they wasted no time in saying what their opinion was of the Pétain régime. It was hardly flattering. The accommodation at the farm was quite basic but the Wojakovskis were relaxed and happy to have found somewhere friendly and secure. They had lived for nearly a year in a state of some stress, partly because they worried about Simon and about his future prospects and his well-being. They worried about reports emanating from the north about Jews and others being rounded up and shipped off to the east and now, more recently, their own survival had begun to look precarious. It had quite unexpectedly changed for the better thanks to their hosts Monsieur and Madame Allier.

'So how did they manage to find where you were Simon?' asked Isabelle.

'I gave my Mama the doctor's address in Domvent so when I made it to the doctor's house and met up with Guy again the doctor knew that they might get in touch.

'It sounds like a dangerous thing to have done Simon, passing the doctor's address to your parents. Suppose they had been rounded up, had searched the house and found Doctor Lovas' address written down on a scrap of paper?'

'I took the precaution of making sure they both memorized his address and got them to swear they would not write it down. I trust them completely so if the police search their house they will not find anything that leads to any of us.'

'I hope you are right Simon – everything hangs on that.'

Isabelle's interjection had the effect of lowering the celebratory mood amongst them and it was only lifted when Guy said,

'What did you have to tell us Cherie? Has something new come up?'

Isabelle began by telling them about Eric Farbres' report to Boudeau and his self-evident total trust and belief in Lieutenant Boyer's abilities. She said that Boudeau was only waiting for a suitable opportunity to get one over on Farbres and were Boudeau able to unearth something that Boyer had missed, he could stir up trouble for her papa. Eric's closing remarks in his report were an attempt to dissuade him from going down that route. She followed up by saying, 'I have a copy of his report in my bag if you would like to see it. It makes quite interesting reading in the light of what the doctor told Guy.' She paused for a moment and then continued, 'Now I have some very interesting news to tell you. My Papa had to go down to Toulouse again on Tuesday so there was an opportunity to quiz Boyer about his mysterious approach to me the day before. He was a bit nervous first of all and didn't know how to start, but eventually he plucked up enough courage to give me some of his innermost thoughts.' Isabelle recounted his outpourings to her, starting with his admission that he felt much of Farbres' belief in his abilities was misplaced. He didn't actually say it but he felt he was out of his depth when speaking to Lovas and everything the doctor had said to Guy confirmed it. He said he presumed my Papa thought that, because he had gone through the Officer Training College and had because he had been given the job of second in command to the

Domvent unit, this magically qualified him as a trained interrogator. So far as Boyer is concerned nothing could be further from the truth. He went on to say that he had the impression that my dear Papa considered that everyone not working for the government at some level, was to be considered suspect. Not only that, but Boyer said he was unhappy with some aspects of the Vichy government and that he gained the impression that Lovas felt much the same way. He told me he had seen a pamphlet (our pamphlet) currently circulating in Domvent and was obviously impressed with what it had to say.'

'How did you react to his confession Cherie?' asked Guy.

'I was dumbfounded for a few moments. I had to be careful and not own up to anything that could be used in whatever circumstances so I spoke in very vague terms about these difficult times and that we should all be aware of saying the wrong thing to the wrong person. It might sound a little far-fetched but I think we could fairly easily bring him round to our way of thinking.'

'It's possible,' said Guy.

They all began to talk at the same time after these revelations by Isabelle. Guy raised his voice slightly and said 'We are lucky to have you to do the job you do Cherie. I can't imagine what your papa would do or say if he ever found out what was happening in his own home, let alone in his office. We raise our glasses to you Isabelle, Cherie!'

There was plenty to think about now and Jacques, David and Henrietta made their exits shortly after. The Gaillard family, together with Simon and Isabelle sat for a while pondering how they could best put to use certain elements of the accumulated knowledge they now had of some people's views of the Vichy régime.

They had now learned a great deal about the Mayor's take on things generally, but it was too early to make any guesses about Boyer. He seemed to be facing in the right direction, which was extremely encouraging but it would entail a massive turn-around for him to come over to their side. It was possible to read this as early signs of a groundswell of discontent beyond the confines of Chalhac and Domvent but it was too early to quantify.

On Monday morning in Clermont, Colonel Boudeau had several items awaiting his attention. One such item stood out from the others, partly because the envelope differed in colour from the rest.

He drew it towards him across his desk and saw it carried the gendarmerie crest on the corner. He scoured through the covering letter from Farbres and his report very quickly.

'He need not have bothered going through all that stuff – I have already set in motion a full scale operation to look at the Domvent unit in detail. I feel that Major Farbres needs to be woken up a little! We have received nothing of any substance which might have pointed to the existence of a resistance group or dissident activity since he took charge down there.' He announced this in the general direction of his assistant. 'I cannot believe there that there is not something happening down there that could have been picked up.'

It was a familiar response. His assistant, Lieutenant René Jouve had heard much of this on several occasions when Boudeau had felt the need to demonstrate his authority and policing abilities. The schemes rarely came to fruition and mostly died on the stem. When his boss spoke to his underlings, either face to face or on the phone, he was invariably objectionable. The Lieutenant had been aware of his attitude towards Major Farbres in Domvent for a long time and was always slightly embarrassed whenever he happened to overhear their conversations. He had been secretly impressed with the way Farbres had dealt with his abruptness and general rudeness.

'I suppose it's possible that Major Farbres has a firm enough grip on the situation in and around his area, and that any potential dissident activity is being quietly and quickly stamped on. The resulting peace and quiet down there could simply be the result of an efficient operation already in place,' suggested Jouve, knowing very well that this would probably induce an angry response from his boss. Predictably Boudeau was enraged. 'I would remind you Lieutenant, that I have been in this job for the past fifteen years and I have gained an immense amount of experience over the years. My instincts have rarely failed me when confronted with this type of issue. I will make the necessary decisions on this occasion, as I have in the past and similarly, I will make the correct decisions in the future. I will not have you trying to tell me what to do. You have had very little experience in this direction during the short time you have been here and I do not intend to be damn well advised by the likes of you or anybody else! Is that clear? You may not know it, but we are under a lot of pressure at the moment from the people in

Vichy. They are pushing us all the time for more arrests of various undesirables at present in the country and it is up to us to comply as much as possible. I hope you will realise that these orders are politically inspired and are emerging at greater frequency than ever before. Orders though are orders.'

'I quite understand Sir and I apologise if it sounded as though I were trying to interfere with your decision making. Nothing could be further than the truth. May I ask if you have fixed a suitable date for this operation to start?' he asked.

Boudeau shook his head. 'I don't have a date yet – there are several items which are making demands on our resources at the moment, but I'll give you enough notice when I believe we can make a start.'

'Thank you, Sir!' said Jouve.

It was a familiar story and the young Lieutenant went on with routine work. Lieutenant Jouve did not leave the subject alone however. He remembered that a fellow recruit into the gendarmerie had become the assistant and second in command to none other than Major Farbres in Domvent. He caught sight of his name in the report from Farbres that his boss Roger Boudeau had received the previous morning. What he remembered of Boyer, he quite liked and he wondered whether he could somehow warn Farbres about Boudeau's plans. He had never been told by Boudeau what had transpired several years before, that had caused the on-going feud between the two men and it was not very likely that Boudeau would ever confide in him about the matter. Whatever happened, his boss's antagonism towards Farbres seemed to be a permanent feature of their professional relationship. It seemed to Jouve that whatever the rights or wrongs in the matter, it appeared to be entering a new phase which could destroy, or at the very least, damage Farbres' position in the service. As Michel Boyer was also closely involved, he too could find himself in trouble.

As René Jouve was about the same age and had been on the same training course as Boyer, he felt an instinctive allegiance to him. His sense of fairness outweighed any feelings of duty towards Boudeau. He seriously doubted whether Boudeau had ever possessed any sense of fairness and had simply bullied his way to the top of his profession. It seemed the same process was about to be used against Farbres.

As luck had it, Boudeau told Jouve a day or so later that he had to go to Vichy. The meeting involved heads of departments in the service and he was needed there. He would be away overnight and would be on his way in the morning. It gave the Lieutenant a golden opportunity to contact Boyer to see what he would have to say when he explained what Boyer had in mind. In the morning when he knew that his boss was safely on the train to Vichy, he telephoned Eric Farbres' office. Luckily Farbres was still in Toulouse and Boyer answered the phone.

'Good morning! Would I be right in thinking I am speaking to Lieutenant Boyer?'

'Exactly right. And who are you, may I ask?'

'My name is René Jouve. You and I were on the same officer training course four years ago. I am now, for my sins, assistant to Colonel Boudeau here in Clermont.'

'Really! How very interesting. How can I help you Lieutenant? I am afraid Major Farbres is down in Toulouse at the present time, but I'll try to answer your queries.'

'Well Lieutenant, I want to sound you out about your boss and to warn you that Boudeau is contemplating making a surprise visit on you, with a detachment of several people, to make a thorough investigation into the way your unit is being run. It will almost inevitably involve re-checking some of the searches already performed, including the most recent one on the Hungarian doctor there in Domvent. My boss feels that there should have been more examples of wrong doing appearing over the last year but there has been very little evidence of that being the case. As a matter of interest, do you know what all this ill feeling is about the two of them? He's never told me, but it might end up very messily if my boss does serious damage to yours – and to you as a side effect. I can tell you, he has really got it in for Major Farbres.'

'I've known that for some time and I cannot tell you what it is all about. You and I are on dangerous ground here Jouve and some of us are becoming a bit edgy at the present time and likely to hit out at easy targets. Do you think it's possible that your Colonel Boudeau is in a situation where he feels vulnerable and would like to score some points over our Major Farbres, in order to re-establish his authority? Does that fit with what you know?'

'It fits very well and I am in fact relieved to know that we are thinking along similar lines. Boudeau is not an easy man to work for – something you already know as he is your boss. I have overheard some of the conversations he has had with Major Farbres and I have been impressed with the way Farbres has dealt with his bullying.'

'Do you know for sure that a surprise visit down here is a certainty and if so, do you know when it could take place?'

'Unfortunately I don't. Boudeau could change direction on something like this, as he has done many times before to my certain knowledge. I asked him when he planned to move on it but he dodged the question saying that they were already heavily committed and that manpower was at a premium, so it may not come off at all. On the other hand, if he decides to go ahead it would probably take about a week to set up the operation which would not give anyone much opportunity for warnings. If you agree with what I am saying and would find it helpful to receive notice about an operation of this nature, I would do my best to let you know about it upfront.'

'You are very kind Jouve. You understand that it would be a mistake to mention any of this to either of our superiors or that we have spoken at all.'

'I agree. I will ring off now – we can't be sure where our telephone operators' sympathies lie and an unduly long conversation might attract someone's curiosity. It's been good speaking to you again, and I hope we might meet up sometime.' He rang off.

Isabelle had been listening to this conversation from her usual place outside Farbres' doorway. She could only hear Boyer's half but she managed to get the drift of what was being said and discussed. The name Jouve meant nothing to her so she had to establish who he was from Boyer somehow. The question was solved when Boyer came into her office where she had already returned to her desk.

'I have just had a very interesting call from Lieutenant Jouve in Domvent. He is the assistant to Colonel Boudeau who is away in Vichy at the moment and Jouve decided to call us in his absence.' Boyer filled Isabelle in with the main points of their conversation.

'So, it seems that Boudeau had it in mind to stir up serious trouble for your papa. If he were to uncover any damning evidence here, that our unit had not managed to discover, he could accuse your papa of running a sloppily organised unit. We could all be in trouble were that to happen and I think we should tread very carefully for the moment. Jouve and I were on the same officer training course a few years ago and he remembered my name. This was how he came to ring me. Boudeau must be less than easy to work for directly and he felt justified in calling us as a result of Boudeau's behaviour and his spiteful intentions. So, what do you think of that Isabelle?'

Isabelle could hardly believe her ears and tried to make sense of Boyer's attitude into the bargain. Did it mean that Boyer had finally come round to thinking the same way as her friends? Was he now worried that he himself might be considered to perhaps have been too easy going with the doctor, when he questioned him a few days before? There was much to think about: the letter opening operation, Doctor Lovas, the quarry inspection, the search of the chateau and the 'bogus' Comte and the pamphlet. Every one of these issues presented risks, which had so far been handled as carefully as they could. However, they could become unstuck very badly if Boudeau and his investigating team really pursued matters as it sounded they might.

'I don't know what to say right now Michel. It appears your pal Jouve has a conscience and is unwilling to let Boudeau trample over everybody for his own ends. His scheme to turn everything over here, has little to do with security of the state or dissidence or anything else, but simply points to sheer vindictiveness. One big question looms: what do we say to my Papa or do we stay quiet? If we tell him he will want to know how we have come by this information. He will want to know how I know about it as well since it means you and I have been discussing it – something of which he would strongly disapprove. It is a tricky situation.'

'I think we should stay silent. Until we know if Boudeau really is going to try to take it further, there seems to be no point in upsetting your father's applecart any more than necessary. We will have to hope that we will get enough notice from Jouve. Meanwhile I think we should stay quiet. While I have the chance, I am going to call on Doctor Lovas. I'm sure he would appreciate it if I told him what was being hatched in Clermont. I feel he needs some sort of apology from me as well, for wasting his time last week.'

'I wouldn't think that was called for, but if you feel more comfortable about it there's no harm done,' said Isabelle. She was already thinking that it would give Lovas an early warning to be on his guard and would be hearing it first hand from Boyer.

'I am going round to the doctor's house now Isabelle. I'll leave you in charge for a short while. I hope your papa does not suddenly arrive back early.

'OK Lieutenant but don't spend too much time round there in case Papa appears,' and then Boyer was out of the door.

He knocked a little nervously on the doctor's door. Lovas opened it and was surprised to see Boyer standing there. 'May I come in Doctor?' asked the young Lieutenant.

'Of course,' replied Lovas, who was already wondering what this second visit signified. Was it some sort of cunning ruse to take the suspicious doctor off guard, or simply a social call, which seemed unlikely?' 'Please come in – my first patient this morning will not be here before midday. Can I offer you a coffee?'

Boyer began to relax a little at this warm welcome and stepped inside as bidden. 'A coffee would be welcome. Thank you.'

'So how can I help you Lieutenant? Is there anything we didn't cover last week when you were here – I felt it was a fairly comprehensive grilling you gave me but perhaps your boss feels differently?'

'On the contrary,' said Boyer. 'He felt that I had covered all aspects very well and said so in his report to his superior in Clermont. However, I have it from an impeccable source that our gendarmerie unit here in Domvent will quite possibly be investigated for what is considered to be a sloppily run unit. Only one man – my boss's immediate superior in Clermont, Colonel Boudeau has voiced that opinion. There has been and still is, some sort of private feud going on between my boss, Major Farbres, and Colonel Boudeau and I believe that Boudeau could use an investigation of this nature, as a device to get one over on Farbres. If it does go ahead, and there remain slight doubts being expressed about it actually happening, then it is entirely possible that there could be a re-run of my investigations conducted over the last few months, which includes you. I hope you understand that no one here, in our unit, has any cause to think that you are anything but honest and innocent. I feel this most strongly which is why I am here now to offer some explanation and apologies, for what would be a complete waste of time, for everyone concerned. Colonel Boudeau is a nasty piece of work and would be delighted to turn up something about you or your friends and colleagues, which I am not.'

'You are an honourable man Lieutenant and thank heavens there are still people like you in this country who believe in right and wrong. We are now living in a situation where some of these definitions are becoming a little blurred. Could I ask, did you get sight of a pamphlet doing the rounds in the town at the present time, which gives the low down on what the author thinks about the new régime?

'I have and perhaps I shouldn't say this, but I think it is first rate. Whoever put that together has some good sources of information. It made me think about things more clearly.'

Lovas inwardly smiled. He felt just a small twinge of guilt about fooling Boyer so effectively. He meant it when he had said he regarded him to be an honourable man and only wished he could come straight out with the unvarnished truth about his involvement with the local Resistance group. He would love to have been able to invite him to become a member, but it was much too risky a move at the present time so he stayed silent. The pamphlet had obviously rung bells with him, which only went to confirm that there existed an unknown number of supporters for their cause. 'I wonder how many people there are in our country now who wished they had not been quite so enthusiastic in their support for le Maréchal and his ideas.' He tried to get a bit more from Boyer, but the young man had begun to feel a sense of anxiety, lest he walked into some sort of verbal trap, added to which he was now worrying about Farbres' returning.

'Yes, I wonder. I think I should be getting back Doctor. Major Farbres is expected back sometime today and I don't want him asking me where I have been and what I have been doing. I am glad I have spoken to you and that you are now forewarned.'

'OK' said Lovas, 'Just one more thing. Do you think there would be an opportunity to pass a copy of the pamphlet to your contact in Clermont? They might find it interesting and I think I have a copy here.'

'I'll see what I can do. I must be off now. Should you find yourself speaking to Major Farbres, don't say you have been talking to me – he had no idea I planned to come here today – nor did I until an hour ago.' Au revoir.'

'Bonne chance and thank you Lieutenant!' said Lovas pressing a folded pamphlet into his hand as he shook it.

When Boyer got back to the gendarmerie there was no sign of Farbres so Isabelle had a chance to quiz him about the doctor's reaction to his revelations. 'How did he take it, calmly or what?'

'Calmly I'd say. He showed no signs of agitation at all and was keen to let me know that he thought I was an honourable man. It was almost as if he was at the point of inviting me to join his club or something – if that was where he was heading he must have thought the better of it, because he changed the subject. We had both seen that pamphlet and he fished one out of a drawer and asked if I could get one into Boudeau's office in Clermont. I was careful not to drop Lieutenant Jouve into the mire and simply told him my information had come from a very reliable source. If we do try to spread the word with the pamphlet we will have to take great care that there is nothing that might link our office here with it. Boudeau might jump to the conclusion that we are all members of a resistance organisation of some kind in Domvent. We couldn't chance that.'

'No indeed!' said Isabelle who was almost choking with laughter inside as Boyer now seemed to be openly edging all the time towards membership of a resistance group. It appeared that he hadn't suspected that Isabelle might already be involved in something of the sort. As she was Eric Farbres' daughter, he evidently took it for granted that she blindly followed in his footsteps despite the fact that some of the conversations they had had could have been interpreted as an indication that her sympathies lay other than with her papa.

Farbres arrived back in the late afternoon and was disinclined to want to talk or discuss how his several days spent near Toulouse had gone. He was sick and tired of talking about concentration camps and just wanted to forget all about it for a day or two. 'I'll talk to you tomorrow Lieutenant.'

Twenty-two

Overnight the temperature had dropped considerably and by the morning some flurries of snow could be seen. It did not bode well for the winter to come. In Clermont the HQ offices were cold and the heating system was not fired up. Everybody looked miserable and some still wore their overcoats.

Colonel Boudeau was expected back from Vichy before midday and the prospect only added to the general sense of gloom. Lieutenant Jouve sat at his desk idly playing with a pencil. He did not relish Boudeau's arrival very much as it would only be another opportunity for the Colonel to demonstrate to all within earshot, how essential his presence in Vichy had been. They had all heard some of his monologues before and they were all along the same lines; "So I told them what I thought was the best way forward in the matter and they were forced to agree," etc. etc. It provided him with an ideal platform from which he could vent his self-importance. He appeared shortly before noon and made immediately for his room, giving a cursory nod to Jouve as he passed by his desk. Ten minutes later he opened his door and beckoned to Jouve to come in.

Jouve's first thought was, 'Here we go again – another lecture extolling the Colonel's leadership qualities.' But no, not this time.

'Shut the door Lieutenant. Thank you. I just want to outline what went on in Vichy while I was there, as you probably need to get some idea of the sort of people we are working for. The main meeting was arranged to take place in the Hotel du Parc – Maréchal Pétain's HQ. The whole place was crawling with security police and the military, but there was no sign of him while I was there. What became clear was that there is a great deal of argument taking place between Pétain and Laval. Laval has a lot of political friends - some he has known for years and Pétain has a lot of military friends. Laval has been cultivating a German man called Abetz. He is the German Ambassador in Paris and he seems to like Laval. I think he has made all sorts of promises to him, in the event of England being defeated and France sharing power with Hitler's Germany. If you had been at the meetings yesterday, you would hardly have missed the way things are shaping. One of the first things that Abetz wants is the early introduction of anti-Jewish laws and Laval evidently goes along with the idea. They all know that there is a lot of anti-Semitism in our country, so the Nazis are simply exploiting any points of weakness they can, to make the population feel easier about the German takeover. Laval is obviously intent on getting the top job in France and he is using Abetz and anyone else, to achieve that end. So, they are both trying to exploit one another's position. There were others there yesterday who were not very enchanted with the way things were going. Some of them are supporters of Pétain and will give him their views when he returns. I don't suppose we will ever know.'

Jouve had been listening intently to Boudeau and began to wonder what all this was about. Could Boudeau think his own little empire in Clermont could be threatened if the planned offensive against England was successful and Hitler's view of France changed in some way. Either way Boudeau seemed to have returned in an unexpectedly gloomy mood.

'Were you able to offer your opinion on any of the points raised by the Colonel?'

'Absolutely not. I am not entirely sure why we were invited to attend this meeting in the first place. We were politely told to be quiet and not to make waves. I think we were simply window dressing so that Laval could demonstrate he had the support of the Police. There were several others of my rank there and none of those I managed to speak to were much impressed by what they had witnessed. There was plenty I could have said, but it was clearly little more than a propaganda exercise and I was blocked before I could say a word. I was quite disappointed.'

'I bet you were,' thought Jouve. 'I can understand how you felt about what must have seemed a complete waste of time,' he said. 'On the other hand, it may have given you an insight into some of the machinations taking place behind closed doors. The general public are getting very little hard information about our government's plans after all. I don't know how they can be expected to understand why some of the moves are being made. Le Maréchal makes various speeches which are meant to reassure the

French people that all will be well in the end, but I cannot but feel that he is being manipulated by devious Nazis, including Hitler.'

'You are talking sense Lieutenant,' said Boudeau.

Lieutenant René Jouve had just heard, for the first time since becoming appointed to Boudeau as his assistant and second in command, five words of praise. It was totally unprecedented and he was unprepared for such a change of tune. It was clear that the charade Boudeau had attended, had somehow opened his eyes to the sort of people that France was now deeply involved with and he did not care much for what he had seen. Jouve was not sure whether to try to secure a more permanent change of attitude by Boudeau, or simply to let the ideas now churning in his head, settle and mature. He decided to take the second route and to leave the whole subject alone for the time being.

'Well! I'm sorry you feel you wasted your time up there Sir, but I'm also grateful to you for letting me know how you saw things. Not everyone gets the opportunity to gain an insight into the inner workings of government, whatever its form. We may never know the motives behind your invitation to attend but your conclusions ring true somehow.'

'Thank you Lieutenant. Forgive me for bending your ear. I must get down to some real work now. I don't want to be disturbed for a while.'

Jouve left him to it and went back to his own desk in his little office. It was still very cold and the skies looked heavy with snow. He picked up the phone and asked the operator to connect him to the Domvent HQ. It was an opportunity to speak to Boyer if he could get him without being intercepted by Farbres, or interrupted by Boudeau, who was bent over paperwork at his desk. He could hear the phone ringing at the other end. The light female voice of Isabelle answered: 'Good afternoon. Major Farbres' office. How can I help you?'

'Isabelle! This is René Jouve in Clermont. I can't spend too much time, but I think the heat might be off now – it is certainly off in our office! It's damn cold here. Is Michel about? I need to speak to him briefly.'

'Just a moment René, I'll get him – he is in Papa's office – Papa is out at the moment and Michel is holding the fort.' Boyer picked up the extension phone, which had only been installed the previous evening. He greeted Jouve warmly. Jouve quickly explained that it was his hope that Boudeau would change his mind altogether about the plans discussed earlier, so he thought the heat was off.

'What happened?' asked Michel.

'There's not time to explain right now but I'll write to you.'

'OK. I want to send you some literature which I think might be of interest to you and some of your colleagues. It is important that its origins are not revealed. Do you have your own in-tray? I'd like to catch up with you sometime; we have a lot of common ground to talk about. Thanks for your information. Stay well and out of trouble. Au revoir, my friend.'

'Thanks Michel. I have taken due note and yes, I do have my own in tray, so it's fairly safe. I hope to see you before very long. Au revoir,' and he rang off.

Isabelle had been listening to the conversation on the new extension phone in her office. She had heard all of it, but was left wondering what had occurred that seemed to have changed Boudeau's mind about his project to unearth, if he could, evidence of dissent in the Domvent area. 'What do you think Michel? Unfortunately, he must have been a little too close for René to speak for so long and freely to you. So, we still don't really know do we?'

'No it's maddening. Still it seems like good news but we must be careful not to let anything slip to your papa. I am still carrying the copy of the pamphlet that Doctor Lovas had lying around. I wonder who wrote and printed it? There must have been several made because quite a few people locally have seen it. I hope that René can make good use of it.'

Isabelle had to stop herself from saying too much to Boyer, in case the signals he seemed to be sending out to her could not be substantiated. The pamphlet had made its mark on him without doubt, but it required a bigger jump by him to convince Isabelle of his sincerity when he declared his sympathy with its contents. She stayed silent.

'Let's get this pamphlet in the post to René,' said Boyer. 'It makes me nervous just carrying it around in my pocket and I'll feel better once it is on its way.' Isabelle typed out René Jouve's official title and address onto an envelope with the Gendarmerie crest on the corner, carefully smoothed out the precious pamphlet which had gathered more creases in Boyer's pocket, folded it and slid it into the envelope.

'Done,' said Isabelle. 'I hope Boudeau doesn't look at René's in-tray too often and spot it. It would be just our luck.'

'René sounded fairly confident about it didn't he? In any case it will only be there for moments before it gets put into someone else's tray for general distribution. It wouldn't be easy to track after that.' He paused for a moment or two and finally said, 'I've just been thinking. I wonder if there is an existing group anywhere close by, only I feel quite strongly about the way things are right now and having talked to René makes me think more than ever that something should be done to try to prevent the Germans from stealing everything from us. Our beloved Maréchal can't see the wood for the trees it seems. I can't help feeling that he is being manipulated by the likes of Laval with the blessings of Hitler's gang in Berlin or Paris. Laval should be ashamed of himself – he was born down this way after all. You'd think he'd have more respect and sympathy for country folk across France, but no, he is aiding and abetting our Nazi invaders and encouraging them to take whatever they want back to Germany. Can't Pétain understand what is going on? What do you really think Isabelle?'

She was stunned and tried to conjure a suitable response to Boyer's outpourings. Before she could say anything else, he began again:

'Doctor Lovas is probably in the know about any local protest groups. I might tackle him again. For all I know he might even be in one himself. He wasn't going to tell me when I quizzed him of course, but he did show signs of wavering somehow. It was almost as if he was at the point of inviting me to join his club or something.'

Isabelle was still struggling with these revelatory comments and she had to sidestep them. It may have all been pure invention designed to trap her, her father, and anybody else she knew, into revealing hidden information about illegal activities. If he was working for Colonel Boudeau in Clermont, then the pamphlet would drop René Jouve into the mire, and would probably then be easily traced back to a printer in Domvent. Lovas would be interrogated in

Vichy and everything would fall to pieces. The entire situation began to look like a nightmare again.

She finally found her voice and said, 'If Doctor Lovas were to be in the know about some illegal organisation, do you think he would be likely to invite you to become a member simply because you showed some interest? As soon as it was known you were an officer in the gendarmerie, do you think they would say, "Welcome Lieutenant, we were just discussing plans to blow up the gendarmerie barracks". I very much doubt it Michel. If you were really of a mind to join some sort of group like that, you would have to ask around without letting on you were a gendarme. Even if you got that far, you would have to prove that you were totally against the régime now in place and wanted to do something about it. That's what I think anyway.'

'You are probably right Isabelle. I hadn't thought that far ahead.' He had hardly stopped speaking when Eric Farbres walked back through the door from Toulouse.

'Good morning Isabelle, good morning Lieutenant. My God it's cold out there. Anything been happening?'

'Not a lot,' lied Boyer.

'No, not much to report Papa,' said Isabelle. 'How was your trip to Toulouse this time?'

'Much the same. I am being pushed by Vichy to make preparations for more undesirables, as they call them. This means another concentration camp somewhere. I don't know what's available down there and have spent most of my time speaking to people with land or buildings which could be utilised for that sort of thing. I've tried to get Vichy to give me some idea of numbers they anticipate. No one has the remotest idea. So, I am left with an insolvable problem. I'm heartily sick of it all. I see the phone extension has arrived so that should help.'

Isabelle could hardly wait to get out of the office which was still unheated and she wanted to get home in the warm. It was Friday again and she planned to go down to Chalhac, see Guy and bring the rest of them up to date with events over the last day or two. She would also see her grandmother and Tantetta. It was still only early afternoon but she hadn't much work waiting to be typed or needing urgent attention apart from making sure the post got away which would have in it the leaflet to René Jouve. 'Do you need me anymore today Papa? I'd like to go home early for once.'

'No Cherie, I can't see any reason to hold you here any longer. You run along. You can tell your Mama that I will definitely be home on time this evening. I'm just going to make a few notes about Toulouse, then I am going home myself. I'll leave you in charge Lieutenant.'

Overnight and in the early morning it snowed. The world was suddenly deadened by a thick blanket of dazzling snow. Nothing escaped its shroud and Isabelle looked out of the window and wondered what the chances were of making it down to the village without the obvious problem of keeping on the road and not drifting into a ditch by mistake.

Anne-Marie was watching her as she gazed out of the window.

'You aren't thinking of going down to Chalhac today are you Cherie? The snow will be even thicker down the road and you would find it heavy going trying to cycle through it anyway. Why don't you leave it until tomorrow and see if it looks better? I know you want to see Grand-mère and Tantetta, but I'm sure they would understand if you didn't show up.' She gave Isabelle a quick wink as she said it. Eric was sitting there at the breakfast table and unable to see the wink.

'Maybe you are right Maman, it does look a bit risky. It might even start again before I make it to Chalhac.'

Eric added, 'You are being wise Isabelle. There is no reason why anyone would expect you to turn out in this weather. Put your feet up for a change and look out of the window.'

There was no way she could escape staying where she was and decided to make the best of it. 'How can I help you Maman – is there anything I can do?' Ann-Marie replied, 'No Cherie, I am up to date with my mending and washing so you can sit quietly, with a clear conscience.' It snowed again in the afternoon and evening, and there were snow drifts building up against hedges, trees, walls and fences. By Sunday morning the entire landscape was unrecognisable.

'Just as well you didn't try to visit Chalhac yesterday Isabelle,' said Eric. 'You'd have been stuck down there for heaven knows how long.' The forecast this morning said this might continue for a while yet. It raises a few questions about how we can keep the gendarmerie working properly. I left young Boyer in charge on Thursday evening before I left and hopefully he is there right now keeping some sort of law and order. I don't imagine there will be an upsurge in crime while this is still with us, so I'm not unduly worried.'

'What will you do Papa if this goes on for a long time? You can't send out patrols or anything like that. Perhaps the men could be used to keep some of the main roads running but while it keeps snowing they won't make much headway.'

Farbres agreed. It would present problems but he was fairly philosophical about it. He had to be because very little could be done which could make a difference.

In Clermont the weather was virtually the same and there was a heavy blanket of snow right across the city. The main roads were mostly open but were now covered in rutted ice. The gendarmerie HQ had its heating going now so everyone had made it into the office where it was, in many cases, better to be at work than at home, where fuel shortages made heating a private house an unaffordable luxury. On Monday morning, by some miracle, the post was delivered – a little later than usual but nevertheless delivered. René Jouve was anxious to get his post in case it was intercepted by chance by someone else. He wanted the pamphlet in his hand before it was spotted. He had a small pile of letters, all official looking and the slightly different coloured envelope was quickly identified. He removed the folded pamphlet and placed it in his pocket and tore up the envelope and dumped it in the basket below his desk. Boudeau was not in yet, so he had a little time to decide how best to get the propaganda pamphlet circulated without it being traced back to him. He had considered that putting it into the circulation system would be easiest but when he thought about it, it would not have taken a genius to track it back to him – something he did not need to happen. Boudeau had just arrived and went directly into his office. Jouve made up his mind then. He knocked on Boudeau's office door.

'In!' said Boudeau. 'Good morning Lieutenant. Take a seat.'

'Good morning Sir. Better now the heating is on.'

'Anything happened I should know about? This snow has upset some of our patrols.'

'Yes it has rather but we can get over that fairly quickly provided the snow doesn't go on forever. I found this on the floor in the outside office near my desk. You had better read it.'

Boudeau took it from René's hand, flattened it a little and began to read. 'Do we have any idea where this might have come from?' was his first reaction.

René shook his head and said, 'Not the faintest.'

'Leave it with me will you Jouve? I'd like to take a quiet look at it.'

'Of course, Sir. I'll speak to you later.'

Five minutes later Boudeau asked René Jouve to come back into his office.

'We have both seen some of the so-called newspapers that do the rounds occasionally, but this one is a little different. Whoever wrote it has some excellent contacts in Paris and elsewhere and it strikes me as an authentic account of what we already think is going on at the present time. It confirms in many ways what was being spoken about in Vichy when I was there a few days ago. Sadly, their view was mostly one of self-congratulation and not regret. Perhaps I shouldn't say this but I am largely in agreement with the sentiments being expressed here. I am expected to blindly carry out orders from our fascistic superiors in Vichy, and it takes a lot of swallowing. Have you actually read this pamphlet Lieutenant? You brought it directly to me so you may not have had a chance to see what it says – take a look.'

René said, 'Thank you Sir,' and took it from his hand. He carefully went through it and was impressed with what it contained. It was no surprise that Boudeau reacted the way he did in the light of the Vichy meeting he had attended. The timing could hardly have been better. He finished reading and returned it to the desk.

'Makes you think Sir, doesn't it?' He was being a little wary in his response.

'It does indeed Lieutenant. Have a look round to see if anyone knows anything about it. It came into this office so someone here must know something. I would very much like to know who the author is and speak to him.'

'I'll see what I can do, Sir.' With that he returned to his desk to ponder the situation. Unless Boudeau was playing some sort of complicated game to try and entrap him into owning up to some clandestine involvement beyond the confines of the policing service, it had to mean that his boss had been hugely shaken by what he had seen and heard in Vichy, compounded not a little by the pamphlet. He was seemingly wavering in his long held beliefs in the rightness of what he was doing. René began to seriously wonder if he could even be pushed into reverse and to lend his undeniable experience for the benefit of some dissident organisation. He would have the perfect cover with his rank, long service and wide experience. He would also have access to many of the plans being hatched by Laval and his associates in Vichy and Paris. There was much to consider. René's biggest problem now was deciding who he could safely speak to within easy range. There was Boyer in Domvent but there were risks involved in telephoning him which could prove difficult to explain away for both of them. If Farbres discovered there had been conversations of some sort going on between Boudeau's second in command and Michel Boyer, while he was away in Toulouse not to mention talking to his daughter, a lot of explaining would be necessary. He decided to put the issue to one side for the moment and walked over to the window. It had stopped snowing for the moment, but the partly melted snow had begun to freeze again.

Boudeau came to his office door and beckoned René to join him. 'Come in Lieutenant and close the door. Take a seat.' René did as bidden and was momentarily anxious that he was about to be confronted with accusations against himself. He need not have worried. Boudeau continued: 'Let me make it quite clear what I'm about to say must never go beyond these four walls. You understand?' René nodded his agreement.

'Right. I have been giving some thought to my position here, in the light of what I picked up in Vichy. This pamphlet only serves to confirm my doubts about everything we are being made to do in the name of our aging Maréchal. It is only my opinion, but I think the man is becoming senile and has been making mistaken decisions aided and abetted by Laval and some of his cronies, about what the future role of our country should be. The criminal gangs in Paris and in Berlin have an entirely different agenda. All they want is to drain our country of all its resources and take everything back to Germany. Germany, Germany! Hitler's henchmen applaud all of this. The expectation is that England will eventually be overrun despite the Luftwaffe getting a bloody nose in September and October. Our Pierre Laval still has the ear of le Maréchal and is a prize manipulator. He is also an excellent orator, to which I can testify, having watched him in action. Sadly, he is saying the wrong things. So, with all this on my mind, I am giving very serious thought to joining the opposition with a view to persuading Pétain to change direction.'

René was stunned and unable to say anything that might cause even greater confusion in their minds.

Boudeau could see that René was shocked by his confession or that he should see fit to confide in his young Lieutenant. 'So, I want to get a younger opinion of what must seem like total madness on my part. It's giving you no notice I realise, but it is just possible that you have a different opinion of everything including me, Pétain and his new administration, Laval, the Germans and the pamphlet. Can I ask you if you have any connections with a dissident group?'

René's heart skipped a beat. 'Well Sir, I do have some sort of loose association with someone I got to know on the officer training course four or five years ago. While you were away in Vichy I took the liberty of telephoning him to see if he remembered me. He did and we had a friendly conversation in which he made it pretty clear that he didn't think very highly of the new administration either. He could be a useful ally.'

'That could be a starting point couldn't it? Where is this fellow?'

'Here goes' thought René. 'In Domvent, working under Major Farbres.'

'That will be Lieutenant Boyer no doubt.' It had slowed Boudeau a little while he digested that news. 'And what about Farbres, is he in cahoots with Boyer?'

'I very much doubt it Sir and there has been no discussion between them, although his daughter is very much on Boyer's side. I think Farbres would go mad if he got to know that.'

Boudeau agreed. 'It does raise problems of course. Our on-going feud will have to stop before we could make any approaches.'

'May I be so bold as to ask if you would continue with your earlier plan to investigate the entire Domvent unit?' asked René, who was still carrying about a recent memory of being accused by Boudeau of interference.

'That little scheme was a bit of mischief on my part to score points over Farbres – I'm sure you had realised that. No Lieutenant, that is no longer going to happen. I am quite certain there are better things for me and for you to do, without making their lives a misery for no good reason. I wonder if any of them down there have seen this pamphlet? Perhaps we could post this one to them to get their reaction?'

'Why not?' said René, suppressing a laugh as he said it. 'I'd like to copy the words before we send it off, or we will not remember the way it was written, which we both agree is appropriate for the present time.'

'Do that René,' said Boudeau. He had never addressed Jouve by his first name and that alone was quite a milestone in their relationship. He stood and held his hand out to René and shook his hand. René thanked him and said, 'Let me know Sir, how you get on with Major Farbres. It is high time you both made it up, you'll agree?'

Jouve returned to his room and pondered the new circumstances which had started to change the entire picture. His own relationship with Boudeau had gone from being on the receiving end of his short-tempered comments and general rudeness, to his becoming something more akin to being a friend – and all within the space of the last hour or two. He could hardly believe it. What was becoming clear to him was that Boudeau had been even more deeply shocked by the events at the Vichy meeting than he at first thought. It almost seemed it had turned his mind. He just hoped he was careful when speaking to Farbres.

* * * * *

'Good morning! That will be Lieutenant Boyer no doubt? This is Colonel Boudeau in Clermont.'

'Good morning Sir. How can I help you?'

'I would like to speak to the Major if I may?'

'I'm afraid you have just missed him but he will be back shortly and I'll get him to call you back if that's OK?

'Thank you Lieutenant. Do that.' The phone was put down more gently than was the usual case.

'That was our old friend Boudeau, asking very politely to speak to your papa Isabelle.' He was in her office when the call came in so he had to take it. 'I barely knew who it was at first, he was so polite. I wonder what he wants?'

'Sounds interesting,' said Isabelle.

Five minutes later Farbres returned.

'Colonel Boudeau rang asking to speak to you Sir and I promised to get you to call him.'

'Thank you Boyer,' and Eric went into his office and closed the door.

'I must hear this,' said Boyer to Isabelle. He took the extension phone off the hook very carefully as Eric was asking the operator to get him Boudeau's number. It rang and Boudeau answered almost immediately.

'Boudeau speaking.'

'Good morning Colonel - this is Farbres in Domvent. You wished to speak to me Sir?'

'Yes, thank you Major Farbres. I just wanted a brief chat with you - and very much off the record you understand.'

'That's fine by me – it sounds very mysterious.'

'Good. Now first of all I feel it is high time that you and I stopped behaving like a pair of children and tried to forget all of the bad feeling we, perhaps I should say I, have generated over the last few years. It is in no way helpful in our working relationship and I'm sure you would be happier to know that I now accept that you were exceptionally lucky to have had a father who could pull strings for you. So, I would like to call that a day and try to forget about it. How do you feel about that?'

Eric Farbres was struck dumb by this unexpected reversal in their personal relationship. Their ill feelings towards one another had become a habit over the years and now it seemed, for some good reason or other, that Boudeau wanted to be finished with it. His first thought was: 'What does he want?' When he regained his power of speech he said, 'I think that is a very noble idea Colonel and I'll be only too glad to get back to normality again. Could I ask you what set this going after all this time?'

'Well, you see I was invited to attend a meeting of top Vichy politicians and police in Vichy last week.' Boudeau gave Farbres a résumé of what was said and by whom and how it was delivered. He told Farbres what he felt about it at the time and that a number of fellow police felt much the same way. He also felt sure that he and they were only there to impress the very right-wing attendees with what they hoped would be interpreted by the German Ambassador Abetz and several others, as having the support of the police services. He indicated very clearly that he disagreed with much that was said. There had been no discussion or questions allowed so altogether it was a complete waste of time. Nevertheless, it had been an eye opener as well to the true nature of the present régime, as personified by le Maréchal Pétain and Pierre Laval.

When I returned to my office in Clermont the next day I was handed a pamphlet which only went to confirm what I had been hearing the previous day in Vichy. I have since given a great deal of thought to everything that you and I are expected to do and how to behave in the name of the new government. If you would like to see it I'll send the pamphlet to you by post. You may find it of interest.'

'Why are you telling me all this Colonel? If I may say so, it sounds very much as though you are being persuaded by certain people, to become a dissident supporter which hardly sits comfortably with your professional role. And what do you expect me to say or do?'

There was a pause by Boudeau at this. He was not altogether sure where to go from there. Farbres' reaction had been measured and was neither angry, nor enthusiastic.

'I will send this pamphlet down to you anyway and you may like to consider the content. Perhaps we could speak again soon?' He rang off.

Isabelle and Boyer had heard every word on the extension. They carefully placed the earpiece back on its hook and sat waiting for a signal from Farbres. The door to their office finally opened and Eric said to them both, 'I have just had a very peculiar phone conversation with our friend Boudeau. I'm not sure what it is all about but his attitude towards me seems to have fundamentally changed. He was friendly, polite and quite expansive. He had been to a meeting last week in Vichy and whatever went on there appears to have affected him. It almost sounded as if he was out to recruit me into some sort of dissident organisation. I really do not know what to make of it. He is proposing to send down a pamphlet of some sort which has turned up in their office. He wants me to read it.'

'There are quite a lot of pamphlets going around at the moment Papa,' said Isabelle, 'and they are all telling much the same story, namely that the Germans are emptying our country of everything they can lay their hands on. They are literally plundering coal, iron, copper, food, animals and animal foodstuff. Prisoners are also being taken back to Germany to work as forced labour in their factories and elsewhere. In the occupied zone our fellow countrymen are suffering considerable hardship as a result. Do you think le Maréchal Pétain really understands what is he is doing? I don't mind telling you Papa that I have serious misgivings about the way things are panning out, and I know I'm not alone. There are millions of people now questioning their judgement when they thought Pétain was the perfect choice to protect our country.'

'What do you think about it Boyer?' asked Eric.

'I'm inclined to agree Sir.'

'So, it's beginning to look as though I'm in the minority here,' said Eric. 'I hope you understand where le Maréchal is coming from in the present situation – he has vowed never to allow the wholesale slaughter of Frenchmen again, if he can somehow prevent it. He saw more than enough in the last war in Verdun to convince himself that it was not worth it. We emerged from that conflict having lost millions of young men and women and even now we have not made up the numbers of people lost or injured. He decided that if he were able to keep Hitler and his friends more or less on our side, they would repay France, by making us partners in an enlarged Europe. That, as I understand it, is where our Maréchal is coming from.'

'We all know his motives Papa, but he has not apparently been given the whole truth by his fellow government members. Pierre Laval, who should know better as he comes from our part of the world, has his own agenda in all this. He is busily ingratiating himself with a man called Abetz who is the German ambassador in

Paris. As a result, Hitler is in favour of Laval and is pressurising Pétain to retain him within the Vichy cabinet. I am also given to understand, and unknown to Laval, that the Germans have no intention whatsoever of handing over a share of power to France when the present conflicts are over, but having taken everything worth taking back to Germany, they will simply use France to give access to the Atlantic, the Mediterranean and North Africa.'

'You seem to have a lot of information about all this Isabelle. You and I haven't had this sort of discussion ever before. Perhaps the opportunities haven't been there or I still think of you as my little girl. You clearly have your own circle of friends, none of whom I have any knowledge of. We really must talk together more.'

Alarm bells were ringing for Isabelle. She had perhaps been a little too frank with her father by openly offering her opinions about the current political set up which she assumed were at odds with his. He could hardly get her arrested on the basis of suspected dissent, nor was he very likely to sack her from the job she was doing. He would therefore have a problem. He had discovered that Michel Boyer was sympathetic to her views as well. This would leave him feeling more than a little isolated.

'I will have to give some serious thought to all of this Isabelle and I need a little time to mull over what has been said. What about some coffee Cherie?' He wanted to escape into his office for a while.

* * * * *

There was a pause in the snowfall that night and by the morning a slight thaw was underway. In the town the rutted dirty snow remained soft and was beginning to drain away a little. Isabelle was itching to get down to Chalhac. There was much to say and she had not seen Guy or anyone else for two weeks.

'Do you think I could have the day off tomorrow Papa?' she asked. 'The snow seems to be melting at the moment and the sky is looking lighter than it has for over a week. I would really like to get down to the village to see Grand-mère and Tantetta. They are important to me,' she added, hoping that an appeal to his sense of family unity would help heal any wounds inflicted by their conversation the previous day.

'Well if you feel sure that you can make it safely down and back on your bike, I'll let you go. The road down there will not be as clear as they are up here. I wouldn't think much traffic has attempted it yet, so it will be pretty difficult. But if you must, then OK. If it snows again tonight then you must stay put. A deal?'

'A deal, Papa! You are a dear. Thank you!'

Eric was beginning to wonder if there were other reasons drawing her down to Chalhac than met the eye. Was it just her grandmother and Henrietta who were the magnet, much as she obviously loved them both? She seemed to be extraordinarily devoted to them and even faced with the prospect of a snowy and icy journey on a bicycle, she was evidently undeterred. He resolved to speak to Ann-Marie about it.

Overnight it snowed again and it looked as though it was going to continue for a while. Isabelle had been up, dressed and ready to go but as daylight broke revealing the true extent of the snow, she realised it would be impossible to make it to Chalhac as she had hoped. Then she remembered that Monsieur Bonnet, Chalhac's baker had a telephone. So far as she knew he was the only one in the village who did.

'Papa. I am going over to Domvent as I would like to use the phone from our office to ring Bonnet the baker in Chalhac. I know he will be happy enough to pass on my best wishes to Grand-mère and Tantetta and anyone else who might be anxious for us with all the snow. Do you think the road down to the town is clear enough at the moment?'

'Yes, I think you will be ok to do that. You will have to ask the operator for his number – I had no idea there was a phone in the village. You can check on the post while you're there, although Boyer will no doubt be keeping things in order.'

So Isabelle set out for Domvent on her bicycle. It was snowing quite hard by the time she got there and she was glad to get into the comparative comfort of the gendarmerie office. She stamped on the floor to shake some of the snow off and chunks of it fell on the floor.

'Good morning Michel. Is there any coffee in the offing?'

Boyer quickly made some and brought two mugs through to her room. 'So, what brings you here today Isabelle? I'd have thought you would stay holed up at home instead of trailing down here in this foul weather.'

She explained that she really wanted to go down to the village to visit her aunt Henrietta and Grandmother and one or two friends but the snow would make it too risky, so she intended to ring Bonnet, Chalhac's baker, to pass on her best wishes to everyone. 'Papa asked me to check on the post for anything important.'

Apart from the well-travelled pamphlet addressed to Eric, there was nothing of any real significance. They both laughed at the thought of the pamphlet coming all the way back again when there were enough examples Eric could have seen from around the town, plus at least one in the gendarmerie. Isabelle picked up her phone and asked the operator to connect her to Monsieur Bonnet the baker in Chalhac. She explained she had no number for him. The operator was happy enough to look him up somehow and before she connected her she said to Isabelle, 'The number is Domvent two seven.'

Isabelle spoke to Bonnet who was pleasantly surprised to find himself speaking to her on his phone. It was something that had never happened before. She explained the purpose of her call, in that it was partly to pass on her best wishes to her aunt Henrietta Suau and her grandmother Hortense Hubert. The other reason was to tell Jacques Fournier that things were developing in an unexpected way in Domvent. She would need time to explain eventually but that it was not all bad news. She asked Bonnet if he would be kind enough to pass on these two messages, which would involve braving the snow. Bonnet was pleased enough to agree despite the snow that was piling up outside his shop window as he spoke.

Isabelle stayed on for another hour or two chatting with Boyer. They went over again some of the ground they had covered following the conversation with Farbres and Boyer. She eventually said, 'I am going to get away before it all freezes up again. Frozen slush doesn't make for easy cycling.' Ten minutes later she was back on her bike heading for home.

While she was out Eric took the opportunity to speak to Anne-Marie about their daughter. 'She seems to be inordinately keen to get down to Chalhac at the moment doesn't she? Do you think she has a boyfriend or someone she is anxious to see?'

Anne-Marie was a little taken aback by Eric's unexpected question. Isabelle's love affair with Guy was a matter never mentioned or even hinted at within Eric's hearing. He still saw his daughter as a dutiful little girl, visiting her grandmother and Aunt Henrietta on a regular weekly basis at the weekend. His involvement in his chosen profession took up most of his time and the world beyond barely existed. His marriage had been severely tested sometimes because of it, but had somehow been repaired before real damage had been inflicted. He had taken Isabelle for granted. She had never been the cause for concern and now she worked for him in the gendarmerie, she appeared to be happy in what she was doing.

'Anne-Marie was obliged to dodge the question. She said, 'She's come to know quite a lot of people in Chalhac over the years that she has been visiting her Grand-mère and Henrietta, so she's bound to have become fond of some of them – it would be strange if she hadn't.'

'That is almost certainly true, but it has become a sort of obsession with her now and I can't help feeling there's more to it than that. Who would want to get on a bike and try to cycle through thick snow or slush for about fifteen kilometres and then cycle back again, uphill mostly, in order to see her grandmother and aunt plus an odd friend or two? It doesn't quite ring true to me.'

'Well you know what Isabelle is like; she gives it her all when she gets an idea into her head.' Anne-Marie hoped she hadn't overdone it or made matters more complicated than they need be.

'Well I think our daughter needs watching that she doesn't become involved with the wrong people.'

'And who would they be in your view Eric? Chalhac is hardly a breeding ground for gangsters I'm sure.'

'Maybe not but these days we must all be careful not to say things or do things that might run counter to the new régime. There are severe penalties for serious infringements of new laws now being enacted and I would not want any of us to be accused of something beyond our ability to control or answer. It would be too easy and very difficult to deny.'

'So, are you telling me Eric that you are prepared to go along with the extreme measures being taken by le Maréchal's régime which now seems to be holding hands with the Nazi crowd in Paris? Surely you know what they are doing in the north don't you? Are you going along with all that to simply preserve your job, or what? Tell me Eric, I would like to know.'

Eric was about to reply when Isabelle arrived home from the gendarmerie. She said 'It's damned cold out there again – I'm nearly frozen.' It took her no time at all to sense some sort of argument had been taking place in her absence. 'Everything OK here, or perhaps I shouldn't ask?'

Anne-Marie answered, 'No Cherie, we were discussing things in general – we don't always see things eye to eye,'

'I have the pamphlet they have sent you from Clermont, Papa. It is the same as the one that has been circulated in and around Domvent for the last week. You will find it quite interesting.' She pulled from her jacket pocket a copy of the original but in better condition.

'Thank you, Isabelle, I'll take a look at it later. Everything OK at the unit?'

'Yes. Everything is under control, but it is nearly impossible for any patrols to get out in this snow. The roads outside the town are virtually impassable, so there is not much point. This bad weather will not last forever.'

'You managed to speak to the baker on the phone I take it?'

'I did and he promised to see Grand-mère and Tantetta to tell them all's well.'

'Good.' He said he would make a point of looking at the pamphlet later and if the weather continued to improve a little he might go over to the unit in the morning.

On Friday morning the weather looked more settled and the frozen slush was beginning to melt. Eric decided he would go over to the unit as he felt sure there were things to do over there. He donned his warmest jumpers and outdoor jacket and set out on his motorbike. It was slippery but possible, and he made it with no particular problems.

When he was safely out of the house Anne-Marie told Isabelle about her talk with Eric. She said that Eric's sudden questioning her about Isabelle's determination to get down to Chalhac despite the atrocious weather, had led him to ask whether she thought their daughter had a boyfriend. 'What was I to say Isabelle? It took me off guard and I told you had made a lot of friends over the years. He was concerned lest your friends were the 'wrong people', meaning, I suppose, dissidents. I pushed him about this and was about to get some answers when you arrived home. He has not returned to the matter since, which means he either can't answer or would rather not answer. It will at least give him time to read the pamphlet and take on board some of its statements. Who knows? It might make him think again.'

'We can hope so, Maman.'

By Saturday the weather seemed to be improving. It had not snowed for at least a day and a night and it had begun to thaw. The roads were reduced to a dirty slush but at least it showed no signs of freezing again. The road to Chalhac had seen a few vehicles pass along and it was now useable. Isabelle was keen to get down there to see Guy, Tantetta and her Grand-mère and also to update her roguish friends about events in Clermont and Domvent.

'You are going to go down to the village then Isabelle?' said Anne-Marie. It was more a confirming statement than a question.

Isabelle said she was going to see how it was. If it became too dangerous she might come back. She was dressed in her warmest clothes and finally set out. She quickly discovered that the going was difficult but she was determined not to be beaten. It was almost impossible to identify where the lane finished and the forest edging began. There was a shallow ditch somewhere in between, but it was nowhere to be seen, so she was obliged to stay somewhere as close to the middle as she could and where earlier intrepid drivers had also been. It meant that she was sliding about on packed slush which had not yet had enough time to really melt, since the forest both sides was keeping out any vestiges of sunlight. She finally made it into the village without falling off, despite a number of near misses. On the way down, she had been able to identify their 'message tree' but it remained bent to a 'No' and she did not stop. The village was deserted when she arrived. Only Jacques' bar showed any sign of life and even that was deserted. The single oil lamp inside the door was alight, giving some sort of invitation to the frozen traveller. Outside his door La Place appeared not to have been walked on since the snow started days ago. She put her head around the door and called out to him: 'Jacques!'

Marie came through from the salon, saw Isabelle and could hardly believe her eyes. 'Isabelle! Come in, come in! Have you just got here? I'll get Jacques – he is trying to get warm. Jacques! Guess who's here?' Jacques appeared, looking a little bleary eyed.

When he saw her, standing there in her wintry clothes, looking just a little frozen, he could not think who she was for a moment. 'Isabelle, it's you!' She was ushered through to their little salon behind the bar. 'What would you like? A coffee, a marc? I'm having a marc – very warming! How about you, Marie?'

'I'll have a coffee if you have some,' said Isabelle. She followed up by saying 'Is everybody OK? You are my first call at the moment, so I must not stay very long.' She briefly outlined her journey down on the unthawed icy lane and how she had waited for the first opportunity to get out and down the road.

Jacques said that everyone was feeling the cold and even more so now, as there was no paraffin oil to be had. If you were lucky enough to have some trees or old wood it was possible to stay fairly comfortable but if not, life was a bit miserable. 'I can't remember it being this cold or snowing like this at any time.'

Isabelle said that she was most grateful for the coffee and was glad they were OK, but she was anxious to see her aunt Tantetta and her grandmother. Would they mind if she left them now? No, they didn't mind in the least, so she took her leave and pushed the bike over to Hortense and Henrietta's little house. The door opened and Hortense was shocked to see her granddaughter standing there looking distinctly cold now.

'Cherie! Come in quickly and keep the cold out!' More explanations followed and some of her grandmother's coffee was promised. Isabelle explained she had just finished a coffee at Jacques and Marie Fournier's bar, so she was happy to be able to refuse with a clear conscience. The little house felt quite warm, partly because there was a small fire burning with the old cooking pot slowly simmering away over it, and partly because the house was small. A little house was definitely easier to warm than a large one, so Hortense was a winner for once. Henrietta was at the chateau and was now wondering whether or not to stay there overnight. Pierre had cut a plentiful supply of logs for the fire in the salon and made a massive fire in the big fireplace. Even that had hardly been enough to counteract the cold weather outside. The road was very quiet and almost unused even in the summer. It was the same road that David Markovich had cycled down into Chalhac the first time. Hortense told Isabelle that she wasn't too happy to be by herself for once, but she could understand how Henrietta felt.

Isabelle eventually told her grandmother that she has better go and see the Gaillard family before the weather changed again. Hortense understood perfectly well and asked Isabelle to pass on her best wishes to them all. With that, Isabelle carefully cycled across La Place, around the corner, on to the Domvent road and to Jules and Sarah's house. They were all amazed to see her standing there on their doorstep. She was getting cold again now and shivered a little as she went inside. It may have been the thought of seeing Guy again that made her tremble, but she made for the open fire which had on it the last remnants of the original bits of furniture supplemented by logs that Jules and Marcel had found just beyond the perimeter of the quarry. They had trimmed them and tied them to their bikes and walked home with them. It took them nearly an hour to walk it but it had given them some very handy wood to burn.

'Where's Guy?' was her next question.

'He's up in his bedroom. Go upstairs and surprise him Isabelle. Don't be too long though as we want to hear what's been happening in Domvent,' said Sarah.

She crept up the creaky stairs and quietly pushed open the bedroom door. Guy was asleep on his back with an open book on his chest, pages down. She bent over him and blew gently onto his eyes. He stirred slightly but did not wake up. Stronger measures were required. She kissed him on his partly opened mouth, inserting her tongue between his lips. He woke, trying to focus on her for a moment and then smiled at her very close face. He raised his arms and pulled her down to him.

'Cherie! You really are here aren't you? I thought I was dreaming!'

'Yes, it really is me. Your maman suggested I might like to wake you – she guessed you were asleep when you didn't hear me arrive. It is still damned cold. Is there room for me in there with you? I could do with a warm.' She knew very well what she was saying. She was already taking her boots off as she said it.

'Jump in quickly before you freeze.' She had taken more than her boots off by then and Guy threw back the bedclothes for her. She slid down into the little bed beside him.

'You feel lovely and warm Guy.' They did not say much for the next few minutes. They both knew what the other wanted and it did not require much by the way of polite conversation. Less than half an hour later they both stirred having dozed off after their love making. Isabelle reminded him later that it had been the first time they had made love in a bed. They both quickly dressed and came down into the living room where the rest of the family had been waiting patiently. No one seemed in the least embarrassed by what must have taken place upstairs. It had been understood from the first moment she arrived.

'Have some coffee Isabelle. Have you eaten anything?'

'No Maman Sarah – there hasn't been much time. I had breakfast before I left home but that was over three hours ago. Is there any bread?'

Sarah brought in a bowl of soup, some pieces of bread and coffee. Isabelle devoured the lot. At the end she said, 'I must tell you now about what's been going on in Domvent.' She began with Lieutenant René Jouve's telephone call from Clermont, to Michel Boyer. She had to explain that he had met Michel when they were training together on an officer training course for the Gendarmerie. She explained that Boyer was able to speak to him because her Papa was away in Toulouse. Later Colonel Boudeau, Jouve's unlikeable boss in Clermont, had rung and spoken to Boyer and later to Eric. A copy of Doctor Lovas' pamphlet had been posted to Jouve who had passed it on to Boudeau and he had reacted favourably to what it said. It had rung bells with him because he had been to a meeting of senior people in Vichy and had come back very disenchanted. The pamphlet's appearance was beautifully timed and went to confirm Boudeau's thoughts about the Vichy government, Pétain and his ill-conceived notion to cosy up to Hitler and his henchmen in Paris.

Her Papa now had a copy of the pamphlet which it was hoped would persuade him to change direction, politically at least.

It was a rapid and confusing tale she had to tell and it was obvious that Jules, for one, had difficulty in following the moves that had taken place. She then brought up her Papa's suspicion that she, Isabelle might have a boyfriend or someone she was prepared to go down to Chalhac in the snow to see. 'What a far-fetched idea!' she said with a laugh and a grin at Guy. She said it gave her Mama an opportunity to challenge him about his political position and his job. 'I arrived home just as he was about to tell all. I spoilt the moment unfortunately and at the moment I'm not sure what he will say. The pamphlet might help to swing him, but it is too early to say. There is a great number of questions hanging in the air at the present time and until I am able to get back and into the office there is no way I can draw any firm conclusions about the direction in which it is all going.' She told them that the road down to the village was icy and rutted. It was also difficult to see where the road finished and the forest began because of snow drifts. She would like to stay a lot longer but she was anxious to get started. 'So I am going to get dressed in my warm things and get going.'

Sarah had been drying some of her damp outer clothes almost since she arrived, upon a rack in front of the fire. They still smelt of damp wool, but were much better than when she arrived earlier.

Guy said he would come part of the way with her but it would be stupid to attempt both directions if the conditions were as bad as she described. She said it was a nice thought but she really did not mind if he stayed where he was and let her do it in her own time at her own pace. She was perfectly happy with that.

Reluctantly Guy said, 'Ok. If that's what you would prefer, I'll go with it.'

With many 'Farewells' and kisses she set out once more for home. It was anything but a pleasure. Uphill most of the way, still slippery and fast freezing slush. She was kept warm partly by her memory of being in bed with Guy: something she would always cherish. The light had almost gone by the time she arrived, but the hard work involved cycling uphill nearly all the way, had kept her warm and she was happy to have made it unscathed. Anne-Marie was hugely relieved to see her arrive. She wanted to know how everything went and Isabelle gave her a brief run down on it – the journey down, her Grandmother, Guy and his family and finally the journey home.

'Is Papa back from the Gendarmerie yet?'

'Not yet – anytime now I would think.'

Fifteen minutes later Eric Farbres arrived home looking weary, drawn and pale.

'Are you alright Cherie?' asked Anne-Marie.

'Yes, I'm alright but Grand-père Farbres is seriously ill with pneumonia. I had a phone call from their doctor saying he was fighting for his life and to be prepared for anything. I really want to get over there but the roads are treacherous and it is dark now, so we will have to wait and see.' Until then he had barely acknowledged Isabelle.

'Isabelle Cherie! You made it down to the village then to see your Grand-mère and Aunt Henrietta? How was the road?'

Isabelle gave him the briefest of reports. She had not seen Tantetta who was probably staying at the chateau tonight because of the road situation.

'And you caught up with one or two special friends I hope?'

'Yes I did. It was very cold down there and the snow had barely begun to thaw because most of the way has forest on both sides so the sun hasn't a chance. I am so sorry to hear about poor Grand-père. We can only hope he will pull through. He is such a lovely man.'

Anne-Marie made a robust stew for their dinner and afterwards Isabelle said she would go to bed as she was quite tired. It was Sunday the next day and Eric said he might try to get to church for a change and offer a prayer for his father's recovery. That he had voiced the idea of going to church was a clear indication that he was desperately anxious about his father. In the normal way of things he would never go near a church let alone say a prayer in one. His father had been an important figure throughout Eric's life and the thought that he might no longer be there, was something he had rarely contemplated, if ever.

In the morning the weather had improved. Although it was only December it felt almost like spring. The thaw continued and Eric said he intended to go to his parents' house to see his father and maybe speak to the doctor. The roads were still thickly-covered with slush and were not easy to negotiate, but he arrived safely at their door. It was opened by a stranger to Eric – not the family doctor.

'I'm so sorry Monsieur Farbres. I am afraid you are too late. Your father passed away at four this morning.'

Eric was stunned. 'Dear God. Where is my mother?' He was led through to the salon where his mother was sitting with a long standing family member who was holding her hand. He embraced his mother as she sat there and gently wiped her tear-wetted face with his own handkerchief. He was lost for words and simply sat there with her as she gave the occasional sob. He suddenly became aware that the room felt intensely cold. There was no fire alight and no oil heater.

'I'll light a fire Maman. The house feels terribly cold.'

His mother managed to say that there was nothing to light a fire with and there was no oil for the heater.

'What do you mean Maman – no fuel or oil? She nodded a yes.

'How long have you been without heat?'

'For over a week now. That is how your papa caught a chill and now look what's happened.' Eric considered this for a moment or two and said, 'Is the doctor still here Maman? I want to speak to him.' She responded with a nod of the head indicating he was still upstairs with his father.

He quickly went up to their bedroom. The doctor was there with the stranger, now identified as the funeral director. Old Farbres' body was discretely covered with a sheet over his face. Eric went over and kissed his forehead. He wiped away a tear as he stood up again.

'Thank you Doctor for looking after my father. It was a losing battle though. Can you say how it was he succumbed so quickly? He has always been a pretty tough man and rarely caught a cold.'

'Well of course he was no longer young and less resilient than he may have been in the past. Unfortunately the lack of heat in the house was a major contributory factor. It coincided with all this very cold weather and he could not deal with it.'

Eric had heard enough. He was boiling with anger inside. Lack of fuel!

'Thank you Doctor, it explains quite a lot. I will try to arrange for some fuel to be delivered to warm the place up. In the meantime perhaps her friend who is with her at the moment will be able to get her to a warmer house, always assuming that her house has some fuel.' So it was arranged and Eric was just a little relieved to be able to escape his parents' house and go home. There was much to think about and he needed time. He arrived back home to be greeted by Anne-Marie and Isabelle.

'Have some coffee Cherie. You look drained. I'm afraid the coffee has nearly gone but you can have what there is. We will have to make do with some sort of substitute for a while.' He recovered himself with the aid of the coffee and recounted how things had gone. He also repeated the doctor's conclusion that the lack of heating oil or other fuel was a major contributory factor to his father's demise. 'The house was terribly cold while I was there and I will try to arrange for that to be put right tomorrow.' He was still boiling with anger when he considered the situation. No fuel for heating, no coffee. He had read the pamphlet at the gendarmerie and the events last night and this morning had overshadowed anything it had said. Then he began to recall some of its conclusions.

'I intend to phone Boudeau in Clermont in the morning Isabelle. I feel he and I can find a lot of common ground at the present time. I might even go up there for a meeting with him. I read that pamphlet yesterday and I must say there is much common sense within it that needs discussion.'

Isabelle was thrilled to hear her father's latest and seemingly changing views. Now he was going to call his arch enemy Boudeau on the phone with a view to meeting him. It all seemed too good to be true.

'Excellent, Papa. But remember you and he will be skating on very thin ice here and if you are going to discuss things that I imagine you will, you must take great care to cover your tracks. Michel Boyer will be very interested to hear all about this.'

'Thank you, Isabelle. You certainly seem to be familiar with the current position of people who are, shall we say, just a little dissident in their views. I'll say no more for the moment but I will be pleased to take your advice.'

271

Twenty-three

In the morning the weather was still staying reasonably bearable. Eric marched
in ready to do battle it seemed.

'Good morning Lieutenant – not so bad today out there.'

Boyer made all the right responses he hoped. 'What happened about your father Sir?' he asked.

'Dead,' said Eric. 'And do you know why? Because our wonderful régime is giving away all our precious resources to the damned Nazis in Paris and Berlin. My beloved father died of the cold. That's why he is dead Lieutenant. That's why.' He slammed the door to his office. Isabelle had just arrived and was taking off her outdoor clothes.

'Good morning Michel. It's a better day out there today. How does my father seem to you this morning?'

'In a word: angry. He is angry at the government for killing his father and angry for them giving away everything to the Nazis. He slammed the door and is in there now. Fuming I should imagine, I was very sorry to hear about your Grand-père – you were fond of him weren't you?'

'Thank you Michel. Yes, I liked him a lot. He was a good man. My Mama and I have already been treated to a tirade by Papa at breakfast this morning. He has read the pamphlet and it has stirred things up in him particularly since my lovely Grand-père died from the cold, because they had run out of supplies of oil and coal, which he rightly blames on the régime. I'll go in and talk to him. He is planning to ring Colonel Boudeau this morning with a view to meeting him sometime. I have warned him to be very wary if he goes to Clermont, because the whole city is swarming with spies listening out for signs of dissent. It's almost comic to think that much of that situation is Boudeau's handiwork anyway, so he should know what he is up against.'

Isabelle gave a gentle tap on Eric's door. 'Come in!' said Eric.

'Could you manage another coffee Papa before you get started? The one at breakfast was very weak. It's all gone now.'

'Thank you, Cherie. What do you really think about all this Isabelle? I can tell you behind this closed door that I have been having serious doubts about Pétain and his so-called supporters for a while now. Pierre Laval is not such a big ally and reading between the lines, I think all he wants to be is the top man. Boudeau briefly told me he had been to a meeting in Vichy last week, presided over by Laval. It was all bad news according to Boudeau. The gang in Paris and Berlin want more undesirables rounded up and put into concentration camps in France – particularly in our unoccupied zone and I am going to be pushed by Vichy to build more. I am heartily tired of the whole thing. They are obsessed with rounding up 'undesirables.' Laval spelt it out in Vichy when he said 'I mean Jews, gypsies, freemasons and left-wing trade unionists.' We, the Fèch are being told by another Frenchman to do the Nazis' dirty work for them. I can tell you Isabelle, I am totally sick of the whole bunch of them, especially Laval.'

Isabelle made no comment. Instead she said, 'I'll get that coffee Papa.'

As she went back into her office she rolled her eyes to Michel Boyer, indicating that she had been treated to another rant. 'I'll tell you later,' was all she said.

They could hear Eric Farbres asking to be connected to Gendarmerie HQ in Clermont. Michel carefully took the extension phone off the hook as he held a finger to his lips to not breathe while they listened.

'Colonel Boudeau, please!' said Eric.

'Good morning Colonel. This is Eric Farbres speaking. I would like to speak to you on a matter of some importance, one that we touched on a day or two ago.'

Boudeau responded politely and indicated he remembered the conversation very clearly.

'I would be happy to see you in either Clermont or possibly Domvent,' said Eric. 'It looks as though this snow is beginning to disappear for a while. The main roads are being kept more or less usable and I could see you there but you would be welcome to come here. What do you think?'

Boudeau said he would like to come down to Domvent and they could talk things through. They had both been careful not to voice

273

anything that could be construed as plotting or mysterious. They both knew that telephone operators were able to listen in on conversations and were frequently used as a means of information gathering.

'Excellent!' said Eric. They agreed that Boudeau would arrive mid-morning on Wednesday, subject to weather conditions. 'I look forward to it Colonel.'

Boyer carefully returned the phone earpiece to its cradle as Eric was doing the same.

Eric came into Isabelle's office and told them both that they could expect a visitor on Wednesday – none other than Boudeau. Isabelle and Michel both feigned surprise:

'A bit sudden Papa isn't it? I thought you were planning to see him in Clermont.'

'I decided to give him the option of coming here or my going there. I didn't relish the thought of trailing up there again anyway. If this weather were to worsen I'd rather he had to deal with it than me. I fancy he would welcome the chance to see for himself what we are up to here, in any case. Not that there is anything here to cause him concern, but you know what policemen are like!'

'Is nosey the right word Papa?' suggested Isabelle with a smile.

* * * * *

Boudeau stepped out from a small standard Gendarmerie patrol van. The snow had stayed away for the last few days and some of the main roads were beginning to dry out revealing their surfaces which were a varied mixture of tar macadam and concrete. Isabelle saw them arrive from her window and called out to Eric Farbres 'They are here Papa.' She greeted them at the main doorway and led them through to her office where Lieutenant Boyer was waiting and standing by her desk.

'Good morning Colonel. I am Lieutenant Michel Boyer, second in command to Major Farbres. We have spoken briefly now and then but only on the phone. It is always interesting to match the face to the voice! If you will excuse me Sir, I'll tell the Major you are here.'

Eric joined them and said to Boudeau, 'Good to see you Colonel. I imagine you had a reasonable journey down here. It generally takes about three hours – you left Clermont before eight this morning? You and your driver could use a coffee I expect. Isabelle, would you make some coffee for the Colonel and his man, and I daresay you would like some Lieutenant? Make enough for five. Thank you, Cherie.' By way of explanation he added, 'My daughter.'

'I gathered as much Eric,' said Boudeau. Three more chairs were brought through from the barrack block over the wall and arranged in a rough circle in front of Eric's desk. The driver was politely dismissed and asked to sit in the van for a while and to take his coffee with him.

'Where do we start?' said Eric, who was curious to hear more detailed evidence which might go to explain Boudeau's change of attitude, manner and general outlook. Boudeau began by describing the meeting he had been invited to attend in Vichy.

'It was quite a revelation to see some of the main characters speak openly about what was driving them in the direction they were following. It was a pity that le Maréchal was not there because he would have seen what was being perpetrated in his name. It had clearly been arranged beforehand that he would be unable to attend. If he had been there he would have had a great deal to say about it all. He would also have been able to more clearly identify who were his real supporters. He does have some real supporters, but pursuing the idea of keeping Hitler sweet is totally misguided.'

Eric spoke up, 'What makes you think it is misguided Colonel?'

'We have some very reliable informers in Paris, in Vichy and Berlin. They have access to many communications between Nazis which have clearly stated that they have no intention to stop the transfer of raw materials, foodstuffs, machinery and livestock out of France and into the 'Fatherland.' At this very moment there are trainloads of coal, iron, copper, oil, petrol, machine tools and food going eastwards. Their intention is to reduce France to the role of becoming little more than the means to provide seaports on the Channel, the west coast and the Mediterranean. At the Vichy meeting I attended last week Laval, Darlan and other notables in our new régime were openly congratulating themselves on how

275

successfully the operation was proceeding. The German Ambassador in Paris, a man called Otto Abetz, was also present in Vichy. Laval has been cultivating him for the past several weeks and months as a means to gaining access to Ribbentrop and hence to Hitler. As Abetz has the ear of Ribbentrop and Hitler, it is Laval's intention to meet with Hitler to discuss further moves as they affect France. Laval believes his ideas to protect France's relationship with an enlarged and victorious Germany are central to Abetz's plans assuming the defeat of the British. He thinks that Abetz is on his side in all of this but we know that he is playing a double game with Laval because we have had access to a circulated note from Abetz sent by him to all departments in the German Embassy in Paris. He clearly stated that, "Everything possible must be done to weaken France and to reduce it to becoming no more than a mere satellite of an enlarged Reich." Laval has no idea that this is the real intention of Abetz, his carefully cultivated 'friend' and of his bosses in Paris and Berlin and he still imagines he will gain some exalted position in a new Nazi dominated Europe.

Meanwhile our fellow countrymen in the occupied north are already suffering from lack of food and heating materials like oil and coal. This is now becoming a serious issue here in the unoccupied south. Food is not yet a major problem but oil and coal supplies are beginning to be difficult and there are many more problems arising from the invasion of our country. The demarcation line is only one such issue. It seems that it is now virtually impossible to get a permit allowing travel between the two zones. We are told that one of the very few people getting permits is none other than Laval. When we were invaded, the German soldiers were instructed to behave impeccably, and they did as they were told. It is a different story now because there are brutal punishments being meted out for quite minor offences including making attempts to cross the line without an "Ausweis" permit. People have been shot as a result. This, my friend, is all part of the new reality of the German takeover.' He continued:

'There are, of course, a number of Resistance groups in the north who find themselves blamed as being the root cause of some of the brutality. Sadly, our Maréchal seems to be unaware of much of this and is being sidelined by some of the people he trusts.'

Boudeau sat back for a moment or two to give those present a little time to digest this information. The only sound came from a coffee cup being returned to its saucer.

Eric Farbres turned away from them and gazed out of the window, gently scratching the side of his nose as he did so. After what seemed to be a long time he slowly turned back again to face the conspirators.

'It seems to me that I must have been totally out of step with an awful lot of people. Your evidence, Colonel, tells me a very convincing story which it would be extremely difficult to repudiate. It also chimes in with my situation at home, namely that my own father, Isabelle's grandfather, died at the weekend. His doctor put the primary cause of death to be lack of heat in their house. They were unable to locate any coal or heating oil and he simply could not deal with it. Why was there no fuel? The answer is very clear to me now: it was on its way to Germany, sealed with a loving kiss from Laval. My only reservation about all of this lies in the fact that our Maréchal has chosen the course he set out upon, because he was, and still is, convinced that without the Armistice, the conflict would continue and France would lose more men than ever. He did it for our benefit. Now of course, we are seeing the whole of his strategy being manipulated by the likes of Laval, Darlan and others hoping that they will be favoured by the Nazis and they will inherit plum jobs in a redesigned French state. We appear to be in the privileged position that most of them are not. We know how the Nazis intend to play it. They know the age of our Maréchal and that time is not on his side. They also still believe they will defeat the British, despite the Luftwaffe taking a hammering in August and September. Their planned invasion of England is now temporarily on the back burner and their Führer is looking at Russia, as the next possible target instead.

We are seeing our country being emptied of all its precious resources and watching some of our fellow countrymen cheering them on as they do it. It is all terribly wrong and a mistaken path the administration is following.'

Boudeau asked, 'Are we to take it Farbres, which you have come around to agreeing with us on the main issues here? If you have, we can begin to examine how we can best advance countermeasures which might be recognized by le Maréchal, as a better way forward. He remains a respected figure by many although that respect is beginning to wear a little thin now. He would perhaps be comforted if he were to be encouraged to change direction and regain the support lost over the last few months. It would demand some courage on his part and he would find that some of his avowed supporters in his government would abandon him, but the man is a determined creature and if he made his mind up to change direction, I believe he would. He is a pretty shrewd assessor of people and right now he probably has a list of people he would like to get rid of.'

'Could I just say a word?' said Isabelle who had been watching and listening to everything as it emerged from both Boudeau and her father. It was almost like a dream she was having and she hoped she wouldn't suddenly wake up. 'I simply want to remind you again that we are playing an extremely dangerous game here. If any hint of this came out, it would mean curtains for all of us, and not only us. I have several friends who are playing the same game and they are well aware that the stakes are high. Some of your less appetizing associates Colonel, in Clermont and Vichy, think nothing of using torture to make prisoners or suspects tell all. The Hotel Algeria in Vichy is well known for much of this violence. As head of the Commissariat Général aux Questions Juives, Xavier Vallet presides over this horrible organisation and he evidently enjoys doing the job he does. He is well known for his anti-semitic stance and is now empowered to bully and eliminate Jews for no other reason than that they are simply Jews. It is another sad reflection on the way le Maréchal allowed such an organisation to be established in the first place.' There was nodded agreement with her comment.

'Major Farbres. I did not get a response to my question,' said Boudeau. 'I asked if we can take if from some of your answers that you are in agreement with us on the main points of issue. If you do agree we can move forward a little to deciding how we might best persuade le Maréchal to change direction for the better. If you have serious doubts about any of it or about what you have now learned about our little gathering here today, it means that Lieutenant Boyer, your daughter and me, plus many others are in real jeopardy. A word in the ear of the security people in Clermont would be enough to bring down the full weight of the newly drafted legislation onto our backs. I need hardly remind you that it would also mean that your own viability could then be at risk if reprisals were taken.'

'Of course,' said Eric. 'I recognize that, and you can take it that I am prepared to go with you all the way. Isabelle will be somewhat relieved to know that her papa is now firmly on her side. What about you Lieutenant? You have not had much to say today. How do you feel now that our innermost thoughts have been so comprehensively aired? It is important that we know where you stand on all this. Your career in the police service may very well become one of the shortest on record were you to be identified as an undercover agent of some dissident organisation. Not only would your career be terminated but your life would probably be terminated into the bargain. You must be sure in your own mind that in becoming mixed up in an enterprise such as this that you will face some very real life threatening risks. So what do you think?'

'Well Sir, I would like to live in a France that is a free democracy, governed by decent people and not remotely resembling the set-up we are stuck with now. I don't believe that Hitler and his thuggish gang will succeed in the end. To my way of thinking Hitler is a maniac, driven by ambition and twisted notions borrowed from legends. He has attracted a very unsavoury bunch of bullies and I don't wish to be ruled by them under any circumstances. I am happy to join whatever means become necessary to prevent that occurring. Count me in.'

Isabelle was transfixed by what happened that morning. She was still trying to take on board her papa's conversion from being an out and out supporter of Pétain's new French state to something very different, and it was proving almost impossible to believe. Finally, she stood and made her way round the back of Farbres' chair where she put her arms around him as he sat, kissed the top of his head and said,

'I love you Papa. I love you now more than ever.'

Eric turned his head and beamed at her. 'Thank you, Cherie.'

Boudeau said, 'We are all very proud to have you on our side Major Farbres. We all recognise how difficult a decision of this importance can be. I think I can say that we have all wrestled with our consciences at some time over this matter but having now arrived at the decision we have, it will give us all greater impetus to succeed. I would like to add my personal thanks to you Major.'

Before the meeting finally broke up, it was agreed that they would all continue to do their jobs as before and not change their behaviour in any significant way that might give cause for suspicion. Boudeau reminded them that he would need to tell Jouve about today's events, adding that Jouve would be certain to agreeing to join in. Likewise Isabelle said she had to tell a number of people about the day's decisions and to get their views in return.

It stayed cold for several days, but there was no more serious snow. Isabelle was able to get to Chalhac on Saturday morning as the road to the village had seen enough traffic to flatten the earlier snow and although it was not clear it was at least usable. La Place in Chalhac still had an even covering and had hardly been disturbed since the heavy falls of the week before. She called first on her grandmother. She was delighted to see her granddaughter. Henrietta was also at home and greeted Isabelle warmly with a big hug. They both wanted to hear the news from Domvent and were saddened to hear that Eric's father had died. Isabelle told them that her father was very angry indeed to learn from the doctor that he had died because they had run out of heating fuels, namely coal and oil. It had produced an unexpected turnaround for her papa and he was now contemplating joining a resistance group somewhere. She did not want to go into a lot of detail about the Wednesday meeting until she could explain it fully with the rest of the Chalhac resistance and out of earshot of her grandmother. Before she left she made sure that the little house had enough fuel to keep it warm and that Hortense had enough food and supplies to keep her going. After a cup of her grandmother's dreadful 'coffee' and a bowl of soup, she departed for the Gaillard house.

They were all there including Guy, David Markovich and Jacques Fournier.

'Tell us what you have been doing - anything exciting been happening?' asked Guy after he had given her a specially reserved embrace that no one else received.

Isabelle hardly knew where to begin. She said their pamphlet had been seen by Colonel Boudeau in Clermont. He had declared total agreement with it having the previous day witnessed the appalling spectacle of some of Pétain's supposed supporters including Laval, congratulating themselves about how well the movement of materials to Germany was going. She explained his anger and total change of attitude and the telephone calls leading finally to Boudeau's visit to Domvent on Wednesday. She also told them about Eric's father's death last weekend and the family doctor's conclusion that it was the result of trying to survive in a very cold house because they had run out of heating oil and coal.

Her Papa had also read 'the pamphlet' and was nearly white with anger when he saw the Vichy régime was aiding and abetting the German occupiers by sending massive consignments of coal to Germany. Not just coal of course but Eric's anger was focused on coal and fuel which was going to Germany instead of onto his dear father's fire. She then continued with her account of Wednesday's meeting in Domvent, culminating with her father's declaration to join their attempt to force Pétain to change direction from the present course he seemed determined to follow. She ended by saying that if their group or the doctor's associates will have them, they would have four new recruits to their little band. 'They could be an extremely valuable addition because they would be the last people to be suspected of any wrong doing and Boudeau in particular, has some very useful contacts in Vichy and in Paris. All four would have my vote.'

A long discussion followed. Everyone was amazed to learn how quickly Isabelle's father had changed his attitude about Pétain's solution to the takeover by the German army. Isabelle said there was no single reason for his conversion. She said that he was becoming weary of endless orders from Vichy demanding the construction of more concentration camps to house 'undesirables.' He had spent days and weeks attempting to find likely suitable locations, but with little to show for it. She thought her papa was already becoming more than a little disenchanted and when he read their pamphlet and then it was followed almost immediately by the death of his father, it had been the last straw. When his long running argument with Colonel Boudeau came to an end, Boudeau said that he was thoroughly sick of the way the régime was behaving and wanted to do something about it. That had been enough to switch his allegiance away from its current direction.

Guy said, 'We will have to speak to Doctor Lovas now because he will know nothing of any of this new development. He in turn will have to tell his contacts to let them know how things are likely to change in and around Domvent. I'll visit him on Monday to bring him up to date. I'll ask him if he thinks we should all volunteer to become members of their group, always assuming they would want us, or should we remain apart from them and simply use what information we can glean? With luck and with Isabelle as our early warning system, it might work rather well if Boudeau, René Jouve and your papa get access to possible moves against resistance groups in our area and beyond. I'll sound out the doctor about it.'

The discussions continued for some time, analysing the motives of Boudeau, Jouve and Eric Farbres and questioning whether all three would remain as enthusiastic in the face of real danger. If any of them became suspected of passing state secrets to terrorists then extreme measures would be taken against them and their close friends and associates. It could prove to be terribly dangerous for everyone. They resolved to sleep on it and wait until they had an idea how Doctor Lovas would react and advise.

On Monday morning Guy called on the doctor. There were no complications at his door and Lovas warmly welcomed him. They had not been able to move about much because of the snow. The town was still piled with half frozen slush and what few people there were, looked a little forlorn as they picked their way across the road. The doctor's house felt cold but he quickly made some black market coffee, which Guy thanked him for. 'So, what's been happening since we last met – anything of importance?'

Guy said, 'How long have you got? There's a lot to tell you.' Trying to remember everything that had taken place since the time they last met was challenging, but he managed most of it. The effect of the pamphlet on Colonel Boudeau, and his subsequent disenchantment with the entire Pétain set up, after the meeting in Vichy and his remarkable turnaround in his attitude, were all worthy of discussion. But there was more to tell. The meeting with Eric Farbres in Domvent was central to his total conversion with him, together with the death of Farbres senior because of lack of heating, had made a profound difference to Eric Farbres' view. 'An unbelievable situation has now arrived where Boudeau, his young

Lieutenant Boyer, and Major Eric Farbres are all seriously looking for membership of a suitable Resistance Group. If Isabelle hadn't told you with a straight face on Saturday, that this had taken place on Wednesday, I would have dismissed it outright as a crude plot to uncover our group here. But Isabelle knows her father very well and had witnessed how upset he had been at his father's death. His upset and anger had been exacerbated by the family doctor's view that the shortage of heating materials in the house had been the primary reason for his demise. It had brought home to him the essential truth about what was going on in the north, and which the leaflet had flagged up.'

Lovas had listened intently to Guy's update and nodded approval or frowned at some contentious points in his narrative. Finally, he asked Guy, 'Does Farbres have any idea how close Isabelle is to you? And does he still cling to his view that the Jews are some sort of second class humans? If that is the case I can't quite see how he can be part of a dissident group which could, for instance, find itself rescuing a Jewish family from the clutches of the Nazis. How can we square that circle?'

'Right now, I have no idea how this can be done. Perhaps Isabelle will be able to talk him around to a more tolerant frame of mind. I'll have to discuss it with her. It would certainly be better if she could tone down his anti-semitism stance before she tells him about our relationship. She may have to resort to some half-truths first of all, because his life has already been turned upside down. If he were to be told that his daughter was not only in love but sleeping with a half-breed Jew, he might blow a fuse.'

'I am sure you're right Guy. Let her handle it the best way she can for the moment. I will need to speak to the principal leaders of our group about the possibilities of recruiting four officers in the Gendarmerie service, together with your gang of dissenting people in Chalhac. I can tell you now they will be very wary. Officially you are not members of anything at the moment and it would be more satisfactory if you could join our activities, which are likely to become rather more interesting in the future. I can't say more than that and it is better that you know nothing anyway. Your Gendarmerie connections could be extremely useful if they can all be trusted. We have to be certain that Isabelle's assessment is accurate and that she has not unwittingly been used as a bait to uncover our activities down here. I'm not sure how we can test that, but keep it in mind.' The doctor expected a patient to arrive shortly after this and Guy was obliged to leave so he headed back down to the village.

'So, what did the doctor have to say?' asked Jacques when Guy walked into the bar.

Guy outlined the way Lovas had responded. 'It was naturally quite predictable. He took it all very calmly in the circumstances. He is by nature a very calm person- something to do with his medical training I suppose. He did say that it would be better if all of us here became fully joined up with the resistance group that he belongs to. He also thought that our four gendarmerie mutineers would be a tremendously useful addition provided they could be trusted. He hoped Isabelle hadn't been duped by them to expose the rest of us and the main group. Personally, Jacques, I don't think that can be the case. Farbres could not arrange for his father to die when he did after all. We will have to discuss this again with Isabelle.'

There was an unsettled feeling in the gendarmerie office ever since Boudeau's visit and Eric Farbres' decision to try to locate a resistance organisation which would be likely to enlist him and his fellow conspirators as members. He had asked Isabelle about it and all she would say was that she would ask her friends in Chalhac if they could help. She explained to her papa that she might encounter problems, since the dangers were such that asking anyone for a way into a group of that nature, would probably be met with a shake of the head. It was not quite true of course, but she was still on the defensive even towards her papa. She was well aware of the possibility of being used as the bait to lead authorities into a dissident organisation. The death of her grandfather might even have been seen as a bonus by her papa and that his grief and anger could have simply been play acting. She had given a lot of thought over the last few days to the various scenarios but had been unable to draw any firm conclusions. She decided she would speak to her mother about it since she would know for sure how Eric really felt about his father's death.

She tackled her mama about the subject the following day:

'Mama, has Papa spoken to you about his idea to join a resistance group if he can find one?' Anne-Marie paused for a moment before answering.

'Yes he has talked to me about it and he also told me about Colonel Boudeau's decision to become some sort of undercover agent for the Resistance. Your Papa is still very angry about your Grand-père's death. He blames it totally on the new government. He had read that pamphlet only hours before he was told about his papa's death and when the doctor said it was all because there was no heat in the house it did not take him long to know whom to blame. His attitude seems to have completely changed since then as I'm sure you have noticed.'

Isabelle's doubts and questions about her papa's motives became unnecessary after that. All she could say to her mama was that she suddenly had overwhelming feelings of guilt towards her papa. In the normal course of things, none of this would have come about, but these were not normal times. Fear of speaking out about political matters tainted everyone's judgements and motives were being questioned.

'I even began to doubt Papa's motives in asking me about resistance groups. Although I know a number of people who are very close to groups like that, I can identify no one who is definitely a member. It is very dangerous to hold any information about this because we know that the interrogation methods used in Vichy against 'resistance' suspects are less than civilised. My only problem now, is how I can tell Papa about Guy and his family. I know Papa has always been anti-semitic. Ever since I was a little girl and discovered Guy on his swing everyone has been careful to keep our friendship and subsequent love affair hidden from him. It's become a habit for everyone now and he may feel, to say the least, aggrieved when he learns that everyone has been holding out on him.'

'I am sure Papa has guessed that there is now someone in your life who means a lot to you,' said Anne-Marie. 'I'm equally sure it would never cross his mind that whoever it is would have any Jewish connections, so it might take a bit of digesting on his part. If I can find a way to broach the subject, I'll do what I can, but it will have to be done very carefully.'

'Thank you Maman, I know you will be very diplomatic if you do tackle the subject. You know very well what Guy means to me. As you probably know his family have almost adopted me as a daughter, so there exist even stronger ties in Chalhac – not just Grand-mère and Tantetta.'

'I promise you Cherie that I will be very careful in what I say to your Papa. I fully understand the difficulties and dangers.'

The snow had ceased to fall for nearly a week now and the roads were becoming usable again. Even the road from Domvent to Chalhac was better now and less of a trial. The Christmas celebrations had taken place and people were beginning to look forward to the spring. Guy made his mind up to speak to Doctor Lovas to ask if he had anything like a favourable response from his resistance group. Lovas opened the door to Guy and after the normal password recitation said,

'I'm glad you have come Guy, there are some important developments you will want to know about. We have heard on good authority that le Maréchal has got rid of Laval. It has been a tricky move for the old man to make but he's gone. It all happened before Christmas on the thirteenth. As Head of State, Pétain had already made his mind up to sack Laval. In his view he was becoming too close to the Germans running the occupied zone, which includes Abetz, the Ambassador in Paris. Abetz has bribed some of the newspapers in Paris to go along with the Nazi line. Laval believed that in cultivating Abetz, who is a friend of Ribbentrop, that he would be able to extract better deals from Hitler after England had been defeated. They still believe that the English can be easily over-run, a line pursued by the newspapers. With England out of the way France and Germany would jointly run a new enlarged Europe. However, Abetz has been playing a double game with Laval and we have firm documentary evidence that Hitler intends to reduce France economically and militarily to little more than a satellite country, conveniently placed to provide sea access to the Mediterranean, the English Channel and the west coast ports. Laval had no idea this was the real German intention.

Fortunately, le Maréchal has some excellent sources of information about the intentions of Paris and Berlin, as we do, and he has managed to keep what he has learned close to his chest. For all his cunning and natural political abilities Laval had been totally unaware of le Maréchal's plot to oust him and it must have been a considerable shock when he was arrested just as soon as he was sacked. He is now residing under house arrest at Chateau de Châteldon in the little Auvergnat town where he was born.'

'That is very interesting Doctor. As you know we already had knowledge of Laval's intentions to a large degree, but his sacking and arrest is quite something else. It seems le Maréchal's wits are not as impaired as we imagined. Perhaps we should try to reinforce his position in the future, remembering that he has not changed his mind about keeping Hitler with a sense of obligation towards France. He is still determined to ensure that no more French lives are lost. Sadly, Hitler's attitude and that of Pétain's cronies, don't quite match up with his own. I am sure it has made for some sleepless nights as he ponders his earlier pronouncements.'

Lovas said, 'I doubt if Hitler has ever felt any sense of obligation to le Maréchal or to the French nation and is doubtless happy to find that the French Head of State is actively encouraging the plunder of French natural resources. Hitler will not be able to believe his luck.'

'It is all very sad. Have you had an opportunity to speak to your friends about our aim to join in a little more actively? It seems to us that the sooner we can put some sort of brake on what's happening in the north, the better. It must be possible to slow down or stop the draining of our country's wealth and resources even if it means making a fight of it. Pétain will not change his mind – not publicly at least, but I'm certain he must be having serious doubts about his avowed policy now that he is aware of the real German strategy of weakening France as much as possible.'

'Yes I have spoken to the ring leaders and they would like to meet you, Eric Farbres and possibly Boudeau to get some first-hand knowledge about their motives and yours. They are naturally curious to learn at first-hand what is driving these people including yourself, into the direction you are all intent on going. I explained your own reasons but they are still slightly baffled about Boudeau and Farbres. Do you think we can arrange an interview with them both? They are of course being very careful and will have to choose somewhere for you all to meet which will be safe for them and for you.'

Guy understood perfectly how tricky all this was becoming and promised he would speak to Isabelle who would have to discuss with her papa the possibility of a meeting. Guy left shortly after and made his way home. On the way he stopped at the post box tree, scribbled a note for Isabelle saying that they needed to speak and continued on his way. He went to Jacques' bar first of all. He told Jacques about Laval's dismissal and that he was no longer part of the Vichy régime. This was met with the general approval of one or two of Jacques' regular customers. They were all familiar to him, so he could speak fairly freely. He did not mention the resistance group south of Domvent or their possible joining. Then David appeared on his bicycle with a bag containing repaired clothes over his shoulder. When he was told about Laval he said simply, 'Good', made more effective with a deep nodding of his head. Guy said he would be back later, with his father and Marcel, saying there were other things he needed to tell them about.

Meanwhile at the Farbres house Anne-Marie had made her mind up to speak to Eric about their daughter's relationship with Guy Gaillard. They were having breakfast, Isabelle was still upstairs and Eric seemed to be in a good mood, so she said,

'You know Eric that Isabelle has a lot of friends in and around Chalhac? She is a naturally gregarious creature and there is a very friendly family living there called Gaillard who have practically adopted her as a daughter. Jules Gaillard is a stonemason and works down at the local quarry with one of his two sons. He was left the house by a distant cousin and they got out of Russia soon after the Revolution. There was a lot of violence being meted out by Bolsheviks where they had lived for several years, but they took the opportunity to move back to France in about 1920 and have lived in Chalhac ever since. Sarah Gaillard is actually Jewish and she and Jules met up when he was working on a Tsarist palace somewhere. Her family had disappeared during the revolution and his parents had died some time before, so they were both orphans in a manner of speaking. Isabelle got to know the family when she was a child and made a friend of Guy, the other son. He is very intelligent and was studying to be a teacher in Clermont until he was thrown off the course because he was partly Jewish. It was very unfair and a bit of a disaster for all of them. Over the years Isabelle and Guy have become very close and she has admitted to me that she and Guy are now in love.'

'Stop there Ann-Marie,' said Eric in mid mouthful. 'This explains her regular visits to see her Grand-mère and Henrietta.'

'Of course. Isabelle was anxious that you should know the truth of the situation. She is well aware of your long-held dislike of Jews generally and was unsure how you would react when you were told about her close relationship with Guy.'

'Over the last recent weeks I have become increasingly sympathetic towards the Jews. This has partly come about because I have been exhorted to arrange for more concentration camps to house "Jews and other undesirables". The orders are coming indirectly via Boudeau in Clermont, but it is clear to me that they originate in Paris or Berlin. I don't like any of it, so you can tell our daughter she can relax about it and that I still love her.'

'She will be tremendously relieved Cheri and grateful for your understanding and love.'

Eric departed for the gendarmerie shortly after. A minute of two later Isabelle appeared and asked Anne-Marie how he had taken it. Her mama told her she could relax about it all and that he was coming down on the side of the Jews as a result of getting orders from Paris or Berlin for more concentration camps. He was heartily sickened by it all. 'And I am to tell you that he still loves you.'

Isabelle's eyes filled with tears on hearing this and threw her arms around Anne-Marie in gratitude for being able to explain to Eric about the Gaillard family and Guy. It could have gone badly wrong. 'Thank you Maman – I can't begin to tell you how grateful I am.'

In Chalhac Guy told their little gang about his conversation with the doctor and that his group was predictably wary of taking anyone into their circle who could be a 'plant' and whose sole interest could be the uncovering and destruction of the group. They wanted therefore to meet face to face with Colonel Boudeau and Eric Farbres to try to establish their sincerity, motives and willingness to face considerable danger and the probable end of their careers as gendarmerie officers. He also recounted the sacking of Pierre Laval by Pétain and his immediate arrest and confinement in his own chateau in Châteldon. Isabelle was expected on Saturday and he had already left a note for her on the way back here this afternoon. There was much to discuss and she would have to ask her Papa to arrange with Boudeau possible dates for a joint meeting in a safe location with the resistance group. There was a sense of excitement in the Gaillard house following Guy's report. They all felt that something was happening at last which might make a real contribution to their long held aims.

On Saturday Isabelle arrived in the village as expected and called on her grand-mère and Tantetta where she was treated to a coffee of Hortense's devising. They covered the usual topic and finally Isabelle said she would have to leave now because there were things to be discussed with the Gaillard family. Henrietta said she would be over there shortly as well. When she arrived, Isabelle was warmly embraced by everyone, not least by Guy. He explained what had taken place at the doctor's and that she was asked to speak to her papa to arrange with Boudeau a date for a meeting. It would necessarily be somewhere south of Domvent in a safe house of the group's choosing. He also told Isabelle about Laval's sacking and his confinement in his chateau in Châteldon. Isabelle's eyebrows went up at that unexpected news.

'I'll bet he didn't expect that. How on earth did le Maréchal manage that I wonder?'

Guy said that although they knew it was true they had no idea how the old man had managed it. Isabelle said she would speak to her papa when she got home and tell him that the doctor's group wanted to speak directly to him and to Boudeau before they would consider accepting them as recruits. So, it was agreed that it seemed to be going to move forward in the very near future. Everyone was happy with the way both Isabelle and Guy were handling the situation. It was all risky but they appeared to have kept some sort of control of the operation. They broke up after that and Isabelle said her farewells to Guy and made for home. The road was still icy at the intervals where the sun could not penetrate but it was now passable again. She explained to her papa what was demanded by the resistance group and he happily agreed and understood their anxieties.

Within a few weeks Boudeau and Farbres were collected from the Domvent Gendarmerie in a small van. A short way out of the town they were both blindfolded by their new acquaintances and their journey continued. The second man stayed with them in the back of the van to ensure the blindfolds were not interfered with. Boudeau said to Eric Farbres, 'Can you follow where we are?' Farbres said he was able to at first but had lost all sense of direction now. They had been travelling for over half an hour when the van stopped. They could hear a gate being opened, a short drive again, and finally stopping. They were led over some soft ground to a building of some sort. Doors were opened and closed behind them and finally another door opened and whoever it was said in an educated voice, 'I apologise for the cloak and dagger arrangements gentlemen, but I am sure you will understand the reasons for our extreme wariness. He asked another person, 'Would you remove the blindfolds from our guests please?'

They were temporarily dazzled by the light again. The windows to the room they were in were heavily curtained and it must have been part of the farmhouse. They had already identified the place as being some sort of farm because the strong smells which emanated from the cattle could hardly be missed. Their host was wearing large and heavily framed dark glasses, a traditional beret pulled down low over his forehead and a heavy military overcoat with collar turned up all round. There was little of his face left exposed as a result, which hid his identity very effectively without resorting to false beards or moustaches. He sat at a plain table with his back to an unlit fire. Boudeau and Farbres sat on not very comfortable wooden chairs, facing him.

'To you gentlemen my name is Abricot. I will not burden you with my actual name which would mean little to you in any event. I lead what might be termed a dissident group, which is totally opposed to the policies introduced by le Maréchal Pétain when he took the reins of the new régime. You will be familiar with his stated aims and he seems determined to pursue those ideas come what may. It has resulted in the Nazi invaders removing from our country everything of value as quickly as they can. We know, as you do, probably, that Hitler's gang of thieves has not the slightest intention of favouring France with a power sharing arrangement in the event of their defeating our allies, which include England. This brings us to the question of where you stand in this mess. We have always assumed that serving members of the Gendarmerie will always behave impeccably, following the existing laws and obeying orders while ensuring that the rest of society does the same. That you have apparently chosen to step out of line, to risk your careers and lives, needs some explanation. You, Colonel Boudeau, would you tell me how and why this about face has come about?' He sat back in his chair, and placed finger tips together, gently exercising his fingers.

Boudeau was anxious to tell 'Abricot' about the meeting in Vichy and the pamphlet's coincidental arrival at the right moment. He said he was already fuming with anger with what he had witnessed in the Vichy meeting and the pamphlet had been the straw that broke the camel's back. He had spoken at length to his assistant Lieutenant René Jouve about it and discovered that he too was becoming disenchanted with current events. Jouve let it be known that he had been talking to a fellow student from when they were both in training for the Gendarmerie service and he too was increasingly doubtful about the way the new régime was behaving. The student was none other than Major Farbres' assistant Lieutenant Michel Boyer. 'Major Farbres will be pleased to expand on this slightly unlikely tale I'm sure.'

'Yes. Perhaps you would like to give me your reasons Major for what seems to me to be a bit of a fairy tale,' said Abricot.

'It's no fairy tale, Monsieur. I was becoming a little doubtful myself although I hadn't voiced it to anyone. However, my daughter Isabelle was signalling that she was already firmly against everything taking place and was talking to Lieutenant Boyer about it. I discovered that I was the only one facing the other way. I phoned the Colonel at this point and we agreed to meet and talk things through. To crown it all my father died of exposure because they had run short of heating oil and coal. Suddenly what the leaflet had said became a reality. I saw very clearly that my father had died because there was no coal and that the Germans were taking all the coal, oil and everything else back to the Fatherland. I was exceedingly angry and wanted to speak at length to Colonel Boudeau. We eventually had our meeting Domvent. I was totally converted to the cause and I am prepared to do whatever becomes necessary to bring down the present régime and Pétain with it.'

Abricot remained slightly skeptical about what he had been told by both men. Their sudden change of view seemed a little unreal and he had to give some serious thought to what could turn out to be no more than an attempt by the gendarmerie to uncover the group. He finally said, 'I will let you know how we are going to advance in this matter, gentlemen. Say nothing to anyone about today. We have our own network of people working for us. You might be surprised how much we know about the workings of the gendarmerie service in Clermont and elsewhere. Don't assume you are safe in your offices because you are being quietly monitored most of the time. Thank you for your time today – I will be in touch.' He turned to the person who had been silently watching and listening to everything that was said.

'Will you replace the blindfolds and accompany these gentlemen out to the van? Thank you.'

They found themselves being led through the various doors and across the soft ground to the van once more. The smell of cattle seemed to be stronger somehow. They were soon on their way back to Domvent. It was still only early afternoon which gave Boudeau time to get back to Clermont before it froze up again in the evening. They had said very little in the van going back, in case their guard reported some misinterpreted comment, so they had tacitly agreed to leave it until back in Farbres' office. They had been quietly impressed by Abricot. He exuded authority and was clearly firmly in control of their group. It was vital of course because any slip up could mean death or very long term imprisonment. Abricot was well aware of the game he and his friends were playing and they played by his rules.

Isabelle was impatient to hear from her papa how it had gone that morning and together with Michel Boyer they sat in Farbres' office and listened as he recounted what took place. He said they had been very impressed with the leader of their group and that he wished to be known as Abricot. He had exuded authority and was obviously well educated judging by his manner of speech.

'How was it left then? Have you been enrolled?' asked Isabelle.

'Not yet. He wanted to think about it so he said. I would imagine he needs to confer with one or two other group members about it. I can't say I blame him – he only met us today for the first time and it would need the Wisdom of Job to make a snap decision. Before they blindfolded us, we were able to see the registration number of the van. I would be surprised if they were that careless not to have thought about that and it is a certainty the numbers are from some vehicle that no longer exists. We'll check it out anyway. We were told not to say a word to anyone about today – again I can see his reasons. I would guess that he wants to discuss this with our Doctor Lovas. He seems to be in the know about it all and is in it up to his neck. That's about all I can tell you at the moment.'

Boyer and Isabelle thanked him for the update. They both agreed that the doctor was likely to be Abricot's confidant. How they could come to a decision remained to be seen.

Abricot had waited until Boudeau and Farbres were safely on their way and then phoned Doctor Lovas.

'They have just left and are on their way back. We need to meet soon before the prognosis is confirmed.' Their telephone conversations were always couched in pseudo medical jargon. Telephone operators were notorious for their nosiness and for their ability to listen in to phone conversations. Lovas and Abricot had made it a rule never to mention names and always to speak in medical terms as far as possible. It seemed to have paid off so far as nothing had come back which would have alerted them to the possibility that telephone operators had been listening into their conversations.

'I take it the patients are aware of the seriousness of their condition? Their lives could be in jeopardy if we make a mistaken diagnosis. You have explained the problems no doubt?'

'I left them in little doubt that if the treatment doesn't work the future could be bleak.'

They arranged to meet at a favoured place between Domvent and the farm the following week. Lovas thanked him for his professional advice and rang off. They met the next week in a charcoal burner's hut in the forest. The owner was not in residence, so they could speak freely, confident that they were alone and not overheard.

'Good to see you again Charles,' said Lovas. 'How are things down here? In Domvent and the surrounding villages I think we have stirred things up quite effectively. That leaflet we devised has done the rounds and has resulted in waking a lot of people up to what's going on in their name by le Maréchal and they don't like it. It has rung bells even louder since the cold weather started as many people have been left without heating. Our Major Farbres in the Gendarmerie was totally converted against the régime when he was told by the doctor that his father had died of hypothermia in his home after their fuel supplies ran out. He probably told you about that last week?'

'Yes, he did. I must say he could hardly contrive to have his father die to order. That part of his reasons to become a conspirator rings true but I am not entirely convinced. The daughter's motives sound real enough. Her half-Jewish boyfriend would be a good reason for the girl to try to protect him and his family from the latest batch of laws from Paris aimed at the Jewish population and at their property and businesses. Then there is young Lieutenant Boyer in Farbres' unit. He is clearly friendly with the daughter Isabelle and says he would like to join in with us. He could be a weak point although he has been privy to all the discussions in Farbres' office, I gather. In the light of that he may have to be taken out. We'll think about that.'

Lovas was a little shocked to hear that Abricot was prepared to eliminate an intelligent, civilized young person like Boyer because he had been in on the discussions with Boudeau and Farbres. 'That sounds a bit drastic Charles. Would you really go that far?'

'My dear old friend; we are not playing some sort of gentle board game here. If we are uncovered by either Pétain's pals or the Germans, they will not hesitate to eliminate us. We would be either shot on the spot or dragged before some bogus magistrate, who would pronounce death sentences without any legal representation available to us and we would almost certainly be shot or imprisoned as slave labourers in Germany somewhere. We know this is happening now in the occupied zone and that Pétain would follow suit if he thought it would go down well with Hitler's cronies. We therefore have to guard our backs against any possibility of our cover being blown, even if it means shooting an otherwise admirable friend. Which takes us to Colonel Boudeau in Clermont. He told me about the meeting he had attended in Vichy. I'm sure you know all about that and how angry he had been on his return. Then I understand his assistant René Jouve gave him a slightly creased copy of our leaflet. It certainly got around! When he read it, he too was incensed by what we had said particularly in the light of his witnessing the Nazi supporting crowd at the Vichy meeting. It does sound feasible that he had been sufficiently aggrieved to want to do something about it.

Boudeau did not know it, but we had one of our members at that meeting. He confirmed that Boudeau was clearly angry and that the meeting was little more than a propaganda exercise. Our man was dressed up as a high-ranking policeman from Paris and he fooled everyone.'

'What about Lieutenant Jouve? Is he to be trusted?'

'He is young of course but he must have realised that when his boss reacted the way he did to the Vichy meeting and then to the leaflet, that these were good enough reasons to fall in line. When he spoke to Boyer in Domvent and discovered they were all looking the same way that probably clinched it. It would mean that he would be throwing away a promising career with the added risks we all acknowledge and accept. I am inclined to accept him as a possible recruit,'

'OK,' said the Doctor. 'So, shall we say that Boudeau, Farbres, Isabelle Farbres, René Jouve and Lieutenant Boyer are all acceptable? What about Isabelle's boyfriend Guy Gaillard, do we include him in the unholy bunch? There is, in addition, the little clique in Chalhac. They would like to think they could join in on this. Personally I feel we should dissuade them for the moment. It will become more difficult to control if we suddenly add a dozen or more to our ranks – some of whom we barely know other than through hearsay from Isabelle.'

'I'll go along with that. I think we can safely say that we can also recruit Guy Gaillard. He has plenty of good reasons to oppose the régime. When he next appears at your surgery you can tell him what we have decided today. They will all be keen to know where they stand and he can inform them. We will have to gather them all together at the farm to explain the set up here.'

Lovas thanked him for his efforts and they parted for the time being.

Twenty-four

The wintry weather finally ceased by the end of March. The trees began to show their pale green young foliage again. The population emerged into the sunlight once more. Some blinked in the sunlight as if they had been shut in the entire time and had remained in a state of hibernation over the winter months. They may have been the clever ones, since there seemed to be no sensible reason to go outside other than the essentials like provisions or fuel.

In Chalhac the village began to wake up in much the same fashion as in Domvent. The only constant had been Jacques' little bar which had remained open throughout. Even Bonnet's bakery had shut up shop for a day or two during the worst of the weather. It was clearly understood by the local populace who had been obliged to survive on slightly stale bread for a day or so. It could barely be described as hardship.

Guy had been fully briefed by the doctor who asked him to let the people concerned know who had been accepted as members of the resistance group. It was greeted with a mixture of disappointment and mild relief. When they were told the reasons they understood better. A gathering of the new recruits was arranged at the farm. No blindfolds were asked for but they were not told exactly where they were when they arrived. A small convoy of three vehicles took them down there led by the little van from the farm, together with the gendarmerie small van and Doctor Lovas' own car, a small and well-used Renault. Boudeau had driven himself down from Clermont in the gendarmerie van and left it parked at the Domvent gendarmerie. They were welcomed by Abricot and ushered into the big salon where Boudeau and Farbres had been interrogated a week or two before. The fire remained unlit and Abricot addressed them from behind his wooden table. He still wore his heavily framed dark glasses and beret but had abandoned the military overcoat, wearing instead a casual much used jacket.

'Welcome to our farm gentlemen and Isabelle,' – he acknowledged her with a smile. 'I know all of you and a lot about you so I do have the advantage. You will probably have never come across me before and all I can say is that I wish it to remain that way. To you I am 'Abricot.' I am the head of our motley gang and as from today you are enrolled as well. In joining us you must accept and understand that you and we are into a dangerous and unforgiving game. We are dedicated to getting France out from under the control of Adolf Hitler and his friends.

Some of his 'friends' are Frenchmen and include le Maréchal Pétain who has deluded himself into believing that if he dances to the Nazi tune, they will repay France by sharing power with them in a new, enlarged Nazi empire. Sadly, this is not what the Führer intends. We have verified documentary evidence which totally disproves everything the Nazis have said or hinted they will do. France will not be a favoured ally and will simply become a poor, weakened colony of an enlarged and stronger Germany. Most of you will be aware of this already but I am repeating it now to remind you what we are about. As your leader here, I demand total obedience. My orders and instructions must be obeyed without question. It is the only way we can remain strong and not infiltrated. We know of many cases in the occupied zone where resistance groups have been broken up, their members shot or imprisoned. I have no intention of letting that happen here. We must all trust one another. Our lives are on the line here. My second in command of the group is Doctor Lovas. Few of you have met him and from now he must be known as 'Silas.' You will probably receive my instructions via Silas in future. As most of you live within the range of Domvent this seems to be the safest way. Orders are mostly given verbally and we expect a verbal acknowledgement. Written orders are very dangerous items and should always be avoided if possible. Any questions so far?'

'Is it possible to say when or where the next operation will be mounted Sir?' asked Guy.

'Impossible for me to answer. It all depends on our intelligence people giving us up front notice of troop movements or arms deliveries and so on. Our intelligence capabilities will, we hope, be enhanced by our recruitment today of Colonel Boudeau and Lieutenant Jouve in Clermont. They will contact Major Farbres, Lieutenant Boyer or Isabelle in Domvent if they uncover information useful to us. The gendarmerie phone lines should be safe enough but operators do listen in on telephone conversations, even in the Gendarmerie Headquarters. I think and hope that you will be ultra-careful in future. Any other questions?'

'Will we all be given an alternative name? Isabelle has already opted for Giraffe although I can't remember an occasion when we have ever used it,' said Guy.

Abricot considered the question. 'I'll think about it. We don't want to make lives more complicated for the sake of it. I'll let you know what I decide. Just one other thing; there remain more people in Chalhac who are keen to become involved. Silas and I have discussed this and we drew the conclusion that it could be clumsy to have too many new recruits from one location. The dangers of talking to friends are such that we should try to limit casual conversations wherever possible.'

The meeting came to a close. Abricot bid them farewell for the moment and they all departed for Domvent and Chalhac. Boudeau picked up his van from the gendarmerie and made for Clermont with Jouve. Guy collected his bicycle and headed for Chalhac. Everyone was quite thoughtful following the meeting. It had brought into focus for all of them, how dangerous their lives were becoming.

Isabelle had been very impressed with Abricot. 'Our Abricot is quite a guy isn't he? Born and bred a leader of men I would say; and a disciplinarian from the way he talks. I wonder what his regular job is? An army officer of some sort? Or someone from the Aristocracy perhaps? He certainly laid it on the line without any holding back. Very confident in what he believes.'

Farbres agreed with his daughter's assessment. He was happy to leave the decision making to Abricot and not be responsible for all their lives. 'What did you think about him Boyer? Do you think you'll be happy to be led by the man?'

'Well he gave out large confident signals to us and tried to instill some sense of responsibility in us and for each other. We would be hard put to find anyone of quite the same calibre. Yes, I'm happy to be led by him.'

When Guy arrived back at Chalhac they were all agog to hear what went on. Guy said first of all that they were all firmly instructed not to say a word to anyone – not even families and close friends. So, what he was about to say they didn't actually hear. He chuckled at that and said, 'How could he expect anyone to simply clam up after a day like that I can't imagine! Anyway that's what the man wanted. I am afraid I am about to disobey him regardless. He is a very likeable person. Tall and medium build. I could not see much of his face because he was wearing sunglasses and a beret pulled down over his eyes. He speaks beautiful French – with an almost Parisien upper class dialect. He must have been well educated. He absolutely exuded authority. He did not want to be recognised – hence the sunglasses and so on. We have to call him Abricot. The doctor is known as Silas and we already have Giraffe in the shape of Isabelle. I asked him if we were all going to be given funny names and he said he would have to think about it. None of us was able to identify him, but he is evidently well-known in some circles.'

'When are you going into action then Guy?' asked Jacques Fournier.

'He did not know. He was waiting for information about troop movements and things of that nature that we could somehow delay. Colonel Boudeau in Clermont is one of our sources of information now so we may have to wait for his reports to come in. It seems everybody is spying on everyone else these days. Abricot said that they already had spies in the Gendarmerie Headquarters, keeping an eye open for weaknesses in the system that could be exploited, and Boudeau and Jouve were both quite shocked to hear that. It will make them look at their working colleagues very differently now.' He went on to explain that the headquarters of operations was a farm about forty or fifty kilometres south of Domvent. The names of the occasional village had meant nothing to them as they drew close to the farm, so he was unable to say where they had been. It seemed to most of them that there was no more information to be got from Guy and the little meeting dispersed.

* * * * *

In Chalhac, Domvent and the surrounding area it was strangely quiet during that spring. There had been little or no activity being carried out by Abricot, or at least none that demanded extra efforts from the Domvent direction. People were beginning to get impatient, waiting for operations to take place that might alleviate the day to day boredom. The temperatures began to climb again and the summer rhythms were becoming re-established. In the village Jacques' bar took on its familiar character - one or two regulars leaning against the little metal-topped bar and a few more at the table under the awning. The Wednesday market always brought in the stall holders one or two at a time. Thirsts needed slaking after standing in the sunshine for several hours. Apart from the old tree in the middle of La Place, which had become the long established private domain of Madame Meral on Wednesdays, there was no other shade.

The sense of expectation that something would begin to happen at any time was suddenly rewarded by the arrival of an unidentified man on a battered old bicycle. He had an unshaven and gaunt face and dressed in a mixture of very well-worn farmer's clothes. A dirty black beret was perched on his head. He made immediately for Jacques' bar.

'Good morning Jacques! I thought I would never get here!' said the stranger.

Jacques was completely taken aback by this person's total familiarity with him. He looked hard at him again and there was a face he knew behind the whiskery stubble that had him floored for a minute or two. Then he suddenly fell in.

'Of course! You are one of Malet's sons.'

'Correct! I am Claude but I am saddened to have to tell you that my brother Daniel was captured, and killed when he tried to escape. They gunned him down as he ran for the trees. I was in a work camp up until four months ago, but I managed to get away. I'll tell you about it later. How are my father and sister? I have not dared go to the mill in case they were no longer about. I've had no post since we were captured so I have no idea what's been going on. Are they OK?'

'Yes, they are alright. Your father comes in here most days and we are all members of a dissident group. You will be roped in as well eventually. You look terrible Claude. How have you managed to get here unscathed – it must have been very difficult?'

'I will not bore you to death with it right now Jacques. I must get over and see my father. I'll see you all a bit later.' With that he got back onto the bike and wobbled over La Place, past the church to the old mill. It hadn't fallen down entirely but was in urgent need of repairs to prevent what could be an imminent collapse. Malet had seen him arrive and was waiting to welcome him at a side door.

'Claude my son!' He hugged him fiercely. 'Where's Daniel – is he with you?'

Claude took him by both arms and shook his head sadly. Nothing had to be said at that moment. Malet's eyes filled with tears. 'What happened?'

Claude explained that they had both been taken prisoner near Rouen in June the previous year. Hundreds from their unit had been captured and were kept temporarily in a disused French camp guarded by a German unit. They were going to be transported out to an unknown destination eventually. In July they were loaded into a convoy of lorries under a heavily armed guard and begun to drive eastwards. Daniel had said to him that he was going to make a run for it and could he distract the guard somehow? So he had pretended to vomit on the floor of the truck. The guard was distracted for enough time for Daniel to jump over the side of the truck and run for a small wooded area at the side of the road. He had reached the trees as the guard opened fire. His legs went first and then his body caught a hail of fire from their guard and from the lorry behind them. He stood no chance.

'He gave them a good run for their money then, didn't he Claude? He was a brave man, your brother,' the old man managed to say between the tears. He sufficiently gathered himself to ask his son what happened then.

Claude told him that a long and exhausting journey had followed, ending up somewhere near the Belgian border. Their new quarters were an old army camp that had been quickly surrounded by barbed wire together with a number of newly built watch towers. The work they were eventually given to do comprised mostly of hand sawing timber, turning the wood into railway sleepers. It was a two man job, using a double ended very large panel saw – a man at each end, pulling and then pushing. It was slow, heavy and wearying work and could have been suitable as hard labour punishment in other circumstances. Their food was minimal. Mostly thin potato soup with a small chunk of bread.

In these circumstances it had not taken him long to begin to formulate an escape plan. It would rely upon hiding in or under a lorry or van going out through the gates. He had watched as closely as he could what went on at the gates when any sort of transport had to go through them to the outside. Two guards were always present. One had to examine the exit documents while the other was supposed to inspect the vehicle for any would be escapees. He had detected almost at once the obvious boredom that came with the job they were ordered to do, and that their hearts were not in it. One or two were still fairly keen and wanted to be noticed as possible candidates for promotion, but the majority had no such ambition. There were about three vehicles that were possible sources of transportation. One was a French or Belgian military vehicle. He had rejected it as it would be too high to get into and get down from. It was also too open underneath to supply any cover. The second choice was a small civilian van, used to bring in food and supplies for the guarding personnel. Unfortunately, he had been unable to make any contact with the driver, nor could he ever. That idea was dismissed. The third was a refuse truck. It had sliding openings which slid from one side to the other to facilitate the dumping of waste products, some of which would end up as pig swill. This seemed to be the best bet in Claude's estimation. It would involve hiding under an amount of rotting food from the staff and prisoners' tables, plus anything else that had to be disposed of. He would have to stay under the rubbish all night before being ferried through the gates. The gate guard hardly ever examined the rubbish vehicle because of its intensely smelly nature. It was an aspect of Claude's escape plan that was the least attractive.

It took courage to climb into the filthy truck containing who knows what and to cover up with a heap of food scraps and rotting material and then to wait until morning and hope that a guard behaved in much the same way as he had been witnessing. His luck held. He heard the guttural voices of the German guards and their final OK. He had no idea where the truck was heading but decided to stay where he was until he was well away from the prison camp. He eventually managed very gingerly to slide open the side panel. The fresh air was like nectar and he drank it in for a few minutes as he tried to rid himself of some of the muck he had been covered with all night. The truck slowed down and he could hear Flemish voices shouting instructions. He felt it was going to be extremely risky to stay in the truck till he was tipped out, so he took pot luck and leapt out of the side opening. No one had seen him as he jumped. He was just in time as the whole of the rear section was being automatically inverted over a pit of sorts. He ran for his life away from the waste disposal area and into a nearby wood. He still wore his French army uniform – now barely recognizable having been the only item of clothing he still possessed. He carefully unpeeled it, then his shirt, also army issue, and then finally his pants. He shook everything as violently as he could in the effort to remove the remnants of sticky food. He finally draped everything over some bushes in the hope they would be sufficiently clean and would dry out. He lay down on a patch of grass and went to sleep in the sunshine.

He woke up about an hour later feeling much better. He began to think about washing himself but there was neither the time, nor a source of water nearby for the niceties of life just then. His clothes had dried and appeared to be mostly free of the previous night's exposures. They were still very smelly but he was going to have to put up with it for the time being. He was aware that he was still within range of the prison camp. There was a morning head count every day so they would be down by one but he had sensed a fundamental lack of concern by their captors about numbers of prisoners in their care. He had heard no sirens or bells ringing so he assumed that at that moment at least he was fairly safe. He emerged from the little copse he had fled into and found he was on the edge of a field of some green vegetable crop. It was still only March and the crop was not going to give him a free meal. He got rough bearings from the sun and began to move southwards. His eyes and ears were strained lest he were spotted and he tried as far as possible to stay clear of the main roads. He also needed to be able to drop into a ditch or into some trees. Now and then a military vehicle would pass. He got plenty of warning of its approach and was able to hide quite easily which in an odd way was slightly exhilarating, in the knowledge that he could see them but they could not or did not see him. He kept walking for the rest of that day but realised that he would have to eat something before long and began to survey the scene ahead. He was still very close to the border between Belgium and France. If he came upon a house and asked if there was any chance they could give him something, anything, to eat, who would he trust the most, his own countrymen or the Belgians? He considered the matter as he trudged along in the fading light. Then a little way ahead some sign of habitation appeared. There was a house with a small light in the window. He hesitated for a while and then drew closer. He eventually got close enough to the front door so he was able to listen for any conversation. There were muffled voices but obviously there was another door in between. One was German and the other Belgian French. He quietly retreated and began walking again. He needed food and he needed to sleep.

It was very dark now and he had been on his feet since dawn and he was desperately tired. He could see in the near distance the outlines of a farm building which might offer something by way of sheltering him from a heavy dampening dew which would silently soak him through by the morning. He made for its general direction and was rewarded with the remains of a barn, in a near state of total collapse. He climbed over pieces of broken structure and found a corner which looked strong enough to remain intact for another few hours at least. The floor was baked mud and not very even but he was beyond caring and quickly settled down to several hours of sound sleep. In daylight he could see that the barn was even more precarious than he imagined and he picked his way gingerly over the old timbers and out into the safety of a field. There was a house on the far side of the field and he resolved to knock on their door regardless of the chance of encountering an unfriendly local or a German soldier. The door was opened by a rather wizened female.

'Good morning,' he said.

'Good morning,' replied the lady in a local French dialect. 'What do you want?' It was not a particularly friendly response. She was suspicious of this scruffy young man at her door at six in the morning. 'I've no food if that's what you are after.'

Claude was a little thrown by her rapid assessment of him and his intentions. She had effectively closed the door on the very thing he was after. 'Madame, I am an escaped prisoner of war. I managed to get away yesterday and have been walking ever since. I slept in your barn last night. I hope you don't mind me taking liberties with your property. I now have the problem of feeling half-starved as I have eaten nothing now for at least two days.' He decided to try to appeal to the good lady's instincts.

'A prisoner of war? Where have you been since you were captured?

'In a work camp or however they are described. Hand sawing railway sleepers. Hard work.'

'You had better come in.'

Claude felt he was beginning to break down the old lady's defences. Inside it was comparatively warm. He suddenly felt extremely dirty.

'I am unable to give you much I'm afraid. Much as I would like to. I can see you are a genuine person and I am keen to help as much as I can but you will perhaps know that the damned Germans are keeping all the food for themselves. Some of my friends are nearly starving but the Boche don't care. My two grandsons are also in a prison camp somewhere which has left me to manage as best I can, but it is very difficult.' Claude felt immense sympathy for the good lady and wondered whether he could strike some deal with her. A bit of work for some food. He put it to her and she was immediately taken with the idea.

'Oh yes. There is plenty to be done here. I lost my husband in the Great War when he was still quite a young man. We had run the farm here together. We had cattle then and pigs. I still had the cattle when the Germans walked in last year but they took them from me after a few months and I suppose they ended up in their country with everything else they have stolen.'

A deal was struck. If he could make the old barn safe, remove some of the broken timber and cut it up for the fire, she in turn would feed him as best she could. He could also sleep in an old bed which had been redundant since her grandsons had been enlisted. She would also try to wash the worst of the accumulated and now dried remnants of food from his clothes and he could take a stand up wash in the tub outside. Claude felt he had the better side of the deal but she was adamant and insisted he did as agreed. It worked out very well. The barn did not take much to push it over completely and his sawing experience had given him stronger arms and shoulders and was thus comfortable cutting up the resulting pieces of timber for her heating and cooking. He stayed there for three days eventually and he felt that his hostess had become quite attached to him. He had eaten remarkably well whilst there and when he finally left she had sent him on his way with a small parcel containing some bread, a piece of cheese and a lump of ham. She had also given him some old working clothes which had once graced the back of her late husband. A small parcel was also included containing his freshly washed uniform. She was obviously sad to see him go but it was a considerably risky situation for her because the invaders made the occasional unexpected inspection of people's homes in order to ensure that no rules were being broken. Hiding an escaped prisoner would have resulted in death by firing squad for them both. She knew this.

He left dressed as a peasant farmer with an old beret on top to complete the ensemble. He had deliberately stayed unshaven for nearly a week. Black stubble had resulted and he felt the part.

'So, I was on my way home Papa!'

Old Malet said, 'Do you know where you were, compared to now Claude?' You can't have got very far from that prison camp.'

'No, it was not that far. It seemed much further as I had walked a long way. I had to dodge the odd army vehicle as they came trundling past. That delayed me quite a lot.'

Claude continued his account of where he had been on the way back home and what he had endured. He had continually dodged the German military all the way until he arrived at the Demarcation line, something he knew very little about. He quickly realised that it was being heavily patrolled and there were not many exit points. People were being asked to show some kind of permit and it looked a highly dangerous place to be.

There were French Police on the southern side and Germans on the north from where he had arrived. He could not get too close, because there were raised guard posts at intervals and the occupants carried guns. He decided that it would be a waste of time trying to get through, either over it or under it, and retreated to a safe distance to consider the situation. He was aware that the Saone river was close by and that the town of Chalon crossed it. He guessed that the line must cross it somewhere and that he was already close to Chalon. So he deduced that the line ran through, or close to the town. The river looked like the best bet to get past the line even if it meant another soaking. He was a strong swimmer having taught himself in the mill pond at his father's mill. As it happened there was no moon to illuminate the river, so he decided that he would attempt it that night. He made his way through a small thicket and found the river bank. He tied his change of clothes in their bag to his waist, realising that everything would get soaked no matter what he did, but it had to be done. He waded carefully into the cold water and was just in time to meet a large piece of wood floating past. He grabbed it and partly swam and partly floated with it in front of him. He could see the lights on the river bridge a little way ahead and prepared himself for what might be a dangerous few minutes. If he were spotted, there would be a hail of bullets to greet him, so he decided he would use the piece of timber and swim beneath it, hopefully to disguise his shape in the water and to give protection if they opened fire. He floated with the timber above him and made no attempt to hurry which would have given the game away if anyone were interested. His luck held. Either no one saw the innocuous piece of wood floating by, or if they did see it, they had dismissed it as innocent. He stayed in the water until he was out of visible range and got out of the river and stood for a moment or two shivering and very wet. He peeled off his clothes, hung them in the branch of a nearby tree, together with his army uniform and hoped they would be partly dry by the morning. He then did some physical exercise to try to get warm again. There was no real shelter to be found close by and he curled into a ball in a slight hollow under the tree and attempted to sleep.

He was awakened in the early hours by someone dressed in a sort of semi-military uniform. He was brusquely shaken by the shoulder.

'Don't speak. Someone may hear. My name is Jambon to you and I belong to a group which I hope can help you get to wherever you are going. Where are you going? Don't bother to tell me yet. Put my jacket on for the moment, you look frozen. These are your clothes? When you are ready we must go before the patrols start.'

Claude was thoroughly confused and meekly followed the man through the undergrowth. 'I have a motorbike along here and that will get us away from this danger zone.' Claude obediently took his seat on the back of the motorbike and was whisked away from Chalon and the Demarcation line. They arrived at a modest house twenty minutes later. The house was one of a small line of similar houses. It felt wonderfully warm inside and he positioned himself in front of a coal fire burning in the grate.

'I'll make us some coffee,' said his host. 'Just get warm for the moment. We'll talk later. I must warn you that if I have any reason to suspect you are not what you appear to be, I'll shoot you. It is a firm rule we all follow. Understood?'

The brief announcement was clear enough, so he fully understood, and was confident that he would be able to convince his new ally without much trouble. His wet clothes had been hung on a rack in front of the fire and were now steaming as the last vestiges of the river Saone were silently removed in a small cloud of steam. His host had thoughtfully given him a blanket to keep him reasonably comfortable. The interrogation began.

'Can you give me your name please?' asked the man, 'and where is your home?'

'My name is Claude Malet and I live with my brother, sister and father in my father's water mill in Chalhac–sur–Bache. Chalhac is a small village about fifteen kilometres from Domvent d'Olt. We are one hundred and fifty kilometres from Clermont. My brother Daniel was shot when he tried to get away while we were being transported to a labour camp just outside the Belgian border. My sister is Monique. She is the youngest of us. My mother died about fifteen years ago.'

'And where were you captured?'

'The battalion was just outside Rouen and we were overwhelmed by the Germans in less than a week. Then they called an Armistice and we were told to lay down our arms, so that was that. We were prisoners in our own country. Then they began to take us away from Rouen in lorries. No one told us where we were going but we could see it was eastwards. My brother and I had stayed together right up to when he said he was going to make a run for it. Moments later he leapt over the side of the truck and began to make for some trees. The guards on the lorries opened fire before he could make it and I saw him fall. Another truck picked him up but it was too late. We were eventually delivered to a disused army camp close to the Belgian border. That's where I was stuck until about March, when I decided I'd had enough.' He gave his host a potted version of his escape and what he had done up until he had been rescued less than six hours before.

'Well it sounds real enough to me. I was just in time when I found you because the border guards on our side of the Demarcation line are less than sympathetic. They are all French but are prepared to hand over their fellow countrymen to the occupiers for some misbegotten reasons. So welcome back home my friend! Let's have something to eat.' He reappeared from the kitchen with some sausage, a chunk of cheese and a loaf. 'I'm sorry it's not more but the food situation is becoming more difficult. Some wine?' He produced a jug with red wine and two glasses. 'Santé!'

'Now we must think about getting you home. I have a network of friends who can be trusted to pass you down the line to their own connections down south. I think you'll find the system works quite well. I am unable to give you names or where most of them are but it seems to work. You are not the only person we have helped in the cause of freedom.'

'I want to thank you Jambon for rescuing me from the clutches of the border guards and for your kindness in feeding me. I'll never be able to repay you. So, thank you again.'

Jambon shrugged his shoulders and said, 'It is my pleasure and my duty to help however I can.'

Malet senior had been transfixed by Claude's tale of escape and listened carefully as he recounted his enforced swim in the Saone and his timely rescue by the local resistance group. It had taken Claude a further six weeks to make it back to Chalhac, during which time he had been hidden under a heap of dung, and in a box buried in a mound of potatoes. Malet could hardly wait to tell the regulars in Jacques' bar and the members of their resistance group. Claude was ravenously hungry when he arrived. He had been given the old bicycle on 'permanent loan' by one of the last links in the carefully worked out chain dedicated to getting people out of the country and into Spain. The last seventy or eighty kilometres had been done on an empty stomach and he needed feeding quite urgently. His father asked Monique to put a meal together for her brother. She had been listening as he recounted his story to old Malet. She had been considerably upset when she heard that Daniel had been killed while trying to escape.

'Hurry up Monique. Your brother is nearly dropping here for lack of food.'

He was eventually fed, washed and clean clothes dug out for him. He was allowed to sleep for several hours. He would need time to pick up his health and strength again as Malet began to realise the full extent of what his son had been through. Claude had become quite emaciated since leaving for the army and Malet was a little shocked to see how much his son had changed as he sat in the old zinc bath washing himself.

'We'll have to feed you up Claude, you're as thin as a rake.'

During the next few days Claude and his father spent some time in Jacques' bar telling the local inhabitants about his sometimes exciting experiences as he escaped incarceration in the work camp near Belgium and his subsequent journey southwards. They were both treated to beer, red wine and the occasional marc. Claude's sister Monique managed to produce some nourishing food despite the limitations that were becoming more apparent in the food supply. Old Malet had managed to lay by a store of hams and sausage together with local cheeses. His foresight in doing so was now paying off as Claude was being given the best food available in the village. He quickly began to put on weight and his strength returned. Inside three weeks he was more or less back to his normal physical condition. The dissidents in Chalhac were told in detail what had transpired from the time he was enlisted until his escape and journey south. He was much admired by all as a result. Guy said he would be a welcome addition to their part membership of Abricot's Resistance Group. He felt sure that Claude would welcome the opportunity to settle a few scores given the chance and promised to tell Silas about the escapee.

Twenty-five

Three weeks into June, Hitler's armies invaded Russia. The French Communist party joined up with the resistance in occupied Northern France. The most visible effect was an upsurge in assassinations. The Germans' answer was brutal and for every German killed, a hundred random French civilians were arrested and sentenced to death by firing squad as reprisals. It was guaranteed to turn French public opinion against the occupiers and le Maréchal Pétain must have begun to wonder what his stated aims for France were now worth. The death sentences were not always carried out completely but never the less many innocent people were put to death.

None of this had gone unnoticed in Vichy, France, where resistance groups were flexing their muscles. In Domvent, Doctor Lovas alias Silas, had received a message from Abricot saying a plan was being prepared to sabotage an important railway line. It involved collapsing part of the tunnel which opened almost immediately on to a viaduct. The viaduct too would be put out of action. It would be dangerous for all concerned but the ensuing chaos would be worth it. Explosives would be needed and if he knew where a ready supply of dynamite or similar could be made available to supplement what they already had, it would be helpful. Lovas telephoned Farbres' office. Isabelle answered the call.

Lovas announced who it was. 'This is Doctor Lovas speaking. I have an appointment here in my diary for Madamoiselle Farbres to see me at my surgery at four o'clock this afternoon. Would you be so kind as to remind her? Thank you,' and put the phone down.

They were all aware of the simple but effective disguised telephone message to be used, to prevent possible nosiness by operators. Farbres was in his room and she told him that the doctor had rung and needed to speak to someone – not necessarily him but he expected to see one of them at four o'clock that day. Farbres said, 'OK. I'll go round there and tell you what's up when I get back. You could pass on the message to Guy and anyone else in the village if necessary.' So it was arranged. The doctor told Eric what was being planned and that it might involve more people. He also said that they were looking for more explosives. Eric hadn't been told by Isabelle that she, Marcel and Guy had hidden a substantial quantity from Jules' quarry in the cave under the escarpment. Eric was unable to offer any help with that issue as he did not know of its existence. When he returned to the Gendarmerie and told Isabelle about it she said,

'Sorry Papa. I just assumed you had been told about the dynamite. We took most of it away from the quarry when Boyer made his inspection last year. You weren't to know. The plan to blow up a tunnel or viaduct sounds exciting. We will have to get orders from Abricot sooner or later. I wonder where he plans to do it?'

'He didn't say but I would guess it may take some time to set up. If he's only just thinking about where they can lay their hands on more explosives it must mean there's a lot to do yet.'

'There will have to be a planning meeting eventually to discuss some of the detail. There are a few things we need to know, for example do we have detonators, a lot of wire and a spark generator? We have detonators and a spark generator, but no wire. We also need enough notice to be able to get the dynamite and detonators from where they are all hidden.' Eric Farbres was faintly amazed at his daughter's familiarity with all the terminology and still had no idea she had been very close to the Gaillard family for a long time. Jules Gaillard was a quarry man as was Guy's brother Marcel, so it was almost a certainty that she would have learned about dynamite which would have been part of their day to day conversation. Isabelle was kind enough not to remind her Papa that she had been instrumental in warning Jules and Marcel that the quarry was about to be inspected by the Gendarmerie and that the inspection team had been led by Michel Boyer.

'You certainly seemed to have picked up a great deal of knowledge about explosives and so on over the years Isabelle! I am more impressed than I can say.'

'Well Papa if I can put some of it to good use then I feel I will not have wasted my time.'

Meanwhile in Clermont, Boudeau and Jouve had their ears attuned for any information that could prove useful for operations further south, but there was little to report. Most of the news concerned the increasingly murderous activities of the Resistance in the Occupied Zone. This was taking place since Hitler's armies had attacked Russia. French communists were joining with the resistance and were prepared to behave more violently towards the occupiers. Assassinations began against selected Germans, particularly in Paris. The Nazis responded by ordering one hundred randomly chosen French people to be executed. The figure was later modified slightly to fifty and some escaped with their lives after legal wrangling.

The telephone rang in Doctor Lovas' surgery.

'Good morning Doctor,' said Abricot. 'I have to tell you that the treatment we discussed earlier has been changed. Your patient will no longer require the medicines I had ordered. Would it be possible to see you and your patient so that he knows about a revised schedule of treatment? Perhaps you will contact me, but you can assure your patient that he is in no danger, however the treatment will change when I have had the opportunity to discuss it with you. I wish you good day Doctor.' The phone went down.

Lovas rang him back. They arranged to meet again at the charcoal burner's hut. It seemed that after long discussions it had been decided that to disable the railway line now would be premature. It would be better to see if the occupiers moved across the Demarcation line into the south. It was widely thought that this would happen eventually, which would then be a more appropriate time to do some real damage to railway communications. The basic plan would remain unchanged, but would be put on hold until it became clearer what transpired in the north. Meanwhile the group would look at the best way to rescue 'undesirables' from buses which were being used to ship people northwards from the concentration camps in the south, and which were becoming over-populated ever since the latest orders to round up Jews and others seen to be undesirable, had been implemented. Abricot apologised to Lovas for the change of direction and hoped it would not be too much of a disappointment for others in the group. Lovas assured him there would be no problem, in fact it would be welcomed by the Gaillard family and others in the village. Rescuing dispossessed

Jewish people would be seen as very worthwhile. When he got back to Domvent he phoned the gendarmerie. Isabelle took the call.

'Could you ask Guy to come by, I have some important news for him.' He was careful not to say anything over the phone, which was now an ingrained habit for everyone.

'Of course, Doctor. Thank you.' She guessed wrongly this time, imagining there was a date arranged for their demolition schemes. Farbres was in his office when the doctor spoke to Isabelle so she told her Papa that she needed to tell Guy that she had been asked by Lovas to come to see him. There was movement of some sort going on, which it was necessary to discuss with Guy and the others. Eric Farbres said, 'Go down to the village and tell Guy that something's afoot. I'll go round to the doctor's to see if he knows anymore about it.' With that, Eric left Boyer in charge and walked around to the doctor's house and Isabelle got on her bicycle and went down to Chalhac. She found Guy at the back of the house cutting the remains of some old trees into logs in anticipation of another cold winter.

'Cherie! What brings you here? How lovely to see you!'

Isabelle quickly explained her sudden appearance and that Doctor Lovas wanted to see him fairly urgently. She assumed that it was about the planned attack on the tunnel and viaduct. She told him that her Papa was going round to the doctor's house and that he would know by now what was going on. She thought it would be best if they both made it back up to Domvent to hear it first hand from the doctor or from her Papa. Guy agreed and they both set off up the hill to the doctor's house. Eric Farbres was still there when they arrived.

'Quite a little family gathering!' said Eric. Doctor Lovas was making some coffee when they arrived and called from the kitchen. 'Give them an outline Eric about Abricot's change of mind.' Farbres rapidly explained that the tunnel and viaduct attack was being shelved for the time being. He began to tell them the reasoning behind it when the doctor appeared with a jug of coffee.

'I take it you would like a coffee? I can explain the rest of it to them, Eric.' They settled themselves as Lovas explained Abricot's latest thinking. Discussions had taken place with some of the established members and it became more and more clear that it

315

would be a wasted effort to sabotage the tunnel and viaduct at this time. There remained a strong feeling that the oppressors were likely to try to take over the rest of the country eventually. Ever since Germany attacked Russia, resulting in the Communists in France joining in with the Resistance in the occupied north, the Germans had been becoming increasingly vicious when handing out reprisal punishments to wrongdoers. The consensus was that it would be more damaging to German schemes if and when they walked into our unoccupied zone, if serious damage could be inflicted on them then, rather than now. Instead it is thought that we should put our time and energy into reversing some of the rounding up of innocent families, who happen to be mainly Jewish. This we know is inspired by the gang in Paris. New laws have been enacted during the last few months which are specifically aimed at Jews, communists and masonic members. Jews in particular are to be dispossessed of businesses and property. If a business is seen to be a valuable addition to the Reich it is to be taken over and run by a Nazi appointed manager and its products passed on to its new masters. That was the new thinking.

'May I ask you for your feelings on the matter?'

Guy was the first to air his feelings. 'It is sensible that we should hold back from attacking the railways at this time. If you really believe the occupiers will try to take over the rest of the country eventually, it would disrupt their communications very effectively. As for trying to rescue rounded-up people, before they are sent off to become slave labourers, I am all for it. We'll have to consider the best way to tackle it. It may be that plans already exist, in which case we would like to get sight of what's proposed.'

Lovas thanked him for his approval of the change of strategy and promised that they would all have a chance to approve or improve upon existing plans. 'How do you see this Isabelle?'

'I agree completely with Guy on this. His family has lived with the unspoken threat since June last year when the country was overrun. We must not forget David Markovich at the chateau who will almost certainly agree with the present plans. He is still out for his own revenge against the Germans for what he witnessed on his way here from Rouen. There are very few Jews living down here, but those who do, will be feeling very vulnerable these days having heard about well documented examples of families being swept up and taken away in buses to unknown destinations.

Monsieur Bastien, the Mayor of Chalhac, has the responsibility of knowing who lives in the village and he is obliged to inform the authorities in Domvent, of details of any Jews, masonic members or communists living there. They will know about Guy's parents – how long they have lived in the village, where they came from and so on. They know about Guy but somehow Marcel slipped through the net. It has resulted in Marcel not qualifying for a ration card when they were being issued. David Markovich at the chateau is not recorded anywhere. When the Mayor was told about him he said he was under the impression that David was only a very temporary resident. He was living at the Gaillard's house at the time. Monsieur Bastien didn't think it warranted all the paperwork the authorities would demand, so he left David out of the reckoning. It means that the only identifiable people at risk are the Gaillard family, including Guy.'

The doctor said, 'I don't see you doing the bidding of anyone in Clermont. Your father knows perfectly well about your relationship with Guy and in any event, I would not expect him to obey the orders coming down the line from Vichy and elsewhere. If the Germans do move into our area the situation could become a lot trickier. That will not happen tomorrow or the next day, but there would be a clamp down by the Gestapo and Nazi military. We cannot plan for that since we don't really know how they will behave. There has to be a rethink about our group's next moves. Abricot and others down there have been giving thought to frustrating the authority's plans to round up more Jews and others. The gendarmerie in Toulouse will be involved in arresting people and, at the moment, they seem to be following the régime's orders. There is no evidence of dissent in their branch, so we will have to regard them as our opponents. I have my own ideas about a rescue scheme which I need to discuss with Abricot, before other plans are activated. Everything we do carries a risk of course so we must be careful to hide our involvement. If my idea is used, the gendarmerie in Toulouse will be considerably upset and will want to know who instigated the operation. We will have to play this by ear for the moment, so bear with me.'

'Are you able to give us some clue regarding your thinking Doctor?' said Farbres. 'We are agog to know how it might work.'

Lovas was reluctant to say too much but explained that it would involve a bogus gendarmerie unit showing up at the right moment, carrying bogus orders from Vichy countermanding instructions from Toulouse. It would take an amount of preparation but it might be a safer approach because it would be difficult to trace where our organisation is based. 'It will rely on Colonel Boudeau's organisational skills to supply suitable vehicles, disguised registration plates and to obtain if possible, a copy of the orders to Toulouse about the round up. Perhaps you Eric, could speak to Boudeau about that part of the scheme? I will speak to Abricot to tell him what we have in mind here. I cannot see him giving it the thumbs down. If nobody else has further questions I will send you on your way. I am expecting to see a patient shortly and we don't want questions being asked.'

The meeting broke up then and Isabelle and her father walked back to the gendarmerie while Guy returned to Chalhac. He told his parents and Marcel what was being hatched by the doctor and Abricot. He also told them about the decision to cancel the attack on the railway tunnel and viaduct. They understood why this had been decided and were gratified to learn that they planned now to offer some protection to Jewish families and their businesses. He left them for a while then called by Jacques' bar, to see if anyone was there and finally cycled up to the chateau to keep David and Henrietta up to date.

At the gendarmerie in Domvent, Eric Farbres had spoken to Boudeau. He had a simple message for him: Could he get down to Domvent as there were matters he needed to know about. Boudeau arrived the following morning before ten o'clock. Eric and Isabelle outlined the doctor's plans, emphasised that Abricot had to approve them before detailed preparations could begin. Eric said to Boudeau, 'Would you have any problems in borrowing one of Clermont's vans or trucks?'

'I would not think so. I would have to dream up an imaginary investigation involving a number of personnel, who could be picked up further down the road. As for producing forged documents from Vichy, there would be no difficulties. We have several expert forgers on our books who would be keen to do work for me if I promise to help them reduce their sentences. I will see if we can locate the actual order from Vichy which authorised Toulouse to arrest and imprison as many Jews and others as possible. I have the picture Eric. Let me know in good time when you propose to mount the operation. The bogus paperwork will take some time to prepare but there should be no problems.' Eric thanked him for his efforts and shortly afterwards Boudeau left Domvent and headed back to Clermont.

The starting date had been fixed for the operation, but it was subject to finalising information about when Toulouse was going to implement the orders concerning mass arrests. The usual pattern for mass arrests involved demanding a local bus company to supply a bus for about thirty people, together with a driver. There would be an armed guard on the bus and it would be accompanied by a small contingent of gendarmes to assist in getting people out of their houses and on to the bus. The victims naturally protested their innocence of any crimes but their distress was met with, 'We have our orders.'

The plan was to waylay the bus with its passengers. This would be achieved by waving it down by 'bogus' gendarmes' – provided by other members of their group. They would ask the bus driver to pull into the side of the road while they spoke to the officer in charge of the real gendarmes, showing him the last minute change of plans, which would supposedly have come from Vichy. The driver was to go directly to the gendarmerie in Domvent, where they would be locked up overnight and collected the next day for transfer to the nearest railway station. The bogus gendarmes would be dressed in borrowed, authentic uniforms and boots, and would not be suspected by anyone. The gendarmes from Toulouse were to return to their unit and the bus would be safely accompanied onwards by the unit responsible for delivering the orders.

Boudeau's connections in Vichy sent him a copy of an order originally from Vichy and addressed to the senior officer in Toulouse. It was a short item on an entirely different topic. It gave them the pattern to make a forgery of an original blank order which could then be filled in and typed by Abricot's group. It would be rubber stamped and dated the day of the exercise. The borrowed order was to go back to Clermont, where Boudeau would get it back to Vichy. It looked like it might work on this occasion. Everything would be in place ahead of the starting date.

A little over a month elapsed and Abricot rang Farbres to say that they now had a starting date near the end of November. Farbres called Boudeau saying that everything was in order and was the paperwork complete? It was, said Boudeau, and he would send it down to him. If a telephone operator was listening during a similar conversation, there was little or nothing to report to the supervisor. The forged paperwork arrived two days later.

There was a meeting at Abricot's farm when the final orders were given to all those involved in the operation. Everyone was excited at the thought of doing something worthwhile at last. Abricot explained that following the new 'orders' being carried out and accepted by the Toulouse officer in charge, the situation would then be explained to the passengers. The bus driver would be asked to retrace their journey and individuals would be dropped off back at their homes if they wished. It was his belief that they would be better advised to go into hiding if possible because when the truth dawned on the powers that be in Toulouse, there would be an all-out effort to carry out the original orders. But it was the best they could do.

Guy Gaillard volunteered to be a 'gendarme' dressed in the standard uniform and boots. The other bogus gendarmes were people known to Abricot who had been with his resistance group from the beginning. They came from all walks of life but all shared the same attitude towards the Pétain régime, namely to get him to change his mind in his dealings with the Nazis. On the evening of the bus hijack, Guy cycled up to Domvent and awaited final orders. They would be taken in the lorry to the road junction where the deception would take place. The lorry was from the Domvent gendarmerie, and not from Clermont. It had been fitted with false registration plates and any other markings that might identify it were painted over with the insignia of an imaginary gendarmerie. A new and non-existent gendarmerie unit was supposedly in an imaginary town between Domvent and Clermont. It seemed that Abricot had re-thought some of the details of the entire operation and was intent on protecting his team as best he could.

Guy made for the doctor's house. The usual preliminaries were recited and Lovas invited him in. 'Ready for the off then Guy?' Guy was clearly a little jumpy about the whole thing but was calmed by the doctor's quiet confidence.

'Yes Doctor. I was feeling a bit apprehensive as I cycled up here, but then I realised that if I dropped out at the last moment, I would never be trusted again. Your presence has helped calm my nerves.'

Lovas said he understood how he felt and that he'd had slight qualms himself. 'I'm sure the rest of the team feel much the same. It would not be natural to feel other than the way we do. I am playing the part of officer in charge of this exercise and will sit with the driver. I have the forged documents and they look very authentic. You will get the drift of things once we start. We can hope that none of the Toulouse squad are too inquisitive and that they will blindly accept the revised 'orders.' I am going to change into my uniform now, the one on loan from Major Farbres. He will not be taking part in the operation in case someone from Toulouse should recognise him. He has spent some time trying to arrange another concentration camp near there and has been in and out of their headquarters. It is a chance we cannot afford to take.'

Shortly after midnight Lovas told Guy to put on his boots and the rest of his uniform, as they needed to get down to the farm. Farbres was going to drive the gendarmerie lorry down there and collect the rest of the 'gendarmes.' The farm had been arranged to make it their 'rendezvous' as most of them were from the surrounding area. They had already established that the bus company habitually used the road where they planned to waylay the bus. At about half past one they had assembled at their road block location with the gendarmerie lorry with ten men on board, carrying suitable handguns. Lovas wore Farbres' uniform and sat with the driver. Blue lanterns were arranged to divert the bus to the side of the road. Lovas carried a heavy duty torch. Eric Farbres was to remain out of sight at the farm with Abricot until they returned from the expedition.

At about two o'clock the bus appeared, accompanied by a small van similar to the one in daily use by the Domvent unit. So far, they could see it carried the driver, an officer and three gendarmes. Lovas was directing operations and the bus slowed to a stop. The Toulouse van stopped immediately behind the bus. The officer in charge stepped out of the van and approached Lovas. 'What seems to be the trouble Sir?'

'There is no problem Lieutenant, but we have had to stop you in order to give you some last minute revised orders from Vichy. I have the paperwork here.' He handed the forged orders to the young Lieutenant. 'As I understand it we will have to take the arrested people on from here and keep them in our gendarmerie at St. Maurice-de-Periac until the morning when they will be collected and taken to a nearby railway station. Our responsibilities will cease there. Your men will not be unhappy I'm sure, to get back to their barracks and get some sleep.'

The young officer examined the orders and said, 'Very well Sir and thank you. What about the bus and the driver? Can you deal with that?' Lovas said he could foresee no problems arising. The driver would know the area well enough and would make his way back when he had dropped off the people in St. Maurice.'

It had gone better than anyone dared to hope. The Lieutenant was a little too trusting, never imagining that a forged, bogus order would end up in his hand. 'Very well Sir. If you are happy to take over from here I will wish you goodnight Sir.' With that he ordered the van driver to head back to Toulouse.

In the bus the very unhappy and anxious passengers had been trying to understand what had been going on. When the small van turned around carrying with it the armed guard, and had headed back the way they had just come, their confusion was total. The doctor came to the door of the bus and got in. The driver was baffled as well and Lovas stood at the front of the bus and explained.

He said he and his fellow gendarmes were not what they seemed to be. The 'gendarmes' were not gendarmes at all, nor was he. 'We are all members of a resistance group in the area, dedicated to rescuing people like you from the clutches of the police and Gestapo. The Vichy régime has sought favours from the German aggressors all along in a policy inspired by le Maréchal Pétain. Your arrest tonight is the direct result of Pétain's eagerness to keep the Nazis happy with the way he is running things. But we happen to know that there will be no favours coming from the Nazis. Quite the contrary in fact, as fresh orders have gone out to gendarmeries in both the occupied and unoccupied zones to round up as many Jewish people as possible. Not just Jews, but masonic members, communists and anybody else the régime sees as a threat to its future. You though, are now free again and we are taking you back to your homes and businesses. We suggest you get away from your existing homes as quickly as possible because the Toulouse gendarmerie appears eager to follow the orders issued in Paris and Berlin. You can be sure that when they discover what transpired tonight they will try to pick you up again. If you have friends or colleagues who might be prepared to hide you for a few weeks that would be the best solution. The driver here will retrace his steps and take you home, if we ask him nicely! He may have to answer some awkward questions at some time, and he would be well advised to be unable to explain what took place.'

The driver stood up and shook Lovas' hand vigorously, saying, 'You are a true patriot Monsieur.' The passengers also wanted to thank him but he said they should get back to their homes as quickly as possible because they may not have a lot of time to play with. He wished them all luck and thanked them in turn before he got off the bus which then reversed and headed into the darkness. Lovas briefly told his team of renegades that everything had gone to plan and suggested they return to Abricot's farm. When they arrived Abricot was chatting to Eric Farbres in a very comfortable sitting room which the others hadn't seen before. It was clearly his private domain. A log fire was burning in the grate and both men held a glass of brandy. They were both relieved to see Miklos Lovas and Guy walk in, wearing broad smiles.

'I take it everything went to plan then?'

'It did, thanks to your planning Abricot,' said Miklos. 'We managed to get about thirty people back to their homes tonight, but I warned them that once the gendarmerie in Toulouse wakes up to what has happened they will shift heaven and earth to try to recapture them. I advised they should leave their homes and businesses as quickly as possible and try to find friends prepared to hide them. I think they got the message.'

'Excellent,' said Abricot, who turned to Guy and asked him for his impressions of the operation. Guy said he was impressed with the whole thing. 'We can expect some intensive questioning now and we should prepare our answers carefully. They should have no

323

reasons to suspect any of us of course, but they will be desperate to get to the bottom of it. The fact that a gendarmerie vehicle was being used will throw suspicion onto the gendarmerie service as having people in their ranks who do not altogether agree with the party line. I would imagine the poor Lieutenant in charge of the Toulouse side of the affair will receive a severe talking to. The bus driver turned out to be completely on our side and he could be a weak point when his interrogators are told that he delivered the captives back to their homes in his bus. I suggested he could plead ignorant of the felony and was only doing what he was ordered by a middle ranking officer of the Gendarmerie. I hope we covered our tracks well enough.'

Abricot thanked everybody for their efforts and apologised for keeping them up late. He thought they were safe enough for the moment but also thought that as a group, they should stay out of sight for a month or two and let any fuss die down.

With that he said he would be in touch eventually, with a similar scheme to consider, but he had nothing specific in mind at the moment. Politely dismissed, they all headed back to Domvent, Chalhac and a number of small towns and villages where the rest of the bogus gendarmerie officers lived.

When Guy got back to Chalhac the lamps were still burning in Jacques Fournier's bar. He had decided to stay open until Guy returned. Marcel, David Markovich and Henrietta were installed drinking a variety of refreshments, provided mostly by Jacques. When Guy arrived, he was greeted by everyone as the conquering hero. When he appeared, they were, for the briefest of moments, taken aback to see a gendarme walk in, as Guy was still wearing his borrowed uniform and boots.

'How did it go Guy?' asked Marcel, who had been anxiously waiting at home and then later in the bar. They were all impatient to hear what had resulted as well as being desperately tired.

Guy said, 'I will be as brief as I can. It went better than we hoped. We were able to release about thirty people and return them to their homes. There was a lot of driving involved for the bus driver as well as helping people out of the bus to retrieve their bundles of clothes and so on. The young Toulouse gendarmerie officer was completely taken in by the forged documents and actually thanked the doctor for giving him and his men an earlier night than they expected! I'll tell you all about it tomorrow. I'm absolutely exhausted right now and I'm sure you must all feel the same. Thank you for staying up for me and thank you Jacques for keeping your bar open.' The evening finally drew to an end and as they left the sky was beginning to lighten in the east, reminding them that another day was due to start in another hour or two.

In the Domvent gendarmerie there was a palpable sense of relief and jubilation. Eric Farbres had related in detail to Lieutenant Boyer how it had all progressed. Isabelle already knew that everything had gone to plan when her Papa came home in the early hours to find Anne-Marie and Isabelle waiting for him in the kitchen. They were both anxious to know all about it and he quickly filled them in with the details. 'They'd all held their breath when the doctor produced the forged orders from Vichy, authorising us to take over responsibility for the poor souls in the bus who were all terrified and confused. The doctor told the young Lieutenant from Toulouse that he and his small team of gendarmes could safely leave the busload to us and we would see to it that the revised orders were carried out. The young officer in charge was only too happy to be able to tell his men that they were going back to Toulouse where they could catch up on their sleep. I don't suppose the young man had ever held in his hand what appeared to be direct orders from Vichy. He may even have felt slightly flattered.'

Eric said he would have liked to have witnessed some of this action but had been obliged to stay out of sight in Abricot's headquarters in case anyone from Toulouse spotted him. He had become a familiar face to a few people down there when seeking likely sites for a concentration camp.

Isabelle wanted to know what became of the bus and its passengers.

Eric said they were all taken back by the driver and delivered to their homes again. They were warned to try to arrange for someone to keep them hidden until the initial enthusiasm to find them again had faded. Isabelle wanted to know how the bus driver would explain away his part in the deception since he was bound to be questioned. Eric said that the man would plead total ignorance to it and had simply obeyed the orders that the gendarmerie officer had given him.

'I hope he will be believed,' said Isabelle.

The following morning in the Toulouse Gendarmerie Headquarters, Colonel Jean Bastide sat at his desk quietly fuming. Standing in front of him were the bus driver and the young Lieutenant in charge of the previous night's fiasco.

'It seems to me,' said Bastide, 'that you were just a little naïve Lieutenant. Did you not read the so-called orders that made fools of us here? Did it not even occur to you that they may have been forgeries?' The forged papers lay on his desk now and Bastide emphasised his questions by thumping the papers with the fingers of his open fist.

'It did occur to me of course, but they were handed to me by someone dressed as an officer of the gendarmerie – a Major in fact. They appeared to be real enough, so what was I to do? He might have taken me to task and reported me to Vichy where they seemed to have come from. You can see for yourself, Sir, that they would fool anyone and at two o'clock in the morning, they certainly fooled me.'

The Colonel picked them up again and closely scrutinised them. 'I have to agree that whoever made these knew what they were doing. They even had the date on the rubber stamp right. Alright Lieutenant, go back to whatever you should be doing for now and we will discuss this more fully later.'

'Thank you Sir.' He produced a smart salute and let himself out of the office.

'Now Monsieur Eldin, perhaps you would give me your account of what happened last night. You have heard what the Lieutenant had to say. You did not see these 'orders' of course but you did get instructions from the Major telling you what to do after the Lieutenant had left you with the bus. What did he say?'

'He said that there had been a rethink in Vichy and I was therefore to take the bus with the passengers back to their homes or wherever we collected them from, and then to go home. It did strike me that it had all been a terrible waste of time, but who was I to question it? The Major giving orders looked like the real thing so I had no choice in the matter.'

Colonel Bastide was less than convinced but it was such a simple tale that he could do nothing for the moment which would weaken Eldin's account. He told him to stay within range of Toulouse as there may be further questions to answer in due course. Bastide picked up the phone and called back the Lieutenant. 'How did the people you rounded up last night react when they heard they would be transferred to another gendarmerie in the morning and then put on a train for somewhere else?'

The Lieutenant explained that they were unable to hear all the details because he and the 'Major' were outside the bus when he was given the revised orders from Vichy. They could probably hear some of it but they were all very upset and worried for their future. 'They would have been very confused when they saw the armed guard we had stationed in the bus being dismissed and sent with me and the rest of our party back the way we had come. I had no idea that the entire operation was a hoax at that time so the pretence that they would be shipped further on in the morning would have been explained to them as a lot of lies. I have just been checking where St. Maurice-de-Peyriac is supposed to be and there is no such place. It seems they thought of everything.'

'Evidently,' said Bastide. 'What is your opinion of the bus driver – do you believe he is being truthful in his version of last night's events? I don't see how we can break down his story which seems entirely plausible to me. If he thought he was being given new instructions by an officer of the gendarmerie, he could have been arrested there and then had he disobeyed. So, he did as he was told and returned the busload to wherever they had come from. Have you made any attempt to check out their addresses this morning yet? It will probably be a waste of time now because they will have been warned that we will come looking for them. It's a damned mess Lieutenant.'

'I have given orders to some of our officers to check out a number of last night's addresses and they have not returned yet. I don't hold out much hope that any of them will remain where they were living before they were picked up. I'm afraid we will have to start all over again if we are to keep Vichy off our backs.'

'Of course. You do realise Lieutenant, that somewhere in the gendarmerie service there exists more than one person who disagrees with the way le Maréchal is running the régime. How else could a gendarmerie truck, uniforms, guns and all the paraphernalia be so effectively arranged? Then there's the forged 'orders', very authentic looking I have to say. It has all the makings of a very professional group of people that we will be up against some time in the future.'

It had indeed occurred to the Lieutenant.

In the Clermont headquarters of the gendarmerie Boudeau's source of information seemed to have dried up. He had received legitimate information and orders from Vichy but there appeared to be very little coming directly from Paris or from Brussels. He began to wonder if he and Jouve had become suspects, since he had been making odd absences from the office without any apparent reason to do so. He also borrowed one of the small vans occasionally, returning it later in the day and saying nothing. He remembered that Abricot had said there were people watching everyone else these days and some were Abricot's associates. He asked Jouve to come into his office and invited him to take a seat.

'What do you think is going on René? I don't know about you but I have a strong feeling that you and I are being watched and suspected of possible dissent. It seems strange to me that our normal contacts in Paris and Brussels have completely dried up. I find that worrying.'

Jouve agreed. He felt that the telephone operators were monitoring their calls. He'd become aware of a change in the sound of his calls coming through the earpiece, as if another person had joined the operator with another handset. 'I think we should be very careful when we speak to our friends in Domvent. If it is necessary to call them sometimes we must always dress up our calls to sound like legitimate police business, but if they suspect we are mixed up in something shady, then it will be very dangerous for all concerned. I would like to speak to them at Domvent and to warn them about the way we are thinking. Should I ring them or maybe go down and discuss it? They need to know because if they are on to us then the entire operation being run by Abricot could be jeopardised,'

'I think it would be safer to go down there. I'll dream up a reason for you to use the van to make a visit. I'll think about it tonight and you could go down in the morning.' Overnight he invented an imaginary villain who they had been watching for some time and Lieutenant Jouve was to be given the job of filling in some of the detail and background of the person to their counterparts in Domvent. They had seen the suspect heading in that direction and had followed him at a distance but he had given them the slip at some point. In the morning Boudeau outlined the story to him so he would be prepared with an explanation should it become necessary. Jouve left for Domvent shortly after.

When he arrived at the gendarmerie he was greeted warmly by everyone including Eric Farbres. 'What brings you here at this ungodly hour René?' asked Eric.

Jouve told them what he and Boudeau had begun to suspect in the light of the apparent drying up of information from Paris, Brussels and from Vichy. There may, of course, be a perfectly rational explanation such as their informant being arrested for some similar misdemeanor, but they were playing safe.

'I can understand your anxieties René, and you are very wise to play it this way', said Eric. 'You may not have seen it yet but gendarmes in this part of the world have all been sent a memo from the top man in Toulouse. We received our copy this morning. It asks all heads of gendarmeries to be alert for any signs of dissent within the service. It briefly gives details of the hijacking of a busload of Jews and others by what appears to be an active and clever resistance organisation within range of Toulouse. A real gendarmerie lorry had been used and the hijackers were all dressed in authentic gendarmerie uniforms including the bogus officer in charge. It's thought that somewhere in the service there is more than one rotten apple prepared to go along with plans to disrupt government authority. When it reaches your office later it will only confirm what someone at the top already suspects, namely there are people within its ranks who don't wish to toe the line. Abricot and Silas, the doctor, have already said that we should keep our heads down for a few weeks or at least until the heat comes off. I respect that decision because at the moment they will do anything to uncover who and where we are.'

René Jouve had listened intently to Eric Farbres' precis of the memo. It had also contained more information about the forgeries and the bus driver's explanations. Eric assumed that the copy for the

Clermont office would come into their hands and they could read it for themselves.

René said that someone had evidently been taking note of the journeys being taken by Boudeau and for which he had offered no explanation. The group all knew it was necessary in order to establish its growth under Abricot. It was important for them to feel a sense of togetherness and to know they were all looking in the same direction. 'Do you think Abricot would be prepared to tell us who our spy is in the Clermont office or would he feel there would be too many risks involved?' he asked. He had not discussed this with Boudeau and the thought had only occurred to him while sitting here in Farbres' office. 'I'll ask the doctor about it,' said Eric. He added that they too should step back a little for the time being or at least until Abricot felt a little more confident that the efforts to uncover the group were fading somewhat. He thanked René for driving down for the sole purpose of warning them. The young Lieutenant left for Clermont shortly afterwards. He arrived back in his office shortly after lunch to find Boudeau was standing and gazing out of his window. The memo from Toulouse had reached their office and it was now in general circulation within the building. It had made Boudeau feel a little uncomfortable when he read it as it only went to confirm that the head man in Toulouse was now dedicated to uncovering Abricot's group. If, as it seemed to be the case, that he and Jouve were already suspected of doing something off the record and were being watched, then the contents of the memo this morning could be interpreted as further evidence of wrong doing in the Clermont office. It all looked very dangerous to Boudeau. René Jouve tapped on his door and Boudeau beckoned to him to come in.

'How did it go?'

'OK,' said Jouve. He told his boss that they were grateful to him for driving all the way down to Domvent simply to warn them that he thought they had become suspects by someone within the Clermont office. They had received a memo from Toulouse fishing for information about anyone who could be out of line with the régime policies.

'We received our copy this morning after you had left and I find it slightly worrying. If you and I are being watched already, it will not take a genius to put two and two together after reading the Toulouse memo and to consider us seriously out of step with the rules and régime. We will both have to take several steps backwards in order to take the heat off us. I am thinking that we can make a start by circulating our own report explaining some of our activities including the pursuit of our imaginary 'suspected' villain down the road on more than one occasion in the general direction of Domvent. He has so far managed to avoid being stopped for questioning after giving us the slip each time. That is the story – what do you think?'

'Sounds OK to me Sir,' said René. 'It would be a relief to feel the cloud above us lifting a little. There are other issues that we must be prepared to answer, for example, how did we come to think our imagined suspect was up to no good in the first place? I feel that if it gets to the point when we are both being interrogated, we will have to be sure of our answers and that we both have the same story.

Boudeau felt much better for speaking to his young assistant. He had begun to mentally run around in circles before he had arrived back from Domvent and had achieved nothing. Now they had a plan. 'Thank you René. I am grateful to you for your input. I will draft a suitable story in rough which we can both agree to. I'll see to it that it gets circulated. Hopefully the right person or persons will get sight of it in its final report form. We can also hope that it never gets to the point where we find ourselves being officially questioned.'

In Domvent Eric Farbres had been considering the dangers surrounding the operations that had been planned, and now wisely delayed by Abricot and Silas. Toulouse was obviously smarting as a result of the bus hijacking and was determined to show that it would not happen again. That morning's memo to various gendarmeries was written not only to try to demonstrate their determination in that direction but was intended also to make an attempt to uncover possible weaknesses within the service. The hijacking had hit a raw nerve in Toulouse where it had always been assumed that gendarmeries and their employees were above any wrongdoing. Farbres inwardly smiled at the damage it may have done to his counterpart in Toulouse. Abricot had said that one of the group's members was employed in the Toulouse gendarmerie and as such was a prime example of the very thing that Colonel Bastide most feared, but had been forced to acknowledge, while never believing that his own unit in Toulouse would have employed such a person. Eric wondered if the group could make more use of the man in some future operation. He voiced his thoughts to Michel Boyer who also had been mulling over the implications of the Toulouse memo.

Boyer had wondered what Abricot had in mind for another operation against the régime. He fervently hoped that it would not be set in motion too soon and would be so devised to deflect suspicion away from Domvent and its immediate neighbours. In his view the last operation was sufficiently dangerous and could not be repeated with any degree of safety for the perpetrators. 'It would be worthwhile speaking to the doctor about it as it would be a pity to have to waste an opportunity of finding a way of wrecking some of Toulouse's schemes. The orders they are receiving from Vichy are becoming more extreme and if it's possible, we should try to obstruct some of them, always given sensible planning and a bit of luck.'

Doctor Lovas, alias Silas, was happy to discuss further ideas with Eric Farbres. He too had been giving serious thought about ways of utilising their member in the Toulouse gendarmerie. 'We could create further chaos if we were able to discover the names of those next on their list to be gathered up by bus, by simply collecting the people a day or so before they tried to. That way they could not be sure whether their list was out of date or whether the party concerned had been away or may have got the wind up and moved out having heard about people or their friends' adventures a few days ago. It would waste a great deal of time and effort and could even lead them into believing that this approach wasn't worth it. The question arises as to how their contact Emile could get hold of their list without instantly being identified? There would be very few people in authority with access to it and he would be exposed very quickly.'

'Would Vichy have some sort of list for potential collection I wonder?' said Eric. 'A month or so ago a new law was published telling all Jews to identify themselves with their local authority. This would have given them a comprehensive resource for all local gendarmeries and would also provide us with the ability to mess up some of their plans. Do you think Abricot's spies in Vichy or elsewhere could investigate the likelihood of a list? If the Jewish population did as they were told and reported their whereabouts to their local Mayor or someone, there should by now be a substantial list which could be exploited by gendarmeries. Toulouse might therefore already hold a list of people for rounding up. If this is the case then our member Emile could, with luck, find it and maybe photograph it. It would not be easy for anyone in Toulouse to pin it on him, because the list would have gone to all the gendarmeries wanting it.'

'Leave it with me Eric. I'll speak to Abricot later. Perhaps we have the answer staring us in the face,' said Miklos. 'Thanks for giving it the time and thought Eric. I know that Abricot has been thinking hard about the next moves. This might be the very thing he is looking for.' Farbres left shortly after and returned to his office where he told Isabelle and Michel Boyer how Silas had reacted. He was going to call Abricot later and put it to him.

Abricot was very much in favour and said he would sound out his contacts in Vichy to see if a list or lists had been created as a result of the new registration rules. He called Silas later to arrange a meeting at their usual place in the charcoal burner's hut. Telephoning would be too risky to discuss the subjects he had in mind. His call was dressed up as a pseudo medical enquiry to avoid possible operators listening in. They met up the following day and Abricot was in a happy frame of mind. He had been greatly encouraged to hear that there were minds at work other than his own looking for ways to disrupt the régime and its supporters. He told Silas that he was waiting to hear from his spies in Vichy and Paris to know whether typed lists existed and if they did who held them. 'I have also asked if it is possible to photograph or otherwise obtain a copy for us. It is a long shot and might be too dangerous to attempt in any event, but there is no harm in asking.'

'No indeed,' said Lovas. 'If we were able to get a readymade list from your sources it would be much safer for us to exploit. We would still need to discover exactly when our friends in Toulouse were proposing to begin their next sweep, but that would not be quite so difficult, I imagine. We will just have to wait and see what your contacts can come up with, but it holds great promise. Has there been any word about the last exploit's bus driver's interrogation? Colonel Bastide would have been very happy to have got some useful answers from the man, but if he kept his nerve the driver's story would have been very difficult to break down. Besides which, the young Lieutenant in charge of their operation would be bound to take a lot of the blame, which Bastide was trying to avoid as it would indirectly reflect on his abilities and on the Toulouse unit as well. If we are able to mount a successful operation again, there could be more repercussions in Toulouse, not forgetting that we could save a number of innocent people from being arrested.'

'Quite so,' said Abricot. With that they agreed to call it a day and they went their separate ways.

Twenty-six

The October hijacking exploit was followed by a pause in activities by Abricot's resistance group. They had been obliged to follow his orders and keep their heads down for a while and it appeared to have been sound advice. Colonel Bastide in Toulouse had no success in his attempts to identify the perpetrators of that operation and interest was waning in the matter. There were no new memos being sent to other gendarmeries and he had received little or no response from any of them. It still niggled him that he was unable to uncover the weaknesses within the service. His mind now was beginning to be deflected by what he had begun to recognize as a probable takeover by the Germans of the Southern Free Zone. Rumours persisted that cast doubts about the prospects for a German final victory. Some of the rumours were being deliberately spread by resistant groups like Abricot's and there were confusing stories coming from Vichy concerning French colonial interests in North Africa. There were baffling moves by France, Italy, England, the Nazis and the Americans, who by this time were considering sending troops from North America.

In Domvent a letter arrived for the personal attention of Major Eric Farbres, bearing a Vichy postmark. Isabelle resisted the temptation to open it in case it contained something very personal, so she placed it on her father's desk. He arrived shortly after this and quickly opened it. 'Well, well, well,' he said, 'Abricot will be very pleased to see this.' He walked through to Isabelle's room where she and Michel Boyer were drinking coffee.

'You'll be interested to see this,' said Eric, waving the letter at them. 'It is a list of Jewish people, trades unionists, masonic members and others, in and around the Toulouse area, extending as far as and beyond Domvent. It covers the entire Cantal region. The letter says that, "So far as possible, you are ordered to round up all of the listed people and to keep them under lock and key until arrangements can be made to send them to Paris where they will be held pending further instructions. The list will enable you to avoid duplicated attempts by gendarmeries within close range of each other to round up persons from the same address." 'It would seem the net has been spread more widely than we expected,' said Eric Farbres.

Isabelle said that they should treat the list and letter very warily in case it was a trap to expose the group that did the hijacking in October. 'If our group responded with another scheme and we were the only gendarmerie to have received this list, which might have some bogus names and addresses on it in any event, then Toulouse and Vichy would know instantly who were the villains. Am I right Papa? I think you and the doctor should tackle Abricot about it and see what he has to say.'

'Perhaps you are right Isabelle. What do you think Michel?' Boyer was all for playing it as safe as possible and agreed with Isabelle's cautious views. Eric said he would call on Doctor Lovas straight away. 'Do you want to join me Cherie? You can stay here Michel for the moment,'

'The doctor welcomed them after the usual recitation and Eric handed him the letter and list.

'Come in and sit down. A coffee?' Lovas carefully read the covering letter and looked down the list. 'I would not trust that for one moment. I smell a large rat in that. How do you see it?'

They both expressed their doubts about it and felt it could easily have been set up by Toulouse.

'I agree,' said Lovas. 'Toulouse appears to have lost interest in that whole episode, but they were quick to recognize that a gendarmerie somewhere had been able to set the thing up using real uniforms, a lorry and all the rest of it. We are still keeping our heads down and it is just as well because they would have been very careful not to be caught out again. I will have to give some serious thought to this and speak to Abricot but I imagine he will agree with our thinking.'

When Abricot finally got sight of the list and its covering letter he smiled at Miklos and said, 'I'd lay you money on it that it is a trap. They have drawn a blank in every other direction and now they are desperate to get to the truth. We will have to consider the best and safest way to put it to the test. Do we have some trustworthy friends in the service within the Cantal region who would have received this if it had been sent to all units? We could ask fairly casually if they had had anything from Vichy in the last day or two, and see what they had to say. If any of them had, it might mean that every unit was now suspect and not just us. If, as Isabelle mentioned, a bogus name had been included in only our copy and no one else's, then we could be fairly sure that we were the prime suspects. We would have to ask for a copy or something which we could compare our list with. What do you think Miklos?'

Lovas was impressed with Abricot's rapid grasp of the situation together with his instant solution to putting it to the test.

'It makes sense to me and if we were able to establish for certain that one of the names is an invention and has been inserted into our copy to trap us, then we could carefully leave it out of any scheme we may be hatching and they still would not know which unit was responsible.'

Abricot asked Lovas to speak to Isabelle or her father to see if Boudeau in Clermont had access to a readymade directory of gendarmeries in the Cantal area. It would be a big help in establishing how many there were and it would not arouse suspicions if Boudeau or Jouve asked about a directory which they could then send down to Domvent.

'I think we could still work out another operation aimed at stopping selected people from being rounded up like cattle and being sent off to Paris for dispatch to German or Polish camps. There's not much we can do to help, but we should do everything we can.'

With that, Abricot suggested they should finish their discussion as he felt sure that Miklos would have some patients waiting for him, and they parted company.

Lovas rang Eric Farbres' office from his surgery and briefly explained that he would like to see Major Farbres in his surgery to discuss his new treatment. Isabelle had taken the call and arranged a formal appointment for the next day. In the morning Boudeau appeared at the Domvent gendarmerie. He was by himself and carried a substantial directory under one arm, which he put on Eric's desk. 'Where's the man?' he asked Michel Boyer.

'He and Isabelle have gone to Doctor Lovas' surgery – it's less than two hundred metres from here. They had hoped you would get down here fairly early and would be armed with a list of gendarmeries within the Cantal and other departments close by. I am sure they will find plenty to discuss in your absence Colonel!'

'I'll get around there straight away,' said Boudeau, who had momentarily reverted to a lifetime's habit of answering people of inferior rank to himself, quite abruptly. Boyer was aware and concluded that he was pre-occupied with guarding his own corner. Michel felt much the same way.

'I'll ring them very briefly to let them know you are on your way round there.'

'Thank you Boyer. I am sorry if I sounded rather rude a moment or two ago. It was unforgivable.' Boyer gave an unmistakable Gallic shrug and followed up by saying that he too was sometimes less than relaxed with the way things were shaping. Boudeau nodded his agreement and picked up the folder and left Boyer to ring Lovas. When he got there he struggled to remember the coded message but Boyer had warned Lovas so he was waiting behind the door when he arrived.

'A coffee, Colonel? We have had one already but I can reheat the pot.'

They resettled themselves and Lovas, Eric and Isabelle were keen to see what he had brought with him.

'It will take some time to make sense of all this stuff,' warned Boudeau. 'Take a look.' He opened the main folder which contained many slimmer folders. Each one was identified on the front with the town or commune named and where the gendarmerie was positioned giving road map references.

'Can we take it that each of these slimmer folders represents a gendarmerie which lies more or less within the region we are concerned with Colonel?' asked the doctor.

'Correct. There are about twenty or so covering all of the Cantal plus one this side of Clermont with another outside St Flour plus two a few kilometres north of Toulouse. It is a well spread out area and I think you are fortunate in Domvent to be one of several similar units which answer to the same description in terms of size and strategic law enforcement.' A suggestion of a smile crossed his lips with his last comment.

'And who compiled these folders and their contents? Vichy or further north?'

'Almost certainly Vichy,' said Boudeau.

'OK. Let's get started and see if anything jumps out of the page which doesn't seem to match up with what we know about the area or the inhabitants. One other question Colonel, apart from Lieutenant Jouve and yourself, who knows you asked for the directory today? And who would he or you have spoken to with a view to obtaining it?'

'Only one person, namely Major Maurice Belin. He is in charge of archived material.'

'It could be that you have a possible spy in your Clermont office. I will make a note to further investigate. It might be that Abricot has some information about him and whether he has any connections with the Toulouse unit. So, let's get back to work.'

They each picked up a folder and continued to look for an address or name that was unfamiliar. An hour passed and no one had uncovered anything out of place.

Isabelle said, 'I've found nothing wrong with the names in the Domvent area, and I have looked very hard. I'm beginning to wonder if we are being tricked into wasting more time instead of making plans in some other direction. It doesn't seem to make much sense to me so far. Once we have examined the rest of the folders, perhaps we should think again about our approach.'

Lovas had already begun to wonder about what they were doing, because no one had so far discovered anything of a questionable nature, despite their eagerness. Eric Farbres had found nothing and he felt sure he would have stumbled on anything doubtful within the area which came close to the Limousin in the west. He said:

'Perhaps Isabelle is right. Maybe we should give this a little more thought.'

Boudeau was inclined to agree. When young Jouve asked Major Belin for the directory there was no hesitation by Belin. He had simply unlocked his cupboard and handed it over to him. Boudeau had observed this operation from the partially open door of his office and body language alone would have rung bells with him had Belin felt something was going on.

'How far have we got?' said Lovas. Eric had picked up the remaining folder giving details of eight Jewish families together with a masonic member and a known left wing member of a trade union. They were all spread across an area of about twenty five kilometres. He quickly flicked through the individual names and they were all familiar to him.

'There's nothing here to worry about,' said Eric.

'OK,' said Lovas. 'Looks like we have drawn a blank.'

Isabelle said:

'I've been thinking about what we are doing here today and it strikes me that our 'friends' in Toulouse will have no idea what we are considering as a follow up to our hijacking operation. They must wonder, of course, that nothing has been happening to give them cause for concern. The list from Vichy ordering more rounding up to be carried out will have gone to all gendarmeries, not just Toulouse, so they will have their hands full already sorting out suitable victims for their next sweep. We have the benefit of holding all the details of the people likely to fall foul of the next operation so the sooner we can warn them of what's likely to occur the better. I think we should give Abricot an update about all of this and see what he thinks.'

Lovas agreed with Isabelle's opinion on the matter and said that unless anyone else had a better idea he would contact Abricot right away. He rang Abricot immediately and was rewarded with a total endorsement of their latest thoughts. He added that he could find the necessary manpower to deliver the urgent warnings to as many threatened people as possible. He would leave it to the ample brains in Domvent to devise suitable messages and await their delivery to the farm.

Isabelle asked Lovas how he had disguised the nature of his conversation with Abricot lest operators were listening in.

'I spoke about an epidemic and that as much of the local population should be warned. It was fairly easy to talk about the actual issue after that and I have been given the all clear to go ahead.'

All that remained to be done was to make a list of the people at risk, compose a suitable all-purpose note, type it out and get copies to Abricot.

Isabelle volunteered to write a suitably urgent note and Eric and Lovas would compile a list of people as their recipients. Boudeau still worried a little about Major Belin who had unhesitatingly handed over the directory of listed Jews and others, to Jouve. He had meant to remind Lovas to speak to Abricot about him to see if anything was known that might link him with their opponents.

'Did you speak to Abricot about the man Belin in my office?' asked Boudeau and Lovas said he had and that Abricot was going to look into it.

Another list was assembled after this. It had the address, family name and religion or specific information which might aid Isabelle when writing her warning letters. She had drafted out a letter in no time and she wanted to get their opinions before going further. She said:

'How do you think this sounds?' brandishing her first draft.

"You are warned that the Régime has issued more orders to the authorities to arrest and imprison people in certain categories as quickly as possible. Being Jewish, you lay within their definition. You have very little time to act as local gendarmeries will waste no time in picking up individuals and their families as they have done elsewhere. We are your friends and are dedicated to preventing the authorities from acting in this cruel and callous way. We therefore suggest you abandon your house, taking with you your valuables and cash and asking your non-Jewish friends if they could give you refuge for a while. There is not time to be lost. Do it now."

'It sounds OK to me,' said Lovas. 'Although it might be too long.'

'Can you pare it down a bit Isabelle?' said Eric.

'I agree,' said Boudeau. 'You have to remember that some of these people are just ordinary country folk and will be hardly bothered to read a lot and so they may miss the essential detail, if it looks complicated.'

Isabelle tried again.

'What about this then?'

"The Régime has ordered gendarmeries to arrest and imprison more Jews. You are warned they will give no notice and will arrest you during the night. Ask your non-Jewish friends to offer you

refuge. Abandon your home and go into hiding. There is no time to be lost. From well-wishers."

'What do you think?'

'Much improved Isabelle. The Colonel has it right. Some people will not give it enough time to read and understand it if it looks too long, so this version has to be so much better,' said Eric. 'What's your view, Doctor?'

'Maybe a bit blunt but it does make it clear so I would give it my blessing.'

Boudeau thought it fitted the bill now and was pleased to think that he had helped to inspire the now adopted changes.

Isabelle pointed out that at least two addresses were not Jewish. One was for a   known trade union trouble maker and the other two were remnants of a small masonic lodge. The lodge was now closed and emptied and the two addressees had somehow avoided being arrested when the lodge was raided during a meeting. The warning letter was easily modified to fit both categories. So Isabelle was kept busy for several hours typing copies of the letter. The list had become a little over thirty names and had been handed over to Isabelle, giving her the opportunity to produce the right numbers. The next day Lovas drove down to Abricot's farm headquarters and handed everything over to Abricot for delivery. He was impressed by the speed of the whole operation and congratulated Lovas on his efforts. Within another thirty-six hours all the addresses had received a warning notice.

It took no time for Colonel Bastide in Toulouse to realise that he had been made a fool of again in his attempts to follow orders from Vichy to round up Jews, freemasons and trade union people. They had planned to do the round up two days after the victims had already flown. He had wanted to demonstrate how well the Toulouse unit was working and once again his plans had been thwarted.

'How many houses did you call at before you realised you were wasting your time?' he demanded of the Lieutenant who had been in charge of the earlier operation. Bastide had decided there would be no repeat of that upset and that suitable safeguards had been put in place to ensure that however it might be devised, the latest operation would not fail. The Lieutenant had to gain experience and he decided no harm could be done this time.

'Five houses Sir,' said the Lieutenant. 'I began to feel uncomfortable with the situation and when we banged on the door of the sixth house, I nearly called the men off before they broke in. They found the house in order but certain items were missing like wallets, cash and valuables. They had left in a hurry for sure.'

Jean Bastide realised that there was no way he could attach blame to the Lieutenant this time, so he thanked him for trying to complete a hopeless task and said they would discuss the problem later.

Three days later Abricot received a message from their Toulouse spy that the gendarmerie had only just realised that the planned round up had come apart because the victims had already fled. He had heard that the Colonel was angry but resigned to the fact that there was nothing that could have been done. Abricot rang Lovas to say that patients were responding well following the recent change in their treatment.

Twenty-seven

On November 11th 1942, the German army dismantled key points in the demarcation line and walked into the unoccupied Vichy led 'Free Zone.' They quickly took over important towns and cities, including Pétain's centre of operations in Vichy and had now installed themselves in the Hotel du Parc. Pétain refused to be removed from his office and stated that he would remain there until the end.

In Chalhac the enormity of what had taken place had been almost impossible to grasp. Within a few days there was a contingency of soldiers, and an officer together with two armoured cars and a lorry parked on La Place, awaiting further instructions. It seemed that no one had mentioned the chateau's existence and David Markovich decided he would have to become the Comte de Villebarde for a while as there was a strong possibility that the Germans would come looking for somewhere to sleep. Henrietta had discussed this with him and he had told her that Pierre Brun, the odd job man and general helper at the chateau had devised a deadly scheme aimed at the enemy soldiers, currently lazing around on La Place. Pierre said it would take very little to make the very unsafe corner of the chateau collapse. The space at ground level of the deteriorating structure had been a stable and coach house in earlier days. Two or three generations of children had been forbidden to go anywhere near that part of the house and it had been a danger zone for more than a century. David was very much in favour of such a scheme since he had sworn to get his revenge against the invaders when he had seen the treatment of innocent civilians fleeing their own army.

Pierre and David had together carefully examined the structure. Even to an amateur it looked precarious and Pierre was sure he could further dislodge some of the stonework to the point where the smallest effort would make it come down. Several tonnes of old stonework would collapse into the stable block below given a small nudge and there would be no opportunity to escape with their lives or at the very least, injuries. David said he had better move quickly on it as the Germans would come looking for somewhere at any time. Pierre promised he would get on to it immediately.

Sure enough, a high ranking German officer appeared the same day on La Place. He was dressed in a leather coat, and sitting in the back of a large open top car, accompanied by a lesser officer.

'Who is in charge here?' he demanded. A low ranking soldier stood to attention and saluted.

'Untersturmführer Getz, Sir.'

'Get him!' said the officer.

Getz was happily installed in the bar and imbibing some of Jacques Fournier's marc. It was strong stuff and he was on his third glass. The soldier burst open the door, saluted and said, 'You are wanted by a high ranking officer – he looks like Gestapo to me Sir. He is in his car over there Sir, under the tree.'

Getz struggled to gather himself and walked, what he hoped would appear briskly, over to the car. The occupant sat impatiently striking his gloved hand with his short baton. 'Good afternoon Sir, you wished to speak to me?'

There were no greetings forthcoming from this person.

'Where are your personnel sleeping tonight Untersturmführer? They cannot be expected to sleep under the stars. What is there nearby that would serve the purpose? A hall or an old school?'

Jacques had spoken to Pierre Brun a few days before and the ideas now were coming to fruition. He had voiced to Getz that there could be some accommodation at   the chateau. 'A chateau?' Jacques gave a short rundown about the chateau. It was still fresh in Getz' mind and he was able to suggest it as a possibility.

'That's settled then. Go there now and speak to whoever is in charge and tell them that by order of the Reich you wish to use any available space for the billeting of your troops.'

'Thank you Sir. I will do it right away.' He saluted again. The car moved off without another word.

'Schwein!' said Getz, to no one in particular.

David, Henrietta and Pierre were well prepared for a visit from a German and another charade was quickly set up in anticipation. Pierre would be stationed at the main front gates and Henrietta would play her part in introducing David as le Comte de Villebarde. David was dressed as before in some of the real le Comte's clothes.

Pierre had moved quickly to dislodge what he had identified as a critical piece of masonry above the stabling. He had inserted a small piece of wood and attached it to a length of thin wire. A short tug would be enough to remove the wood and make the entire structure collapse. Whoever was in the stable block at the time would have no opportunity to escape several hundred tonnes of stone falling from above.

A little later that evening, Untersturmerführer Getz appeared at the chateau gates. Pierre had been obliged to wait about in the less than comfortable gatehouse and was relieved to see the car turn up. He emerged from the hut carrying his big key.

'Can I help you Sir?'

'Open the gate please,' said Getz.

'Can you tell me who you are Sir and what is your business?' Getz was less than pleased to be spoken to by an underling.

'Just open the gate man. I will tell whoever is in charge here what I require and who I am.'

Pierre decided that he had pushed the German as far as he dare and yielded to his command. He pushed open the old gates and said, 'I will have to inform le Comte Sir, will you drive to the front of the chateau?' Pierre pulled on the bell which gave its unmusical clonk from within. Henrietta came to the door.

'The officer wishes to speak to Monsieur le Comte Madame.'

'Ask the officer to wait where he is while I see if Monsieur le Comte is available.'

'Pierre turned to Getz who was standing by his shoulder and said, 'She will speak to Monsieur le Comte and see if he is available.'

Getz was becoming increasingly irritated by the whole thing and said to Henrietta,

'I am authorised by the Führer and the German High Command to use what I understand is available here, as accommodation for a small contingent of troops. You can tell le Comte that he has no alternative, other than to obey this order.'

Henrietta was about to turn away from the front door when Le Comte aka David appeared.

'What seems to be the trouble Henrietta?' said David.

Before she could answer Getz pushed Pierre to one side and said to David that he was fully authorised to take command of some space within the building, as accommodation. He needed to examine the area and to get his men inside before it got dark.

'Very well, Lieutenant. Pierre will direct you to the area you are referring to. Good evening and good night.'

Pierre led the way to the old stabling and Getz peered inside. There was no lighting and it smelled of damp wood and stonework. The floor was hardened mud and mostly covered with an accumulation of dried leaves and general detritus from the previous hundred years or more. Getz was less than impressed but decided it would have to do.

'Very well. We will be back in the next thirty minutes and move in. Leave the main gate open please. We will park our vehicles near the front of the building.'

Pierre watched him leave and then made his way around to the salon where David and Henrietta were drinking black market coffee.

'They're going for it and he will be back with his soldiers and their vehicles in the next half hour,' said Pierre.

'Excellent. Revenge will be sweet. Are you fairly sure your booby trap will work Pierre? I don't want you to be in any danger of discovery or injury to yourself,' said David. Pierre assured him he would be well away from the building when he pulled the wire. The wire and wood would be pulled clear so no evidence would remain of any skullduggery.

Half an hour later the lorries, two motorbikes and a car carrying Getz pulled onto the driveway leading up to the front door. Folding beds and blankets were unloaded and carried round to the stable. They got down to sweeping some of the rubbish out of the doorway and then arranged their beds in neat lines. Bedding was set on top of each bed and a portable gas lamp was hung from a protruding wood nail. Getz placed his own bed near the original barn door. By now it was totally dark outside and one by one they took to their beds. The lamp was turned down to a glimmer.

'Early start tomorrow,' announced Getz from his bed, 'Five thirty.'

At about one o'clock, Pierre decided to move. There was no sound apart from occasional snores coming from the stable. His strand of wire was waiting to be pulled a few metres from the danger zone. He gave it a firm tug. For a moment he had the impression it was not going to work but then with a roar the entire corner of the chateau fell in vertically from the roof down. Only a massive cloud of dust was left where moments before there had been an elegant tower nearly four stories high. It had left a clean break at one side and a less than clean break on the other side.

There were shouts for help for a short while and then there was silence. Most of the soldiers including Getz had been crushed to death under the sheer weight of the old stone masonry. Some had simply suffocated under the cloud of ancient dust.

David and Henrietta found Pierre gazing at his handiwork. He still held the wire in his hand and was obviously shocked when he realized there were more than twenty young men either dead or dying in the wreckage, and all because of his actions. David put his arm around him and said:

'Not your fault Pierre. You can blame Hitler and his gang of thugs for this. I wanted revenge for what his Luftwaffe did when they walked into France. I saw some of it and swore I would redress the balance a little. It came down to this in the end. So don't feel bad about it. Blame me if you like!'

There was nothing to be done and all three returned to the comforting warmth of the salon.

'Let's have a drink on the success of the operation. I hope Monsieur le Comte will forgive us for destroying a fifth of his chateau.'

Henrietta went down to the cellar and brought up two bottles of red Bordeaux wine. All three felt better after the wine and went to their beds. In the morning the village was talking about an explosion somewhere. No one could be sure, but at about 1.30 a.m. it sounded like something had blown up not far away. David was the first to hear this and then realised that they had heard the chateau's tower collapsing. He told Jacques about it and said that the young officer Untersturmführer Getz had been killed with the rest of them. He apparently knew there was some vacant space at the chateau and had turned up in the evening and took a quick look inside.

'So all those people out on La Place have been killed?'

'Looks like it.'

'Who knows about it David? What do you plan to do about it? You can't just leave them buried there?'

Before he could answer a German dispatch rider appeared on his motorbike as they spoke. There was no one visible on La Place and he walked over to the bar where he could see Jacques and David talking. 'Where is everyone please? Headquarters have been trying to call the officer in charge of this unit and has been unable to make any contact. Do you know where they have gone?' The dispatch rider was perfectly polite.

David explained that something terrible had happened during the night and part of the chateau had fallen down. He told the young man that his headquarters had better send a heavy crane and medical help. The dispatch rider wrote down the essentials and got back on his motorbike and disappeared down the hill.

'There is not much we can do now David. We will have to see what will happen next,' said Jacques.

Within an hour the Germans had arrived with a large crane and a military ambulance. They were obliged to ask about the chateau, where it was and what had happened in the night. Jacques had to explain its location but said that beyond that he knew nothing. The crane disappeared out of La Place followed by the ambulance. They were shocked when they saw the scale of the catastrophe. David still played the part of Le Comte and described what he heard from his private quarters on the other side of the chateau. He had to portray himself as being intensely shocked at what had happened, not only to his chateau but for the victims now buried beneath the entire corner of the building.

Shortly after, the open-topped staff car arrived with the unpleasant officer on board with his slightly junior companion.

'What's happened here?' he demanded to know. David stepped forward and explained that he was the owner of the chateau and that less than twelve hours before he was informed by the officer in charge of their small unit, that he and his men were authorised by the Führer to take over the stabling. He had no opportunity to do other than comply.

'Did you know that anything like this was likely to occur?'

'Certainly not,' said David. We forbade our children from playing in there because it was dirty and smelly. Had they been allowed to use it as a playground this might have happened sooner. It was as well they did not because we could have lost them just as easily as you will have lost some of your men. The chateau has been here for nearly four hundred years and nothing has ever happened like this. It is a disaster for me and my family.'

'Of course,' conceded the officer. As an afterthought he asked David, 'You Sir are?'

'Le Comte de Villebarde. My ancestor was a high treasury official in the court of Louis the second or third. He was rewarded with land and money for his loyalty.'

'When did you realise it was not safe for your children to play in there?'

It was a trap. David instantly recognised it as such and his defences were up. Gestapo?

'We could not have anticipated the present situation.'

'Where is your family now? There is no sign of them.'

'They are all in Switzerland. We all moved there when the situation in France was becoming difficult and my children needed a proper education. I try to get back here occasionally to ensure my business interests are being properly safeguarded. None of this is easy as I am sure you realise.'

David did not feel it was right to be interrogated standing close to a heap of rubble, now being carefully picked over by a crane and several men from a German engineering unit.

'I need to check that the rest of this part of the house has not been compromised. Do you require my presence here any further?'

The Gestapo officer said there was little any of them could do now. But he would call upon le Comte if he needed any more information. He gave a curt salute as a token of respect for David's title and position, thanked him briefly and turned away.

Back inside he found Henrietta and Pierre waiting about in the salon. The fire had died down to a heap of grey ash and the place felt cold.

'What's been happening?' asked Henrietta.

'There is some sort of engineering unit out there with a crane. I've been quizzed by an unpleasant man who I am sure is Gestapo. He tried to get me to say that I knew this might happen but I did not fall into his casually put question. If you should find yourselves being questioned, don't say anything that might let them off the hook and get us blamed for everything. He has accepted that I am le Comte de Villebarde and I am over here to check that my business interests are being looked after. You, Henrietta did not get mentioned, nor did you Pierre.'

'What do we do now David?' asked Henrietta. David said there was nothing much they could do until the wreckage and the bodies had been removed. After that they would have to think about making sure the rest of the house was safe. We'll have to have a discussion about it all with Jacques and the family. The doctor and Abricot would also need to know as it might have a bearing on their plans.

In Domvent gendarmerie the man from the Gestapo had already made the position clear. Since midnight last night the German army, the police, and administration in Vichy were under the direct rule of the Reich. The gendarmeries in what had been the unoccupied zone were now absorbed by the German police. They would now be administered and controlled by the Gestapo. The old administration in Vichy was now no longer in charge of the zone which was now controlled by the Reich. Le Maréchal Pétain would no longer be responsible and would probably be retired to a suitable location in keeping with a man of his former political stature.

'For the time being I will be in charge of this gendarmerie, until such time that a person of appropriate qualifications can replace me. I have to ask you Major Farbres to remove your personal belongings to the outside office and I will take over your desk.' He went on to tell Eric that part of the chateau had collapsed in Chalhac. Le Comte and his staff were uninjured but there were many casualties in the unit that had only just moved in to use it as sleeping quarters.

'When did this happen?' asked Eric Farbres.

'At about 01.30 hours. Engineers and rescue people are trying to dig people out right now but I think many will be lost. I spoke to le Comte and he had never received any indication that this very unfortunate incident would occur. It must have been in a very precarious condition to have fallen the way it did.'

'Yes,' thought Isabelle. She had already guessed how it had happened and hoped that David felt he had repaid with interest some of the iniquities he had witnessed on his way from Rouen to Chalhac.

'We will need another desk if the Major moves into my office,' said Isabelle. 'I have space but no extra furniture. I didn't catch your name Monsieur?'

'I am Hauptsturmführer Otto Weiss, Waffen SS.'

'Thank you Hauptsturmführer,' said Isabelle. She had to suppress a smile at the complex construction of German words. 'Will you arrange for a desk and at least two more chairs? As you can see, the Régime has not been over generous in the way gendarmeries are supplied with suitable comforts for their staff.' Otto Weiss said he would do as she had asked and made a note on a small pad as an aide-memoire.

Although the arrival of the German army had been anticipated, the local population was not prepared for the effect it would have on their lives. At almost every level, habits of a lifetime were upset. In Chalhac one of the immediate effects was at Jacques' bar, which had been part of the landscape since the early twenties. It had become the favourite meeting place for locals, particularly on Wednesday's market day. In hot weather it was a place of retreat out of the sun. Jacques' opening hours were very casual and if he saw a potential customer heading towards the bar he would make sure they did not leave Chalhac unless suitably refreshed. He received a formal notice from the newly formed German Police Authority based in the old gendarmerie in Domvent telling him he must publish a notice on the front window of the bar, stating his opening hours and on what days. A licence would be issued once this was done, which would be irrevocable.

Jacques voiced his displeasure over the following few weeks to all his customers. He did not want to be controlled and licensed but under the rules now being imposed he decided there was little alternative.

'In any event there is nothing to stop us from having a drink with our friends. I can simply bolt the front door.'

Isabelle's weekly visits to the village were now less easy than before. Otto Weiss had made it clear that she was expected to work on Saturdays. She would have to ask him if she wanted time off. She had explained that her grandmother would be less than happy if she did not appear. Weiss was sympathetic to a degree and said he would do what he could to help. A week elapsed before she asked Weiss if she could take Saturday off. Grudgingly he said, 'Yes,' whilst saying that she would have to keep her grandmother under control. Since the German army had arrived, there was more to do in the gendarmerie. There were endless orders requiring typing and everything seemed to be urgent. That weekend however she escaped the confines of Domvent and cycled down to Chalhac. She was warmly welcomed by Hortense and by Henrietta.

'Have some coffee, child,' said her grandmother.

'Thank you Grand-mère,' said Isabelle and accepted the proffered cup of Hortense's 'coffee' substitute. She could think of no valid reason of turning it away and did her best to register pleasure as she drank it. There followed a well-trodden list of subjects: Eric's welfare, his apparent demotion with the arrival of the German officer, and Eric's mother. Henrietta was keen to hear from Isabelle if the reasons for the collapse of the chateau's tower had been believed by the German officer Weiss. She, David and Pierre were anxious to know if they were considered innocent of any action that could have resulted so effectively in the death of a complete unit. Isabelle assured Tantetta that she heard nothing nor seen anything written that might point to any lurking suspicions. She added that David must be feeling he had redressed some of the wickedness he witnessed on his way from Rouen in 1940. She went on:

'I think you can expect replacements for the people killed last week. They are keen to maintain a presence in the area and someone will appear any day now to look at the village. I've already told Weiss there is no extra space left in the chateau to house their troops and there is nowhere else in Chalhac which would be suitable. He simply shrugged his shoulders and said it wasn't his problem.'

Isabelle explained that there was much to tell the Galliards and Jacques Fournier and that she would have to go. After much hugging she left them and made her way over to the bar to be greeted by Jacques, Guy, and the Mayor, Monsieur Bastien. She tried to give a shortened version of events as seen from Domvent.

'My Papa's position has been taken over by the German officer Hauptsturmführer Otto Weiss, and all orders now emanate from him. He is a fairly short-tempered man and I suspect he would rather be doing something else than being in charge of a police office. Pétain is no longer the Head of State and the Vichy government has been taken over by the occupying powers. Some of the civil servants in Vichy have kept their jobs as they know how to keep the system functioning. The offices in the Hotel du Parc in Vichy are now surrounded by armed guards and Pétain is refusing to come out of his inner sanctum and has said that he will never abandon France or the French people. Since the Germans lost an entire unit when the chateau's stabling came down they want to replace that unit with something similar. I have tried to steer Otto Weiss away by saying Chalhac has nothing the size of the chateau's stables, that there's no school or village hall nearby so I didn't know where they could be housed. He shrugged his shoulders and said, 'It's not my problem.' It looks like he could not care less. He must also realise that Germany is not going to win in this conflict and cannot wait for it to be over. They are now in charge of the Clermont offices of the gendarmerie. As you can imagine Boudeau and Jouve have not been in touch and I cannot see a safe way for them to do so. We can assume that they will have been swept to one side by the Gestapo, so our information sources are now reduced. Abricot's spies up there may find the situation very difficult from now on. We know enough about the Gestapo's methods and punishments to understand that making any risky moves against the Reich is a fool's game.'

Guy said he needed to speak to Doctor Lovas now that Germany had walked in. He wanted to know if Abricot had revived his earlier plan to sabotage the railway. He would also like to know if the Toulouse unit under Colonel Bastide had been absorbed by the German police and how co-operative Bastide might have been in his efforts to uncover the operation here. There were so many unknowns right now. What was certain was the Nazi's intention to eliminate as many Jews, freemasons, communists and trade unionists as possible.

'Our family and David are now once again at real risk of being tracked down. David is in some ways better placed than we are. There is no written record of him anywhere and when he becomes le Comte de Villebarde he looks and behaves as he imagines the real le Comte looks and behaves. Hauptsturmführer Weiss has been taken in by his play acting, that's for sure. I wish I could be as optimistic about our family. They knew enough about Simon Wojakovski and me at the Education Ministry to sack us from the teaching course. They also know that my mother is Russian Jewish. They do not seem to have discovered Marcel yet, who was apparently missed or deleted when we all arrived from Russia in 1926. I think we should begin to look for a safe place, somewhere we could make for in a hurry. Luckily we still have Isabelle in the Domvent gendarmerie and with luck she will still be able to give us some notice of an impending sweep. I hope that is true Cherie?

Isabelle smiled and nodded her agreement.

Guy said he was anxious to speak to the doctor to get an update from that direction and planned to go there on Monday. Isabelle said he would have to be very careful if that was what he planned because Domvent seemed to have German soldiers on every corner.

'Be sure to carry your identity papers with you because they are checking everything and everybody. Your Gaillard name will not give anyone cause for concern but your youthfulness might be of interest.'

'I'll have to say that I have some terrible disease and that I am on my way to see my doctor right now. That might be enough to keep them off me. He would be able to confirm that little fib.'

'With luck,' said Isabelle. She followed up by saying that she was thinking of gathering up some of the dynamite and detonators from their hideaway on the plateau. If Abricot's original ideas were still an option they would be looking for explosives.

'I'll make a point of asking him.'

Twenty-eight

On Monday morning Guy took the long way round to Domvent rather than the direct route from Chalhac. It was a precautionary move with the intention of avoiding as many confrontations with German soldiers as possible. He arrived at the Lovas door and knocked. He recited their greeting message and Lovas said, 'Come in my friend.' He seemed slightly edgy for once and ushered Guy into his salon.

'A coffee? I've just made some.' They settled in their chairs with their coffee.

'I have had a Nazi officer call on me here this morning. A nasty piece of work named Otto Weiss. He is now in charge of our gendarmerie here in Domvent. He was full of questions about me, my background, how long I'd lived in France, my parents, my medical qualifications and my patients. I had to be careful how I responded to this man and not give him any information which could help him reveal anything useful in their search for Jews, freemasons and others. They are dedicated to finding as many as possible and their orders are clearly coming from the top. It is pretty obvious that Hitler is behind all this and what the Führer wants he gets, mostly.'

Guy told Lovas he knew all about Weiss at the gendarmerie as he was now Isabelle's new boss. He also told him about the contrived collapse of the chateau's stable block onto a complete unit of German soldiers during the week – much to David Markovich's satisfaction. David had passed himself off as le Comte de Villebarde and Weiss regards him with a degree of respect for his rank and position. He should know! Guy was keen to know what Abricot was planning to do in the light of the new circumstances.

'I have had long discussions with Abricot and it has been decided that we could cause some real delays to German troops and equipment movements if we collapsed a tunnel which opened onto a bridge or a viaduct. The viaduct could be blown up at the same time as the tunnel. He has asked some of his members to search out likely locations right now. We will need explosives, a spark generator, detonators and wire. Unfortunately the wire was confiscated when your father's quarry was inspected. They also took a small amount of dynamite and some detonators but I am told you and Isabelle have a very dry cave up on the plateau where most of the dynamite and detonators are hidden. The spark generator remains at the quarry. So all we need is wire. Your brother Marcel could be a useful person to advise on the best way to collapse a rock tunnel, so perhaps you could speak to him? A viaduct presents a different problem but perhaps we have someone who has some knowledge of their construction.'

Guy said they would have to take great care now because the Nazis were bound to keep an eye on vulnerable railway lines.

'There have already been some derailments but they only cause a small amount of delays and very often result in people being killed or arrested. I'll suggest to Marcel that he takes an urgent look at the likely locations and even does some preparatory spade work if necessary. My father might be able to help if he feels up to it, because he knows his stuff about rock formations.'

Lovas was happy to know that Guy's family and Isabelle were already in the mood for further and more extreme measures against their oppressors. He also knew that Guy was a careful man and unlikely to take unnecessary risks with his loved ones or friends. He raised the matter of their fellow conspirators Boudeau and Jouve in Clermont, as there had been no contact from either direction. It was known that the Germans had taken over the entire gendarmerie service and enrolled it into part of the German police. Telephone calls were now not possible since operators were watched and overseen by their new bosses. Abricot's contacts in Clermont and Vichy had all but dried up, so they were working in a vacuum.

'I'll speak to Abricot today sometime. He will be pleased to know we are waiting for further instructions. I asked him if he had heard any more from the Toulouse direction and whether Colonel Bastide had kept his job. He had heard nothing. We must assume that our last operation has become past history and best forgotten.'

Guy said he would arrange to pick up their small arsenal of dynamite and detonators from the cave and re-conceal it at his father's house in Chalhac. If Weiss couldn't spare Isabelle on Saturday they may do it instead on Sunday.

357

'Let me know via Isabelle if things begin to move. She can leave a message for me in our post box tree. Also can you give me a name for some obscure malady that I can pretend to be consulting you about, should I be questioned by any of the Germans standing about in the town. One of them might question my youthful appearance and report me for not being in the armed forces or working as a forced labourer somewhere. It needs to be a sufficiently serious illness and enough to prevent me from joining the workforce.' Lovas said, 'Give me a moment. I'll look at my reference books for something suitable. A tropical disease might be the best bet. I suggest Leishmaniasis. It is pretty rare and difficult to treat. I will make a note that it is what you contracted years ago as a child.'

'Thank you Doctor for that rapid diagnosis!' said Guy with a smile. 'I am off to Chalhac now. Stay in close touch if you can!' He took the longer route back to the village and was greeted by his father, Marcel and Jacques.

Jacques said they had another German come to the village while he was in Domvent. He was not a friendly or approachable person. First of all, he asked who was the owner of the small herd of cattle he could see from the village side of the river.

'His name please?' he asked. 'He is our Mayor, Monsieur Bastien. He lives over there in a house in the far corner.'

The German made a note on a small pad, printed with a swastika on the corner.

'Who will know about space for a contingent of troops to sleep within the village?' he asked. 'I understand the best place was destroyed when the chateau's stables fell down. Is there nothing else here like a school, or a hall of some sort?'

Jacques said the Mayor was the best person to ask but he knew there was nothing of the sort.

'None of the houses here are very big – there was only the chateau and that now has been reduced to a ruin on one side. I would guess that Le Comte is nervous sleeping in what remains in case the rest of it collapses.'

'Yes I can imagine that might be so. You are?'

'Jacques Fournier, licensed proprietor of this bar.'

'Very well Monsieur. Thank you for your help. How do I get to Monsieur Bastien's house?'

'Over the footbridge and it is over to the left at the far side of his pasture.' The German gave a token salute on his cap to Jacques and departed.

'Oh dear!' said Guy. 'It looks like he has his eyes on Bastien's cows.'

'I warned him months ago that in the north they were taking cattle out of France and sending them to Germany by the trainload. Bastien did not think there was much chance of that happening here and changed the subject. He is about to have a rude shock I think.'

A half hour later they were standing in Jacques' bar when an irate Bastien arrived. He was clearly shaken and white with rage.

'What do you think?' he managed to say. 'I've had a damned German officer waving a piece of paper at me saying something to the effect that, by order of the Reich and the Führer, he was fully authorised to organise the removal of my herd of cattle and transfer them elsewhere." Elsewhere means Germany no doubt. I said that not all of them were mine and that an elderly lady owned one cow which was precious to her. He simply shrugged his shoulders.'

'Have a marc on me Robert. You look shaken – it will calm your nerves.'

'Thank you Jacques, I can use that.' He took a swig of marc. 'What's to be done then? Is there anything you can suggest?'

'I cannot see any way round it,' said Guy, 'I feel we should get Hortense Hubert's cow out of there before it gets taken away. She would be less than pleased if that happened. There's no time to be wasted because they will show up with large trucks at any time. Do you think other people in the village would be willing to look after a few for you? What about your mother's friend Madame Dumas?'

'It's possible but I don't think we will have enough time to do any of that other than getting Madame Hubert's cow out of harm's way. I think we should do that this evening.'

'OK Monsieur Bastien, I'll go over to her house right now to explain what's happening while you go over to collect her cow. It can all be settled in ten to fifteen minutes.' Hortense was a little taken aback to learn that the cow was to take up residence in the land at the back of her little house, but when she learned that she might lose the beast altogether, she understood.

Shortly after daylight the next morning, two large purpose built lorries appeared and parked close to the footbridge leading to Monsieur Bastien's pasture, his house and his herd of cattle. Beside the driver of the first lorry sat a non-commissioned officer of the Wehrmacht. He carried in his hand a written order from the new headquarters in Vichy, authorising the handover of the cattle to the Reich. Bastien came across his pasture land looking sleepy and angry.

'What time do you call this?' he called to the man in the leading lorry.

'We have our orders,' replied the man.

'I am sure you do,' said Bastien. 'Well let's get on with it then. The cattle are in the area behind the milking shed. They wait there until my man comes to milk them which will not be for another hour. You are going to need some help.'

German orders were shouted and four young soldiers climbed out of the second lorry and were told to follow Monsieur Bastien over to the milking shed. Sure enough the cattle were hanging around, waiting to be milked.

'Sorry girls. Not today. You are going for a ride,' he said. Bastien told the soldiers the best way was to herd them over to the footbridge a few at a time. The backs of the lorries were lowered and they were chased up into the lorries. It took twenty minutes or more to load them all and finally the non-commissioned officer gave Bastien a receipt for his cows. Robert Bastien rarely cried but he was quite tearful as he saw his herd driven off. He was also still angry and was left feeling totally helpless. It was not yet six o'clock but he looked over to Jacques' bar. There was a light burning within which meant that Jacques was ready to start his day. Bastien walked over to the bar and could see Jacques moving about. He tapped tentatively on the door. Jacques came immediately and pulled the bolts.

'Come in my friend. You look done in. I have some coffee brewing at the moment, will you join me or would you like something stronger?' Bastien said a coffee would go down well for the moment. 'I hope I did not wake you Jacques. The lorries arrived when it was barely light.'

'I was awake already when they showed up. It was as well we rescued Hortense's cow last evening or she would have lost her precious cow for good.' They discussed the situation over several cups of coffee. They looked towards Bonnet's bakery. He had been up before either of them and could be seen standing loaves on their ends to cool.

'How about some breakfast now you are here? Get a loaf from Bonnet – I've a piece of ham in the cupboard and we'll start the day with some food.'

Bastien walked the few paces over to the bakery. The door was unlocked and he bought a large loaf. Bonnet was very sympathetic about his having his herd of cows confiscated by the Germans. 'Let's hope this will not go on for much longer.'

In Domvent a message had been delivered to Lovas from Abricot saying he would like to gather together the key players in their next exploit. If possible it was to assemble the team at the farm to explain in detail what was planned and where. A location had been identified for the best effects but it required the expertise of one or two individuals to arrange the final positioning. Your response is required with some urgency.

Miklos Lovas had no alternative other than a drive down to Chalhac and explain that Abricot was making final preparations for their attack on the railway. He called first at the bar where Jacques and Bastien were still finishing their breakfast. He introduced himself.

'I am Doctor Miklos Lovas from Domvent, and you must be Jacques Fournier!'

'What a pleasure Doctor! This gentleman is our Mayor Robert Bastien.' Hands were shaken and brief explanations were made by Lovas for his sudden appearance in the village. He explained he needed to speak to Guy, to his brother Marcel and his father Jules. Jacques said the best way to achieve this was to go round to the Gaillard house where Guy would probably be, and to get up to the quarry. It was arranged that Marie would look after the bar while Jacques took Lovas round to the Gaillard house. More explanations followed and expressions of delight at meeting the doctor for the first time.

361

'Jules and Marcel have just left for the quarry on their bikes. You might even overtake them,' said Sarah. Lovas and Guy took the road to the quarry and left Jacques to walk round the corner back to the bar. They arrived at almost the same moment outside the gates of the quarry. Introductions were made and Lovas explained he had an urgent message from Abricot in which some key players were required to meet up at the farm. The key players were Marcel and Jules. There would be more no doubt, but the specifics about explosives and their positioning was critical and Marcel and Jules were regarded as experts in this field. Guy reminded them that they still needed a lot of wire and that the spark generator was still in the quarry's security cupboard. Guy said he would help Isabelle to bring back the dynamite and detonators from their hide out on the plateau. He would have difficulty finding the cave without her help so they would have to wait until she could get out of the office. Tomorrow looked the best they could hope for.

'It will have to do,' said Lovas. 'While I'm here I'll take the spark generator with me. If you Guy, could call by my house tomorrow, I hope I will be able to give you a firm date for the off. We can begin to work around that. I'll drop you off at the village now and make it back to Domvent. I'll be in touch – it's been a pleasure to meet some of you. Au revoir.'

Isabelle had got ahead of her work for once and asked Weiss if she could go home early. It was barely half past four. A little ungracefully he agreed and she wasted no time in cycling down to their message tree. It was upright indicating a message in the hollow tree stump behind. 'Come straight down – important. Love x.' She wasted no time and went at top speed to the Gaillard house.

'We are going up to our cave to collect as much of our arsenal as we can manage. I'll explain to you as we go,' said Guy. She was excited by what she had heard from Guy and they loaded as much as possible into Isabelle's basket, covering it with a cloth. Guy had a satchel which he filled to capacity with the rest of the stuff. There was nothing remaining on the shelf and they both needed to sit for a moment or two for a break. The light was beginning to fade now and Isabelle suggested they made for home. Guy had slightly different ideas however. He said, 'Got your breath back? How about a quick cuddle?'

She agreed to a cuddle but the cuddle turned into a passionate ten minutes or more, partly against the cave wall and partly on the dusty floor.

'We have not done that for ages Cherie. I've been looking for a chance but there has been no opportunity. I hope you approve.'

'I should say I approved. Of course I approved, Cherie. I just wish we had more time for more of the same!' They brushed themselves down and finally made their way back to Chalhac. Guy's satchel was unpacked and Isabelle's basket was carefully unloaded. It was quite dark now and Isabelle had to get home. The road was dry and still rutted but she was familiar with some of the particularly difficult places and she made it home quite quickly. Eric Farbres greeted her warmly as did her mother.

She said there was a lot to tell them about but she needed to wash and eat something before she dropped because she had eaten nothing since breakfast that morning. Fifteen minutes later she reappeared and sat at the table opposite her Papa and Mama. Ann-Marie had produced a very filling and nutritious casserole. She ate hungrily.

'So let's have it then Isabelle. We are both waiting to hear what you have learned since this afternoon.'

Isabelle told them as much as she could remember. The most important item though was the proposed attack on the railway. Abricot had a plan and a particular location and he needed Jules and Marcel Gaillard to take a careful look and make their recommendations regarding the rock strata surrounding a tunnel. She and Guy had collected the dynamite from their secret cave on the plateau. Doctor Lovas had come down to Chalhac that afternoon for the first time and he had to inform them both there would be a meeting at Abricot's farm for a briefing. It had become so much more difficult since Weiss was in the gendarmerie, and they were all hoping that an allied invasion would take place before long.

Farbres thanked Isabelle for the information. It had become much more difficult with German soldiers walking about the streets and standing watching on street corners. With the arrival of Weiss in the gendarmerie Eric's ability to contact the doctor was dramatically curtailed.

The phone rang in Isabelle's office. It was the Doctor.

'This is Doctor Lovas. I wish to speak to your superior.'

'Hold the line please, Doctor.' She leaned over to Farbres and said she had Doctor Lovas on the line and he wished to speak to her superior. 'I'll take it,' said Eric.

'Good afternoon Doctor. What can I do for you?'

Lovas said that he wished to see Mademoiselle Farbres in his surgery as there were aspects to her treatment that required explaining. 'Would you authorise her to call by later today? I will be expecting her. Thank you.' His phone was put down and Otto Weiss put down his extension phone just after, with a faint click. He had been listening.

Eric signaled to his daughter that Weiss had been listening before he said, 'Isabelle your doctor wants to see you sometime today about a treatment he is prescribing for you. It's OK by me but I will need to speak to Hauptsturmführer to give you a little time out of the office. I'll speak to him right now.' Weiss' office door was slightly ajar and he tapped on it. 'In,' said Weiss. 'Isabelle's doctor wants to see her at his surgery about a treatment he is prescribing. He said he would expect her today. I have said it is OK by me but I need your authority Sir.'

'Very well, Major. She will not be long will she?' Eric thanked him dutifully.

Isabelle quickly put on her coat and walked briskly round to the Doctor Lovas house. She began to recite the coded message but Lovas stopped her and said,

'Come in Isabelle - it's all clear here.' He told her he had spoken to Abricot and that he had arranged a briefing at the farm with the rest of the sabotage team. Jules, Marcel and Guy needed to be told to be ready to be collected in the morning and he would take them in his car, sometime before mid-morning He would take the dynamite and detonators at the same time and would collect it all by eight a.m. Isabelle said she would go down to the village as soon as she could get out of the gendarmerie. She added, 'Otto Weiss overheard your conversation with my papa – he doesn't trust anyone any more.'

As arranged, Lovas arrived back in Chalhac by eight o'clock in the morning. Jules, Marcel and Guy were waiting for him and all four got into the car having loaded the spark generator, dynamite and detonators in the boot. They made good time to the farm and were warmly welcomed by Abricot. There were six more gathered already in the big room including one or two familiar faces from the earlier high-jacking exploit. Abricot introduced the three from Chalhac and explained that Jules Gaillard, the older man was a quarrying expert. 'He will advise about the local rock formations in the vicinity of our proposed target and the most vulnerable place for explosives to be placed to achieve the best results where the railway emerges from the tunnel onto the viaduct. We are lucky to have with us today Jean Bouchet who has spent his entire life building beautiful brick and stone arches in some elegant structures across the country, including road and rail viaducts. He has told me his work has never included the destruction of a viaduct until now, so it will be a new experience for him. Could I ask you now to gather around the table and I will show you on the map the exact location of my suggested target. There are several similar locations offering similar opportunities but this particular one could be expected to cause the greatest disruption to the enemy's troop and equipment movements.' He produced a wooden ruler and leaned over, pointing at a tunnel exiting onto a viaduct, which stretched across a valley for about three hundred metres before once again vanishing into a similar tunnel on the other side. He continued:

'If I wished to move a large contingent of troops and armoured equipment from the south up to the north of the country, in the best possible time, this route, using this tunnel on the way, would be the one I'd choose. Alternative lines heading from south to north are no way as efficient in terms of distance and attack by enemies. Any questions so far?' There were no questions so he continued:

'The farm is here and the target is here,' he said, pointing with the ruler to the railway line as it emerged from the tunnel onto a viaduct. 'There is no road access very close to the target so it will mean carrying all the equipment by hand and on our backs. There appears to be sufficient ground cover to hide our activities. I suggest we begin the preparations as soon as we can which will enable us to react quickly if we are alerted to the anticipated movement of troops and equipment. We are unable to do more at this stage because the Allied invasion has not yet become a fact, although I can tell you it is about to become so. Our enemies will be looking to re-enforce their existing defences and I hope we can frustrate at least some of their efforts. The main road to Toulouse and the south is on the other side of the valley, as you can see, so our opponents will be more actively engaged on that side, rather than on this side. It means a lot of leg work for us but if we can succeed it will have been worth the effort. If Jules, Marcel and Jean could reconnoiter the nature of the rock formation above the tunnel exit while Jean can look at the viaduct for any specific difficulties, we will be able to make final preparations. Am I talking sense?'

All three voiced and nodded their approval so far.

'Good,' said Abricot. He went on to explain that subject to agreement on the target, he had instructed that a bogus anonymous note be left in the new police office in Toulouse, giving warning of a planned derailment on the line somewhere south of Limoges. It would help to divert attention and manpower away from the real target. They all agreed that anything to make their operation safer was worthwhile doing.

Two days later Jules and Marcel were collected again by Lovas and taken down to the farm where Jean Bouchet was waiting for them. Jean had all his equipment ready and waiting including ropes, crampons etc. Abricot explained that Doctor Lovas would take them to nearer the target where they would be met by five other group members who would do their best to protect them against possible enemy guards watching for just the sort of activity they were embarked upon. The five were all to be armed with rifles and pistols in case it came down to an open fight.

'When you have satisfied yourselves that this is the best location and that the rock formation above the tunnel will collapse into the tunnel when dynamited, come back here and we will wait for word from our informer in Toulouse. I will remain here at the farm and you will be able to tell me how the preparations have gone when you return.' He wished them luck and they left shortly afterwards. Lovas got them as close as he could to the viaduct and tunnel and hid the car in an indentation surrounded by thick undergrowth where they began to unload the car boot. Jean Bouchet put on his spiked boots, picked up a long coil of rope, a length of wire, three detonators and three sticks of dynamite still wrapped in waxed paper. In his belted waist he tucked in a small hammer, a chisel and a grappling hook. The others took the spark generator, a long coil of wire, the remainder of the dynamite and detonators plus a rock drill, a spade and an axe. They all made their way carefully through the undergrowth towards the abrupt edge of the valley near the viaduct. They were met by their five guarding companions who were hidden in the thicket of brambles and gorse. They had not seen any activity that might have given them early warning of enemy watchfulness and the saboteurs told them they would get started on their allotted tasks.

Jean Bouchet made his way to the edge and climbed down to the top of the viaduct at the tunnel exit. He disappeared beneath the first arch of the viaduct and could be heard hammering at the brickwork. Half an hour later he swung himself out from beneath the arch and gave a thumbs up signal. He had fixed the dynamite and detonators into the space vacated by the two bricks, now laying in the undergrowth below. The wire was attached to the detonators and he took the loose end with him and explained to Jules that the wire would need to be positioned and fixed to the rest of the wiring.

'That should bring down the first arch quite nicely. It seems almost criminal to destroy a nice bit of brickwork like that but we must turn a blind eye to the morality in the circumstances,' he said ruefully. Jules and Marcel had identified the rock above the tunnel as limestone and had drilled five or six holes down into it close to a natural crack. Each hole now contained dynamite, a detonator with a loop of wire attached from the end of Jean Bouchet's arrangements. The rest of the wire was hidden under the overgrown surface of the land and was ready to be fixed to the spark generator when the go ahead was given. The generator was carefully concealed in a dip in the terrain a safe distance from the expected small landslide. They stood back and looked at their handiwork. Nothing was now showing of their efforts and they all decided to get back to the farm as instructed. Lovas was very impressed with the speed and professionalism the little team had displayed. He had imagined a much lengthier preparatory operation and knew that Abricot would be equally impressed when they reappeared. He was indeed impressed with the speed and efficiency in which the entire operation had advanced. He had hoped for little more than an exploratory examination of the rock face and the viaduct construction and had not anticipated that they would return telling him that all they had to do was to push down the plunger on the spark generator. It all sounded too good to be true.

Four days later the phone rang in Eric Farbres' office. It was Doctor Michel Lovas saying that Mademoiselle Farbres' prescription was ready to be collected at his surgery. Farbres said to Otto Weiss that she would need to go round to the surgery to pick it up. Grudgingly Weiss agreed and followed up by saying, 'Do you know what your daughter's problem is Major Farbres?'

'Not precisely. Some sort of female problem I think.'

Weiss was becoming increasingly suspicious of Isabelle's 'female problems' and despite listening to telephone conversations between Farbres and the doctor, had been unable to glean any useful information. He had instructed the local telephone exchange to record all calls from and to the doctor's number. This move had produced a number traceable to a farm about thirty kilometres south of Domvent. There were confusing conversations between the doctor and the farmer. There had been occasional references to a hut and Weiss decided to put a tail on the doctor when he had planned to meet the mysterious farmer at the 'hut.' Lovas had spotted the police van as it followed him towards the charcoal burner's hut and was able to throw it off by making for the intersection of four roads in the woods. He chose one which would lead him eventually back to the hut. There was no sign of the police van and it was safe to meet up again with Abricot. Weiss was unable to do much about it now because it would spell out to Eric Farbres that he was watching their every move. He was yet to investigate the farm and that was his next target.

When Lovas was followed it had sent warning signals to him and Abricot to be on their guard and they agreed that the farm was likely to be investigated, either openly or secretly. All traces of Abricot's plotting would have to be erased and he would have to return to being the gentleman farmer for the time being. Communications were the biggest problem and would have to rely on Eric Farbres' daughter Isabelle to deliver orders and information about further moves. It was in these circumstances that Lovas phoned Farbres' office to arrange for Isabelle to collect a prescription. Weiss had intercepted the call as usual but granted her his permission to leave the office for a short while. Isabelle walked quickly round to Lovas' surgery. He told her that the invasion had begun in Normandy and it had triggered frenzied activity in the south to move re-enforcements northwards. Lovas said he would collect Jules and Marcel from the village in the morning and get them over to the viaduct site. He would be ready for them by six o'clock.

Isabelle said she would be glad to do so but would have to get out of the office as soon as possible and not be deliberately delayed by Otto Weiss. There could therefore be a slight pause before the message was delivered. Weiss did his best to hold Isabelle in the office longer than usual without knowing the urgency behind Isabelle's eagerness to depart. She arrived in Chalhac and went directly to the Gaillard house. She quickly explained to Sarah and was told that Marcel, Jules and Guy were all in Jacques' bar, having listened illicitly to his wireless for the latest reports on the Normandy landings. Isabelle told them they would be needed in the morning and they were to be ready by six o'clock. The gathering dispersed after that and Guy said he would tell David Markovich and Henrietta what was happening.

Twenty-nine

In the morning everything went to plan. Lovas dropped Marcel and Jules off at the road nearest the viaduct and they carefully picked their way through the vegetation. The group's spy in the Toulouse headquarters had managed to get an indication of when a train was likely to leave and which could be imminent. It would comprise mostly field guns, tanks and lorries plus nearly two thousand troops. The Germans had anticipated that the resistance would probably try to delay it, but had been unable to identify what would be attempted. Small units had been consigned to keep an eye on possible vulnerable points and the viaduct had been selected for their attention. The preparations by the conspirators four days earlier had paid off and were all installed before the Germans were in place. By the time they arrived there was no sign of any activities that might have called for a response. High on the hill above the viaduct three people sat, taking it in turn with a pair of very powerful field glasses. One had seen slight movement in the undergrowth above the tunnel exit but it did not happen again and he decided it must have been an animal or a bird.

There was a distant sound of a steam locomotive labouring to pull a heavy load some way off. Then the sounds seemed to cease quite suddenly. Both groups –the saboteurs and the Germans, realised that it was probably the expected train and that it had already entered the tunnel on the far side of the hill. Jules and Marcel and quickly uncovered the spark generator, attached the wires and waited. They did not have to wait for long because the distinctive sound of a locomotive became clearer by the second. Smoke billowed from the tunnel.

Jules said: 'OK Marcel. A nice steady plunge down on the generator now!' Marcel took a deep breath and firmly pushed down on the plunger. There was a flash of bright light for a moment from beneath the viaduct followed by an explosion as an entire section of the viaduct collapsed into the greenery below. Marcel said, 'I think our part isn't going to . . .' He did not get to finish his comment when a dull roar above the tunnel entrance followed by a massive piece of limestone began to slide almost gracefully downwards towards the now partly wrecked viaduct. The tunnel could no longer be seen and a bigger piece of viaduct collapsed when a massive amount of dislodged limestone fell onto it. Somewhere within the tunnel the train had come to standstill. The locomotive had become derailed and there was heavy choking dust and debris everywhere. The saboteurs had seen enough to be able to report to Abricot that the mission had been a complete success. They grabbed the spark generator and made their way back to the hidden car where Lovas was waiting for them. Jean Bouchet had followed them carrying his equipment with him. He had left his own car at the farm and planned to make his way back from there.

'Judging by the noises and troop movements along the road at the moment, I imagine the scheme has worked out according to plan,' Lovas said. 'We will have to use an alternative route back because there are too many Germans rushing about at the moment. What has become of your protecting group? Have they got their own means to get back?'

Marcel and Jules had all but forgotten they were being guarded by their armed protectors.

'I'm sure they will be OK,' said Marcel. 'They will know this area better than anyone and they have guns to shoot it out if necessary.' They all got back into the car and took a small side road off the main road just in time to avoid a confrontation with a German personnel carrier on its way northwards. The further they went they heard the sounds of machineguns and rifle fire behind them somewhere. It could only mean that their protection team had been uncovered and were having some sort of battle. They eventually came within sight of Abricot's farm gate. Parked outside was the personnel carrier with no one in it other than a driver. As they drew closer a farm worker emerged from the hedge near the gate, waving his arms pointing and shaking his head, silently indicating they should not go in.

'It looks like Abricot has some visitors,' said Lovas. 'It will be best if we get back to Domvent. Perhaps Otto Weiss can enlighten us with what's going on. It doesn't look good at the moment. I think it would be wise to get rid of the spark generator and anything else that might incriminate us.' As they approached Domvent they stopped and unloaded the generator, the axe and spade together with most of Bouchet's kit. Everything was dropped carefully into a ditch. They had remained unarmed so there were no incriminating weapons to be found. When they arrived outside the gendarmerie, the van was nowhere to be seen and there were no gendarmes visible.

Lovas said, 'It will be a mistake to go into the gendarmerie. I want to get back to my house but I'll drop you off in Chalhac first. I suggest you come back with me Jean. Is that OK?' Jean Bouchet nodded his agreement and they carried on to Chalhac. There was nothing to indicate any problems in the village when they arrived but Isabelle immediately emerged from the front door of the Gaillard house as they pulled up.

'Thank God you are all safe. Where's Guy? I thought he would be with you. He planned to go to your surgery Doctor Lovas. There has been no word from him since this morning.' This was deeply worrying for Lovas. He said, 'I'll be in touch as soon as I can.' He and Jean Bouchet disappeared back up the road towards Domvent.

There was much to tell Isabelle and Marcel recounted the events of the day. Jules was very tired and sat back in his chair and closed his eyes, listening to Marcel's narration. At the end Marcel said:

'What's been happening in Domvent Isabelle? We came by the gendarmerie but didn't stop as it would have been unsafe. Where is your papa? And Otto Weiss?'

Isabelle said she went into the gendarmerie in the normal way. Otto Weiss was sitting at his desk with a typed document in front of him. He was deep in thought and tapping his desk with a pencil. Her papa was in her office, sitting at her desk and gazing into the middle distance. Lieutenant Boyer was sitting at the recently imported desk in the corner, doing nothing in particular. She said there seemed to be an indefinable tension within the room when she arrived.

I suggested a coffee for everybody and no one responded. 'Well I am going to make one anyway.' She made her coffee and sat down opposite her papa at her desk.

'What's going on?' she had asked very quietly.

Farbres held his finger to his lips and nodded in the direction of Otto Weiss. The door opened almost immediately and Weiss had appeared.

'I have to go out and will return later today. I am taking the van.' He said.

None of us knew where he was heading but he had looked a little pre-occupied.

The typed document that Otto Weiss had been reading was an official notification from Berlin informing him that the Allies had made the first landings on the beaches of Normandy. 'Every effort must be made to ensure that communications are maintained within the southern zone of France as it might become necessary to utilise equipment and personnel being held in reserve in the south.'

Otto Weiss had already made his mind up that Nazi Germany's enterprise was doomed to failure and the memo did nothing to help change his mind. He drove around to Doctor Lovas' surgery with the intention of asking him if he knew if anything was being hatched by any resistance group. Weiss suspected that something was going on, but had been unable to tie the ends together. The doctor's house looked normal and he gave a firm knock. The door was opened by a middle aged woman.

'I would like to speak to the Doctor. Is he available?' he asked.

'I am afraid the Doctor has had to go out, Officer,' she said. 'Can you leave a message for him?'

Weiss politely declined the offer and was about to get back into the gendarmerie van when Guy Gaillard appeared on his bicycle. He spotted Weiss and the van and realised that something was going on which he had not expected. He did a quick about turn on the bike but it was too late. Weiss had seen him.

'Stay where you are!' ordered Weiss. 'Your papers please.'

'I am afraid I don't have them with me.' said Guy, playing for time.

'I see. Why are you here outside the Doctor's surgery at this time?' demanded Weiss.

'I have an appointment to see him this morning about my illness.'

'What illness is that? You don't look ill.'

'I have a rather nasty tropical disease and it prevents me from working. The Doctor can confirm that.' Guy was beginning to get his act together now. 'Can I produce my identity papers a little later because the Doctor will be expecting me?'

'The doctor is not there. I wish to speak to him myself. Where is your home?'

'In Chalhac, Sir'

'I will take you there and see your papers. Put your bicycle in the back of the van and hurry up about it – I don't have all day.'

This was getting a little out of control now Guy decided. He did as he was told and lay the bike down on the van floor.

'Do you know the way to Chalhac, Sir? asked Guy.

'I do. I had to investigate the collapse of the chateau's tower when twenty of my men were killed.'

Guy suddenly fell in. So this must be Otto Weiss. He had to be sure about the identity of the man now taking him down to Chalhac. If he was Otto Weiss he was also Isabelle's boss.

'Are you based locally Sir?' asked Guy casually, as they drove down the hill towards Chalhac.

'Yes. I am the officer in command of the gendarmerie in Domvent. You are very inquisitive in the circumstances.' said Weiss. 'This is your home?' said Weiss as he pulled up outside the Gaillard house. Jules and Marcel had both gone to bed. Jules was extremely tired having lost hours of sleep over the preceding day or two. Marcel too was knocked out with the efforts made the previous day and in the early hours this day and Sarah had insisted they both got to bed. Father and son were both in deep sleep when Guy and Weiss arrived.

'I will accompany you to ensure you don't try to be clever and try to run off. I want those papers!'

'OK,' said Guy, whose mind was now racing. They both got out of the van and Guy walked to the front door with Weiss at his shoulder. Guy pushed open the door as his mother Sarah appeared from the salon.

'This gentleman is the officer in charge of the Gendarmerie in Domvent Maman. He wishes to see my identity papers.'

'I will get them for you, Sir,' said Sarah who walked briskly up the stairs. She had listened earlier to Jacques' wireless, and heard the announcement from London that the invasion was underway. Extreme measures were called for now and Sarah retrieved from her cupboard an outdated pistol from the earlier war. It was loaded and ready to fire.

She re-appeared in the doorway just as Guy was about to hit Weiss with the sculptured head of Sarah. Weiss turned at the critical moment to see the very heavy piece of polished stone about to descend on him. He pulled his gun from the belt around his waist and was about to pull the trigger when Sarah opened fire with the old pistol. Weiss looked puzzled for a moment and then toppled forwards onto the floor, still holding his own gun. He was dead.

A small puddle of blood was already forming on the floor from his injury.

'You left that a bit late Maman! He was just about to kill me!'

'We'll think about that later Guy. Your Papa and Marcel are both sound asleep upstairs and I am surprised they did not wake up with all the noise.' She had hardly finished speaking when Marcel appeared on the stairs. He took a brief look at the body on the floor with its increasing pool of blood. 'We will have to move this man as quickly as possible in case someone comes looking for him.' The Gendarmerie van remained outside on the road and would have to be moved.

'Can you go over to Jacques' bar and ask for a bit of help Guy?' said Sarah.

Quite suddenly Sarah had begun to take charge of the situation. Until now her role had been fairly passive but some quick thinking was called for. 'While you are about it call in on Henrietta at her mother's house to warn them that things are becoming a little complicated.'

Guy removed his bicycle from the back of the van, leant it against the house front and managed to get the van out of sight around the back of the house. He then went over to Jacques' bar, breathlessly explaining what had happened in the last few minutes and they needed some help. He continued across La Place to Hortense Hubert's house. Henrietta opened the door.

Guy explained briefly what had occurred and that David needed to be warned that things were getting a little out of hand. It occurred to him that no one in the Domvent gendarmerie knew what was going on. Isabelle, Eric Farbres and Michel Boyer were out of the picture for the moment and Guy decided he would have to cycle up to Domvent to alert them about how the situation had suddenly changed. He left Henrietta and explained the need to get up to

Domvent. He also went back to the house where Jacques and Marcel had man-handled the dead Otto Weiss to the rear of the house.

He arrived in Domvent shortly after. There were still no signs of life and he walked straight into Isabelle's office – something he had never been able to do before. He explained that Otto Weiss was dead, shot by Sarah.

He had to explain how that had come about and had Sarah not shot him then both he and Sarah would almost certainly have been shot by Weiss.

When the German authorities became aware that Otto Weiss had gone missing they began to inquire about his last movements. A high-ranking Gestapo officer appeared before Isabelle could leave her office. She explained that Weiss had received a note from Vichy or Berlin that an Allied invasion had begun in Normandy. He had left shortly afterwards without saying where he was going.

'Did he take transport with him or was he on foot?' asked the officer.

'He said he was taking the small gendarmerie van and would return later.'

'Did he confide in you Major Farbres?'

'I did not converse with him at all,' said Eric.

'And you Lieutenant – did you speak with him?' said the officer to Michel Boyer.

'No, Sir.'

'Very well. I will be making further inquiries today. If the Hauptsturmführer appears later, ask him to contact Headquarters in Clermont.' He picked the phone up from Isabelle's desk and gave some orders to someone in very rapid German. 'There will be more soldiers arriving soon,' he said. With that he quickly departed and they watched as his car passed through the old iron gates.

Isabelle said she was going down to the village now on her bike and try to catch up with Guy who had left just before the German officer arrived. Eric Farbres decided to stay in the gendarmerie to avoid unnecessary confrontations. As a precautionary measure, he picked up a hand gun and a rifle from the armory room and suggested to Michel Boyer that he would be wise to do the same in case things turned nastier, as seemed likely.

* * * * *

Doctor Miklos Lovas had decided to visit Abricot's farm to check what appeared, when they drove by earlier, to be some sort of German inspection. He drove carefully along the usual road but was stopped at a temporary check point, manned by two German soldiers. He was close enough to be able to see the gate to the farm about three hundred metres further on. He was waved down as he approached.

'Your papers please,' said the soldier. 'Where are you heading?'

Lovas took out his identity documents and handed them to the man, saying as he did so, 'I am visiting the farm down there,' pointing with his head.

'Why would you visit the farm this particular morning Doctor?'

'The farmer is a friend and a patient of mine and I wished to call on him.'

The soldier said to Lovas, 'Will you please pull over to the side of the road and get out of the car. I must take you to the farm on foot. Here are your papers.'

'What's all this about corporal?' asked Lovas. He already had a good idea what was going on following the sabotage operation a few hours earlier.

'I am not permitted to say,' said the soldier.

The personnel carrier had gone, but there were several military vehicles parked near the front of the farm buildings. A sentry stood outside the main door. Lovas was taken through the hallway to the living room. Sitting tied to an upright chair was Abricot. He looked up as Lovas was brought in. A German Gestapo officer sat opposite Abricot and was smoking a cigarette. An interrogation was in progress and he was slightly put off his stride by Lovas' arrival.

'Take that gentleman out of here and keep watch on him,' he ordered Lovas' guard.

It did not look good thought Lovas. There was no sign of any of the farm staff and Abricot now had no support. In fact the farming staff had all been arrested and loaded into the personnel lorry, under armed guard. Its destination was unknown. The Germans had arrived shortly after the viaduct and tunnel had been wrecked. They had demanded that Abricot would allow them to search the farm for any evidence which might link him or his staff as culprits. They had found a map, not of the viaduct and railway but of the area surrounding the farm.

Abricot was now being interrogated about the ownership of the farm, how long he had been in charge and where he came from originally. It was hardly surprising that Abricot's real identity had been a mystery. He was an English born son of an English aristocrat. His mother was French and he was schooled mostly in Paris and later in the Sorbonne. When Germany began its rapid annexation of neighbouring countries the family left France and returned to their farm in the Cotswolds. It did not take long for the English to identify Charles Whittinger as ideal material to train as an agent of the Secret Service. He was approached and eventually recruited to become a 'sleeper' in France. By the time Germany walked into France Charles Whittinger had become a French farmer. He was also given the name Abricot. He had many French friends in high places in the administration and police and had been able to report back to London on the way Germany was running things in occupied France.

The Gestapo officer questioning Abricot paused for a few moments while he lit another cigarette.

'We know a great deal more about you than you might imagine – Monsieur "Whittinger". My colleagues in Toulouse have done some careful research into your origins and it seems that you have been living in your farm, supplying a steady stream of information back to your English employers in their secret service over a number of years. I am sure you must realise that this is a clear case of espionage, punishable by death. I am disinclined to shoot you myself as I find the whole process distasteful, so I am sending you back to Vichy where you will be further questioned before being executed. While I have you here, can you tell me your relationship with the gentleman just arrived?'

'He is my doctor and has been for nearly ten years. He knows nothing about me other than my state of health. I suggest you release him forthwith.'

'I will make my own decisions on that Monsieur Whittinger.' He stood up and left Abricot tied to the chair. A minute or two later the soldier returned carrying handcuffs and leg irons. His ankles were clamped and linked together with a short chain and his wrists were handcuffed behind his back. The ropes attaching him to the chair were undone and he hobbled out of the building and was pushed roughly into a black Citroen car where he sat between two other plain-clothed men. The car drove off northwards.

The Gestapo officer was waiting for Lovas when he was brought back into the big room.

'Please sit down Doctor. You are Doctor Miklos Lovas?'

'Correct.'

'You are Monsieur Abricot's personal medical doctor, so how long have you known him?'

'Yes, I am his doctor and he has been my patient for nearly ten years.'

The German considered his next question. 'How well do you know him? Do you talk on matters other than his health, such as politics for example?'

'Very rarely,' lied Lovas.

'I can tell you doctor that your patient has been a spy, working for the English for nearly all that time. He is now in serious trouble and will shortly be executed. You don't appear to be very surprised doctor!'

'What do you expect me to say Sir? I am shocked of course but I am beyond being shocked these days. Too much wickedness has been perpetrated over the last few years which has left me numbed.'

'You may like to know that a major sabotage event occurred early this morning. A viaduct and a tunnel have been put out of action. There seems to be every chance that your patient was involved in that operation at some level in view of the proximity of the event. I am curious to know why you should have decided to call on your patient on the very morning that all this took place. Can you offer any explanation for the coincidence doctor?'

'It is pure coincidence as you have suggested. I have had him booked for a visit for some time because I like to keep in regular touch.'

'Very well, 'said the German. 'I am letting you go back to your professional duties. I will instruct the guard to bring over your car to the gate. If there are further questions arising after our chat this morning I will call by your surgery in Domvent.' The soldier accompanied Lovas as far as the farm gate and his car was delivered back. It showed signs of having been carefully examined while he was in the farm, but he was hardly surprised. When he arrived back at Domvent there seemed to be more soldiers than ever. His housekeeper told him that Otto Weiss had called by earlier but had taken young Guy Gaillard with him in the gendarmerie van. Lovas went over to the gendarmerie then and found Eric Farbres and Lieutenant Michel Boyer were still in the office. Both had an automatic pistol and a rifle on their desks in front of them.

'What's been happening?' asked Lovas. 'The town is crawling with Germans.'

'Hauptsturmführer Weiss has been killed,' said Eric. 'Sarah Gaillard shot him as he was about to shoot Guy and Sarah. She'd had an old Great War pistol upstairs.' Guy had given Isabelle a full account of what happened earlier and she in turn had told Farbres all she knew and was planning to return to Chalhac as quickly as possible.

Eric continued, 'Weiss's body was dragged into the ground at the back of the Gaillard house and the gendarmerie van was also moved there. By now they will have found Weiss and the van, and will be demanding to know what happened.'

'No doubt,' said Lovas. He followed up by asking if he could borrow a hand gun, some ammunition and a rifle from the gendarmerie weapons store.

'Of course,' said Eric Farbres. 'I think we should come down with you to the village in case there is a show of strength by the Germans.'

'OK,' said Lovas.

They all got into the doctor's car and drove as quickly as the old road would allow, down towards the village. As they approached they could hear gunfire.

'I think we should see what's happening from the woods. I'll pull in here and try to hide the car,' said Lovas. They crept forwards through the trees and were able to see La Place, Bonnet's Bakery and the Gaillard house. A German was firing a rifle from the side of the church. They could not see his target. Then suddenly he fell forward onto the roadway as a bullet caught him from somewhere. They were unable to see who was where and Boyer said, 'If I can make it across the road to Gaillard's house I might be able to see what's happening a little more clearly.'

'OK but be careful!' said Eric.

There was no one to be seen in the Gaillard house and Boyer realised that he was still too far up the hill to get a good view. He crept carefully through the overgrown greenery towards Bonnet's bakery shop. He arrived at the back door and silently moved through the salon towards the shop front. Bonnet's body lay on the shop floor and there was a German soldier crouching below the counter reloading his gun. Boyer was ready for him however and shot him through the heart. The German had been firing at the front of Jacques' bar, where Jacques and Henrietta were doing their best to hide from the hail of bullets that came first from the direction of the church and then from Bonnets.' Boyer stood up to show them he had silenced the man in Bonnet's shop. A burst of fire from a machine gun from Hortense's house on the other side of La Place, caught Boyer across his chest and stomach. He stood no chance.

Jacques said to Henrietta, 'I am going to get round to the back of your mama's house and try to silence that machine gunner. Don't move from here until I appear over there.' He crawled out of the bar into the salon and out of the back door. He made his way carefully around the back of the old blacksmith's premises and along to the back door of Hortense Hubert's house. He found Hortense tied up on the floor beside the stairs. The German was too busy changing the magazine of his gun to hear or see Jacques arrive. Jacques had no weapons but had picked up a garden fork as he worked his way around the back. The fork had sharp looking prongs after many years of gardening. The German's back presented an even area of thin fabric uniform. Jacques limped quietly towards him with the fork held in his right hand high above his head. The man began to turn but Jacques brought down the fork as forcefully as he could manage into his back. Four prongs penetrated the thin uniform and the fifth prong missed altogether. One prong went through just below his chest and into his heart. Another prong hit his spine and the remaining prongs went into his lung. The man fell forwards onto his machine gun. His heart fatally damaged by the garden fork.

Hortense had watched in ever increasing horror as this was taking place and was close to passing out when she saw what Jacques was about to do.

'Sorry Madame Hubert for making you witness that, but you will understand I'm sure that we have to defend ourselves somehow,' said Jacques, as he untied the ropes around Hortense's wrists. She stood up and swayed a little unsteadily.

Jacques said 'Please sit Madame – you look shaken.' She did as bidden and Jacques went to the window to indicate to Henrietta he was in control of the house again. At that moment Isabelle appeared at the back door. She had been hiding in the garden behind the Hubert cow which had laid down for a doze. The cow was large enough to conceal Isabelle from casual eyes. The girl had tried to make sense of events from the back of the house. Gunfire and machine gun fire and shouts made for a confusing picture.

'What's happening?' she asked Jacques.

Jacques told her that various people had been lost including Bonnet and Michel Boyer. He said there had been a gun fight of sorts in the Gaillard house and was unsure who was involved.

'Have you seen Guy?' Isabelle asked.

'I believe he is still at the house as I haven't seen him leave.'

'I am going to try to get over there to see what's happening. Are you OK Grand-mère? This must be very difficult for you. I must go now.' She left by the back door again and crawled on hands and knees back to Jacques' bar. Henrietta and Maria Fournier were still safe and keeping their heads down.

'Is Jacques OK?' asked Maria.

'Yes, he's fine. He killed the man with the machine gun.'

'How?'

'With a garden fork. Have you seen anything of Guy?'

'I think he is still in his parent's house,' said Henrietta.

Isabelle said no more and left by the back entrance into the wooded area behind. Eric Farbres was still sitting in the doctor's car. He was at a loss to know what to do. Lovas was nowhere to be seen and Boyer had vanished.

'Boyer has been shot Papa,' said Isabelle.

'That is bad news,' said Farbres.

'I suggest you come with me to the house. I might need some cover. I want to find Guy and the rest of the family.' Unknown to Isabelle, Sarah and Marcel had been quickly arrested before all the shooting began. They were obvious suspects and involved in Weiss' death and the gendarmerie van was found on their land at the back of their house. They had no chance to explain anything and were bundled into a black Citroen car and driven off. Guy had taken refuge in the roof room and closed the trap door. He heard the car drive away and the sounds of the Germans departing the house. He had emerged from the roof, found his father Jules dead in bed and had taken a few shots with an abandoned rifle at a German soldier seen running across La Place. He missed and the soldier dived behind the old tree in the centre, giving him enough protection from Guy's firing and allowing him to reload. All had been quiet for a minute or two and the German carefully peered from behind the tree to see who had been shooting at him. Guy knew he was there and waited to get a good shot at him. There were other eyes however looking in Guy's direction and when Guy stood to shoot at his target behind the tree, a bullet hit Guy in his stomach, just missing his heart. Guy staggered across the landing holding his wounded belly and slowly climbed back the rope ladder to the roof room, pulled up the ladder and pushed back the trap door. He laid down beside the door and hoped someone would come to rescue him.

Isabelle and Eric scrambled through the trees towards the road. The Gaillard house was on the other side of the road and it meant a quick dash across. There was a pause in the gunfire and Isabelle said, 'Let's go now, Papa.' She ran with head down across the road and dived onto the grassy edge. Farbres was just behind her but a shot rang out and caught him in one of his legs. He went down in the middle of the road in agony. Isabelle saw it happen and tried to pull him off the road while being almost prone herself. She could not get close enough for a satisfactory tug of his wrist and he was unable to add anything to her efforts.

'It's no good Papa. I can't reach you. Can you slide forwards a little? You must get off the road somehow because you are very exposed where you are.' She had hardly said it when another shot from the village rang out. It hit Farbres in the neck and he slumped lifeless onto the road surface. Isabelle could do nothing more for him and left him lying there as she stumbled around the back of the Gaillard house.

'Is anybody there?' she shouted from the back entrance. There was no response. She decided to get upstairs to make sure there was no one about. The salon showed signs of the earlier shooting of Weiss. There were unmistakable blood stains on the floor and furniture had been moved. She carefully and slowly climbed the old creaky stairs. In Sarah and Jules bedroom the big bed contained Jules. He was dead. His heart had given out in the early hours and had not seen or heard any of the subsequent battles that were still taking place. Isabelle pulled the sheet up over his face and went into Guy's and Marcel's room. There was no sign of them. On the little landing she thought she could hear something from the loft above. The edge of the rope ladder was poking through the wooden loft hatch. She needed a chair or something to reach it. The chair in Guy's room was just high enough and she placed it beneath the rope ladder edge. Reaching up she could get hold of its end. She pulled on it and it obligingly unrolled down towards her. The loft door was still partly shut but she pushed upwards with her shoulder. Close to the opening lay Guy. He was injured in some way and was trying to speak.

Isabelle said, 'You will be OK Cherie. I'll get some water.' She realised that she had no idea what had happened to him then and she said, 'Have you been shot?'

Guy managed to say 'In my side – I am bleeding.'

She carefully pulled away some of his clothes which were soaked in blood. A large wound was revealed which began to run more freely once she had disturbed the clothes around it. He was clearly bleeding to death. Isabelle was at a loss to know the best way to deal the situation. Guy was going to disappear in front of her.

'Don't try to move Cherie – I'll get some water.' In the back bedroom the old water jug and a cracked glass still held some water and she poured some into the glass and re-climbed the rope ladder into the loft. Guy's face was losing its colour and he was moaning. 'I can't make it Cherie – I'm sorry, I . . .' He had died.

Isabelle fell on him, and pulled him towards her. She was instinctively feeling that she could bring him back, using her strength, health and love. It was no good because she could feel his body temperature falling away quickly as she held him and she gently laid him back down again. She was beyond crying out loud but she was screaming inside and almost insane with grief. She took a last look at him, kissed his cold face gently and somehow got back down the rope ladder to the landing. A gun had been abandoned by someone and it was a rifle of some sort, probably German. She released the magazine and it still contained some bullets, so she took it out through the back door with her and tried to discover who was still firing a gun now and then. She could just see the top of David Markovich's head as he dodged behind the remains of the old blacksmith's building in the far corner of La Place. An effort was being made by a German to shoot him but had failed to pick him off. Isabelle looked back across La Place trying to see where the German was hiding and then saw a small puff of smoke come from the upstairs window of Madame Bastien's house. There was no sign of her son Robert Bastien, the Mayor. Isabelle could not quite see the German who had David Markovich trapped. She made a return trip out of the Gaillard house and across the road where her father's body still lay. There was no time or safety margins left for her and she simply wanted to get to the front of Fournier's bar where she could get a shot at the man in the Bastien house. The move was successful in that she could now see the German quite clearly behind the curtain of Madame Bastien's bedroom. She took careful aim. The recoil of the gun made her stagger back but she had hit the German somewhere vital because the bedroom curtain was suddenly dragged down out of sight as the gunman collapsed on the floor. There was silence for a minute or two and Isabelle peered over the top of the windowsills to look for any movement. There seemed to be a pause while decisions were being made by both sides.

Isabelle told Henrietta and Maria that Guy was dead, that Jules Gaillard had died when his heart packed up, Sarah and Marcel had been arrested and had been taken away in a car. They knew that Bonnet had been shot and Lieutenant Michel Boyer.

'What has happened to the Doctor? There has been no word from him since he followed me down to the village over an hour ago. I must speak to David now because he has been pinned down for ages by the man I just shot. I hope he is safe. He might even know what's become of the doctor. She let herself out through the back and resumed her crawling position around to the near derelict blacksmith's building. She called quietly to where she could see David crouching behind some old woodwork.

'Are you OK David?'

'Thank God it's you Isabelle. I thought I was fighting this war by myself. Yes, I am OK, but I am not so sure about the Doctor. I last saw him as he was getting into the house next to your grandmother's. It has been empty for a time now and the doctor evidently felt it would be a good place to hide in. A German had much the same idea and they must have come face to face, because I heard the sound of a gun being fired inside. Who shot who is anyone's guess, but there has been no new firing from there and no sign of the doctor.'

'We'll have to find out David. Leave it with me,' said Isabelle.

She picked her way around the back of Hortense's house, patted the cow as she went past and came to the back of the empty house. She warily raised her head to see in through a downstairs window. She could just make out the figure of a man lying on the floor near the front window. The window was barely transparent so it was impossible to be sure what she was looking at. She tried the back door and it yielded to her push.

She called from the doorway, trying not to shout but not to whisper as well.

'Anybody there?'

No response. She crept in, looked briefly at the figure on the floor and it was not Doctor Lovas. There was no gun anywhere. She went over to the staircase and trod carefully up to the top. The layout was the same as her grandmother's house which had probably been built at the same time. The second room she looked in had the doctor half laying propped up in a corner on the floor. He was clearly not well.

Isabelle said, 'What's been happening doctor? Have you been shot?'

'No,' said Lovas 'but I have had a hell of a fight with that damned man downstairs. He tried to shoot me but I managed to push the gun away from my direction which he then dropped by accident. I grabbed the gun and got up here. Eventually he appeared at the top of the stairs, with the idea of retrieving his gun. I was in no fit state to start fighting him again and warned I'd shoot if he came closer. He tried to rush me but I pulled the trigger. I hit him somewhere because he cried out and ran back down the stairs. Have you seen him?

'Yes he is down there on the floor. He looks dead to me,' said Isabelle. 'So, what is your trouble Doctor? He inflicted some hurt to you presumably?'

'He hit me hard in my chest and stomach. I think I have some sort of internal damage. I need to get to a hospital quite soon.'

'Easier said than done right now,' said Isabelle. As she spoke she could hear a lorry arriving on La Place. There were about twenty fully armed German soldiers with orders to re-establish law and order in the village which had been seen to be putting up resistance to their take over.

Lovas said, 'Get out of here Isabelle and hide somewhere or they will pick you up. Could you make it to the church before they get organised?'

'I'll try. OK Doctor. I'll leave now. Wish me luck.' She ran from the house towards the church and pushed open the door. One of the new arrivals had seen her dashing across the space between the house and the church entrance. He made a mental note.

Père Mulligan greeted her as she pushed open the church door. 'Have they seen you?' he asked. She was unable to say.

'We'll play safe then and get you hidden before they come looking. Quick - into the Confessional and I'll release the panel.' She did as she was told and Mulligan pulled the little catch and slid the panel open.

'There are metal rungs on the wall of the hole. Climb through and take your time. There is some light from the top of the buttress so you will be able to see enough. Stay there until I give you the all clear and you can get out again. I hope it will be sooner than later.' With that, Père Mulligan slid back the panel and took his place near the church doorway.

Isabelle climbed down the old metal rungs. At the bottom the stream was trickling its way out to 'la Bache' and the mill pond. She waited for what seemed a lifetime. No sounds were percolating to her which might have relieved the boredom. As darkness fell outside what little daylight from the tiny glass panel on the buttress top, faded. It was pitch black in her hiding place and she was cold. 'Better cold than dead,' she said to herself.

In the early hours of the morning Père Mulligan's voice called down to her. It's all over Isabelle – you can come out now!'

Her legs had gone to sleep and her feet were numb with the cold. She laboriously climbed out of the hole and into the confessional. Mulligan was waiting for her. He handed her a cup of coffee from his own carefully saved supplies.

He said, 'Not long after the Germans arrived another lot of army vehicles showed up. They were Americans. There was no fighting because the Germans knew they were completely outnumbered. They fled in their lorry and disappeared up the road towards Domvent.'

'So, it's all over then Père? Here, at least?'

'I hope so, yes. You're safe now Isabelle.'

FINIS

In 2006 we had spent a happy relaxed time in our favoured holiday gite in South West France. It was now nearing the time when we were obliged to pack up our belongings and consider getting back to the motorway heading northwards for the ferry and our home in England. Neither of us ever enjoyed the process very much, knowing that it heralded the end of our summer holidays for another year.

Partly to string out the remnants of our holiday, Jan said, 'How about stopping at that village – what was it called? Chalhac - that was it. There is a little restaurant or bar there on the village square. I remember a few years back we were dying of thirst and we both sank a cold glass of beer outside. It would make a break before we pick up the motorway.' I went along with her suggestion and before we finally left the gite we took a careful look at the map to find the best route back to the village.

'It is certainly off the beaten track – it hardly shows on the map,' I said. 'A funny old place altogether.' So we made our way carefully around minor roads up to Chalhac. It was hot again when we got closer but we had time to take in rather more of the surroundings than we had two years before. A little way before we arrived at the village was a small cemetery. Neither of us had noticed it when we must have passed it by two years ago.

'Let's take a look at the cemetery Darling. I find them quite intriguing sometimes.' I pulled up and we walked back a few yards to the wrought iron gate guarding the entrance. There were no spectacular memorials to be seen and we were about to depart when Jan said, 'This is a rather sad one. A man called Guy Gaillard was involved in a gun fight against the Germans towards the end of the occupation. Right next to his grave is a very new grave with a wooden cross. There is a small handwritten notice attached saying, "I'll never forget you my Darling Guy". I'll bet there is more to that than meets the eye.'

We got back to the car and re-parked it under the old tree on the square. There was very little foliage but what remained cast a small shadow across the car roof. We walked the few paces over to the bar. There were no other patrons to be seen and I ordered two beers and offered a third glass for the barman. He gratefully accepted and followed us out to the front and the three of us sat under the faded awning. I asked him to tell us a bit about the village. I asked, 'Is the elderly lady on her bicycle still about? She came by, I remember, on her bike and went into a house over there.' I pointed towards the little house.

'You are just a little too late my friend. We buried my mama just over a week ago. She could have told you a lot more about the village than I can. Yes, she was my mother Isabelle. A tough old thing I can tell you. Her father was an officer in the gendarmerie and she worked for him as a civilian in his office in Domvent. She was up to her ears in the Resistance during that time and he did not get to know about it for a long time.'

'Is you father still alive?' I ventured.

'Sadly no. He was killed in a bit of a battle here in the village just before the Americans arrived. My father was also deeply involved with the Resistance, which was how he came to be shot during the battle here.'

I told him that we had stopped by the cemetery on the way here and had discovered his father's grave in the cemetery together with his mother's alongside. 'It must have been a real love affair between your parents. Did your mama ever speak about it?

'Frequently. He and mama were children when they first met and they became strong friends. A few years later they realised they were in love. They both had bikes and would go up to the plateau above the village. There was a cave somewhere up there where they made love. She said she must have fallen pregnant with me less than two weeks before my papa was injured and died. I would have liked to have known him because he sounded like a very bright, intelligent man. He wanted to become a teacher but was thrown off his teaching course by the anti-semitic régime being run by Pétain at the time. His mother – that is my grandmother, was a Russian Jew but she married my grandfather who was a French-born Gentile. So my father was half-Jewish which was enough to disqualify him from becoming a teacher. It was all very sad.'

I said that we would really like to learn more about Chalhac's recent history but we really had to get going if we weren't going to miss our ferry booking. He said that if and when we were down here again, to come by and he would try to recall some of the stories surrounding the village. He said he felt we would find it quite interesting. We thanked him warmly and I said that we might just do that.

Plus ça change….

Printed in Great Britain
by Amazon